Swimming on Hwy N takes its reader ride through the center of the count convoluted politics, and its isolated souls. Mary Troy had the courage to present her marginal and morally challenged characters without varnish or apology. In these pages, we meet Stalking Badger, Mean Boy, Misery, and the Citizens Against Terror, each of them trailing a rich and painful history of their own. Throughout, Troy exercises her dry wit and dark humor even as she extends empathy to every character, no matter how violent or abject. The novel draws a sharp unsentimental portrait of the human experience, including maternal limitation, romantic disappointment, and political rage. But Troy never leaves her characters—or her readers—in despair. In her confident hands, a road narrative becomes a pilgrimage and a manhunt is transmogrified into a family reunion of misfits and lost souls.

—Trudy Lewis, author of *The Empire Rolls*

Swimming on Hwy N is a novel of forging family. On a journey from Missouri to Washington state, Mary Troy's characters learn to reconcile and love in the least likely of places: in hotel rooms and in cars, in inflatable pools and at roadstops, all while picking up hitchhikers and running from bounty hunters and armed nuns. A travel story of both distance and time, *Swimming on Hwy N* illuminates everything it means for people to be complicated, messy, and tender. Yet, whether she is writing kindness or cruelty, Troy's clarity makes us want to call home, makes us want to right our wrongs. This novel, in addition to being a thrilling read, ultimately challenges readers to reconsider our capacity for empathy and to believe in the power of the people around us.

—Wendy J. Fox, author of *The Pull of It* and *The Seven Stages of Anger and Other Stories*

SWIMMING ON HWY N

moon city press

springfield missouri

MOON CITY PRESS

Department of English
Missouri State University
901 South National Avenue
Springfield, Missouri 65897

The stories contained herein are works of fiction. All incidents, situations, institutions, governments, and people are fictional and any similarity to characters or persons living or dead is strictly coincidental.

First Edition
Copyright © 2016 by Mary Troy
All rights reserved.
Published by Moon City Press, Springfield, Missouri, USA, in 2016.

Library of Congress Cataloging-in- Publication Data

Troy, Mary.
  Swimming on hwy N: a novel by Mary Troy

                                        2016909949

Further Library of Congress information is available upon request.

ISBN-10: 0-913785- 89-X
ISBN-13: 978-0- 913785-89- 8

Cover designed by Charli Barnes
Art: *Swimming on Hwy N* by Charli Barnes

Typesetting designed by Kyle Rutherford
Text copyedited by Karen Craigo

Manufactured in the United States of America.

www.mooncitypress.com

ACKNOWLEDGMENTS

First, thanks to Moon City Press and Michael Czyzniejewski, an astute, intelligent, and hard-working editor, as well as a writer of terrific short stories, and to Karen Craigo, a poet and an amazingly good copyeditor and proofreader. Thanks, too, to Charli Barnes for the cover art. I hope to meet her some day.

I am grateful and lucky to have the support and friendship of my colleagues in MFA program at the University of Missouri-St. Louis—John Dalton, Steven Schreiner, and Shane Seely—talented and giving writers who make meetings fun (and few). I am privileged to have worked with many talented MFA students over the years, and to be working with some now. Their hard work and insights, frustrations and successes and triumphs, convince me over and over that what we all do is important.

Thanks especially to my sister Anne and my two brothers Mark and John, to their spouses Mike, Mary Fran, and Sally, and their children and in-laws and grandchildren, to my sister-in-law Kathy and her husband Dale. Every one of them is gifted and wise and funny and accepting, more friend than family. Thanks to all of you Troys, Millers, Storys, Lewandowskis, Hawns, and Fontenots for including me in your worlds, for making me laugh.

To Pierre Davis, as always.

SWIMMING ON HWY N

ONE

Flesh on a hillside. A body barely covered in water. An old body, Louise's ghost said. Madeline agreed. Sixty was old. Still she spent her days in a bikini, soaking in tepid water in a child-sized pool, in full view of Highway N. Not aging gracefully, Louise's ghost said, and Madeline agreed with that, too. Her pool reminded her of the one Chris, Louise's son and Madeline's first husband, had back when they were both in second or third grade, three blue rings and a flexible plastic bottom. She bought hers in April and spent hours puffing and blowing to make the rings full and bouncy. Then she searched for and found the faded red bikini in an unopened moving box marked *miscellaneous*. The bikini was a concession. She wanted to be bare, wanted her meat and bones blending with the dirt of the Ozarks. She joked with herself this could be a long-delayed adolescent rebellion, a way of not following Louise in all. That she was sixty and Louise had been dead for eight years made it an easier rebellion, to be sure. She smiled in the early morning heat and haze. Here she was, swimming on Highway N, making herself an object, a thing to notice if driving up above. *As you approach downtown Bourbon, look to your right and down the hill and see the old woman in the red bikini, the old woman with three dead husbands and an estranged daughter. The unruined woman.*

She'd not been ruined. Her first mother had not ruined her. She knew it as she sprawled on her hillside in early September 2005. From her pool on Highway N she looked to her past, trying to shape the life of Madeline Dames into a story with a theme and forward movement, even with the last scenes unwritten.

1

She remembered one summer night, 1957.

"I know guns," Wanda, Madeline's mother, said. She stood beside the red plaid wing chair in the living room, the moon bright through the sheers covering the picture window behind her. Madeline heard the snap of her gum. Madeline's father, Phil, sat in the chair and stared straight ahead. The shotgun Wanda held touched his left temple. "Nothing that happens here will be an accident," Wanda said. He closed his eyes. Madeline stood against the far wall that led to the hallway, pressed tight against it. Angie stood on pudgy baby legs beside their father, silent but for her ragged breathing. Wanda laughed, causing Madeline to jump, but kept her eyes on Phil. "All I have to do is pull the trigger."

Madeline contracted her bones and muscles, willed her mass to give way to air, no more noticeable or offensive than the dust underneath the breakfront. She took small sideways steps until she reached the edge of the wall opposite the picture window, then tiptoed into the hall and turned into the kitchen, not breathing until she reached the back door which did not creak and which she closed silently behind her. She then ran across the backyard, about forty feet to the corner and the wire fence she had pried up weeks earlier for emergency escapes. She expected to be shot in the back as she ran, but she didn't turn around until she'd squirmed flat on her stomach under the fence and was in the wooded area beside the unnamed creek. She sat down at the base of an elm and watched her house, listening for the shot. Into the air, she told herself when she heard it, the boom as always louder than she'd prepared for. Mom's shot.

Forty-eight years later, Madeline felt the backwards living was coming to an end; something new was on the way. Later, after the journey, she would say all that wallowing in the past had been like backing up to go forward, moving back for a running start. But until the new arrived, she talked to herself about that night in 1957, knowing memory was false, and *seemed* did not mean *was*. Had her father been afraid that night? Had he said anything about it later? No. That answer was a sure no. Maybe her mother's hormones were out of balance, her diet causing a blood sugar rush. Everyone has a breaking point. Alongside Highway N, Madeline knew it as nonsense. She splashed water up onto a shoulder, squinted into the leaves of the giant oak throwing shade just to her left. The truth was her mother had been exactly herself that night. To pretend there could be an explanation other than that her mother would happily torment her family, wanted to hurt and frighten her father or any of them and often did, was to cultivate a naïveté of the kind that weakened a mind, diminished a soul. And that wasn't the only or the first shotgun incident of Madeline's childhood, nor was the shotgun the sole threat. Kitchen knives, ball bats, plastic belts, screwdrivers, cookware—all became extensions of Wanda's rage. And Madeline understood that 1957 was not hotter or crazier than the other years surrounding it, but that one sticky summer night lived on.

It started with her father asking why there were noodles in the meatloaf. He asked it thrice, and Madeline watched her mother's face change colors. It was a spectacular display, and by the end, Wanda was the gray green of the sky before a tornado, the skin around her eyes and lips gray like the lead pipes in the basement.

Madeline Kneedelseeder was the name given her at birth, but she'd been Dames for forty-four years, each one of them and the eight or nine before those lived according to Louise's advice: "Don't look back." Until now.

An air horn blasted from a semi speeding along Highway N, sixty or so feet above Madeline's pool. She waved. It was that kid from Sullivan who now drove for Schneider. She sipped from her plastic tumbler of Chablis, taken over ice on days like this when the air temperature topped 90. She'd done good. Some girls would have suffered from a mother as bad as Wanda, but Madeline had exchanged her for a better model.

Her first and only plan was to lead Christopher Dames, her childhood buddy, out behind his parents' garage and rub her hand along the zipper in his jeans. They were both fifteen. "And a half," she said then. She kissed him by sticking her tongue in his mouth, just as yucky as she'd imagined it would be, and said he could touch her wherever he wanted, said he could try things. "Intercourse," she said, using the word from the health education filmstrips. He did, but had insisted she call it love. He said he was in love, so she said she was, too, both of them claiming they were in love as they put their under pants back on after. And maybe they were, she thought now. Maybe saying so made it true. The third time was the best because they both claimed to feel like their skin had been lit on fire. Eventually victory. Her periods stopped, a mere seventeen months after they started. She'd chosen Chris for the gently smiling Louise, his mother and her mother number two—she had picked her out years earlier.

She'd awakened this morning at dawn as always, but the feeling that something odd and new was coming kept her from going back to sleep. So she filled her pool earlier than usual and was swimming by seven o'clock. It was why she'd missed Randy's call. *Connect* was the word he used on her answering machine. He was a new friend from the County Fair two weeks past. He'd headed up a committee of some sort, had been in charge of schedules and assignments. She'd been the lowliest of workers, one of the cleanup committee. It's good to seem helpful, Louise's ghost had told her. You can meet people, and on a lowly committee no one's ego gets in the way. Randy'd said he'd connect with her later. She liked that word, *connect*. His eyes were chicory blue and his laugh was soft. He was single.

Another blast from above, another wave.

Chris'd been dead for forty years. He was barely eighteen last time she saw him, tall and lanky with large knuckle and wrist bones, clearly still growing. His wavy caramel brown hair covered his ears, and his bangs merged with his eyebrows. "I can't be married to you for one more minute." They'd played at being married, living in their nest of two rooms in his parents' basement for thirty-seven months. "You don't care about anyone but yourself." Though she denied it out loud, she accepted it then as true. He'd found her out. He was the sacrifice. She'd had to ruin his life to save her own, though if he hadn't gone crazy and joined the Marines, his life wouldn't have been ruined, either, not forever. She could've been a mere hiccup, an interruption. They'd been divorced for three years when he was blown up in a tunnel outside Dong Ha. It was not her fault.

An orange VW bus, an old one she called a hippie-mobile, barreled down her drive, spraying gravel into her pool, finally sliding to a stop thirty or more feet below her. She smiled even though the gravel stung her shoulders. Randy. *Connect*, he'd said. Yes, let's. Maybe he'd be husband number four. Geez, Louise, that was only a joke.

"Am I disturbing you?" he walked up beside her pool, looked down.

She shaded her eyes to see his silhouette against the bluish glare. Even though she was rich in ex-husbands, dead husbands, even though men seemed to like her, she'd never learned the art of flirtation. Too bad. "Sit if you want." She pointed to an aluminum lawn chair webbed with blue plaid strips tilted in the crab grass beside the pool. She wanted to be inviting, so she added, "Please."

He did. "I have a list of things," he said, removing some crumpled pieces of paper from his T-shirt pocket. "The mayor's tired of fielding calls, wants to know if you've seen any of these." He referred to the list of lost items. "A gold-colored locket with photos of horses in it. A pearl-handled pocketknife. Three bill caps, all with names of St. Louis sports teams on them. A pair of rhinestone-encrusted sunglasses. A recipe for gumbo. Sterling silver salad tongs …."

She shook her head at each item as he read more. It was only a two-page list, on it names of things lost forever. He could've called. Any of the other organizers could've called or e-mailed her the list. He had wanted to come by, and she wished she could think of something fascinating to say, something to keep him around since he clearly wanted a reason to visit. "My driveway's sort of dangerous. Sorry." She shaded her eyes with a hand again and squinted up at Highway N and the steep driveway leading to it, made usable only by the flat gravel turnaround beside her mailbox. When she bought the place in December, she'd planned to fix the driveway as soon as the weather got nicer. Ollie had left her not only enough for her dirty white shack and the sixteen acres of hardwood and scrub in the tip top of the Ozarks, but also enough extra for some repairs.

"Yeah," Randy said. "The drop-off surprised me."

Ollie's daughter called her foolish for moving to the sticks, so far from her previous life, fifteen years in the heart of Chicago. Ollie was her third dead husband, but repetition didn't make the loss easier, or so she told herself even as she worried his loss, all the loses, may have been too easy to bear. How sad was sad enough? It wasn't the question she wanted answered anyway. And the hell with introspection. She'd loved all her husbands in her own way. How else but that? Did it matter by now, all of it finished? The sticks, she told Ollie's daughter and others; she wanted the sticks. She wanted to start out as a stranger in some backwards place and see how long before she was one of them. Sometimes when she said it like that, she believed herself.

When Randy shifted his weight in his lawn chair as if he would stand soon and go, she started talking. "Where do they go, all those lost items?" He looked at her and shrugged. That was not a conversation extender. "Tell me something about yourself," she said. It was a line Louise had given her long ago, said would win her friends. As always, it worked, and he began talking. "Tech writer, single, luckless fisherman, bad dancer, like cheap beer." He ran a hand through the hair at the top of his head as he listed his details, creating parts and showing some scalp. He continued, said he was from Pittsburgh, Pennsylvania, but he'd grown accustomed to small towns from his days in western Canada and his escape from the Vietnam draft. She smiled as he talked about being a draft-dodger. His long graying reddish hair hung to his shoulders in waves, inviting touch. She'd missed the hippie era, the clothes and hair and attitude, the drugs and freedom, because she was a mother living in Louise's basement then. Yet now she was passing time with what Chris would have called a peacenik. Randy continued, saying by the time he returned to the States, crowds annoyed him, and he could keep good thoughts about people only if he saw them as individuals and not as part of a group.

He was not it, not the thing she'd been expecting, still was expecting. "There are woods around Pittsburgh, too," she said. "Why these woods?"

He shrugged.

"A woman, is my guess," she said. "Affairs of the heart often guide our destiny." She laughed. In attempting flirtation, she ended up sounding Victorian.

"How long've you been a widow?" he asked.

"You could ask how often, too. Three times."

"Three?" It was his turn to laugh, and he did. "It's not funny. Sorry. So why're you here?"

"Not sure," she said. "But I'm surprised by the people I've met. Accepted wisdom in Chicago is folks here are rabid fundamentalists, NRA members, white-bread-and-iceberg-eating creationists. They warned me before I moved."

"We got those here," he said. "And I like iceberg."

"My sister once told me people take up to four days to digest iceberg.

She was only about ten when she came up with that pearl of wisdom, but it stuck with me. The same weird sister sent me a note when I moved here. 'Hope the big bad wolf doesn't blow your wood house down,' it said. Funny, huh?"

He leaned forward in the lawn chair, hands on his knees. "The truth is if everyone thinks they know what you're like, you're free to be whatever you choose."

"I chose to be who I am back when I was fifteen." A lie, she knew, but who would believe she'd done it at seven? She was a Dames long before the wedding made it official, Louise often calling Wanda to say Madeline was all tuckered out from a day of play, sound asleep on the couch, and could she spend the night.

"I keep choosing, but it never sticks. I usually choose to be wiser." He coughed. "Gotta go," he said, but before he could stand, she reached out and touched his knee.

"Jeans in weather like this?" As she asked it, she suddenly felt naked. Was she covered well enough or had her suit shifted as it sometimes did, letting hair show at the leg holes? "I keep choosing, too. I mean, choose or get chosen, right?" Stay longer, she told him with her eyes, a message he did not get.

"Ha," he said, and stood, coughed once more. "My allergies. I do have to be going."

What did that mean, choose or get chosen? Just jabber. She wasn't as brainless as she sounded, and she almost said so. She could claim heatstroke. "See ya," she said, then closed her eyes. She listened to him back up and turn around, felt gravel ping against a shin. He spun his tires at the top of her drive before gunning it onto Highway N, and belts or something old on the hippie-mobile screeched all the way down the next hill and around the curve.

As she soaked up more September sun, she heard movement behind her, but when she opened her eyes and turned, she saw only trees and rocks. Deer, she thought. Maybe turkey. Not whatever it was that was coming. Maybe just a squirrel, the only creature besides man stupid enough to be moving in the heat of the day. As if she had a clue about Ozark wildlife. She heard a honk from above, turned too fast toward the road, and made the hillside spin. Red spots danced in the oak leaves.

What she'd learned from Louise was how to act. She developed her mild and tinkling laugh, practiced it in the mirror of the Dameses' medicine cabinet to be sure she looked happy as she laughed, kept a journal and gave herself gold stars for days she used it at least once. She learned to smile at people she met in stores, too, and she was patient with clerks and workmen. She dressed up for church, and she collected for the March of Dimes. When she married the second time to Martin, she continued her education. She learned to cook with spices and wine and garlic and give intimate dinner parties as well as the end-of-summer barbecue the two of them became known for. She volunteered to read to children at the local grade school. She learned to be friends with sweet and inoffensive women who drove mini-vans and took Prozac. That was in Houston, where Martin owned a boat repair business. Ollie, number three, was a lover of museums in Chicago, and she learned to love them, too, especially the Art Institute. She volunteered as a docent there, eventually chairing a few fund-raising committees. She knew as she lay in the sun on the side of Highway N that hers could be called a charmed life, and ever since she'd left Wanda to become a Dames, her life had been on track, her track, one she carved out little by little by and for herself. But Chris's death had not erased the validity of his accusation, one echoed by their daughter. She was her first and maybe sole concern. "I'm sorry," bubbled up her throat and she let it out now in the early mornings, sometimes before dawn. Her first words.

What can you say about a mother so bad her daughter leaves for good? She hadn't thought she was that bad, but Trysh was gone, promising not to return, and so far keeping that promise. Trysh said it was Madeline's failure to care for Martin, husband number two and the one who served longest as father to her, that she could not tolerate. But it was more. Madeline knew it couldn't have been one thing; nothing was only one thing.

She closed her eyes again, and in what seemed mere minutes, Martin stood before her. He laughed. "Lazy bones. Jump in." Behind him was a vat of grease. She took his hand, and though she pulled back, he pulled her toward him. "We'll go together. Extra crispy."

"No," she said as his eyes became bullets. She awoke, drained of her strength, unable to stand without the hill spinning around her, her heart pounding. She heard a horn and waved in what she thought was the direction of Highway N. Then she stood halfway and nearly crawled through her front door and all the way back to the cool and dark kitchen. A lumpy bear-like woman humming what seemed a lullaby sat at the table. She turned toward Madeline.

"Angie," Madeline said, her heart still pounding, her legs like dandelion stems.

"I came in the back way. I tripped on your step." She bent over and rubbed at a spot on her calf. She wore running shoes, a black, knee-length, gathered skirt, a fuzzy blue cardigan sweater buttoned all the way up. Rivulets of sweat coursed down her large red face.

"The back way," Madeline said, waving toward the door, "is a mess. Me, too. My blood's dried up. I need something."

"I don't go by Angie any longer. I'm Misery now. Angie has something to do with angels. I'm not like one, never have been."

Madeline stumbled to the refrigerator for the jug of ice water, drank fast until her stomach hurt. She took a deep breath. "I doubt Mom knew what either of our names meant."

"Know what Misery means?"

Madeline raised her glass and dribbled cold water over her head.

"It means I finally know my place in the world. I've accepted my lot."

Madeline refilled the jug and set it and two glasses on the table. She guessed it'd been two years since she'd seen Angie, maybe longer. Angie hadn't been at Ollie's funeral, so it must have been one of the birthday parties her father's new family threw for him on the decades and half-decades. Likely he'd been eighty a few years ago. "Aren't you hot?" Madeline asked now.

"Sure. It adds to my misery."

"What brings you here?"

"My legs. These two sturdy appendages." She stuck them out straight under the table. "They brought me."

"Ha!"

"Remember how the Dameses insisted you move in with them?"

"Of course." Madeline's heart slowed. The spots had changed from red to black and were fading now.

"I think you should do the same." Angie said.

"Same?" Madeline asked.

"You're slow today. Getting old I guess. The same as those old farts. Let me move in."

Madeline felt herself frown, so she pictured the moonlight on Lake Michigan.

"Here's what I've seen while you've been sleeping in the sun. Your place is small and dark. It's the homeland to generations of spiders. It smells like something died under it."

"I think something did."

"The floors squeak. The toilet runs."

"You have to jiggle the handle."

"Clearly, the roof leaks. But I've been living in a cave for a week. On the edge of a city park, so I had to keep way to the back during the day. This shack will suit me. I think you should act like those old goody-goodies you like so much and insist I move in."

Madeline took a breath and thought harder of Lake Michigan. She should not refuse her own sister. Absolutely not. Not again. "I thought you were with Ginny."

"Ginny was a figment of my imagination."

"Angie, what happened?" The picture came to Madeline fast, and she saw herself hugging Angie, rocking her, soothing her. Oh Honey she'd say. Baby Angie. It wasn't a memory, and not quite a wish. She remained standing, made no move to touch or comfort.

"I told you my name. Just like you to pretend I said nothing."

"What happened?"

"The usual. I fucked up. I blame it on Mom, just as I've blamed everything on her."

"If you try, Angie, you can forget the past." Not that Madeline practiced forgetting lately, but it had long been her way. "The mind is strong," Louise often said. "I, for one, have never been depressed, not even sad." Louise said it was a version of shock therapy in which the brain cells that knew the bad things died, but instead of being shocked out of existence, they were ignored to death. Dead cells either way.

"Name's Misery. And don't tell me it's all behind me or some other cliché about moving forward. That was all Ginny could come up with."

"Ginny? The imaginary Ginny?"

"Want to know why I spent three days walking down Highway 44, determined to get to my sister's house? Know what my plan is?"

Madeline shook her head. She did not want to know.

"Revenge. My misery is catching. I've been told that often. Just by being around you, I can make you suffer. After a few months, we'll have to change your name to Misery, too."

Madeline'd often told herself she'd been sorry to leave Angie behind. But Madeline hadn't been much more than a child either, living in fear. It was the excuse she gave herself, and as excuses went it was a good one, yet she'd known she could've thrown Angie a line, could've given the Dameses more details about their life with their parents.

"Anyway," Angie continued, "You may be Little Miss Sunshine, moving with ease from one man to another, but you don't have the nerve to throw me out. Or do you?" Angie sat up straighter. "Try it. Let's just see you try."

"You're welcome here," Madeline said. She focused on the tulip poplar leaves outside her kitchen window and took a deep breath. "No one cried at dinner there. No one turned colors."

"Oh, at that goody-goody house? How nice for you."

"I want you to understand. I used to imagine my vertebrae were ice chunks, one move and they'd crack loud enough for Mom to hear. I remember sitting straight and quiet, around her, holding my breath. I could breathe at the Dameses." She surprised herself with that, but it wasn't a lie. She remembered her ice spine.

"As apologies go, that's a horrible one. Even as an explanation, it's lame." Angie kicked the table leg as she talked, making waves in their water glasses. "Very lame. Who cares anyway? So you knew people who made Mom and Dad seem the cretins they were. Let me tell you something real." Angie smacked the table. "The judge was against my new name. 'Misery is not a positive name,' she said. Ha! What an intellect. But she had to let me be what I wanted. Not a want exactly, but am. Misery is me."

There is a last time for everything. That truism was one Madeline relied on, one that helped her often. The last slap, the last hair pull. She knew those when they happened just before she left home. The last meal of sorrow and anger, she remembered, had been fish sticks. She'd known Ollie's last breath, too, had sat beside his hospital bed so she would see it. This was her last chance to help Angie. She pictured them then as outsiders would, the two weird sisters, Madeline and Misery, M&M. She cupped Angie's chin to make her look up, then smiled that gentle half-smile perfected by Louise. "Everything's fine," she said. "Angie."

TWO

The day Madeline came squalling out, waving her arms within minutes, screaming when held, refusing to be rocked, Wanda knew she'd been rejected. This one already thought she was too good for her own mother. The next one was different but no more loving. From the beginning, Angie'd been a sullen, frightened, ugly child, and she'd grown into a pathetic lumpy dumpy with nothing but the crazy hospital in her future. What the two had in common was Wanda, and she believed they talked about her often, shared complaints and hatreds. She could feel that angry talk as an increased charge in the air, a static not accounted for by humidity or temperatures. The two sisters, one a winner and one a loser, would sit somewhere, wherever they lived now, perched on their butts like old stew hens, and cackle over how Wanda had harmed them. It hurt. Wanda admitted as much to herself. And she knew enough about mother hatred to know all their complaints, even the exaggerated and downright made-up, would be true. The mother was always the ruination of her daughter, just as her mother, the old squaw, the sour and ugly old squaw, the sour and ugly old squaw who was both the joke and the shame of Felt, Oklahoma, had been for her.

Wanda could taste dust, could still smell her mother's acidic sweat that came before and so signaled the dark rages, but the blessing was she could no longer picture the old squaw. Wanda'd had a very few photos of her mother to begin with—one just the side of her head and knife-sharp nose taken by a photographer trying to earn his fame by snapping the poor and downtrodden Okies in front of their shacks—and she'd torn up, thrown out, or burned all she had, so that now the old squaw's face and head and even her shadow were gone from Wanda's mind, too. Well, she worried that perhaps the old squaw was present in her mirror, Wanda's nose jutting out as her eyes sunk deeper into her head, worried that she was aging into the curse of Felt, Oklahoma, but no one would know for sure. Wanda was the old squaw's only living child, so there was likely no other person alive who remembered the squaw, who could call up her face, who would want to.

For Wanda, at seventy-nine, not just her mother, but many other pieces of the past were gone, and she wondered: if she couldn't remember it, did it count as having happened? And was there a difference between what she'd lived through or caused and what she'd seen in movies, what others told her about? So many pieces of her past had become vapor that she could've been starting over.

Yet it was the cranberry juice she drank each morning now for the health of her kidneys that took her back to 1961, the Runway Lounge, and the bartender's specialty, a Scarlett O'Hara—cranberry juice, Southern Comfort, and gin.

"You get down, the old squaw always said, and you never get up." Wanda sipped her Scarlett O'Hara, tilted her head, and winked at Juda. She was only thirty-five, yet had just learned she'd be a grandmother. The Runway Lounge was a new place near the airport with a neon martini glass dancing above the entrance, and she was drinking with her boss, Juda Steinmetz, manager of Fisher's Department store. She'd frosted her hair herself, but knew it looked like a professional job. Her beaded, low-cut sweater showed her healthy cleavage, her breasts full and good looking when squeezed together. She'd been with Juda on and off for five years, and thought of herself as his paramour. It was a word the old squaw'd never heard, a word so pretty no one raised in Felt, Oklahoma, could ever hope to be one. But Wanda was pretty and special and sexy enough. Juda was no pushover either, not like Phil, who after seventeen years was a wet rag tied to her ankle. Yet there she was, sitting in the Runway Lounge, bringing up the old squaw for God knew what reason when she should have been gossiping about her fellow Fisher workers, a conversation Juda found stimulating.

"She had what wasn't more than a lean-to on some ole guy's land, way in the back. She lived there alone, working up at his place during the day, even frying him a steak the day I was born. Then she went back to her shed and had me all by herself. She was tough. Felt was rich the year I was born, wheat farmers just raking it in. Yet our shack had no heat, nothing but oilcloth covering the windows. She was probably forty something when I was born, having lost four or maybe five children before me. Only one, a boy, lived long enough to be named and buried in town. Sam. Though I never did see his grave. Don't know what last name she used for him or any of the others. Mine and hers was Preedy, but though she sometimes claimed to have married him, Art Preedy, other times she said he just used her on his way through town. A few times she forgot and referred to him as Jackson Preedy. Anyway, I never saw him, never knew anyone in town who knew any Preedys but us."

Juda yawned. "You Okies and your scraggly family trees."

It was what she thought, too. Who wanted to hear about a raggedy half-breed who'd made herself a laughing stock of Felt by standing in front of the general store and cursing the white men, throwing rocks at their dogs, spitting on their new cars. Wanda often heard the town matrons (struggling themselves by 1935 and 1936 when Felt gained the distinction of being the epicenter of the Dust Bowl) give their verdict about the old squaw. "Women like her should be sterilized. What good could come from her having children." But now Wanda would be a grandmother barely a month after her thirty-sixth birthday. By the standards of the same kind of right-thinking people who'd spoken about the squaw and Wanda as if both were deaf, Wanda's sixteen-year-old pregnant daughter signified trash, bad breeding, ignorance, and lack of control. But there would be a wedding soon, and then Madeline would be part of one of the nice families in the area, the kind who were uncomfortable with strong emotions and honesty, the kind who would call, but only to themselves, her affair with Juda base. Wanda could see Madeline's attraction to the Dameses, of course, even though she felt jittery around them, dismissed by the gentle half-smiles that left their eyes dull.

Juda leaned across the table and whispered warm and moist in her ear. "Take your girdle off in the restroom before we go. It'll be easier later on."

The warmth moved from her ear to her chest and then spread out in all directions. She wondered if she were glowing in the dark lounge. She loved Juda. Phil didn't even know she wore a girdle.

By the time Madeline's daughter was born, Wanda'd stopped being Juda's paramour. He'd taken up with a younger woman, a beatnik Wanda called her, from the children's clothing department. The beatnik wore her brown hair in braids and had shown up at Fishers Christmas party dressed down in dungarees and a man's white shirt, its tails flapping about her thighs. She didn't wear a girdle. She had slightly crossed eyes and wore pink lipstick that made her look like a deranged kitten.

"I can't see myself with a grandmother," Juda said when he dumped her, and Wanda'd had to shrug and accept his leaving. What choice did she have? Choice diminished with age. That was something Wanda would've told Madeline if they ever talked. She was not entirely without bits of wisdom to pass on. The young had choices too numerous to count, enough to paralyze some, but soon the options narrowed to *this* or *that*. Like with Juda. She could accept his leaving, or make a scene and then eventually accept his leaving. Sure, she could find another to be a paramour for, and she told herself she may choose to do just that, but even then, her choice would've been limited, and she'd be lucky to find a one she could stand to be with. And what was the most unfair part about Juda leaving because she was a grandmother was that she was never allowed to be a grandmother, not by Madeline. Madeline wouldn't bring baby Trysh to Wanda's, and she'd let Wanda hold Trysh only in the Dameses' living room, only while she and usually Louise, too, looked on.

Even later when Madeline separated from her boy husband, she didn't return home, but remained in the Dameses' basement. He moved out, and then went away and got killed. Wanda wasn't even invited to the funeral, though it was in a church and anyone could show up who wanted to, and she did, sitting in the back in a black satin almost backless dress and sobbing as loud as she could in spite of Madeline's dirty looks. But that meanness of Madeline's had not gone unpunished. Wanda knew from Trysh herself that once she'd grown up and left Madeline in Houston, she'd cut off all contact, and would rather "eat a bag of nails" than ever speak to her mother again. The letter that said so was included in Trysh's Christmas card, 1982. Trysh had been twenty-two then and waiting tables in a shrimp restaurant in Galveston. But Trysh hadn't just broken contact with Madeline, but with Wanda, too, for reasons Wanda didn't understand. For now she could only hope Trysh meant it and that Madeline had lost her daughter, too. Fair was fair.

Call her mean. Call her vindictive. So what? Wanda was what she was. And what she was, she knew, was the mistreated stepchild of the universe. She wouldn't have harmed baby Trysh, and the truth was she'd not been all bad for her own girls. Before condemning her, they should know Phil was so bland she would scream out of boredom some evenings, just sit at the kitchen table and shout out nonsense syllables to get the air moving. He could at least have screamed back. He never got a promotion in all the twenty-five years they stayed together, never bringing in quite enough to make ends meet, so she'd had to work at Fishers. And though without warning she could be filled with a rage so bright it nearly blinded her, she'd fed all three of them while working twenty-four hours a week, two afternoons and three evenings. She'd cooked and done the laundry, too, sending her girls off to school in clean blouses and with full stomachs. So let them talk about how she ruined their lives, because no matter how much was true, she could've done a lot worse. Angie'd had braces when she needed them; both girls were taken in for yearly check-ups. She could've bought a mink coat with what their school clothes cost.

******

Louise used to call Madeline a bundle of wants, and now Madeline tilted her head back so she looked at the sky, her head resting on an inflated blue ring, and said "Louise, you did not cure me well enough. " For she wanted again. Or was it still? Not that it was bad to want, Louise usually said, not totally, for it was in wanting that we were most alive. But strong wills were taken down; forces were always reckoned with. Louise said no one need act on her wants. The wanting was usually enough. Of all Madeline's wants, two were most pressing on this the last September Saturday of 2005, and had been for weeks. Angie and Randy.

Her sister should not be such a stranger. A strange stranger. Was she insane or was it an act? Martin used to say knowing another

16

person was a kind of death. "I know you. Poof. No mystery. No pull."
Madeline smiled when she pictured him saying it, squeezing his fingers
up to his pursed mouth and then opening his hand wide for the *poof*,
but she hadn't bought it then, and wasn't buying it now. Sure, Angie
talked all the time, when she wasn't humming some tuneless version
of an old song, but what she said was not enough to build a person
with. She didn't like asparagus, cargo shorts, mint-flavored dental floss,
radishes, pine trees or pinecones, or pork link sausages. To keep the
talk moving, Madeline had added her own list, admitting to not liking
mushrooms, fabric softener, underwire bras, car commercials, and
panty hose. Both sisters liked Chablis and wine of all kind, charred
meat, high-smelling cheeses, ChapStick, and sunshine. Angie also
didn't like Madeline's pool, and wouldn't join her in it, would rarely sit
in the lawn chair beside it, and even then wouldn't cool her feet in the
tepid water beneath the blue rings. And because Madeline called her
Angie, she often refused to respond enough to add to the list of likes or
dislikes. "Who?" she'd ask. "Angie? Used to know someone with that
name. A real mess, she was."

"That new name will make your life worse, not better," Madeline
said. "I cannot use it. It's too sad."

"Boo-hoo," Angie said. "Wouldn't want to make Madeline sad."

Then there was Randy. She'd seen him a half dozen times in the four
weeks since Angie arrived. He first came by with slices of ham, saying he
bought too much and since he lived alone and so did she, it made sense to
share. A few days later he appeared with a watermelon, one he'd grown.
He admitted he didn't like watermelon, grew them because his dad had
done so, and he hoped she'd take it. Angie hid inside for each visit, though
it turned out she liked watermelon and finished Randy's off in a day. He
brought zucchini by twice, a plastic bag of okra, and later some over-ripe
tomatoes. She joked he was her personal farm co-op, so he suggested lunch
at B's diner where she'd had a bowl of bland chili, orange with grease. He
called six days ago, and said he was busy writing a large report on wind
turbines, so wouldn't see her for a while. How much time could a report
take? Day and night? She was not at his mercy, she knew, and could call
him if she so wished, but both times she did, the answering machine told
her to leave a message. His voice on it lied and said he would return her
call. "Come over for a swim," she said, the last time adding, "Call me." She

should be ashamed to know the number of days since his call. He was just some old guy she'd met, a shy and awkward one at that. Maybe he ran out of extra food, she joked to Louise. Yet as she soaked in her pool for each of the six days since his call, she imagined his bus careening down her embankment, scattering gravel and dust.

Dinner this Saturday was Madeline's treat for Angie, spareribs soaked in garlic and honey. The treat grew out of a nostalgia that'd made her briefly forget Randy as she soaked in her pool. For it was now, after the autumnal equinox and at the hoped-for end of the wilting September humidity, when she and Martin threw a barbecue for his employees, suppliers, and friends, one that grew more elaborate each year. The ribs were her specialty. She knew they were good, too, and though Angie hadn't said as much, she'd sucked the meat off five rib bones and offered to do the dishes after.

"I used to visit her," Angie said as they came to the end of the dinner too large for two.

Madeline didn't have to ask who, but she did ask why.

"You know I'm medicated now. If I weren't, I wouldn't be able to put words into sentences."

Madeline nodded. She had not known.

"But this was before it all went bad. I would forget, would think, well, she was a mother and I was a daughter—would think we could be close to normal." She shrugged. "Something stupid like that. Haven't seen her now for three years and nineteen days."

"What happened when you saw her?" Madeline asked wishing she could take it back or that Angie hadn't heard, hoping Angie wouldn't say.

"Shit. Horrid old shit."

"Then be quiet," Madeline said. "Please."

"Okey-dokey," Angie said. She tilted her head and gave Madeline a dopey grin. "Like your second mother claimed. Some pain we do not have to feel. We could talk instead about that surprising piece of so-called opinions."

The latest *Kneedelseeder Report*. It was on the table just inside the front door where Madeline had dropped it when getting the mail. It was two rooms away from the kitchen where they sat, but it may as well have been right there next to the leftover ribs and pasta salad. It was written and published and circulated by Phil himself, Dad.

He must have seen the knives still stuck in the wall above the couch when he came home in the evenings. He had known that Angie slept on a sheet in the hall for close to three months when Wanda took her bed away as punishment. How could he have missed the black eyes each girl had worn at times? Did he notice Angie's blinking? Did he ever wonder why Madeline stayed away?

On its banner, the *Kneedelseeder Report* claimed a circulation of five hundred, which Madeline assumed meant it was sent to five hundred addresses her father knew of, not that five hundred people had asked for it. She certainly had not. The one that arrived this Saturday was Volume One, Number Four. Number Three she'd read last month to pass the time in her pool. It contained what he called truisms, commentaries on a life she hadn't known he paid attention to. One recurring article was titled "The Destruction Report," and was a criticism of new shopping centers and subdivisions that were taking farm and forest land out of use. He insisted *development* was the wrong word for what was so negative. He referred to the new subdivisions as Tyvekvilles for the wrap put up on their pressed-board walls, and took to making fun of so many of the units in them being called Villas, no longer homes, condos, apartments, or townhouses. "Tyvekville Villas" was the title of a song he'd written lyrics for and published. It was to be sung to the tune of "The Battle Hymn of the Republic." Madeline laughed at it in spite of herself, agreeing with some of his observations, yet wondering where this concern had come from. She'd not been sure he'd known Chris's name, and certainly not the Dameses' phone number. Yet now he was an active member of society. Her father's interest in more than his diet and bank account had not been evident at the last birthday dinner his new family had given him.

"It was two years ago in June, " Angie'd said the day she showed up, referring to when she and Madeline had last seen each other. "I remember Dad's socks didn't match. One charcoal gray, one black."

"You, a member of the fashion police?" Madeline had wanted it then to sound like a joke, but by now she knew Angie's black plastic bag contained nothing but the same uniform—black full skirts and fuzzy sweaters and running shoes. The look screamed insane and was not joke material, especially when the sun baked the Ozarks so the air above the dirt waved and wiggled, and the clothes Angie wore seemed deadly.

"Didn't say I disapproved. Just saying what I observed. What you would not notice."

Madeline and Ollie and Angie and Ginny had been invited to one of those expensive St. Louis restaurants where the waiters wore tuxes and walked backwards. His dead second wife's daughter was the organizer, the host, and though she seemed pleased to throw a party for him, she took Madeline aside before the éclairs and said, "I'm not taking care of him if he gets dementia. Just so you know. He's your responsibility." Madeline'd nodded, confused by the urgency of the stepdaughter's announcement. If there were dementia signals, she missed them, though lately she thought maybe it was the socks. He was his usual self that night, smiling like someone just getting over shock treatment. He said, "Well, well," as his part of most conversations, and he'd finish a remark by spreading his hands out, palms up, as if to say, "There you have it, and it doesn't matter."

"Write *Return to sender* across it, and send it back," Angie said. "He's more imaginary than Ginny." She shook her head and looked down at her plate, allowing stands of gray and black hair that had escaped the rubber band at her neck to trail through congealed barbecue sauce.

Misery. Why would a person choose that name, especially a miserable person? Madeline knew she'd have to use it eventually, even if she never understood why. Martin would've called Angie Misery from the first, and would've been confused by Madeline's resistance. His heart was big enough for silliness and error. Well, this was his day, and she knew she'd finally give in, so would do it now for his sake as well as for Angie's. You should be called what you wanted to be called. Period. No matter how wrong. She could hear him say so, see his thin face, the tanned skin cured by moist and salty air, as he explained it to her. As she remembered his gentle drawl, she heard a knock at the back door.

"How odd." Angie said, still looking down. "You have to pass this shack's front door to get to the back."

"Odd, yes, but it was your way in," Madeline said. "Misery."

Misery looked up at Madeline and smiled. Then she pushed her chair back and stood. "Let's see who the idiots are."

Randy stood in the doorway, and a young couple, a boy and a girl, balanced in the dirt and roots beyond the crooked step. The couple laughed in a way people do when nothing is funny.

"These are my cousins," Randy said, pushing his way in the door, all three of them nearly knocking Misery down, crowding into the small kitchen. Randy's shoulder-length hair framing his sunburned face as it did made him look like a chubby, unkempt angel. His pale blue T-shirt, even sweat stained and stretched tight across his belly, picked up the blue in his eyes. Looking at him squeezed into her tiny kitchen, Madeline almost reached for her phone, wished she had a friend or two to send his photo to, say look what turned up in my doorway.

"Come into the front room," she said even as she enjoyed standing pressed up beside him, inhaling his smell of sweat, dry grass, and heat. "Were you climbing the hill?" she asked the three of them.

"What?" Randy sat in the rocker near the front door, and motioned his cousins to take the couch against the opposite wall.

Madeline stood next to Randy, and Misery pushed her way into the room and sat in the straight-backed chair that used to be Grandma Kneedelseeder's. She tilted it and wiggled in it in a way that Grandma would have frowned at. "This should be good," she said.

"You came in the back way, so I thought you must've been climbing the hill."

"Yeah," Randy said. "We were sort of hiking around, ended up behind your place."

"Want some tea? Ribs? I even have some pasta salad left over," Madeline said. "Normally I wouldn't have so many goodies to offer."

"No thanks," Randy said, but the young people said yes at the same time, nodding vigorously, so she laughed at Randy and moved them again, this time to the table in the small and dark dining room, the white cloth already stained with sauce and grease. She carried the leftovers in from the kitchen, put a stack of paper plates down, and told them to dig in. Misery sat at the head of the table the whole time, smiling and humming an advertising jingle for lunch meat.

Randy looked at the spread and said, "I guess we could eat a bite." At that, the two young people filled their plates fast, and the boy ate six ribs, cleaned them off to the glistening bone, before looking up. Even the girl looked at him in wonder.

"You're faster than my sister," Madeline said.

He scowled. "Didn't know how hungry I was." He piled pasta salad on a new paper plate.

"They're from Texas," Randy said. "Been on the road a while. I didn't know they were so hungry, or I would've fed them before we went out exploring."

"Lisette," the girl said, extending her hand across the table to Madeline. "The eating machine is my boyfriend, Henry."

"Madeline," Madeline said. "And my sister Misery." All three nodded at Misery, not even flinching or smirking at the name.

"No use beating around the bush." Randy cleared his throat, talked fast. "These cousins of mine need a place to stay for a few days. My water main broke and my air conditioner quit working and I have termites, and they won't be comfortable with me. I'll probably sleep outside for a while, but these two youngsters could use a better place. Their visit came as a surprise, but I'm pleased to see them, just don't have a place for them. Sure, I could put them in a hotel, but that doesn't sound nearly as friendly as if they stayed here and I could visit them often and we'd all have fun."

Lisette and Henry nodded as Randy spoke, Lisette moving her lips as if she had memorized the same speech. Madeline noted that they'd clearly counted on her wanting to spend time around Randy. He'd judged her as a giver, too, not just a taker. What'd given him that idea? "How are you related to Randy?" she asked Lisette. She hoped Randy was right, hoped she could prove more than a taker.

"His mother and mine are first cousins," Lisette said.

"Misery lives here now. I do have one extra room, more like a closet with a window. It has a futon in it. One I got second hand from that woman who runs the bakery."

"Henry can't go outside," Lisette said. "I mean, we can help around the place to make it easier for you, but Henry has to help inside. He can't go outside."

"He has allergies," Randy said, and Henry and Lisette both nodded.

"And yet you were walking about in the back woods," Madeline said. "Brave of you."

"They're lying," Misery said. "All of us know that."

Lisette blushed to the crown of her head, the red glowing through her thin blonde hair. Henry sighed, then shook his head. "We're sorry to have bothered you."

"Now wait a minute," Randy said. "I guess you've been in the big city too long. Maybe people have to be wary in Chicago, but out here, if a friend needs a favor, he's not usually subjected to such suspicion, not called a liar."

"You mean out here in the meth center of the world where good honest folk pray hard and vote against welfare?" Misery rolled her eyes in such a theatrical gesture all but the boy laughed.

"I didn't say anything," Madeline said. "Misery called you all liars, and she came to me after living not in a big city but in a cave. No reason to be so defensive. As you can see, I don't have resort-like accommodations, but I do have a pool out front, room in it for two at a time. And I can always give you bubbles for your baths."

"OK," Lisette said, looking at Henry. "Sounds wonderful."

Misery stomped her feet under the table and shook her head.

******

"Madame X has cancer of the throat. Help her. Shrink the cancer cells, kill them off. Vaporize them. Turn them into harmless miniature warts. Do whatever whoever you are does. Please, I implore you." Wanda wore what she called her prayer shawl, a tattered patchwork quilt she'd taken from the old squaw, made from scraps of blue-flowered flour sacks, and smelling by now of mold and sweat. Both her babies had crawled about on it. It had been on her and Phil's bed until she bought a rose sateen comforter with her employee discount at Fishers. Wanda'd wrapped it about herself the first time she prayed, grabbing it off Angie's bed that winter afternoon simply because it was handy and she was cold. By now, she was afraid it was a lucky quilt. Her eyes were closed as she rocked back and forth. She wasn't sure if she had said the words, what she called the begging, out loud. Madame X's friend had agreed to one hundred dollars for one prayer a day for ten days. Or maybe Madame X and the friend were the same person and this was a sort of denial. Most of her clients gave the names of the subject of the prayers, but Wanda didn't care. The woman who agreed to pay, the "friend," lived on the street behind Wanda and used to sing in the choir at the ten o'clock mass at St. Dismas. And why ask for ten days? If the prayers worked, they should work right away. What kind of god needed so much repetition? One with attention deficit disorder? Wanda didn't care about that, either. It was some superstitious nonsense connected to numerology like the seven first Fridays and the novenas of nine somethings and the six weeks of Lent, and the three mysteries of the rosary, and the ten beads in groups of fives. Someone had figured all the numbers out long before her, and all she had to do was count.

Wanda charged only for the prayers that worked, one hundred percent satisfaction was her claim. There was no overhead, and if she got paid for every other one, that was still good money. Her rate of success was about fifty percent, though she claimed it at eighty since she didn't factor in the ones that were impossible, prayers to win the lottery or to end all the wars in the world.

She started praying in the late sixties, a good eight years after Juda dumped her and nearly two before Phil decided to leave, back when girdles were no longer in style and bras were worn mainly by middle-aged and old women. She'd had her tubes tied up tight and bought twin beds, had made it clear to Phil not only would she have no more babies, but she would have no more of him, though she may have sex with others if she felt like it. Though she never found someone she could put up with long enough, he needn't know that. She said she was a modern woman. And if he wanted sex, he'd have to figure out some way to get it with someone else. She didn't care how or with whom. But he wanted more of her, and he wanted the part she'd never given him, her attention. He wanted to talk, get to know her again now that Madeline was gone and Angie was, as he said, "old enough to ignore." He'd come home from work and want to tell her what new building he'd passed on the way, what old friend he'd run into in the coffee shop across from his office, how the new guy was getting on. He was an insurance adjuster and had what he believed were funny stories of claims people made. He would laugh as he talked, sometimes spitting on her. He didn't know her hatred of him had no bottom. Shut up, she said. Shut up. She said it over and over. Once she threw a new carving knife at him just before he got to what he said was the funny part. She grabbed him and twisted his ear back until he screamed when he asked her if she'd ever wanted to travel or live in a different part of the country. Out of desperation, she prayed. God, make him give up. Please make him know that I hate him, that the sound of his voice gives me the chills, that the sight of his dopey face with the bulbous nose makes me gag. Please please please make him stop talking to me.

And he did. One evening he entered the house, an evening in February when she was prepared as always to tell him to go to hell, already angry at him for coming home at all, and said nothing. Not even hello, or his annoying, "Honey, I'm home." She traced it back to the prayer she'd uttered that afternoon.

Then she prayed for Angie, already fourteen, failing in school, no friends. It was a mother's curse, but the bad ones, the ones that looked at you without joy or respect, were the ones you had to try harder to fix. Wanda wanted Angie to smile, to be a happy girl for both their sakes. Wanda's prayer for Angie was "Make it so that she is not ruined, that I have not ruined her." Soon Angie began leaving the house most evenings, sharing her mopey face with others, with at least someone else, anyone but Wanda.

Encouraged by what she called a one hundred percent success rate, she prayed for a raise. It was true she also asked Juda for one, but she asked him every year. This time, she prayed as well as asked. And it worked. It wasn't much of a raise, though, twelve cents more an hour, and she decided next time she had to be more forceful in her prayers, clearer and more specific.

A month or so after her raise, a young man in the shoe department, a weaselly sort she usually tried to avoid, walked over during a lag in customers and stood talking to her during what was supposed to be her break. He tossed his head to make the greasy bangs on his forehead move while she prayed for his phone to ring. It did. A week or two later, he stood talking to her again. He said he wanted to get a scholarship to the state university so he wouldn't have to work at Fishers all his life like a loser. In spite of the insult, she decided they'd all be happier if he were in college, and she told him she'd pray for his scholarship. When he got it, he told her he owed her something, and though she laughed it off, other coworkers noticed.

The accountant's wife had an unexplained liver disease and her body filled with fluid. He asked Wanda to pray for his wife, but he asked everyone else in the store to pray, too. Wanda did pray, and told him so. Within weeks the mysterious disease went away as fast as it had come. He jokingly credited Wanda. Then there was a lost dog that came home, a house that sold fast, a rain storm that held off until after a picnic, an engagement, a case of acne clearing up, someone's son-in-law getting a job. Wanda was called the prayer lady, and the joking tone gradually disappeared. After a while, she began to charge for it, just the ones that worked, and just for people she didn't know well. She made about two hundred extra a month this way, all tax free, no advertising but word of mouth. Angie bugged her eyes out when Wanda talked about it. How could this monstrous meanie have a direct line to God? Wanda thought Angie's reaction even better than the money, and she laughed out loud whenever she thought of Angie reassessing this god she'd been taught to believe in, wondering what kind of higher power it could be if it listened to Wanda. Wanda wondered, too. She knew what she was, knew if there was a god and its opposite, as most believed, she was closer to the opposite.

THREE

"I'd be counting the hours until we get out of this dump, if anyone knew when that would be." Lisette was stretched out across the rock-hard futon in Madeline's back bedroom, a room so small the futon frame had been pushed up against the wall so the door could open. She raised up on an elbow and looked at herself in the mirror above the powder blue vanity. The short blond curls made her look sweet like a kindergarten teacher, though her skin was too sallow for blond. "I mean it's hard to breathe in here. And that window thingy doesn't cool much." It was her twenty-first birthday, but clearly his life was too sad for him to remember that.

Henry sat at the end of the futon, up against the window. He watched a flock of blue birds as the air conditioning unit blew swirls on his faded red T-shirt. "I wish I could sit outside, not in that stupid pool the old lady has, but back here with the birds."

"Of course you can. Don't get paranoid on me."

"We're too close to home, you know."

His new blond shaggy hairdo made him look like a skateboard dude, either that or a creep, but she sat up and hugged him from behind. When he sounded so pitiful, so full of confusion, her blood pumped faster. She wanted to kick in the recruiting office door, bash in the heads of every person in the place, him included. Any recruiting office would do, the one nearby in the shopping center in Sullivan, or the one he had actually walked into in Terre Haute, back when he was Kenny and she was Anna.

She'd said nothing the evening he came by and told her he'd withdrawn from Indiana State and signed up. Surely he knew the war

27

was a mistake. They'd talked about it together, wondering why so many people, including their parents, fell for it, fell for it at least enough to hope for the best even as they wished it would end. "You don't approve, I know," he'd said. "But there is such a thing as duty."

She couldn't find a single word or phrase that would work as a reply.

"You still love me," he'd said, as if it were mostly a question, and she nodded.

He'd gone from Terre Haute to Fort Jackson, South Carolina, for his nine weeks of basic training. Then after a brief two-week home visit, he was shipped to Iraq. They'd e-mailed and called each other throughout his first tour, and in the beginning his notes and his voice were filled with hope and optimism. He told her he'd met Iraqi families who were grateful to the U.S., loved the soldiers, believed their country was on the way to a fair and just government. She wanted to say, What about us, when do we get a government that cares about fairness and justice? She wanted to say, I guess it's OK to kill them and ruin their towns if it will someday make them happier. The cynical remarks lined up in her mind, ready to pour out, but she knew enough not to be cruel to someone who could die any moment. She swallowed and told him to stay safe. She also knew she wouldn't stay with him if he made it back.

After fourteen months he was sent back to the states for a break, four months back at Fort Jackson where she visited him for weeks at a time, a week back in Terre Haute, and suddenly, or so it seemed to her, he changed again. He couldn't go back to Iraq. Those were the words he left in his farewell note the army captain showed her when he came to Terre Haute. "No one's ever sent me a note before," the captain said. "He even added a 'sorry.'" It made her love Kenny again. Soon the Sheriff of Vigo County came by as well, once with and once without the captain. Kenny was wanted, both men said, but they assured her he would be forgiven upon his voluntary return. They understood he was afraid, many young men were, but he shouldn't let his fear ruin his life. She told them both the truth. She had no idea where he was, but she knew Kenny, and yes, Kenny may be afraid, but one thing he was for sure was disgusted. The sheriff was a tall man with his hair in a buzz cut, more scalp than hair showing. He leaned down toward her and shook his fuzz-covered head slowly. He said even though there were now women serving in Iraq and Afghanistan, as a sex, women seldom understood war. She shrugged, knowing anything she said would only encourage more of the sheriff's wisdom. The captain returned a few times, and during one visit, he said Kenny absolutely would not be sent to a combat zone if he turned himself in. He was sure of it. But Kenny would soon be a target of bounty hunters, and could be in more danger than he'd been in in Iraq.

Nine days after the captain's first visit, a letter appeared in the *Indianapolis Star*. "Dear U.S. Citizens, I am a deserter. And I do not know what else. The fourteen months in Iraq have changed me, so I've lost the nouns to describe myself. Killer. Murderer. Coward. Fake. Those come to mind. I know so little, but I do know I don't want to take part in the ruination of a country and a people or myself. My fiancé, Anna Adams, knew this all the time." The letter was two-pages long. He said he was sorry a few more times, talked about forgiveness, about not trusting his country. "This war should be about or for something, but no one knows what that is." The sheriff returned to Anna's apartment, and he and the Captain visited her parents' home, too. A rock was thrown through the window of her parents' TV room. Churches in the area prayed for Anna's family. The letter was called a rant by the local news channels, and the Adamses made the six o'clock news more than once.

She talked to him in her head then, calling him knucklehead, her father's favorite insult, but also saying she was proud. He was a rebel, a man with convictions. If she saw him again, she'd say his naïve insights were not for the newspapers. But she'd also say yes, stand up and testify.

Two weeks after the first letter, another appeared, shorter but sadder, riddled with regret and confusion. He described an operation gone wrong, a family killed who were probably on the side of the U.S., though it was hard to know. Four days after that, a Kenny letter was printed in *The New York Times*, this one about supplies not being where needed, private contractors diverting goods, an unreported suicide, and the power of fear. "What is it for?" he asked in the beginning and at the end of his letter, underlined and in bold type each time. The next day, Anna received what looked like an invitation to a bridal shower, but inside was a note she was supposed to destroy. Kenny wanted to see her. If she wanted to be with him, she should fly to Chicago, where she'd be met by a friend. If she didn't show up in Chicago on September twenty-third, seven days from the invitation postmark, Kenny would understand. She responded by sending the RSVP card to a P.O. box in Leasburg, Missouri. She checked the line that said she'd be there, changed her mind immediately, then changed it again and bought the ticket, reaching her credit card limit with the last-minute flight.

Randy was waiting at the baggage claim holding a sign: "Anna: Bridal Shower." She'd expected this "friend" would be a man, an older man, but she'd pictured him like her father and Kenny's father, dapper with neatly trimmed gray hair, clean shaven and slim enough to be in erectile dysfunction commercials. She was afraid to get in the VW bus, afraid of this old guy with long graying reddish hair and pouches under his eyes as if he hadn't slept for days. She told him she wouldn't go with him unless he proved he wasn't a killer or a pervert, so he showed her his driver's license—Randolph Roma printed above his picture—and he showed her the RSVP card. She'd had to surrender her Swiss army knife at the Indianapolis airport, so for the first few hundred miles, she kept her hand in her purse and clutched her keys just in case she had to poke his eyes out.

On the seven-hour drive down to Bourbon, Missouri, Randy told her there may or may not be a federal bounty. The U.S. government was officially looking for Kenny, yes, but not actively, as the military was stretched thin. If caught, though, Kenny would be court marshaled, the book thrown at him. The main threat was that he'd made himself a big deal with his letters, reprinted along with his photo in many newspapers and blogs across the nation and already used in some political ads. At least two patriot groups that Randy knew about had put bounties on him. Postings on their web sites said they expected him to head for Canada. Kenny'd been in hiding in three different places already, but that was all Randy could tell her now. The truth was his case wouldn't die down as easily as most, and he couldn't be Kenny Washburn any more. Randy had two passports with him. "Don't know how they do it, those who help us out and get these fakes. Maybe your names come from dead people. He's now Henry Hobson. You're Lisette Graver. I have a driver's license for him, photo and all. A Missouri license."

Randy said once Kenny got to Canada, he'd not be able to return, not for a long time, not legally anyway, and by helping him, especially by using a fake name and ID, Anna could be called an accomplice. The fake passport alone was a federal offence. Randy wanted her to know all the risks. She released her keys by the time they passed the Springfield, Illinois, exits, but she didn't start crying until they'd cleared Pacific, Missouri. She hated to do it in front of the strange man, and hated it more because it was self-centered and useless. She wanted to tell him she was not sad but angry, that she was not crying for herself, though that would've been a lie. Randy told her she couldn't call her parents or friends, but she should write to her parents immediately and tell them she was off to explore the country for a while, tell them not to worry. He'd see that the letter got posted, probably from somewhere in Wisconsin.

Who'd decided she was going to Canada with Kenny? Had anyone even asked her?

It was after midnight when they arrived at Randy's stone bungalow, just a block from the main street in Bourbon, and she was still sniffling. Kenny was there, waiting in the dark. "Marry me," he said as soon as he saw her, even before the kisses and hugs.

"Could've asked me that before you called me your fiancé in the newspaper." She said it as a joke, lighthearted in the midst of sorrow was what she aimed for. He tasted like berries and yeast as always, but he smelled hot like fear, and she wanted to hurt him. She buried her face in his shoulder, rubbed his back, held him to her, chewed his earlobe, even bit it harder than she should have, anything to keep from talking more. She knew she couldn't marry him. He'd ruined their lives. He walked into that recruiting office on his own. Let him flee to Canada on his own, too

"We'll get married in Canada," he said the next morning as they waited for her hair color to set. Randy was at the diner, so they had the place to themselves.

"You need a gold chain around your neck to go with your blond curls," she said, but he didn't smile. "If we even get in," she said. "It's all so fake."

"Randy and this group are good. We can count on them."

"You're not much of a judge of what's good, falling as you do for blue-eyed recruiters in buzz cuts who say duty and freedom," she said. "And once there we can't come back."

"Not legally. But nothing we're up to is legal anyway. We may get good at sneaking back and forth." He didn't sound as if he believed any of it.

"Your mom wrote a letter that was printed in the *Star*. She said you have to follow through on your commitments, no matter how your mind changes. She said it's part of being a man."

He shrugged.

A lonely life among strangers awaited them, and that was only if everything went well. They were sitting at the scarred wooden dining table, one Randy or someone had carved stars and hearts into, and she suddenly jumped up, pictured herself running away. If she left fast, she'd be free. Instead she turned to face him. "How could you? Why did you do this to us?"

"You can leave if you want." His voice was flat, quiet. She knew he was more lost than she.

"What made you sign up?"

He shrugged. "I told you. I wanted to help. I was tired of being selfish." He stood and put his arms around her. "It sounds stupid now."

She pushed him away. "It would've sounded stupid to me then. I guess I'm with you for now, but I may bail before we get to Canada. I can't say." She looked at him, his shoulders drooping, his formerly bright hazel eyes dull, his blond hair long enough to curl at his temples. "My name is Lisette," she said. She held out her hand for a shake.

That afternoon, before Randy took them to Madeline's, he talked more to Lisette. "Your passports are good ones, I guess, so there's no need to worry. Overall, though, it's harder to get across the border than it was in my day. The Canadians are frightened by the terrorists, too." He laughed. "Not all the folks up there are more rational and cooler than we are. It's a myth. I'm not part of any real organization with a name and all that. We're just human beings trying to help others." He smiled at her, grateful she was finally listening without crying. "Please don't worry so much. He's doing the right thing."

Henry was stretched out on Randy's red leatherette couch. Broken springs caused one end to dip lower than the other, so his head hung low. He closed his eyes and listened to the talk. Maybe more blood would reach his brain, wise him up.

"I can't get used to Lisette," she said.

"It was my mother's name," Randy said. "Maybe that's a good sign. The trip'll be easier if we're a family group and can say we're all traveling north of the border for a wedding or some such. They ask now, you know—want to know the purpose of your trip.

"And sometimes miracles happen in this country. I lived in Armstrong, British Columbia, for twenty-five years, but could've returned much sooner. I wasn't there too long before the U.S. government came as close as governments ever do to admitting error. It offered amnesty for all of us who left the country to avoid one of those endless non-wars we're getting known for." He realized he was preaching, so he stopped for a deep breath. "My point is, maybe when this debacle is over and viewed in hindsight without fear, amnesty will be granted for people like Kenny. Henry I mean."

"But Kenny's not a draft dodger. The idiot signed up!"

"Henry," Randy said.

"Yeah. Whatever. He's AWOL. Or is it called UA now? Was amnesty ever given for that?"

"He's worse than UA," Randy said. "He's what he called himself in the newspaper, a deserter. He's missing from battle."

"Why are you taking us to this odd woman you know? Why should we trust you or her?"

Randy sat up straighter. "I don't know why her. It's a gut thing. Her first response to most things is to laugh. It's a fake laugh, but still, it gets to me. There's more to her than she knows. I don't know beyond that." He wished he had a reason. He explained that they had to stop before Canada to be sure the crossing was safe, for the patriot groups were watching the borders, or claimed to be, anyway. The plan was to go to a house in Michigan first, but some unexpected visiting relatives of the homeowner were causing a delay. "So it's best for us to lay low in Bourbon for a bit, just not at my place," he said. "It's gut thing," he said again.

Henry opened his eyes and sat up, pretending to be refreshed and therefore decisive. "OK. I'm Henry, she's Lisette, some sort of jakeleg cousin."

"Your visit came as a surprise to me," Randy said. "Let's say you're from Texas, OK?"

"We came in from Texas, need a place to stay." Lisette brushed her bangs back, the blond much silkier, finer, than her normal brown. "We got it. Let's go see this laughing woman no one knows very well. We'll worry about the rest of our lives later." She sounded strong, even to herself. How else could she sound?

******

Wanda couldn't believe in miracles, for to do so would mean she believed in a force that could cause them, and if she believed in such, she'd have to wonder why the force that could provide miracles hadn't done so for her. Oh sure, she'd had a few small favors, like Phil deciding to leave her and giving her the house, but, as Juda once said about her offer to pay for a night in the downtown Sheraton, too little, too late. Either she was unworthy, or the god made a mistake and missed her value, or she was just unlucky. And if unlucky was the answer, then the god was merely haphazard, and praying to it or talking about it, appeasing it in some way, would mean nothing at all.

How could any caring god have let a miserable woman like the old squaw have a child? And sure, maybe it was a god who killed all the squaw's other children—that would be the act of a caring force, like drowning a litter of kittens so they wouldn't grow up in starvation—but it had let her live, had missed one of the litter. Was it a god who put the idea of clearing all the grasslands into the heads of the farmers of Felt and those farmers for miles and miles around? Wanda'd heard about it when she lived in Tulsa years later, the old men shaking their heads at one of the causes of the Dust Bowl, blaming it on clearing the land for wheat. Short-sighted, they said, those businessmen who talked around her in the office as if she were a desk or wastebasket. Was there a god who chose not to send rain once the prairies were nude? If Wanda'd had more than corncobs boiled in creek water for her dinners, she may believe in a force that cared. That was the melodramatic way she'd explained it to the blind pastor of St. Dismas church back in the late fifties, the year just before Juda. She'd told the pastor God could've sent down a four-course dinner every Sunday for all the good it would've done her, the old squaw too suspicious to accept help, divine or human. It was true. The old squaw cursed the woman who walked up to the shack one evening with a pot of bean soup, said, "No charity for me or mine," turned the pot upside down, and the woman and Wanda watched the bean soup soak into the gray Oklahoma dirt. Wanda snuck out later that night and ate the dust-coated beans.

But here she was, praying for others and being successful.

And she felt it now, someone listening. She tried not to.

It would be a while before she knew if Madame X recovered from her throat cancer, but a woman she met at Great Clips more than a year ago was now a manager of her bank branch, a job she had been hoping for without much reason. She said her promotion was due to Wanda's prayers, so Wanda was busier than ever as the banker spread the word.

When she told the pastor she didn't believe in God, it was long before she started the praying business. It was at the end of the only year she and Phil took the girls to Sunday mass. They'd dressed up, and they tried to fit in as they greeted other parishioners and nibbled donuts in the basement afterwards. A short-lived experiment. Wanda's white-hot angers had not gone away, and she'd been as bored with the smiling Christians as she was with Phil. When she told the priest her prayers died in the Oklahoma dust, she prepared herself to despise his limp comfort. Yet his response was to ask if she ever prayed for her mother.

"Sure," she answered. "I prayed that she'd lose her throwing arm. She could hit the side of my head with a rock from thirty feet away." The frown that darkened his entire face was her reward.

So now she prayed as she was contracted to, collected only on those that worked. And for a few weeks she'd felt the presence of something or someone else listening to her pleas. She teased herself about her Native blood. She could have been doing one of those rain or crop dances, appeasing the great spirit of whatever tribe the old squaw had been a part of. So Wanda, imagining a listener, sent up a prayer for herself. She could have asked for enough money so she wouldn't end up stacked three deep in a charity ward, dead a week before anyone noticed. Or she could have prayed for her joints to stop hurting, for her stomach to stay tough enough so she could eat all she wanted of whatever she wanted. That sort of thing, indistinguishable from millions of prayers from other self-centered old farts like her, would be easy to ignore. But let's make this interesting, she said to whatever spirit was listening. She knew what she wanted, and that was to be someone else, to have another life entirely, but no use asking for that sleight of hand. Instead, she would put the spirit to the test with something almost as hard. Make my oldest daughter call me. Let her work up the nerve to confront the beast who nurtured her.

******

For three days, Madeline and Misery entertained each other by asking who Henry and Lisette were. They asked it over their morning coffee and again in the evenings as they sat in lawn chairs beside the empty pool and ate bowls of caramel swirl ice cream.

"Drugs," Misery said. Her usual first guess.

"You've seen too much TV," Madeline said.

"Maybe it's the War on Terror, then," Misery said.

"Good," Madeline answered. "If those are the sort of terrorists we have to worry about, we're in the clear."

They laughed about the two liars, three counting Randy, which they always did. He was the ringleader liar. He barreled down the gravel drive all three days the couple had been there, spent a few minutes in the back room with them, then sat out by Madeline as she lounged in her pool. It was the hottest September on record; a semi overturned on 44, closing the highway westbound for two hours; the principal of the middle school went to the Mississippi casino a weekend ago and won two thousand dollars. He said all that vapid nonsense, the sort of stranger talk she herself was good at, to keep her from asking questions, she knew, and so she gave him a break. No questions. By day three, he had interesting things to say as well. He was writing a report on wind turbines and on ways to use them without interrupting bird migration routes. The white pelican, for one, was often caught in blades, seemed unable to see them if they were silver or white, but communities by and large didn't want a hillside of red blades as their backgrounds.

Did she mind being used? She wasn't sure. She should be sure, she knew. Either you mind or you don't, she lectured herself. If you aren't sure, then you don't mind. He wouldn't have to lie if he weren't doing something wrong, Louise's ghost said, and Madeline knew she was right, but that made Randy more appealing. How long had it been since she'd been part of something wrong? Not counting Ollie's death, that is, which was illegal, but not truly wrong.

One afternoon, after Randy had already stood to leave, Misery joined them, carrying a black umbrella as her personal shade. Her fuzzy sweater of the day was orange. "I cannot imagine taking a trip to see a relative, and ending up in a stranger's back room, living like a vampire," she said after dragging another lawn chair up.

"Aren't you hot?" Randy asked.

"I ask her that all the time," Madeline said. "She wears that getup because she wants to suffer."

"Are they vampires?" Misery asked. "That would explain a lot."

Randy laughed. "Vampires?" He looked down at Madeline in her pool. "I have to go. Reports to write," he said.

"Didn't mean to chase you away," Misery said.

"You should park up on top," Madeline said as she had each time he left. "Next time. By the mailbox."

He stuck his head through the window, said, "Vampires," then laughed again.

"I wish they were vampires," Misery said as the bus jerked and squealed up the hill.

On the fourth morning of their so-called vacation, Henry did nothing but watch bluebirds and whine. He had ruined his life. Even when running away you took yourself with you. He wished he could stop thinking. Lisette rubbed his back, listened and agreed, wanted him to get over it, to go forward, whatever it would take. She was not cut out for this, truly did not know how to help him. But she was troubled, too, and no one thought to ask about her, least of all Henry. The question—*Want to go with me?*, or better, *Will you please?*—remained unasked. When she gave up rubbing his back to give her aching arm a rest and headed for the kitchen, she found the crazy sister staring into a her cup of cold coffee. Of the two old women, only this one was truly crazy. Sure, one claimed she was swimming on Highway N each afternoon, but she was only playing at eccentricity. Lisette had an aunt like her, one who'd decided to wear only shades of blue for no reason but attention. The other one, Misery, was not pretending. She hummed when she wasn't talking, cackled rather than laughed, wore clothes that left her drenched in sweat. She'd chosen her own horrible name. The truly crazy one stood up suddenly and blocked Lisette on her way out the back door, made her listen to how noisy the quarrelling squirrels were. "Like fingernails on a blackboard," Misery said, grabbing Lisette by the arm and squeezing. "They make the ugliest sounds. Someone should shoot 'em. Right?"

"I'm twenty-one today." She hadn't planned to tell anyone.

"Whoop-de-do," Misery said. "Hip-hip hooray."

The letter Lisette wrote to her parents on her second day in Bourbon, the one that was carried to someone and to someone else and ended up at a post office in some small Wisconsin town, took two drafts to get right. In it, she said she was fine, and was exploring the country. She said she was flying from one city to the other, renting cars to see the countryside, trying to overcome the attention Kenny'd caused by naming her in his letter. She'd only made it as far as Wisconsin. She may be gone a while, and they should give notice to her landlord and pack up her stuff. She was safe and happy and was sorry to ask for their help with her apartment, but it was time to be impulsive, to do something without endless planning. She said she'd see them soon. She added they should remember she loved them and not miss her much on her birthday. She signed it, Love, Anna, a name she already mourned. Randy made her throw that draft away and write another, exactly the same but without the love and the birthday line. Now, having announced her birthday to the crazy woman, she felt more alone than if she'd kept quiet.

She knew if she were home, the day would be boring and predictable: her mother would bake a ham, buy a sheet cake with "Happy Birthday Anna" in pink glaze surrounded by sugar roses, and give her a heavy winter sweater, possibly with snowflakes appliquéd on it. It would be from both her parents, but her father would not have seen it yet, and her mother would laugh, admit it was not exciting but practical for the coming winter. Anna'd smile, knowing she'd not wear it.

But she was Lisette and the crazy one had told the bikini one and unfortunately her birthday was the excuse for a party that evening— anything, she guessed, for the bikini one to get Randy to show up twice in one day. And he did, bringing in two large pepperoni/ mushroom pizzas with extra cheese from Rocket Boys in downtown Bourbon, five salads, and two bottles of wine. Misery said she wouldn't eat her salad. Before grabbing slices of pizza, they toasted her birthday.

As the bikini woman carried on about what good pizzas they were, better than almost anything she'd ever found in Chicago even, Lisette remembered how touched she'd been last year by the e-card Kenny had sent, remembering her birthday even from Fallujah. He was Henry now, and he joined the conversation about pizzas, saying the best he'd ever had had come from Bandolino's in downtown Terre Haute. He covered himself, awkwardly she thought, by saying he had a great uncle who lived there.

"What about Texas?" Misery asked. "Abilene wasn't it? Any good pizza places there?"

Henry shrugged. "I guess."

"Funny you being from Texas anyway, Harvey," Misery said. "Madeline's favorite husband was from Texas."

"It's Henry," Randy said. "Not Harvey."

"How many husbands have you had?" Lisette asked.

"Too many to count," Misery said

"Three," Madeline said.

"Did you have a favorite?" Randy asked. He reached across the table for the wine.

"Well, the first one will always be special because I got my last name, Dames, from him. I became someone else."

"My name change was for my first name," Misery explained to the others, looking mostly at Henry. "But now I wonder why I didn't do the last name, too. Why did I keep Kneedelseeder? What about you, Howard? Have you ever thought of a name change?"

"It's Henry," Lisette said. "*You* keep giving him name changes."

"I had one wife," Randy said. "So I guess she's the favorite, even though we didn't like each other much."

Misery cackled and hiccupped. "I have no favorites because I've had no one but me. A tumbleweed, wanderer, vagabond, lone wolf. That's me."

"The self-made woman?" Randy asked.

"Oh, I was made, all right. I didn't do this all by myself." Misery pointed to her head. "I was definitely made."

"Did you say Needle-seater?" Lisette asked.

"In my grade school," Randy said, "we would have called you needle butt."

"How clever," Madeline said. "We've never heard that before, have we, Misery?"

"It's just adorable," Misery said. "I'll have to write it down."

As the dinner wound down and they ran out of the Cabernet Randy brought so had to break into Madeline's stash of Chablis, they talked about their favorite foods, the heat, when the sugar maples would finally turn gold. Misery filled any silences, no matter how slight, by tossing meaningless facts into the void. "The first time rubber gloves were used in an operating room was in 1860," she said.

"So what?" Lisette asked.

"Well, it may not mean much to you, Miss Priss, but it saved lives, I'm sure."

"They're all dead by now," Henry said, and Madeline laughed. Henry's first joke.

Henry had told Randy exactly what kind of sheet cake to order, pink and white and fancy, and Randy had brought it over earlier and hidden it in the pantry. Madeline planned to carry the cake in from the kitchen with a *Ta-da* or something as silly, but just as she reached for it, her phone played a tune. Trysh. She grabbed her phone instead of the cake, her blood saying Trysh, though she didn't know why. Her last and only premonition had been Misery, a surprise. This was merely a wish, she reminded herself. But she wished for the call always, and this feeling of Trysh coming closer was new and powerful. Please, she whispered. I want to see you, baby mine. I cannot have been so horrid that you will never forgive me.

Instead, it was Alexandra, Ollie's daughter.

"I'm a goner," she said instead of hello. "I'm the same as dead. Kicking the bucket. Buying the farm." It was cancer of the pancreas, and she'd been given the diagnosis two weeks earlier, but with hope leading her, she'd gone to the Mayo Clinic for the second opinion. It was the same as the first. No good treatment existed, nor did any real hope. She was undergoing chemotherapy and radiation, eating bushels of herbs and swallowing handfuls of vitamins, meditating and doing yoga, but was running out of time. She was just this side of large doses of morphine, the sweet end. "You know, they can almost pinpoint how many days I have left," she said. "Well, months is what they count in. Six is my magic number. Maybe eight if I'm lucky." She was just forty and didn't want to die, she said, then laughed and admitted there seemed to be no good age for death. She said she would make a deal with god or the devil or whoever controlled things like this, and yearned for that puff of smoke that came before the wish-granting deity appeared.

Alexandra's news made Madeline's home grow small, the walls move in, so she escaped to the front yard where she sat in the grass beside her empty pool, taking deep breaths as she listened. Life was a puny thing people clung to. All it took were a few renegade cells acting up and it was over. Or like Martin, a decision. As he said, it was like leaving a party. You just knew when to go. Some evenings Madeline put herself to sleep by naming all the dead she knew. Who wants to live forever, Ollie'd asked near his end, and she'd shaken her head each time, said, "Yeah, really a bad idea. No thanks," but she had wanted to; she did want to. Still wanted to. And Alexandra must as well.

Eventually Madeline said the expected, "Let me know if there's anything I can do," and Alexandra was ready.

"I need your mother," Alexandra said. "You used to joke about her prayers, but I need prayers now, no matter how worthless you may think they are. I'm trying it all. I want more time. Please call your mother."

"OK," Madeline said, for she'd meant the offer. She would do anything, no matter that it would be useless.

By the time Madeline made it back inside, Misery was telling them that the doctor who treated John Wilkes Booth was named Mudd, and so maybe that was where the phrase "Your name is mud" as an insult had come from. They appeared flat, the four of them, two dimensional, pasted onto the background of the dining room. Misery spoke from underwater. The rest nodded as if their heads were helium-filled balloons. Not one of them had met Alexandra.

Henry went to the kitchen for the sheet cake that read *Happy Birthday Lisette* in pink glaze with sugar roses along the borders. Randy smiled at the coming surprise. Henry set the cake down, then spread his arms out, and said *Ta-da*. Lisette looked at the cake, jumped up, knocked her chair over, and ran out the back door. "I cannot do this," she shouted just before slamming the door. Henry took off in the other direction and shut himself up in the back room with an answering slam.

Alexandra was dying fast. Madeline wanted to say so, to put the high drama of children in love in perspective, but Randy spoke first.

"Youth," Randy said. "Young love. What can you do?" Then he clapped his hands and said, "More for us. I'll take a giant corner piece with one of those roses on it. How about you two?"

He was no good at smoothing things over. His clapping was silly. "Hell," she said. "Give me a big piece. Eat, drink, and be merry, blah blah blah."

FOUR

Through the normal 'round-about way, all in letters that could be and were shredded, absolutely no e-mail, Randy'd heard that it would soon be safe for him to take the two kids up toward Canada. The group he was part of was loosely organized. It didn't have a name and no one was in charge, at least not as far as he could learn. It was a mere few hundred strong, started by a priest. Some in it kept track of police and military bulletins, others monitored the bounty hunters and bounties, some dove down into the truly illegal for the false documents. Others, like Randy, helped by moving the escapees from one safe house to another. He got involved through an electrical engineering professor at UMR who judged Randy—the hair, the flight to Canada—correctly as someone who would help. Randy'd been advised by the professor that his house was being watched, just a fear of one of the jumpier members most likely, but the professor was not foolhardy enough to ignore it. The work bred nervous speculation. Randy wasn't entirely above the fear himself. The mere speculation his place was known was the reason he used Madeline's place. He'd planned to take the kids up to a house in Pearl Beach, Michigan, and would in a few more days once the unexpected visitors left it. Pearl Beach would likely be Henry's last stop in the States, and Randy planned to ask Madeline to go with them to give the illusion of a family group. He liked Madeline's face, thin and honest, just the hint of a dimple in her right cheek, was intrigued by the string of dead husbands.

He was drawn to the crazy sister, too. He understood she suffered, but thought the self she displayed was also partly an act, a funny version of crazy complete with a silly name and all that humming and those ugly clothes. Big, ugly women like her reminded him of his mother, who'd worn black tent-like dresses most her life, unlaced buckskin hiking boots beneath the dresses. His father said it was a reactionary response to being named Lisette. She died a month after Randy slipped across the border in 1967. She was setting the dinner table and fell down dead of a brain aneurism. She was only forty-eight. She was up, then down, his father said over and over, unable at first to accept the suddenness of her death. Her last words were, "I've never cared for this flatware."

******

Trysh was sixteen the last time Madeline'd spoken to her own mother, heard her nasal voice. It was Martin who'd wanted Madeline to call and let Trysh talk to her grandmother, sixteen being a special birthday and the beginning of being grown up. "She has one good grandmother in Louise," Madeline answered then to end the conversation. "And another in your mother." But the conversation continued, and Martin's argument that a third one wouldn't hurt was one he could make only if he'd disregarded all Madeline had told him. All Wanda did was hurt. Did he think Madeline's stories fake or merely exaggerated, she asked, her anger closer to the surface than she'd known. That he had not believed her tales of life with Wanda reduced her words, her life, to chit-chat, and reduced her to an insignificant noise Martin lived with. She said as much and more. She amazed herself by screaming, kicking furniture, throwing dishes, and cursing as she had seen and heard her mother do, had done herself only in her dreams. He should believe her. She wasn't making Wanda into any more of a monster than she really was. Trysh hid on the stairway landing to watch, but eventually joined in, said she remembered her grandmother as a nice woman. Madeline turned on her then as she never had before. "You were eight last time you saw her. Eight-year-olds like everyone. They all seem nice when you're eight!" She threw a cake plate in the direction of the landing. Not at Trysh, she knew. Never at Trysh. It was that part of a tantrum where nonsense was screamed as if it were truth, but even as she heard herself say it, she knew when she was eight, she'd not have called her mother nice, by then was already staying at the Dameses' as much as possible. She bit the inside of her mouth until she tasted blood to make herself stop screaming. She left the house and drove around for a few hours, returning to find the glass and ceramic shards swept up, but her loved ones gone, her home quiet as a stage set. A day later, she apologized to her husband and daughter, though still feeling bruised and trodden upon. To prove she meant the apology, though, she made the call to her mother, saying only, "Here's Trysh."

That was twenty-eight years ago. Since then, Madeline's only contact with her mother was the Christmas card she sent to her childhood address each year, her signature and nothing else under the card maker's printed message. She'd used various P.O. boxes as her return address. Wanda answered each card within weeks, putting down her year's worth of news in small cramped writing. Her news was not new—everyone hated her, she deserved better, she'd never had a break. Madeline knew the refrain without having to read the verses.

******

"I'm very old," Wanda said on the phone. "You're old, too. You can get over hating me now."

"I need a favor."

"Boo! Did I frighten the poor little baby?"

"I was recently married to a man named Ollie."

"Did he kill himself, too?"

"He died. Cancer of the brain." But Wanda was right, suicide was right, assisted suicide. There'd not been enough morphine in the world to stop Ollie's pain. He cried with it for days before his heart could finally be made to stop pumping. Only Alexandra and Madeline and the doctor at Columbia Hospital who defied the law and administered the drip knew. "His daughter has cancer now and she wants you to pray for her."

"You got involved with a family with defective genes. Good thing you're too old to reproduce."

"Will you pray for her, for Alexandra?" Madeline looked at her kitchen clock. By the time the little hand hit the six, eight minutes and some seconds, this conversation would be over and she would have survived it.

"I make a lot of money praying. You probably know that."

"You've said. She'll pay. I'll pay. Someone will pay."

"It's the oddest thing. Can I tell you something real? Someone's there."

"What?"

"Whatever it is I pray to is listening."

"That's the idea, right?"

"No. I mean yes, it's the idea, but it's been pretend, superstition, luck. But now there may be a listener."

"Her name's Alexandra Stuckey, Ollie's daughter. Cancer of the pancreas. She doesn't have much hope. Can you start today?" Why was she going through the motions as if she believed? Today, tomorrow, next week, never—what difference would it make? But she'd promised, and she had to tell Alexandra the prayers were already being said. If not out of fear and desperation, Alexandra wouldn't have asked for this voodoo.

"That's just it. I can start, but I'm worried now. There may be a god."

"Please just pray. Or at least say you will so I can tell her. Do you picture them, the ones you try to help? Alexandra's a blond, mostly natural. She has gray eyes and a pointed chin. She's thin with no waist."

"OK. You don't care about what I'm trying to tell you, but why should that be a surprise." Wanda's voice changed, grew younger and harder. "I have a price, you know."

"I'll pay. I'll pay. Didn't I just say so?"

"Good. You're still a simpleton. Learned it from Louise probably. I've never been stupid enough to promise something before I knew what it was. Want to know my price?"

"Yes." Madeline would hang up in five more minutes. It was her limit. If she did it before Misery's nap was over, she could avoid that scene.

"I want you to invite me to your home. Just once. I want an invitation."

"I live maybe eighty, ninety miles from you. Do you still drive? Even if you do, you can't get on the highway and come all this way."

"An invitation. I want to be asked. You're right. I probably can't make it."

"I'll pay twice what you usually charge."

"You just told me I can't make it. So why not at least invite me? I want to hear what that would sound like. Say it. Say, 'Come to dinner, Mom.'"

Madeline took a breath. A Wisconsin farmer made a goat cheese from non-pasteurized milk and aged it underground. It tasted like sweet and spicy grass, and because it was Madeline's favorite, Alexandra made the long drive from Chicago to the Wisconsin farm and sent Madeline at least two pounds each month. "OK. Come to dinner, Mom."

"When? You have to say when."

"Tomorrow night."

"Love to. Can you come and get me?"

"No. That's not the deal. I invited you. You can't make it."

"I can if you come and get me. As you said, only about ninety miles. I hadn't known you were so close."

"I can't."

"Then I can't pray. If you told Alexandra I was praying for her, it'd be a lie. Now, you're not above lying, I know, but then you'd be sad that you told a dying woman, one you seem to care for, a lie. You'd have to do your pretending a lot harder, do that Louise stuff of living forward so hard your brain would explode. Easier to come and get me."

"Misery's here."

"Misery's everywhere," Wanda said. "So what if I'm a mean old woman. BFD, you scaredey cat. I have *not* harmed you. You've done that all by yourself."

"I meant Angie," Madeline said. "And I am not harmed. Was not harmed. You didn't do it because I left. In case you don't recall, I stayed with the Dameses as much as I could, even before I moved in their basement. For most of my life, I was mostly gone. But Angie is here. And Angie was harmed."

"You want prayers or not?"

"I want prayers. But I invited you and you cannot come. So sorry. Now pray."

"No."

Madeline knew the one who wanted something was the one who had to give in. Could she put up with Wanda for a day, part of a day? She could if she had to. And when she was with Wanda, she wouldn't listen to one syllable that came from that old mouth, that rotten heart. But she could not pick Wanda up. She knew that much. Spending time in a car would make her want to head directly into the side of a bridge. Pretending had limits. And more than that, she couldn't look at that house where she'd grown up again, not when she'd managed by sheer force of will to stop dreaming about it. But one of the kids could collect Wanda. Randy owed her that much and more for his lies. "OK. Let's make it lunch. Be ready at ten-thirty tomorrow. We'll eat at noon and get you back home by three. A friend will pick you up. He's young, but he's a sullen liar so you should get along fine. He'll be in a red Escort."

"This proves it," Wanda said. "I prayed for you to call. But how could I ever expect this prayer to be answered? After all this time? And with an invitation. Never in a million years would I expect you to call. There is something or someone listening. There must be. Why now, I don't know. Better late than never? Anyway, this is the answer I needed." She laughed, sounding like a happy child, throwing Madeline off balance. "I may be born again."

"Just start praying, " Madeline said. It was time to hang up, so she did.

Madeline asked it first as a favor. Could Henry pick her mother up? Randy said absolutely not. It wasn't safe, he said, and she asked for whom, but he didn't answer. Instead, he offered to do it. No, she said. She didn't know him well enough yet, and meeting Wanda could scare him off. Or he could believe the lies Wanda would tell. It had to be the kids, one of them. She begged. He refused. She promised to repay the favor, but just as she said it, she knew she already was doing more than normal, above and beyond. She remembered the truism she'd come to earlier. Whoever wants a favor more has to give in. She changed her method. It wasn't a request. It was a condition.

"They're running from the government," he said. "And patriots." He'd been planning to tell her all anyway. The daily reports from the engineering professor claimed some people and groups were interested in Henry, strongly interested was what he'd heard, but no one was looking for the one called Lisette. She looked different anyway, and would be just a young blond woman in a red Escort, so he gave in, ninety percent sure she'd be safe. "Lisette can do it, " he said, "if she's willing."

"Willing?" Lisette said when she was given the choice. She laughed like a child, dancing and grinning at the chance to get out. The dark and smelly shack, the crazy women, a depressed Henry, the intense boredom—who wouldn't want to leave that?

Randy told her she had to drive carefully, always following the speed limit, because she didn't have a license for who she was now.

In this way, the deal was made, and as Lisette skipped back to the guest room to tell Henry the good news—that she at least was getting a field trip—Madeline smiled in spite of the impending visit, pleased to have bargained so well. When she smiled in victory, looking into Randy's eyes and cocking her head, so clearly pleased with herself, Randy smiled back, and on the sort of impulse he thought was in his past, he pulled her toward him and kissed her. She returned the kiss, his lips hot and firm and salty.

How do two sixty-year olds make love? That was the setup to Madeline's joke to herself. And the answer, the punch line, was fast. They didn't need time for thought, seduction, a built-up yearning that could finally not be restrained. They just did it. They were old, and if they didn't know what they were doing now, who cared anyway. They didn't have to consider their futures too carefully for they had more past than future by then, and the truth of that made them freer.

There was one moment of hesitation. "I don't think we can do this," Randy said when they were already naked in her bedroom.

"Of course, we can," Madeline said. "I have K-Y lubrication."

He laughed. "Think I meant *should*, not *can*."

So it was quick and explosive. She'd forgotten how much fun. He smelled like freshly baked bread. He went home soon after to work on a report on the number of pelicans who could be caught in wind turbine blades, and she sat on a dark and damp back step and drank a tumbler of Chablis quickly, willing the alcohol to preserve her new memories but to kill her oldest brain cells. Misery sat on a step and drank, too, but Madeline barely knew she was there. Rather she looked out into the green that filled the space all the way to the horizon and imagined herself on a South Pacific island with Randy and no one else.

Lisette took off at eight the next morning, though Madeline told her it was no more than an hour and a half to Wanda's home in the St. Louis suburb of Florissant. The sun was alone in the blue sky that morning, nearly blinding Lisette at times as she headed east on 44, and as it lit up the hillsides. Yellows and the rare reds, mainly sumac, shone, glistened, winked at her. Hardwoods and limestone and quartz cradled her. She'd been cooped up in the bikini woman's home, cooped up with Henry and no one else the least bit interesting for so long, she'd forgotten the thrill of driving down a highway with the radio on and the windows open. She didn't mind that the only station she could get played contemporary country and was full of singers who whined like Henry. And she didn't mind the tailgating trucks, the slowpokes pulling campers, or the women in SUVs speeding by while on their phones. For five days she'd sat beside Henry and listened to his sorrow about the trouble he'd gotten himself into, hardly ever remembering to include her. He was frightened to leave the house, to do much more than watch the birds through the dirty windows. He said he hadn't thought being on the run would be so boring. They'd only made love once, and that not with an ounce of the old joy, and she felt duller, more confused for that. She was most herself when she was desired. Before he signed up, even when she visited him in North Carolina, some of her best thinking, her clearest ideas, had come as she sucked his penis, the repetitive action clearing space in her brain, making her nerves crackle faster. She once wrote a paper in her head, positing Grendel in Beowulf as the real Christ figure, as she tongued his uncircumcised head. Now he seemed uninterested.

She laughed out loud. All of them back in that crazy house on the steep hill had to know how strong the temptation would be. A car, a road, an atlas, fresh air in her hair. No one sulking and brooding and sighing beside her, no need to hide. Or yes, she still had to hide. Randy had made that clear. But she was hiding in the open. She knew how to get to Indiana from here, could pick up Interstate 70 in St. Louis and be home by dinner. She'd never tell where Henry was, and surely he knew that much, knew she'd protect him even if she cut him loose. Randy's group or someone could buy the bikini woman another car, not that the ten-year-old Escort was worth much anyway. She'd not thought it out, this living in Canada, changing names. Could she spend her life with someone like Henry, so needy and sad? Frightened and stupid. Why had he enlisted? Still, no matter how many ways he said *duty* and *responsibility* and claimed he'd been tired of being selfish, no matter how many times he explained, she didn't get it. There was no responsibility in killing just because others were signing up to do it. If no one signed up, it would have to stop faster. She yelled all that to him, whispered it to him, even wrote it out for him, though she knew it was simplistic, redundant, and worse, beside the point. He already agreed with her now. And the past could not be undone.

But she needn't suffer for his mistake.

Nevertheless, she did as she'd been instructed. First though, she drove around the downtown part of St. Louis for a half-hour, passing the signs for Interstate 70 three times, and finally stopping in the museum underneath the Arch. She bought a post card and mailed it to her parents. Not that they'd be impressed by the Arch, for as a family, they'd been to it twice, up the cable cars to the top both times. They'd wonder at her traveling the country and stopping there, but she liked to imagine them putting up a bulletin board in the kitchen over the buffet as soon as they got her letter, planning to use it to track her travels. She wanted to be connected to them this way. So she sent the Arch, and she wrote on it that she'd been to the middle of Missouri, spent some time in Bourbon. She believed she'd not given her position away, for she didn't say she was there now, and no one would think that having been there she'd go back. Finally she pulled up in front of Wanda's small box with its brick facade, just fifteen or twenty minutes early.

Why had she followed her instructions and not taken off? She had to answer that for herself before she could leave the car, go up and ring the bell. She knew her own habit of obedience, taught early and reinforced in grade school, was partly to blame. She'd been able to sit with her hands folded on top of her desk all day long if the nuns at St. Catherine's told her to. She believed she could be impulsive like Henry and the recruiting office, but it wasn't likely. She was a thinker first, then a doer. And what were her thoughts?

Well, for one thing, she could run away any time, and for now she was doing something noble by reuniting the bikini woman with her poor old mother. OK, that was one thought, and a good one. And even if the Madeline's mother was a mean old thing as Madeline said, Madeline deserved some pain. Anna or Lisette or whoever she was supposed to be now had pain, was confused and in hiding, and all the others in that nut house, excepting Randy, she guessed, should have it, too, feel the swirls of confusion that seemed to lodge in her chest and stomach as they churned nonstop. Number two was that Henry may stop whining, and then being with him would be as nice as she remembered and she may in fact go to Canada with him. Number three was that they would worry if she didn't return, think she'd been killed on the roadway, and not only did she not want to worry Randy, but when she finally left, it would have to be in the open with time to say good-bye. Pleased she had three good reasons already, she moved to what she now knew was the big one, number four. It was an important part of the struggle to help Henry escape. She was a hero of the resistance. She nearly strutted up to the front door, leaned on the doorbell.

Wanda looked older than Lisette expected. Her dark and colorless eyes were at the bottoms of deep pockets of dark brown velour in a face white and cracked like dried Elmer's glue. Her cheekbones were high and pronounced structures the rest of her face hung from. Her nose was straight and large. Her hair was gauzy and her skull shone underneath it. Her ears were large, the lobes yellow and waxy. She had two dark hairs on her chin. She wore a royal blue nylon running suit and blindingly white athletic shoes. She smiled at Lisette, said she was cute like a blond version of Trysh, whoever that was, said the blond was as fake as a barn cat wearing a bow and no one would be fooled, but she was happy her ride wasn't a sullen young man. She carried a foil-covered pumpkin pie, which she held on her lap the entire way back to Bourbon.

"I've made a pumpkin pie every year the day before Thanksgiving, thinking it possible I'd get a call at the last minute—'Mom, come for dinner'—and I wanted to be ready, to have something to take. It's rude to arrive empty-handed, you know. But the call never came. Not once. I've spent the Thanksgivings alone since my youngest left home. My pie always ready. Not to mention all the other holidays and birthdays and regular weekends or weeknights when company would've been appreciated. I think of Thanksgiving as the day for families. But I always eat my pie alone. My family hates me, in spite of the sacrifices I've made." She sniffed. "I know I won't get invited to Thanksgiving this year. I mean, an invitation by Madeline is a once-in-a-lifetime event. So though it's October, this will have to be like a mini-Thanksgiving."

Lisette's face clouded, her lips flattened, and Wanda called her a decent young girl who no doubt paid attention to her parents and grandparents. "You're probably misunderstood, like me. But you always do the right thing. I haven't seen Madeline for thirty-six years.

Can you imagine not seeing your mother for that long?"

Lisette shook her head, and Wanda noticed a tear running down the side of her face. Old age was mostly a series of losing out, except, that was, for the ability to inspire pity. Old folks' stories of neglect and loneliness were automatic tear-jerkers. It was one more power Wanda was gaining, growing into. "Anyway, once the so-looked-for invitation came, I had to bake the pie." She was careful not to laugh. The last pie she'd made was Key lime for one of Juda's birthdays, a desperate attempt to make him look at her with a touch of the old fondness. Too many years ago to count.

"I understand," Lisette said. "It's a wonderful thing, that pie."

"I may have put too much cinnamon in the first one, wasn't sure, but I was afraid I'd ruined it, so I made another. From scratch. I was up all night baking."

"I'm sure it's a delicious pie."

"Couldn't take the chance, see. If the pie was bad, Madeline would think it was on purpose, would think I was trying to hurt her with a bad pie, didn't want to come, didn't love her. She's hard to please, and I get so few chances."

"We'll all love the pie," Lisette said. She was doing a good deed, uniting this family. The poor old thing beside her needed attention and love. She hoped odd Madeline would get over whatever it was that made her neglect her mother so. Maybe Lisette would have a talk with Madeline before she left them all, her way of saying good-bye, her parting gift.

Madeline had spent the afternoon in her pool, her heart jumping at each gear change from above, each whoosh, each toot.

The Escort, when it did arrive, seemed to plunge off Highway N, skidding past Madeline, spraying gravel the way Randy usually did. Madeline stood up, dried off, took a deep breath, and before turning toward her mother, she faced her house. There, she saw Misery's face pressed up against the living room window, her mouth hanging open.

Lisette leaned against the car, holding tight to the pie, and Madeline turned her gaze, focused on how the foil caught the sunlight and bounced it back to the trim around the car's windows. Then she looked at her mother, a small shapeless elf in blue nylon who stood on the other side by the passenger side door and squinted across to Madeline and the pool.

"The Great Spirit sent me," Wanda said. "But I should've been prepared for a trick. I finally hook onto to some power, and get a trip to this dump."

FIVE

Randy took Madeline's car and left his VW so they all could be ready to go when he came by early in the morning. Misery and Wanda and Lisette and Henry were supposed to be putting whatever meager belongings they had in the bus as Madeline emptied her pool for the season, stepping on the blue rings to flatten them. She folded it up so it fit in around the spare tire under the third seat. Lisette sat on the bus's floor, just inside the sliding door, and Wanda in a lawn chair she'd drawn up. Misery leaned against the side of the bus, pushed the side mirror back and forth as she talked. Her black bag of sweaters and black skirts was already in the back next to Henry's duffel, but Lisette hadn't thrown her suitcase in yet. Wanda had nothing.

"I won't have many more chances," Wanda said. "Now is my time. I have to get to my people, the Cherokees."

"Cherokee? You?" Misery said. "One of the civilized tribes?" She tilted the mirror down to her feet.

"I have the gift. The calling. I have to go back to Oklahoma."

"Course, your mother may have been renegade from her own people. Could be anything—Navajo, hell, even Iroquois." Misery looked up and laughed. "Which are the meanest? Probably that one."

Wanda snarled. "Stop. This is not about the old squaw. I don't care who she was. This is about me. Me." She stood. "I can do miracles. I can. I'm here, aren't I, traveling with my two daughters? My powers will only grow as we get to Oklahoma."

"Let's go the other way, then," Madeline said, but none of them acknowledged her. Just as well. Jokes and smart remarks were superfluous in the absurd situation. Wanda had not been able to go home after lunch; her dizzy spells made her their problem. Surprise, surprise. Madeline cursed herself for not anticipating the ploy, though anticipating would not have been enough. The first fake spell came during lunch, but it was a day later, just after the fourth one, each hammier than the previous, that Lisette insisted they take Wanda on this trip north, said she wouldn't go without her, and Henry said he wouldn't go without Lisette. Randy said, *Surely an extra person for a day or so, the course of least resistance, the more the merrier,* and other phrases only an innocent could come up with. Now Wanda wanted a detour.

"Maybe Randy'll take us to Oklahoma first. Or maybe we'll go to Oklahoma on the way back," Lisette said.

"Oklahoma's not on the way back from Michigan," Misery said. "Seems odd to have to say so."

"How long will you have to stay in your homeland to connect with the spirits?" Lisette asked.

"I don't think there's a set time," Wanda said.

Lisette and Wanda and Misery went in just after the lightning bugs stopped showing off, but Misery came back, dragged a chair over beside Madeline, sitting next to the brown spot where the pool had been. She brought a bottle of Chablis and two glasses. "Let me tell you about my rape," she said.

"I was never pretty, you know. I've always looked more like Dad than like you or Mom. Meaning even as a child I resembled a gorilla with a ponytail. When I got to college, though, for a brief time, I thought my fortunes had turned. The good thing was I was away from home. Of the two of us, I was the one getting a degree, so I had something on you, too. People seemed to care, at least some few I met, that I was smart. But that thing we're all supposed to want, happiness, eluded me. I could talk myself into it, but I never could feel it." Misery laughed, gulped her Chablis. "I worried about it more than it was worth. It's probably not even a condition natural to our species.

"Anyway, likely I was already crazy, ruined in the crib as they say, but after trying the chorus and then athletics—did you even know I was briefly on the university's track-and-field team as a shot-putter?—I did the typical and found religion. God promised

me peace, all that stuff. Since we'd once been Catholic, I joined
the Newman Club and was suddenly part of a group of people my
age who had in common their need to belong to something and a
background of masses and sacraments. The most active were cheerful
and serious, but some were in it just for fun, for the conventions and
the so-called retreats, which were rumored to be wild overnights. Sex,
of course, was everywhere, and this being after the sexual revolution
and before the AIDS scare, no one, not even the priests, were shocked
or even greatly concerned. Not that I had any sex, being big and
ugly, but I created a character who was loud and crude and funny. I
learned lots of dirty jokes, and thought of myself as the combination
truck driver/prostitute. Not just *come* and *blow*, but *meat* and *fizz* and
sandwich and *jump shot* and any word or phrase you could think I
gave a double meaning to. I made myself unshockable, a sort of living
joke. The big ugly girl who knows the score."

Madeline stared at a pair of eyes, shining in the darkness of the
hill on her right. Fox, raccoon? Who could tell? Back when Misery
was making herself into a character, Madeline was working at an art
supply store. Having left the Dameses' basement shortly after Chris'
death, she and Trysh lived in a efficiency near her work, and the
woman who would fix her up with Martin was already her coworker
and friend. She lived like someone with no sister, no parents, either,
except for Louise and Ray Dames. Had she known then what
university Misery attended?

"It wasn't really rape," Misery said. "But it may have been worse.
We were in a Holiday Inn in Carbondale for some sort of regional
conference on living our religion, all of us holy young people. I shared
a room with a quiet German exchange student, but everyone else was
paired up boy-girl. On the first night there, we drank a lot and were
sitting around my room—that was my thing, being party central—and
one guy just coming in stumbled over a vacuum cleaner hose left out
in the hall by the cleaning crew. He brought it in, hanging out of his
pants, pretended it was pulling him, that he was led by his penis. We
all laughed, and then he pointed it at me, said he had to have the big
girl, and we all laughed again. I kept laughing as the joke continued,
and I was pushed down, held on the bed by some of the others, my legs
spread, and the hose pushed up against my panties. Even the other

girls laughed. I knew the joke meant I was too ugly for a real penis, and I was embarrassed by my panties, wondering if they were stained. I knew not one of those holy people would be aware of my humiliation.

"I left that night after the fun was over. I hitchhiked home. A woman who said she was running away from her children gave me a ride. Never set foot in the Newman Club again."

They sat in silence, and Madeline poured more wine. "I'm sorry."

"Sure. Me, too. I used to spend lots of time wishing every one of the people in that room would end up with a horror of a life. I used to be able to go through them by name, but now I can't. And from what I know of life, it's a safe bet theirs all have been horrors without my wishing for it. I did stop wanting to be happy, though. Stopped expecting it. I may have fallen into the expecting trap a little bit with Ginny, but not much or for long."

"Tell me more about Ginny."

"Ha! You think we're friends now? I only told you that story to explain why, since I've been here, I've never vacuumed the place. I've got an equally good one to explain why I have not cleaned the bathroom." Well, that was funny, Misery thought. If she could make jokes, she was OK. And she did feel funnier lately. There should've been a warning on her pills—"Stopping suddenly may cause funniness." She'd run out of her pills three days earlier, so decided to stop at least for a while. It was a test. How could she know the devil would show up that very day? In person, too, not in her dreams as usual. How could she know they'd all be taking a trip? Nonetheless, she functioned—doctors' speak for not causing too much trouble, for being able to pass as normal enough. "I function," she said out loud beside the brown spot where the pool'd been. "I am functioning tonight. I will be functioning tomorrow." Madeline looked worried, so Misery laughed for reassurance. "More jokes. I'm full of them. I tell functioning jokes."

******

The previous night, Randy told Madeline he'd chosen hers as the hiding place, chosen her as the traveling companion, because she was unconventional enough to understand how unfair it was to hold a young man accountable for a mistake. They were in her bed for the second time. She felt lighter, when he spoke, knew her smile stretched across her face. How good of him to consider her swimming on Highway N as a sign of unconventionality. He'd be confused to know she'd tried for most of her sixty years to be conventional, to know what conventional was and how far she could venture from it. She'd once given a dress to Goodwill because Louise said it was the wrong kind for a young mother to wear, and it was a brand new dress, worn by Madeline only up the stairs from her bedroom to the kitchen and Louise's frown. It was too short, too low cut, too sheer.

"Misery can come, too," Randy'd said. "Up north. Michigan. Into Canada. It'll be a week at most. We can walk around the dunes while there. We'll go the day after tomorrow."

******

When Randy opened the door, B was on his doorstep, rubbing his right foot along his left calf. He said he was in the neighborhood and thought he'd drop in. Randy's mostly packed duffel was on the couch, in it a University of Missouri-Rolla student ID for Lisette. Three copies of the report on a trial wind farm and bird migration were in a bubble mailer on the chair by the door. Randy shrugged. "Sit if you can find a place."

B did, setting a three-ring binder full of photos of wind farms on the floor beside the rocker, then easing himself down into the chair as if he were an old man. He was nearly the same age as Randy, but his stomach covered his belt as he sat, and when he leaned over to push the binder farther from his feet, Randy could see he soon would be completely bald, only a few brown strands hovering over his scalp.

"I'm taking a trip tomorrow," Randy said, motioning to the duffel. "Nothing too much. Can I get you a beer?"

"You can't go to Pearl Beach," B said. "The plans have been changed."

"What? Who said anything about Pearl Beach? Where's that? I'm heading south."

"Sorry, Randy." B laughed. "I'm not trying to be all mysterious, not really. Just wanted to freak you out for a minute. I know about the kid. I know about the trips. I've gone on two myself recently. Last summer when the diner was closed for what I said was my nephew's wedding? We went to Seattle then."

"I'm not used to the cloak-and-dagger stuff, B. I don't want to get used to it either. It's a child's game."

"Trust me," B said, and Randy nodded. He did. After all, he ate breakfast with B two, three days a week, had for more than a decade.

"You know the professor, I take it."

"We were in the seminary together. He told me about you. But we got word there's a large reward out finally. Large enough to attract real hunters. A group called Citizens Against Terror. CAT. They use a panther-looking animal on their web pages, all claws and teeth. Weirdly mean looking. But they won't let this kid fade away. That makes Michigan unsafe now because one notice on the web site says the kid may go up there. They're recruiting help in stopping him."

Randy sat on top of his bag on the couch. He felt like a character in a movie. "Where should we go now?"

"Montana. Up near Butte. I got the address at home."

Randy laughed and B joined in. "I hate this spy crap."

"I'll take that beer now," B said.

"You, a priest?" Randy said when he handed B the Old Milwaukee. "You don't seem the type to believe in miracles. Bourbon would've missed your good gravy."

"I'm not much for miracles," B said. He told Randy he'd joined the seminary because there was nothing else he could think of he wanted to do. Priests at least got to give money to the poor. All other jobs, even fireman, seemed boring to him. "My word back then was *bogus*. Anything any adult did seemed *bogus*. And I think I wanted to go to a school where I'd have to board, too. I wanted to get away from the house. I was only thirteen when I decided, but, no, I didn't hear the call, not as some in my class claimed to. I was eighteen when I left the seminary, and I left for sex, of course. I didn't get to board in the seminary, anyway. That doesn't come until the college level."

An hour and one additional beer later, B said he should go to Montana, too, drive some of them up in his car, follow the bus so they wouldn't be so crowded. He hadn't known Randy was taking such a large group. It was a good plan, would make it easier to split up at the border, those with papers getting across, the others waiting somewhere.

Randy agreed. He hoped Madeline's unlovable mother would ride with B.

******

Oklahoma? Okla By God Homa? Going there would be like
revisiting a torture chamber. How unaware her daughters were to
think she meant it. She enjoyed stirring Lisette up about her need to go
to her "people," and her so-called need also provided a reason not to be
rushed back to her house in Florissant and her isolation. Well, that and
her not entirely fake heart condition. She wanted to find some special
use for her special gift. As she lay on Madeline's couch the night before
the trip, the stuffing in the seat cushions like fists striking her back, she
wondered what spectacular action she could cause. If she knew the real
purpose of this journey, she'd arrive at her role in it sooner. "Please,
Great Spirit, get rid of Alexandra's tumors, cleanse her pancreas."
She whispered that prayer, sent it up to the cobwebs and the cracked
ceiling. "I mean it, whoever you are," she added. "That woman's cancer
has helped me a lot. Give her a break."

******

Before she climbed into the bus, Madeline took one last look at
her house and saw Trysh's dimpled and foxlike face hidden among
the purple spikes of the false dragon head beside the house. The face
disappeared, but came back. Then she heard a crow caw "Mom, mom."
Escape from her mother was not possible for Madeline, though she had
once thought so. Here she was at sixty still tied to the mother she'd
plotted all her life to dump. But maybe that meant escape was not
be possible for Trysh, either. She pictured the soul like a boomerang,
returning to its origins no matter how long or far the throw. The body
had to follow the soul. Trysh may already be on the rebound, willing
to talk to her own mother, to forgive. If Lisette pictured Oklahoma as
a small detour on the way to Michigan, what would she think of Texas,
Galveston to be exact? Could Madeline talk Randy into going there
once they made Henry the problem of another nation? Yes, she already
guessed she could talk Randy into almost anything, but she'd have to
be ready to explain Martin and her way of letting him go. Perhaps she
could if she had to. It was time for Trysh. Letters returned but calls not;
it was a firm good-bye, yes, though clearly not a wish in it for a good
anything. Madeline worked hard at not thinking the word *never*.

SIX

As close as B followed Randy's bus, the storm followed them all. At nearly noon, when they pulled out onto Highway N, Madeline knew if she'd been asked, she would have called the clouds filling their rearview mirrors beautiful. The series of ever-darkening semi-circles were a giant scallop shell, inside out, as seen by the scallop. By the time they got to Interstate 70 and headed west, the shell was almost black, and it hovered on their left side. At Independence, where they turned north again, it was back behind them, and Madeline decided it had changed into a giant pipe, one of those drainage pipes leading off from Cold Water Creek, which she and Chris had crawled through as children, daring each other to go farther, their hearts beating in fear of being stuck or drowned. Surely the storm would overtake them. Madeline was surprised only that they got past Independence, Missouri, before being caught.

Hour after hour, she'd ridden in the short middle seat of the bus, Lisette having claimed the shotgun spot first. Madeline leaned back against the window and stretched her legs out, watched the woods pass by. Gold and orange and red, set off by still green but browning oaks. Because the thirty-six-year-old VW was less powerful than most cars and trucks on the highway, Randy stayed in the right lane, so Madeline's view of the Ozark river valleys and bluffs was interrupted only by the billboards. And from her position, what she could see of those was mostly their supports and, for a few, the bottom lines of their messages. No matter. She knew them all well. Some read JESUS, making it clear the name was enough. Some advertised free showers for truckers and as an added incentive, the largest assortment of porn in the Midwest. Home cookin', without the G, was claimed by nearly every restaurant. She laughed at the missing G implying tasty food. Her view, though, was mostly woods, limestone and granite rock faces, ponds, and then eventually pastures that seemed high and flat with cows and goats as focal points. She saw four red-tailed hawks swoop down low, dozens of vultures. One open field was dotted with sheep. She didn't listen to Wanda complain, nor did she pay attention to the assorted facts Misery offered now and then—"Weasels have bones in their penises," she said as they passed something furry and dead on the road. Not paying attention was the same as not listening and that was the same as if no one was talking and that was like being in the sixth and seventh grade when her father would drive her to school in the mornings in total silence. She'd stare from the window then, too, imagine what it would be like to be someone besides Madeline Kneedelseeder.

By the time they turned north at Independence, just before they were sucked into the black tunnel, Wanda said, "Something's burning." She repeated herself twice before Misery agreed.

"This should be fun," Misery said.

"Let's ignore it for now," Randy called back to them. "Think positive."

Lisette said nothing. Like Randy, she'd sat quietly so far in the front of the bus while Wanda and Misery, sharing the long back seat, had talked enough for them all.

The first drops were large and loud splatters, but within seconds the bus and the highway were underwater. The violent drenching of the world drowned out all other sound, and Madeline knew Randy, though driving at fifty-five, a bit slower than the rest of the traffic that must still surround them, could see only every half second out of the two it took the wipers to complete their path. She knew they were all holding their breaths.

Traffic slowed to a creep just outside St. Joseph, and even then visibility was no more than ten feet. As they crept past all six exits, Wanda started talking again. "Get off here," she said for each one. "We're burning up. Madeline, talk some sense into your man. We're about to burn up in the rain."

Madeline faced the side of the bus and tried to glimpse the woods through the water. Wanda was probably right about the smell being dangerous, but not listening was a habit by then, a pleasant habit. So we'll burn up, Madeline thought, and that will be one more in a series of hardships Wanda could bitch about.

What she had heard so far from her mother, even without listening, was the ride was rough; the other drivers were stupid or mean; it was too hot or too cold; they were lying to her and not planning on stopping in Oklahoma; Angie's blue sweater smelled like freshly killed skunk, and Angie did, too; it was a slap in her own face that Angie had chosen that odious name; both of her daughters were ungrateful; Phil had used her; no one ever liked her because she told the truth and because she was Indian; her feet and legs swelled because Randy wouldn't stop often enough; she should be paid lots more for her prayers than she was.

Misery, the only other one who had anything to say so far, had not once responded to Wanda's complaints, but rather gave them all pieces of what was in her brain. Besides telling them about a weasel's penis, she told them Saturn was three times the size of the earth. She told them that the wife of the man who wrote "Home Sweet Home" ran away from home. She said Caligula meant "small boots," a name the Roman ruler was given by his men. When she wasn't talking, she emitted a low hum that sounded somewhat like "The Battle Hymn of the Republic."

The burning smell nearly disappeared when the traffic began moving again, and for more than one hundred miles it was so faint they could ignore it, wish it away in those positive thoughts Randy had asked for. But when they were just across the Iowa border, three miles from Route 2, the smell grew so intense it stung their noses, and before even Wanda could complain, the bus bucked, jumped, and screeched, then stopped entirely. Randy guided them to the shoulder and cursed. "Clutch's gone," he said. "Where are we anyway?"

"Nowhere," Wanda said. "Absolutely nowhere."

They were on Highway 29 in Iowa, just six miles from Nebraska City. B, who had Henry in his front seat, told Wanda, Misery, and Lisette to squeeze into the back of his Cavalier, and he'd take them into town, come back with a tow truck for Randy, Madeline, and the bus. Misery insisted on taking her black plastic bag with her, and Lisette spoke up finally and said she, too, would take her luggage now, would need some of it at the hotel before the bus was towed, and then Wanda said she'd take the bag they'd made up for her that morning—a few extra underpants of Misery's, a pair of socks—and so almost all of them, including Randy and Madeline but not Henry who remained seated and staring forward during the transfer, got soaked trying to stuff and rearrange bags in B's trunk.

When the five of them finally drove off down Highway 29, peace descended on the bus. Even the drumming of the rain was softer. As Madeline sat with Randy, she apologized for her mother, something she'd not had to do since before she became a Dames. "She's not my fault, but I guess I am responsible for her being here now. I'm sorry."

"Luckily I can't hear well when I drive," Randy said. "This old bus rattles, and there's a constant whoosh of wind around my head, even with all the windows up." He took her hand. "But we'll make Lisette sit elsewhere from now on."

"I shouldn't have gotten my mother involved anyway. I know Alexandra's as good as dead. Alexandra knows it, too."

"Maybe we're all as good as, but until we are, we're not." He leaned in and kissed her then, his tongue tasting as salty as always. When he finished, she took his hand, and half stooping, half crawling, guided him to the back of the bus. "I've never done it in a VW, bus or otherwise," she said. "I mean, not in all my sixty years."

"Sad," he said as he pulled her shorts and panties off, tossed them up toward the driver's seat. "So sad."

******

The Pear Tree Inn was not really an inn, but rather one of those groupings of stone cabins, some connected and some separate, called motor courts when they were built sixty years earlier. The cottages had been renovated a few times since, and now had microwaves and mini-fridges, as well as cable television and brownish-red indoor/outdoor carpeting throughout. The walls were the original knotty pine, darkened by the years but still glossy enough that they reflected outside light. The black mildew stains between the bathroom tiles and around the shower stall were permanent, and on damp days the rooms smelled of pine mixed with the faint urine scent of the carpets.

It was 10 p.m. by the time Madeline and Randy checked in. B had dropped the others off at about eight. In spite of their choice of separate vehicles for the drive up, Henry and Lisette took one cabin with a double bed. Misery took the one next to theirs, way in the back by the Dumpsters, and when she asked that Wanda's cabin be close to the lobby and far from hers, Wanda said she was used to being hated, pushed aside, having her feelings count for one hundred percent zero, but in fact, she'd never asked to be dragged up here or to have her life put in jeopardy in a burning bus on the side of a highway in a monsoon. Was it too much for someone to consider her once in a while? She was old. She needed care. She should be next to her daughter.

"Your daughter Misery?" Misery asked. "Or your daughter Angie, who doesn't exist?"

B said he'd take a room next to Wanda's if it would calm her, or he could be put wherever else they needed him, but he'd let them sort it out, as he had to get a tow truck out to the highway where Randy and Madeline waited in some danger. After he left, Wanda said it wouldn't help her much to be next to him, a virtual stranger, and they'd better put Madeline next to her, which would be much better, being next to the only daughter of the two who could take care of herself. By the time they all had keys and had dragged their bags to their agreed-upon cabins, the pizza place across the street closed. Misery, Henry, and Lisette resorted to candy bars from the lobby for dinner, but Wanda said chocolate gave her headaches, and her people were used to doing without, had survived many moons of famine, so she was not as weak as the other three.

******

"Seventy percent of dust is shed human skin," Madeline said to Randy. She was stretched across the bed in cabin 2 of the Pear Tree Inn. "Misery told me that last time I dusted."

Randy laughed. He sat in one of the two straight-backed chairs beside the table at the foot of the bed. He drank a bottle of beer from the cooler that had been in B's trunk. His shirt was still damp, and he wore a towel draped over his head.

It wasn't even close to what she wanted to say. You make things better, was what she meant. Or they can go on without us. Can't B take Henry to Canada by himself? Or who are we when we're with them? "How long will we be in Nebraska City?"

"We'll find out tomorrow." B hadn't found a garage that was still open, so they'd left the bus on the highway. "We'll try the one called Grovers on the corner first. It's close and looks decent. I've been expecting the clutch to go out for a while, but hoped we could make this trip. Pressing my luck, I guess. Now I just wish we'd made it to Grand Island. We'd have a better chance of getting a clutch faster."

"Sorry about your bus," she said.

He laughed again. "Strangest thing, getting your sister's rags from the back, I found your pool. All sad looking and deflated. Planning a swimming party?"

Wanda sat on the bed in cabin one, wrapped the purple comforter around her, and prepared to pray. The old squaw used to say everyone hated Wanda because she was the old squaw's daughter, and they hated the old squaw because she was "injun." Wanda had known better even then. If the old squaw had been as white as one of those Mayflower pilgrims, or if her ancestor has signed the Declaration of Independence, anyone with any sense would still have hated her. It was true, they may have hidden their hatred better; smiling and bowing and groveling would have replaced spitting and throwing rocks.

Wanda was a chip off the old squaw, couldn't deny it. The only one who'd ever liked her was Phil, and that said nothing good about her. Nonetheless, if she didn't win the hearts of humans, she was favored by the gods, not by all of them maybe, but by one or a few. Her prayers worked. The grackles that congregated in the trees around Madeline's shack started their raucous banter before four in the morning, but that first morning, she prayed for them to shut up, and they did. The next morning, they didn't even drop by. The god that liked her must be the one who directed nature, or maybe he or she was in charge of noise. It was why she believed a few of the gods cared about her. She was successful praying about illness and jobs and personal relationships, too. Or maybe there was only one god and she could be successful in any area, its liking of her so firm. How could she use her power? What should she ask for now? Well, one thing was her mind. When they'd stopped at that family buffet restaurant in Herman, Missouri, she'd been confused by the bus. It'd been orange when she got out, yellow when she got back in. And at that rest stop on Interstate 70, the bus grew while she was out of it, managing to be twice as long by the time she climbed back in. She said as much, said it was hard to travel in something so changeable, but none of them were listening. She knew they'd closed their minds to her, and this time she was relieved by their inattention. Obviously, her brain was crumbling, but her daughters had so long ago stopped caring, so she was her own confidant in the matter. How would she know when her mind was truly lost, against what would she measure?

It was like hitting that car a few weeks ago. Oh, Madeline had acted concerned when she said Wanda couldn't get on Interstate 44 and drive to Bourbon, but where was that concern when Wanda needed groceries or had to make a doctor's appointment or had to escape the goddamned house she spent endless hours in? Precisely nowhere. For half a lifetime, Wanda hadn't even seen Madeline. So Wanda had to drive herself, no matter if her eyes were failing her. Even after she hit the streetlight standard and couldn't tell her patronizing and censorious insurance agent, so her car had only one headlight, she had to drive. But to be safe she decided to drive only during the day and would have made it home before dark if the checker at Food Shoppe had been faster, but as it was, she'd been nearly blinded by an oncoming car's headlights, and so had slammed into the car parked on St. Denis Street, only two blocks from her own driveway. She shook so from the impact, she'd wondered if her head would ever stop bobbing on her neck made of mashed fruit. But as soon as she stopped seeing double, she sped away, and seemed to have gotten off scot-free. The owner probably had insurance anyway with an agent who wouldn't condemn him for getting hit, children who loved him, and besides, he was probably descended from one of those white men who'd made her and her kind's life so full of sorrow.

"Let Alexandra's pancreatic cancer disappear as if it never existed. I need a miracle here, and need it soon. Blow the cancer cells away like so much dandelion fluff." She rocked while she prayed. Her lucky quilt was back at home, but she wasn't worried. She was the lucky one. "And heal my broken mind. Don't let any of them ever notice my weakness." She chanted that out loud, repeated it a number of times she'd meant to be ten but lost count. When she finished, she stood, then remembered one more prayer. She plopped back on the bed and said, "And that boy. Reveal his secret. And I don't mean that he's not a natural blond. Amen." She fell backwards, lying sideways across the bed, laughing out loud, wondering if the gods that favored her had a sense of humor. She laughed more. Wanda as a favorite was a joke itself. "Seriously, Great Spirit, tell me what he's running from." Still chuckling to herself, she fell into what she considered the troubled sleep of the simultaneously blessed and persecuted, slept all night wrapped in the comforter with her legs dangling off the bed until morning. Both of her feet were numb when she awoke.

******

"One girl would stand up on the top of her desk and scream," B said. "Every now and then. For no reason I could figure. Story was she'd been abandoned, had emotional problems, saw a counselor every day. But I was supposed to teach her English, and I wanted to. I didn't know how else to help her, but I thought if she had the tools, you know, sentences, punctuation, vocabulary, then she could tell her story, or tell her ideas, or get involved in another world and get over herself. I had another one who jumped out the window when I turned my back to write on the board. We were on the second floor. They give the new teachers the problem classes. I really thought if he could learn to understand what he read, he wouldn't feel alone. For him, I thought the puns in Shakespeare would be fun. But they all fought me too much. I gave it two years, then found something else."

B was talking to them at breakfast in a diner on the square. It was a place like his own, same major food groups of fat, sugar, and salt, same clientele, but with newer starched and flowered curtains and a brass chandelier. The question he'd started to answer, was answering, was why he'd opened a diner. Part of the answer was *no, he did not like to cook* and wasn't much good at it, either. The high school cafeteria served better food. He admitted to liking the diner, though—the chatter, the groups and the couples, the regulars and the tourists. The complete answer went all the way back to his seminary days, his sudden loneliness when leaving the seminary, his education certification, and his failure as a high school teacher.

"If I'd known you were one of those holy Catholics," Misery said, "I'd have gone to another table, another diner."

"Don't hold my past against me," B said.

Five of them shared a table. Randy and Madeline had gone to the garage instead of breakfast.

"So," Lisette said, "you made at least two mistakes, the seminary and the high school, and they didn't ruin your life. Imagine that."

"Some mistakes are easier to get over than others," Henry said.

"I never saw any of it as a mistake," B said. But the high school teaching had once seemed one large one made up of many small ones. He'd been fired for approving and directing a play the remedial class wrote about the vice principal. The play involved a game of strip poker and brief full-frontal nudity, which upset the vice principal far less than his own characterization as a buffoon. "I may not be quite so dim-witted as portrayed," the vice principal said after he advised B to look for work elsewhere. B laughed at it all now, one of the advantages of being alive for sixty-three years. "I consider it all, even the firing, as merely changes in direction."

"How sweet of you," Misery said. "Such a greeting card attitude."

"My menu has syrup on the back, keeps sticking to my hand," Wanda said.

Lisette looked down at her plate, the scrambled eggs already rubbery and cold. Some changes in direction *were* mistakes, yet not the kind that ruined your life. All during the ride she'd been thinking that when a person died, he was no longer alive. You would be foolish to pretend he was still there, to try to live with anything but the memories. This was the same: this stupidity of Henry's was like a death. If he'd been stupid enough to step out in front of a semi, had tried to cross Interstate 70 on foot and been killed, she'd be in mourning now, but would not be giving up her family and friends. In fact, she'd be wallowing in whatever comfort they could provide. So Henry'd done something as irrevocably stupid as crossing the highway in front of a semi, and just because he didn't die, she'd become someone else and lived with no comfort at all. Even now, she heard him sigh while B managed to get the crazy one and the old one laughing. She forced herself to look up again, to pay attention.

"We're telling stories," B said, looking at her, seeming to know she had gone inside herself for a time. "About bad meals in restaurants. Misery once found a fingernail floating in her split pea soup."

70

"Even large ones with paint and glitter will float," Misery said.

Lisette smiled at B. He was as old as Randy and as her and Henry's grandfathers, and more than that, he was round and balding, had that northern European skin that after sixty-plus years was full of rough patches and blotches. Nevertheless, he took problems in stride, clearly saw living as fun. When he laughed, she wanted to kiss him. If he promised to laugh every day, she would be his. That feeling surprised her, but she knew it was true. She would gladly give up confused and sad young men whose skin fit their bodies.

******

A simple man thinks simple thoughts, Randy teased himself. Here was his simple thought: sex was fun. Well, he was a man, and common belief was he would enjoy sex with anyone. Maybe that was true, maybe not. He didn't know, for he'd never had the chance with many anyones, and had had no chances at all for a while. But he liked sex with Madeline. And the reason was he liked her. So much for profundity.

She seemed to agree. "Old people sex is fun," she'd said as they were falling asleep the night before. "Because I don't have to wonder if I'm good at it any more." She confessed she'd never felt good at it. He said he hadn't known women cared about their performance. All they had to be was willing, or at least able to be talked into it, then they had to move a bit to show they were at least alive. The man did all the rest. She kissed his earlobe and set him straight. All that advice in the women's magazines, men's magazines, too, about muscle contractions and positions and rhythms was hard on a girl who couldn't dance because her hands and feet seldom worked together. "Now I just enjoy it. Nothing forced. No more worrying about my rhythm or my skills. I'm too old to get better."

When he said he guessed she was unusual, that most women didn't worry about being good in bed, she snorted.

"Here's another news flash. Freud was either stupid or very mean. Clitoral sex is the best."

Well, he'd known that from his first wife, but had fallen asleep before he could tell her so. The next morning as he listened to her singing "Camptown Races" in the shower, he wondered at his luck.

Clutches for 1969 VW buses were a rarity, especially for Grover's Garage, just off the square in Nebraska City. Still, it was only Tuesday, and Grover was sure if he ordered the clutch that morning, it'd be in by Wednesday afternoon, Thursday at the latest. Randy would be on his way by Friday morning without fail. Randy and Madeline took that news to the diner where B still sat with Lisette. They were reading about Nebraska City on his laptop. B didn't know where the other three went, but he knew Nebraska City had once been a major trading center for goods traveling on the Missouri River. Randy said he hoped Henry was being careful. "Ha!" Lisette said. "He's probably hiding in bed watching the cartoon channel and not laughing."

B checked the few listservs he was part of and said CAT had raised its bounty for Henry to two thousand dollars, but was still guessing the Michigan area was where people should look. Another group, Stand and Be Counted, was offering a reward, too, advising its members to keep an eye on all ways into Canada. One of the Democrats campaigning for a senate thirteen months before the election was using Henry's words in his speeches, had Henry's photo on his web site, which prompted letters to the editors and blogs from those on the other side, some of whom noted how many times in his letters Henry admitted he did not know much. They said that ignorance was consistent with this weakest of generations. B said the American memory was short, but not short enough for Henry to be forgotten yet. Lots of ugly rants. Of course, he'd been called Kenny Washburn in all of them. B wouldn't be foolish enough to e-mail the professor in Rolla nor the woman who had the place in Montana nor anyone else connected to the transport of UAs, but as far as he could tell, no one had figured out Henry's connection to Randy or himself. "However," he said to Lisette, "the sheriff of Vigo County has figured out you're not in Wisconsin or St. Louis and were never traveling alone. It's clear, according to him, you're with Henry. Your parents just hope you're safe and will be careful. It's in this article from this morning's *Tribune Star*." He turned the screen her way. "Even has a color photo of you. Nice smile. Brunette suits you. Your postcard from St. Louis arrived yesterday." He paused, rubbed a hand across his face. "The sheriff doesn't buy it."

Lisette looked up from the screen at B. Here was a man who would never in a million years have fallen for a recruiting slogan, yet he helped those who had or would. It was true that if she unfocused her eyes, he looked like an aging river otter, but she'd take him over Kenny who was now Henry any day. She'd trade a boy for a man.

A hot wind had blown the clouds away earlier, and the four of them decided to kill the day by hiking the seven-mile trail on the bluffs up above town, a highlight B had discovered on the Nebraska City web page. Before they left, B said he guessed Misery and Wanda weren't the hiking types, and Madeline said it was a good guess, not telling them that Misery had walked, or claimed to have, for four days down Highway 44 five weeks ago to get to Madeline's home. Lisette said they needn't bother to invite Henry, either, as he wasn't a fan of exercise, though as she spoke she remembered the afternoon three years ago he'd taken her out to Cagles Mill Lake, and they'd hiked the sixteen miles around it, slipping on the muddy banks, getting stuck once in what they called quicksand. It was there, both of them bruised and covered with mud, smelling of dead fish, that he gave her the thin gold band with diamond chips and promised an engagement soon. She wondered whatever happened to that ring, couldn't remember when she'd stopped wearing it.

As they were hiking, Randy said he'd treat all of them, including the three not there, to dinner that evening. Being stranded made him hungry and he wanted meat and potatoes, had spotted what looked like a good steak house just two blocks down the hill from their inn next to the movie theatre. Be there at seven o'clock, he said. Madeline looked out over the Missouri River valley, her breath coming in jagged gulps, her lungs burning from that last steep incline. Her stomach muscles clenching at the thought of dinner.

She would not dine with Wanda tonight.

When they returned to the Pear Tree Inn, the car ride back from the hike having stiffened Madeline so she walked across the parking lot straight-legged like Frankenstein's twin, they noticed Wanda and Misery in the lobby. Wanda, wrapped in one of Misery's black skirts, the waistband up under her arms as if it were a strapless muu muu, had gone there for quarters so she could wash her running suit in the nearby Laundromat. Misery was stocking up on chips and chocolate from the vending machine. Randy wasn't as stiff as Madeline so he got to the lobby first. "Glad to see you both at once," he said. "I'm taking us all out for steaks tonight." Madeline entered the lobby in time to hear Randy name the place and time. Misery grunted her acknowledgement, then kicked the vending machine so the bag of cool ranch corn chips would fall. "Another sign from the gods," Wanda said. "Two signs," she added when the chips landed.

Later, while Randy was in the shower, Madeline called her mother's cabin and said there'd been a change. They'd decided on Mexican, the place across from Grover's Garage, and they should be there at 7:30, not 7:00. It was less than a block from the inn. Wanda could walk that far, couldn't she? The lie was mean and childish, and she knew she should be ashamed, even before Randy and the others found out. She knew she'd act ashamed. But she'd jettisoned her mother all those years ago to save herself, and connecting up now, this late in both of their lives, was asking for pain. Even with the heat of orgasm and Randy's hot breath on her neck all the night before, she'd dreamed of Wanda in her coffin, facing downward, her face in the satin pillow. Alexandra was one of the mourners. When she awoke she imagined herself a jelly doughnut, glazed exterior and mushy insides.

She called Misery with the same lie in case the two talked at the laundromat before dinner.

One evening a few decades ago, after calling on a boat supply warehouse late on an afternoon, she suddenly knew she couldn't go home to Martin. She felt the same now. Not possible was not possible, no matter whom it hurt.

The afternoon of that long ago evening, Martin had come home for lunch, and as he entered their house, he'd tossed his windbreaker across the living room, its zipper hitting the ceramic jar lamp just hard enough to chip the gold flecked paint. "I hate that lamp anyway," he said when she stared at him. "Always have. Why do we live with crap we don't like?"

"We'll replace it," she said. "It's only a lamp. Not worth getting angry about. We'll go out tonight and buy a better one."

"They're all crap," he shouted. "We'll be replacing one piece of crap with another."

She held her breath. The explosions he treated her and Trysh to lately were unlike him. If he'd been angry for the entire ten years of their marriage, she'd be used to it by now. Or else she wouldn't be with him. But this was new for calm and happy Martin, and she knew it had to be the pills. His angers were worse than the one display she'd put on three years earlier about calling Wanda because his were not about anything; there was no subject or circumstance to skirt around in order to avoid his tantrums.

He sat across the wooden kitchen table from her, took one bite of his ham sandwich, and tossed it into the sink. "Why do you buy such tasteless stuff? Don't you care what we eat? Do you like cardboard?"

She sighed, picked at the chipped white paint where the table legs joined the tabletop. The ham tasted fine to her, packaged and processed, yes, but it wasn't as if they'd the time or the inclination to visit a smokehouse every week.

"And King Kustoms is a rip-off joint, changing nearly twice what their parts are worth. Why do we deal with them?" His eyes, usually like the brown underneath of mushroom caps, were hard pellets now, and his neck was flushed. "What kind of life is this?" He pushed his chair back so roughly it toppled over, then stood and shook his head as if to clear it and went upstairs. "I'm not going back in today," he called down. "In case you haven't figured that out."

She cleared the table before following, and found him stretched out on their bed, an arm thrown over his forehead and eyes.

"Why'd you buy these ugly drapes? What kind of fake color is grasshopper anyway? You have absolutely no taste. Not any."

"Sorry," she said, sitting beside him. The drapes had been his choice.

He removed his arm, looked at her with his hard brown eyes, and shouted from where he lay. "I hate living here." He paused to gather breath between each word. "I hate it."

She watched him, waited until he closed his eyes and his color was nearly normal. "It's those muscle relaxers," she said. "They're making you insane." They'd been prescribed for a back strain he'd given himself months ago when installing a window air conditioner in his shop.

"Jesus," he said. "Don't you understand how much my back hurt? Why can't you be happy that I'm pain free?" He said it was just like her to dismiss his agony, as she dismissed everything she found unpleasant.

"How can you be of any help to anyone if your method is to pretend nothing is wrong, not ever?" She was Louise' clone, he said, first and foremost. He shouldn't be surprised she was all pretense and coldness. "Cold," he said. "Ice."

That one night she lied to him was the one she remembered while walking to the steak house with Randy.

She'd called Martin after leaving the warehouse, and had left a message she knew he listened to as he lay in bed. She said she'd been invited to one of their customer's yacht clubs for dinner. Then she'd gone alone to Chester's, a dark and expensive place full of diners so genteel the atmosphere was somber. She chose a table in the corner, her back to two walls, and ordered escargot in butter, then French onion soup, then baby spinach and arugula salad with a raspberry dressing, then Veal Oscar with garlic whipped potatoes, then bread pudding with a hard sauce. She took only a bite or two of each course, pushing the food about on her plate, making designs, building mountains and rivers and roads. She wanted to stay in that corner a long time. His rages were so like Wanda's of old, she found herself holding her breath, moving quietly around him. He was not violent, but the angers that sprouted suddenly from nothing made her want to run. Save herself. He'd probably be himself again once the pills were gone. She worked at believing that. Or maybe before. Maybe she'd go home and find him back to normal. "Holy shit," he'd say. "I've been mean," just as he'd said, "Holy shit, I love you," on their third date.

But when she got home, Martin was sitting at the dining room table, head in his hands. "I'm starting to hear two voices at the same time. In my head. They argue." Her guilt came out as tears as she rubbed his back, told him it would be OK. The next day he stayed in bed, curled up and wrapped so tightly in the sheet only his brown curls were visible. She watched his still form, making sure she could detect breathing, as she spoke to his doctor. The new pills she asked for controlled his pain as well as the others had, and within days his mood lightened. She was certain the old Martin, the real Martin, would soon reappear. But less than a week after the second prescription, he made his dinner table announcement. He looked calm and he smiled after he spoke, not an ironic smile either. They were in the dining room, and the evening sun filtered in through the shutters at his back, making him glow. "When I kill myself, neither of you should feel responsible. I love you both," he said. "But be warned."

Madeline's stomach clenched, but she smiled back at him, pretended it was a joke. "The spaghetti isn't that bad," she said, and he and Trysh laughed politely. But as she lay beside him that night, watching figures move across the ceiling with each set of passing headlights and guessing he was awake, too, she imagined her life without him, the calm that would take over, the orderliness of it. Her imagination shamed her, so she told herself to stop looking forward, urged herself to be his help and support, a shining path through his pain. What would Louise advise beyond survival?

Two days later, Martin did it, using both kinds of muscle relaxers and lots of vodka.

Trysh blamed Madeline. "You heard him. Why didn't you stop him? People who threaten always do it."

Your Introduction to Psychology class is already paying off, Madeline thought, but knew better than to say. She and Trysh had to be a unit now, should comfort each other. And as Trysh cried, Madeline remembered Wanda's regular threats—"Someday I'll kill myself just to get away from you"—but all she said to Trysh was she was sorry. She would have stopped him if she could. That much was true. She was very sorry.

Trysh was nineteen then, old enough to get her own apartment close to the university, and she did, moving out just two months after Martin's death, said she couldn't stay with someone so self-centered and cold, so unfeeling. "When someone changes so suddenly, you cannot just worry about yourself, or do what you did, smile and pretend and hope he gets better," she said. "You should have saved him."

For a few years after she left, Madeline still saw and even fought with Trysh occasionally, heard more about her from Louise who advised hope and said she knew mother and daughter would reunite. "It's as easy to believe all will work out as it is to believe she is gone forever," Louise said. "Give her time, and she'll choose you to be her mother again." So Madeline was surprised and a bit impressed when Trysh made good her threat and finally cut off all contact. By 1982, all letters were marked "Return to sender." All phone calls went unanswered. She knew Lousie was wrong about this one thing, though she pretended to be comforted when Lousie said it was only a setback, and Trysh would return to the fold. Louise died on Madeline and Ollie's seventh anniversary, her card arriving in Chicago after her heart had stopped, and any news of Trysh since then came from Chris's sister, Trysh's aunt, who was irregular with her reports. What Madeline knew: Trysh was still in Galveston and the owner of a restaurant. The spit and image of Madeline, the aunt had reported a few years ago, thick dark hair and a narrow face.

******

In the Cattleman's Reserve Steak House, Madeline shrugged when asked where Misery and her mother were, but because Randy seemed determined to wait for them before ordering, she lied again.

"They decided to go out by themselves. You know how perverse they can be. We've got lots more chances to hear them moan and talk nonsense. For now, let's eat."

B shrugged. "It's your family," he said, and she stiffened, taking that for an insult at first.

"I like your poor old mother," Lisette said, and Madeline smiled across the table at her, her top teeth resting on her tongue in a gentle bite, as Louise taught her, to keep from saying "You sit next to her in the bus then, or you go to the Mexican place and share her burrito."

Randy announced his need for a large, rare porterhouse, but suggested they begin with appetizers. "Whatever you want," he said, and when the waiter appeared, he said, "Let's ask this young man what's good."

The waiter was indeed young, not even out of high school Madeline guessed, with large dark eyes and a hint of fuzz above his lip. His hair was gelled and spiked in the messy-haired toddler style, and she wondered if he knew it made him look even younger. He recommended the stuffed mushrooms and potato skins, then after he took the order for drinks he was too young to serve, he asked where they were from.

"Bourbon, Missouri," they all said at once.

"Just passin' through?" he asked.

"We were," Randy said, "Now we're at the mercy of Grover's Garage."

"My dad hates that place," he said. "But it's mostly personal about Grover himself. I guess they do good work."

His name was Tim, and by the time he took their entrée order, he was moonlighting as a tour guide, telling them about the city park with the waterfall and the community theater production of *The Glass Menagerie* starring his friend's sister. He told them Nebraska City was the original Fort Kearney, the first fort west of the Missouri established by Lewis and Clark. He said Nebraska City was where Arbor Day began, and was known as Arbor City. A four-story tree house just on the edge of town served as an interactive tree museum. His enthusiasm about his hometown was rare for a high school kid, and it added to their enjoyment, especially since the steaks were tough and the baked potatoes mushy. He said he wanted to join the Army after he got out of high school, follow in his brother's footsteps.

"Are you insane?" Lisette asked, but before Tim could say he most certainly was not, B asked where the brother was.

"Fallujah," Tim said, and they all shook their heads.

"It's a hard life," Randy said.

"No doubt about that," B said. "Getting harder."

They were deciding on desserts—Tim recommended the pecan pie or the double fudge brownie sundae—when Misery and Wanda entered.

"Chicken shits," Misery called from the door. "Did you think you could hide in such a small town? Chick Ken Shits."

And even then, when Randy and B and Lisette were saying how sorry they were for the confusion, asking Tim for more chairs and plates, swearing they'd not tried to eat without them, never would try to, joking about one for all and all for one, yet looking at Madeline with accusation that turned to realization, even then, Madeline kept a civilized smile on her face and refused to get dragged into it. She had a right to get rid of her mother. "Don't let sadness in," Louise's ghost said. Avoiding Wanda was the only way Madeline knew to do that.

Even Tim got in on the commotion when he delivered two large glasses of Chablis. "You were sent to Pancho's? That place sucks."

Before she would sit, Misery said she was going to the restroom. "Come with me, Madeline," she said as she walked off toward the corner Tim had pointed out.

Once in the ladies room, Misery said. "You sacrificed me. Again."

"Yeah. Sorry. I guess we could all sneak out of town without her, leave a note, let the cops see that she gets back home."

Misery put her arms around Madeline and hugged her. "Very funny, Sis," she said.

The hug tightened until Madeline found it hard to breathe.

"I don't like being sacrificed."

Madeline wondered if she would actually hear her ribs crack, or just feel the pain.

"If you use me as a sacrifice again, I'll tell the police on the boy. I know all about his Army career. I know these two goody-two-shoes men are being helpful, but I don't care. I'll tell on everyone involved before I get stuck with the Devil's Dance Partner again."

Madeline shrank into herself more and found a way to breathe.

"The waitress at Pancho's spoke to us with quotation marks around 'waiting' and 'the others.' When she went back to the kitchen, she probably called the local insane asylum to see if it was short a couple of inmates." Misery gave Madeline one final hard squeeze, and released her. "Don't fuck with me. I mean it."

******

Tim had talked to the strangers partly out of boredom, partly to get a bigger tip, and mostly because the blond girl directed her smile at him. True, she may consider herself too old for a sixteen-year-old, but that was no reason he couldn't talk to her. Then again, no telling how old she was. He didn't card her when she ordered wine because that would have been rude, but there was a chance she was under twenty-one. Tim was tall and had started to bulk up from the three-a-week workouts he did, and knew he could pass for older than sixteen, maybe four or five years older. Not that he was planning anything, or even imagining much. She was there and she was pretty. The bald guy she talked a lot to was probably her father, and the other old couple were an aunt and uncle. The shaggy orange-haired dork must have been their son or maybe her brother, but was clearly someone she didn't like. The small dark-haired aunt had a sour look on her face during most of the meal, though he could tell she considered it polite. It was as if she kept swallowing her tongue and it tasted bad. He could tell his blond didn't like the aunt much either.

Tim knew he impressed the blond at first, telling all he knew about his town. He even used *The Glass Menagerie*, a play he'd had to read and been bored by his freshman year so would never go to see, to let her know he was cultured. She smiled at him when he talked about the tree house the town was so famous for, so he explained all about Arbor Day and the importance of replanting trees, something the old people at the table agreed with. It wasn't until she said his brother was insane that he started to hate her, and the rest of them, just looking down at their plates, saying too bad or tough luck when he said his brother was in Fallujah. Sure, it was dangerous, but they should have said they were proud of him, that he was doing his duty by defending his country, their country. They'd pray for him. Tim's brother was making sacrifices and so would he when the time came because that was how it worked.

After the really old one and the retard came in so the rest were too busy calming them down to pay him any attention, he had time to think. He'd seen that old hippie bus in Grover's lot, and it had Missouri tags, and of course it had to belong to hippie wimps like them. He'd been on the debate team at school and had won a few blue ribbons, and so could have discussed the war and being a soldier with them, made them see how wrong they were to hate those who gave their lives so the terrorists wouldn't win, but he knew he'd be arguing alone against all five.

So an hour after they left, when he got off work, he went up by Grover's Garage, and sure enough, the bus was in the parking lot on the side of the garage, in full view and unprotected. As he expected, the doors were all unlocked, the locks probably having broken long ago. He jumped in and, using his Swiss army knife, he slashed at each seat, cutting them up as much as he could. What if his brother didn't come back? It was a fear he felt like pin pricks in his neck and shoulders day after day. How dare they look down and mutter into their plates as if ashamed. War was hell, sure. As he slashed their tires, he knew he could have said that to them. But soldiers were heroes. If they weren't heroes, he thought, then the word meant nothing. He used a rock to smash the front windshield, guessing the noise gave him away and the cops would show up soon. Those cops should be chasing hippie terrorist sympathizers instead of a future hero like himself.

SEVEN

Even in adversity, especially in adversity, saints smile, carry on, forgive the perpetrators, do what must be done. B was a saint, at least according to the descriptions of saints Lisette had heard as a child. Not those Catholic saints, either, the ones that had to perform three miracles after their deaths before the old pope would say they were real, the ones that were more like magicians and psychics than just plain old good people. No, Lisette had been taught by her parents and her Sunday school teachers that saints weren't all pious and acting holy, but were real people who were kind and forgiving, never lazy or complaining. Like Firefly girls and the Scouts, saints laughed a lot. Like B.

He chuckled about Tim's vandalism and helped Randy put duct tape all over the seats, teasing Randy all the while for not carrying his own roll of tape in a vehicle like the bus. "A roll of duct tape and a tangle of bailing wire should come standard with these old buses." B said, as he covered holes in the long back seat. Randy laughed, too, an appropriate response, Lisette decided, for the slashings were not serious. Tim had been caught doing it, so he had to pay for the windshield and new tires, better tires than those he'd slashed, and getting new tires wouldn't even cause a delay since the bus was stranded already without a clutch. So Tim had hurt himself, what Lisette knew those Sunday school teachers she remembered—Auntie Alma with her stone gray hair hanging down her back and Mr. Quinn with his trifocals—would have pointed to as a life lesson. Evil was its own undoing. Not that that'd often proven right or true in the world Lisette lived in, but there was a pleasure in justice occurring, however rarely and accidentally.

Or, as the crazy sister called Misery said, there'd been no real harm unless you counted the intent. "When someone who doesn't know you wants to hurt you," Misery said, "when someone is that full of hate and anger, there is harm done. It's frightening."

When she said that, six of them, all but the poor old mother, were standing outside Grover's' Garage, looking at the VW bus. They'd not yet begun taping, and B reached an arm around Misery's shoulders, hugged her. "Spoken like a sheltered innocent," he said.

She pushed him away and glared. "Oh yeah, I was sheltered all right. I've never been ill treated. My name is not an indication of anything."

B shrugged and looked at the others. "My timing must be off. That was meant as a joke."

"Of course it was," Lisette said. "I love jokes."

And Madeline had laughed, of course she had. She knew jokes had to be laughed at, but it was an odd feeling, like a rock or more precisely a boulder high in her stomach where Wanda-pain usually landed. Not counting Wanda, no one had ever wanted to hurt her just for being her. She'd been ignored, easily forgotten, tolerated, put up with. She'd blended in, even been admired for the cool and calm image she projected, but no one had disliked her enough to hurt her, not when there was nothing for her or him to gain. Then again, she told herself as she took big breaths, pictured her pool in the Ozark sun, this anger was not likely aimed at her. She was an innocent bystander. The target was Henry. She was one of the many innocent bystanders. She was collateral damage. She felt the boulder shrinking. She was just along for the ride. She smiled wider.

******

Wanda smiled in her sleep. Phil had looked like the Alpine cow herder in the poster taped to the Tulsa grocery store window to promote Swiss cheese. He wasn't Swiss, though, but German, one hundred percent, something he said with pride as if the national boundaries actually defined a people, and he would not accept the association with Hitler. When he talked about his family back in St. Louis, Wanda pictured not Germans but rather the British Royal Family from the newsreels, servants and doilies and tea in delicate cups. "Oh, is it proper?" they would ask one another. Wanda could just hear them. Phil was lonely in Tulsa and a bit embarrassed by his non-glamorous asthma, the condition that sent him home from North Africa after just one tour of duty, and was why he worked as a civilian soldier, a so-called home-front hero, for Home and Hearth Insurance Company, selling war bonds along with their insurance.

Wanda was in Tulsa with the hordes of other young women who'd come in from the fields and plains to type and file and answer phones, taking the jobs vacated by others like them who'd been promoted to jobs left open by men who'd become real soldiers. Wanda answered phones, her inability to read quickly or well ruling out most secretarial work. She answered phones for the life insurance and war bond salesmen in Home and Hearth's fourth-floor suite. The payroll department had asked if she wanted to send part of her money home, as was common for women coming from the small towns to work in the city. A young unmarried woman could be a valuable means of support for the old folks left behind, and besides, a young country girl with too much money and no supervision could get into trouble. But Wanda had said no, she was an orphan. Her mother was dead. It could've been true.

Before she arrived in Tulsa a year earlier, 1943, she took her clothes, some bedding, a few pots and pans, and half the assorted bills and coins she and the old squaw kept in a tin can in the kitchen, their rewards for cleaning the houses of those rare citizens of Felt who were nearly wealthy once again. If the old squaw could have read, Wanda would have left a note, but she knew there was no need. Taking half the money said it all—good-bye forever. She'd come a far way across the long top of Oklahoma, but not far enough. She knew she'd have to keep going, get completely clear of the state's red dust and despair. The people on the streets of Tulsa looked too much like the ones she wanted to leave behind. The women may have worn their hair in smooth rolls and curls and may have wobbled about on high heels, but Wanda wasn't fooled. In their natural state, they'd be barefoot and in sunbonnets.

Phil was her ticket out, but with so few marriageable-aged men around, her competition was fierce. She'd lost two prospects before him to girls who played the game better, girls in her office she got back at by sending anonymous letters to their new husbands. "She layed with many before you," she printed on Home and Hearth stationary she cut the name from. But she'd also learned from failure. For a few years, she'd known her powers, different ones back then: a pretty face with high cheekbones and large eyes with thick lashes, shapely legs, a small waist for someone as bosomy as she, hair thick and wavy enough to hide her large ears. And she'd noticed the girls who got the men smiled often. She did understand that. She'd often seen the old squaw turn good intentions to disgust with a snarl, so she was determined to smile at everything Phil said or did. And she had learned, too, that by Tulsa standards, she was a hick, so she let him do most of the talking, let him order for both of them when they dined out. In restaurants, she used the forks and spoons he used, and she laughed at his jokes, except the off-color ones he was prone to. "Jesus wouldn't like that joke," she said when he told one about a farmer's daughter and a razorback pig. She made herself look sad thinking of Jesus, too, nails through his hands and feet like that, though all she knew about Jesus she'd picked up from a Pentecostal radio show broadcast out of Tulsa.

And maybe because she didn't use her voice often, he claimed to be in love with it, with what he called her Western twang. He said she was his cowgirl. He wanted to take her home to St. Louis to meet his family, but she knew they wouldn't be so easy. He was dull-witted enough to fool, but the others would see little more than a stupid half-breed standing before them, so she let him drive her out past the edge of town, beyond even the close-in farms, let him roll on top of her on a blanket in a cow pasture as he swore he loved her so it was OK. She wasn't sure she'd get pregnant from just one time, but knew she'd claim it anyway. She knew he'd marry her and imagined his doily-using mother saying, "It is proper, dear. Duty and all that." So by the time she met the rest of the Kneedelseeders, she was carrying Madeline, had been a Kneedelseeder herself for five months, long enough to have let Phil know he'd been her ticket out of Oklahoma and that was all. He was no more to her than Union Pacific.

Wanda was partially awake in Cabin 1, not sure if she'd been remembering or dreaming about Phil, and not sure why she needed so much sleep lately. It was early afternoon. Suddenly, Phil stood at the foot of her bed, took a step back, and sat at the desk by the door. He was no longer the strong Nordic youth of the grocery store cheese poster, but wasn't the dried up saggy bag of a man he'd become by their divorce either. "I'm ready," he said, and unbuttoned his plaid flannel to bare his chest, the hairs on it already graying. She crawled to the end of the bed, leaned over, held him by the shoulders, and placed her lips on his chest, right in the center. His skin was as clammy as always, bitter tasting, but she sucked hard until he disappeared. She fell back across her bed. She'd seen him before, had many times lately sucked the soul out of him as she did now, just as he accused her of when he insisted on the divorce. She'd drained him of what made him him, he'd said, and she laughed at that then as she would now. Nothing made him what he was. He was nothing. She rubbed her eyes to get rid of him. No, he hadn't followed her from Florissant, Missouri, to Nebraska City, Nebraska. She'd conjured him here because the air in the cabin tasted bitter anyway, tasted the way Phil's skin tasted back when she had to put her lips to it.

When she heard the door to the next-door cabin close, she knew Madeline and Randy were back from viewing the destruction she'd heard them lamenting earlier. Evil forces were testing them; the gods were against this journey West. Wanda hoped to find out why, but for now she decided to drop in on her oldest child. She was tired of visiting with her self and her past, so she wrapped the comforter tight around shoulders and knocked on their door. Madeline's face squinched up in a frown when she opened the door, and Wanda hoped she'd broken up a moment of romance.

The rain clouds had been blown away the day before by winds from the southwest, and those winds brought with them hot, dry air. Nebraska City was having an autumn heat wave, and according to the local television station, it was as hot here in September as it'd been all summer. Yet Wanda was dressed in her running suit with a Pear Tree Inn comforter wrapped around her. Maybe, Madeline thought, her old mother was already suffering from heat stroke, something the elderly were more susceptible to. She was pale, too, and she shook, shivered even beneath all those layers.

"Are you sick?" Madeline asked.

"No, I'm fine," Wanda said. "Do I have to be dying for you to welcome me? No, don't answer that. I know your cold heart." She stumbled past Madeline and half sat, half fell onto the bed. "Just thought I'd pass some time with you, especially as we're stuck in nowhere-ville and there is nothing else to do. Let's hope we get out of this old town before the locals decide to attack us again."

"We'll be leaving tomorrow afternoon," Randy said. "Grover'll work faster now. Everyone wants to keep us happy."

"Keep?" Wanda asked.

"You didn't have to come," Madeline said, hearing the whine in her voice, knowing she'd said the same thing many times already, or if she hadn't, she'd meant to, should have.

When Lisette and B knocked and squeezed into the room, Madeline looked behind her for the back entrance she knew didn't exist. "Can we cram anyone else in here?" She sat on the bed next to Wanda, and scooted back toward the wall so B would have a place to stand.

"She dragged me over here," B said, holding up Lisette's hand. "Don't know why."

"Henry's gone," Lisette said. "That's why."

"Gone?" Randy asked. "Cleared out?"

"No. But he's usually in bed watching cartoons, and he's not there. His stuff is still there."

"He's not a prisoner," B said. "It's all right."

"But Tim and probably others here are a danger." She perched on corner of the desk, a strap of her pink camisole tank top dangling off her shoulder. "Tim clearly hates him."

"Who knows why Tim did that," Randy said, and B agreed quickly.

"Could've been too small a tip," B said.

"I do think that's funny," she said, and laughed as proof. "But we all know the reason we're here, know Henry's problem, know ..."

"Wait," Madeline said. "We *all* do not know anything." She nodded toward Wanda, who pretended not to notice.

"By the way," B said to Madeline. "Did you know your sister has her gun with her?" The switch in subjects was so obvious even Wanda laughed.

"It's mine," Madeline said. "Really it was Ollie's, an antique of sorts. Don't know if it's ever been fired. Misery found it, the .22, and decided to keep it under her bed back home. I didn't care, and it must have made her feel better for some reason."

"Well, she brought it along. I noticed it when we were switching the baggage out in the rain the other night. She put it in my trunk."

Madeline had noticed it, too, but could tell by the look on Randy's face, he hadn't. When he raised his eyebrows at her, she shrugged. "Too busy wondering about my pool," she said.

He grinned. "Who'd have thought both you and your sister would bring along useless pieces of luggage."

"Not that it matters," B said. "Just seems odd."

"It matters," Lisette said. She stood, nearly leaning against B's back. "She's crazy. One gun and one crazy woman does not add up well."

"She's not crazy," Madeline said. "She's sad."

"She's not stable," Wanda said. "A mother shouldn't have to admit that about her child, but it's true. I've known it forever."

"Could be," B said. "You misunderstand her. Easy for a parent to do. Maybe she's a good woman deep down, just confused for now, as many of us are."

"She's not dangerous," Madeline said.

"She stabbed Ginny." Wanda cackled, slapped her knee at Madeline's stunned look. "Didn't tell you that, huh? Came at her with a letter opener is what she told me."

"Not everything she says is true," Madeline remembered the hug that took her breath away.

Madeline turned to Lisette. "Did Henry leave a note, say where he went?"

"No." Lisette snorted. "I mean, *if* he had, I wouldn't be worried. I guess I would have shown you the note by now. I am not stupid."

Madeline smiled sweetly toward Lisette but directed her gaze just over her shoulder. "Of course you're not." Louise's ghost nodded, said good girl.

A brief silence descended upon Cabin 2 then. Madeline guessed B would try another subject to keep peace. She knew Wanda wanted a fight to break out. She didn't know what Lisette wanted, but she wanted space. As always, escape. "I'm going for a walk," she said, knowing she couldn't move toward the door without knocking into Wanda, pushing her into Lisette.

"Let's go to the tree house," Randy said. "A four-story tree house. Every little boy's dream."

"I'll see if Misery wants to join us," B said. Lisette followed him out, and Wanda stretched herself out slowly across the bed, and exhaled loudly.

"Of course you'd think of something I can't do. Thanks a lot."

"Oh, sorry," Randy said, and Madeline guessed he meant it. "We can come up with something else to pass the time."

"Hey, don't worry about it, white eyes. I come to smoke'em peace pipe. I'm used to being ignored. I will fight no more today."

"White eyes, Mom? Really?"

"My ancestors whisper to me. I'm no longer in charge of what comes from my mouth."

"Lucky you."

"Sometimes they say silly things in my ears. Not all my ancestors were bright or good with speeches, you know." Wanda kicked her shoes off and wiggled under the bed covers. "Can I sleep here while you're gone? I'm too tired to go back to my room." She pulled the sheet up to her chin. "Turn the light out, close the drapes, on your way out." She had no idea why she needed so much sleep lately. Or why she liked it so. She'd rather sleep than anything.

******

The view from the top of the tree house was one of those that never truly did the trick but were thought to. Oh, they may seem powerful at first, the viewer struck by the beauty of the universe, the grandeur of nature, the insignificance of her own problems. Such vistas were believed capable of providing perspective on one's own life, on the trials and tribulations of the hoi polloi. But mere hours later, the childhood traumas etched deeply because early into the gray matter resurfaced. Misery knew that while she enjoyed the view; it was not a cure. But yes, she was pleased and surprised to have been sought out and asked to join the others on their touring of Nebraska City. Enforced touring, she said to Madeline, for it was either that or go crazy, stuck as they were here for at least one more day. Nevertheless, her being invited to join anyone or anything was a rarity. She was often merely there and included out of politeness, or more likely avoided. And she knew she shouldn't dwell on her traumas, but she also knew the scars, old and crusted over by now, existed without her dwelling on them. And she knew, too, just what Ginny used to say: she should get over herself. She shouldn't have to be ruined. She should at least try to make new pathways for her brain synapses. She sighed as she looked out on the colored tops of the trees, the Missouri river sparkling in the distance. There was no such thing as rebirth. You got the one chance and that was it. Someone screwed you up, and you never recovered.

She remembered a frying pan. It was that memory that fractured her mind this last time, that sent her reeling away from Ginny and before that from her job in the inspector's office. She'd been one of the code inspectors for the town of Webster Groves, a fancy, genteel, close-in suburb of St. Louis with hundred-year-old homes and organic food stands. She drove about in an official car, looking at fascia and embankments and fire doors and railings, at smoke detectors and broken windows and brush not cleaned up. One day her reports made no sense. The houses had pittle pattle, boogie woogie, lacey dacey. One needed snarls and taps and squiggles. Her boss was surprised, then annoyed by her inability to make sense of her own reports. She knew the words, but her mind was in shards, and she couldn't come up with the right things to say. On top of that, she giggled at what she'd written. When she tried again, the reports remained nonsense and just as funny. "You should go home," her boss said. "Hopey dopey," she answered.

Eventually, after a few doctors' appointments and many tests, it was clear she hadn't had a stroke, but her brain waves had become trapped in a dead end. Her mind was spinning its wheels, miring her ever deeper in the muck. "Flopsy mopsy," she said to Ginny on the way home from one of the many psychiatric evaluations, and then she laughed hysterically. "I don't mean that," she said. "I mean pig wig. I mean catty matty." She couldn't stop laughing, even though she saw the frying pan then, was sure it had happened, even though Ginny frowned.

Doses of some high-potency drugs combined with meditation and a high-protein diet gave her back her speech, but once she recovered she was not able to be around Ginny anymore. Ginny said Misery, Angie then, couldn't have been harmed by whatever happened long ago, not so much anyway, hinting that the lack of speech and teetering walk was if not an act, an exaggeration, smirking at the phrase *repressed memory*. After all, Angie worked and thought and lived, had for years. Why now? Misery didn't have an answer. The drugs caused her hair to fall out, caused her vision to blur, caused painful gastritis. The drugs were worse than the nonsense words. Yet Ginny had insisted on the treatments. Insisted. "If you truly are so affected, take the medicine. Get over it," Ginny said. Misery left in the middle of the night, not even leaving a note. She had planned on telling Ginny about the frying pan, but that was before she could talk.

What she'd seen was the frying pan coming at her, and she'd heard it clang on her skull. She couldn't recall any pain, but she knew she'd been in bed for a while in her seventh year, had been told when she came to that she'd hurt her head and would likely never remember falling off her bicycle. And she hadn't remembered for forty-three years. Then, while driving around a back street in Webster Groves, the image came to her. Her mother's face grayish green and her eyes blazing, the frying pan coming down. It was a small pan, large enough for a two-person round of corn bread or two eggs, but it was cast iron, and one blow knocked her out. Who hits a seven-year-old on the head? Someone who hates her, who cannot stand being around her, who doesn't care if the seven-year-old lives or dies. Mother.

Ginny and the doctors all said don't dwell on it. And she tried not to. Don't think, don't remember. She knew it then as the sort of advice Madeline had long tried to live by, that old Louise Dames not one bit original. She'd gone back for pills, though, wanting to speak in sentences again. Now she'd been without for five days, functioning but in her natural condition, miserable, the brief feeling of being funny having passed. If beauty had power, the trees in Nebraska City should be a help. The view from the tree house and the warm air like Ginny's breath on her face, the fact that she was invited to come along—all that should do it, should chase the frying pan away. But no. Not long ago, common belief was that the negative, if harsh enough, worked better than the positive for attitude adjustments. She knew mental patients of old had been given doses of malaria or other convulsive-causing diseases in the hope that the shock of the convulsions would knock out what was lodged in their brains and causing them anxiety. Misery understood she'd tried that method, had given herself the pain of doing without Ginny, being homeless and jobless. But the frying pan wouldn't be chased away by that pain or by this beauty.

******

"Before you go over, they say you'll be fighting *for* your country." Henry spoke through the screen door at the back entrance of the Cattleman's Reserve. Tim was inside at the sink, washing the glass candleholders that would go on each table that evening. He gave no indication of having heard, and Henry couldn't tell if anyone else was in the kitchen. He'd waited in the small brushy wooded area behind the kitchen, and had seen Tim enter, coming to work just after school was out. Henry had first considered hanging around the school, trying to find Tim, having a talk with him there, but decided that was too public. The discussion he intended was best one on one. "They say it just that way, '*For* your country,' and you accept it, but what does it mean. How does your killing children help your country? And even if you don't kill, though you will for sure, even if you don't, how does your work there help your country? Whatever it is you're doing. And no one even knows because the more I think of it, the more I'm sure all the cute phrases are lies—nation-building, giving democracy a chance, enforcing the peace, liberating. Even if all that or even one or those were true, why is it *for* your country?' OK, you can see it, as some do, as I did for a while, as '*for* humanity,' one group of fortunate human beings helping out some less fortunate. But that doesn't hold up long, not when they mostly hate us and try to kill us, and our response is to shoot into crowds of them, not when they haven't had clean water since our invasion and so are dying of diseases they had eradicated a century ago."

Tim made no reply, gave no indication he'd heard, though Henry could tell Tim had stopped washing the candleholders and was standing statue still.

"I'm not trying to take away what your brother's going through. It's rough stuff."

Nothing. Henry wanted someone to listen to him. He'd written letters to the newspaper, but wasn't naïve enough to believe they'd changed any minds, ended up as more than birdcage liners. One person at a time, maybe just one person period. And Tim had made himself that one person.

"But I cannot pretend he's doing anything valuable either, your brother, no matter how much danger he's in. See, nothing is real. The words are not real, and if the words aren't real, how can anything else be? It can't." He reached for the screen door handle. "You think if words aren't real, why am I talking? How can I even try to talk to you? But it's their words I mean. And you know who *they* are—the *they* others tell you don't exist, the *they* that make things up and change the meanings of the words. Get it?"

Two years ago, he'd been a mere kid, and as his father always said, kids had nothing to say, nothing to tell the world. They knew nothing. "Look up the word *kid* in the dictionary, and it says, 'Know-nothing,'" his father would say. Well, maybe so. Back when Henry was a kid he'd not known words meant nothing. He listened to authorities and accepted most of it, their words telling him things. Even grownups, his parents and the news guys on TV and some of his teachers, had said it—"*for* our country." When the dead were sent back to the Indiana airports with flags draped over them, the reporters would say Sergeant or Lieutenant or Private or whatever prefix they had died carrying had died for our country. Well, now he knew something, and he wasn't on TV, wasn't some old fart giving advice to kids. But he could tell one kid the truth. There is no truth. That's what he should say. But he wouldn't say it yet. First he'd try to get Tim to see how fake the words were, that one preposition especially. For.

"Tim," he said. "Tim." He pressed his face against the screen, tasting the old metal and the grime on it carried by a Nebraska wind. "Hey," he said, his voice sounding funny for his face being mashed against the screen. And even that close, he couldn't really see into the kitchen, couldn't see the figure rushing toward him with the aerosol can.

"Hot Shot," Tim said as he sprayed the ant and spider killer through the screen into Henry's face. "The best brand there is for getting rid of pests."

Henry stumbled away, his throat full of hot needles, his eyes skinned raw so he knew he'd been blinded, his stomach tumbling over itself. He took two blind steps and retched, then retched again. He screamed, mainly out of pain, but partly so someone would help him. He couldn't open his eyes, couldn't see to make his way back to the Pear Tree Inn. How he needed Anna now. No longer Anna, but Lisette. Years ago, hundreds of years ago it seemed, they'd been in tune, protecting each other from the rest of the world. He corrected her calculus homework; she gave the teachers his excuses for missing classes, nursed him through the flu one winter. He called her now. "Lisette. Help me. Lisette. Where are you?" he knew no one would come. "Mom," he called. "Someone. Help me." He let himself fall into the dirt and crawled toward the pavement where the restaurant truck was parked. He felt with his hands to find where the pavement began because he knew if he kept to the edge of the pavement, he could crawl around toward the front of the restaurant, then to the road. Surely someone would see him, take him to a doctor. He shouldn't have to lose his sight for finally knowing something worth saying, for trying to keep another kid from ignorance. Was he blinded for his country? Is that what Tim would say?

******

It was only money, Tim knew. Money wasn't the most important part of life. So what if he'd been caught wrecking the already junky bus, and so what if his father had had to buy a new windshield and new tires and even pay for the already ordered new clutch so Grover could get the bus on its way, get it out of town, make amends for the destruction that happened in his garage, charging only for labor? So what if Tim's father said Tim had to pay it back out of his next few paychecks, not being allowed to keep any for fun until the damages were paid off? It was only money, and he'd do it again to stand up for his brother. His brother was fighting so that assholes like that one could go free. That one who said the government was the enemy was allowed to be freer than Tim's brother who had to take orders and be brave all the time. It was an upside-down world. And so what if that asshole ended up blind? Tim's brother could end up dead. The spider spray had been handy. If the owner'd kept a gun in the place, that big nonsensical talk about prepositions and lies would have been answered by a blast, by sudden death. Tim knew he'd have shot and killed.

******

Madeline would just have to inflate her pool. It was clear by now they were never getting out of Nebraska City, not for days longer at least, and then who knew what else would occur. Henry was in the hospital and they were planning a delicate procedure that would require at least a week of recuperation time. His eyes were scarred, and the skin on his eyeballs itself would be peeled off. The doctor said it was possible Henry's vision would return once the scarred tissue was removed and his eyes were allowed to heal. "Hot Shot," Henry said when he was picked up by a Nebraska City policewoman and her dog. "Hot Shot," he repeated when he was admitted to the emergency room. His drivers' license said Henry Hobson, though he insisted his name was Kenny, then changed his mind and said Henry. The policewoman was suspicious, Madeline knew, though she told of his confusion as if it were a joke, a sign of his pain. He'd finally said they should call Randy Roma at the Pear Tree Inn, and should tell Lisette she needn't stay with someone who was blind on top of all the rest. "All the rest?" the policewoman asked when Randy and Madeline showed up at the hospital.

"Lover's stuff," Madeline said. "The rest is the usual."

He'd given his own consent for the surgery, as he claimed to have no family and he was of legal age. The hospital wasn't pleased he had no insurance card, but since he'd come in by way of the emergency room, they had to take his case. Randy and Madeline and B decided to chip in and give the hospital something, but knew they wouldn't be able to cover the cost of what was surely an expensive operation. There was a VA hospital in Lincoln, not far away, but deserters weren't allowed VA privileges.

Lisette cried when she learned about Henry, but wouldn't go to see him. "I'm stuck now," she'd said. "Really stuck."

"He says the opposite," Randy said, but Lisette rolled her eyes at Madeline, who understood. You couldn't leave someone in trouble. The most Lisette could hope for now was that Henry would leave her. At the hospital Madeline had learned that Henry's real name was Kenny, but no one had yet let Lisette's real name slip. Whatever it was, Madeline had sympathy for her for the first time. Sure, she was a do-gooder who pushed Wanda on her daughters because of wrong-headed sentiment, but she was also a young girl, far from home. She was trapped by a man who came to his senses too late, or at least later than she had. She must dream of waking up as whoever she used to be, of hearing her real name on friendly lips.

Henry's surgery was scheduled for Friday, and the recuperation would require at least three days in the hospital, then a few more in bed in the

Pear Tree without moving, no stress or strain. Then the doctor may release him, but she would prefer Henry not travel much farther.

Nebraska City seemed to grow hotter as they waited, and on the day of the surgery, the desk clerk at the Pear Tree and the waitresses in the diner tsk-tsked about global warming, said how much like hell the world was becoming, said doom was around the corner. They smiled when they predicted such, though, pleased Madeline could tell to have something interesting to say, some clever remark to make.

"I'm going swimming," Madeline said that morning. "I'm going to swim right here in town, on the front yard of the Pear Tree Inn." Misery and the waitress Madeline spoke to shook their heads, said it wouldn't be possible, but it was. The manager of the Pear Tree didn't mind. "A senior citizen in a bikini," she said. "Big deal. I guess this town can handle that."

It took two hours for Madeline to blow up her pool so that all three blue rings were round and full, but by the time Henry came out of surgery, she was soaking on the front yard of the inn. She closed her eyes and even though no one honked, she pretended she was back on Highway N. Swimming alone. If Henry was troubled by the word *for*, Madeline worried about the word *my*. My mother, she thought. My burden. "My God," she said into the still and heavy Nebraska air. A bona fide old woman moaning about her mother. "Grow up," she said. "You old bag. Get over yourself," she shouted. "Ga Row Up." Hush now, Louise said.

******

"You can turn him in," Grover said. He half leaned, half sat against a gray metal desk in his garage. Behind him on the desk was a set of distributor wires, an alternator still in its box, and a set of metric-sized wrenches. Grayish light tried to filter in through the grubby window behind him. He stroked his chin where his goatee used to be. "There's a way to get some extra of the money your dad wants."

Grover was talking to Tim who had stopped by to find out the exact amount his dad had paid Grover. It would be just like his dad to charge him more than he'd paid out, trying to teach him a lesson or something. Or maybe he'd do it to turn Tim against Grover. Grover supplemented his income from the garage by turning in runners for the bounty, what made Tim's dad dislike him. "Preying on the downtrodden. The troubled. I'm not even talking guilt or innocence, but the bail bondsmen use poor people with no hope, no friends, no families to go their bail. Then hunt them down, pay others to help. Seems if a man needed money that bad, he could find a more honorable way to get it." Tim's dad said that often, and Tim used to agree, at least in theory, imagining himself more as the hunted, the one in trouble. But now what Grover said made sense. Tim'd learned the kid he'd spayed was an escapee, a deserter, a scum. What would be wrong with turning him in?

"I'd do it myself, but you deserve it. He caused your troubles," Grover said.

Tim nodded. He knew Grover wasn't normally the kind to be nice about money unless the amount was small enough, not really worth Grover's time. But this was two thousand, and that just for "aid" in the capture. The group offering payment was a bunch of old guys who were against terror. They didn't think deserters should get away with it, thought deserters hurt the rest of the men and women fighting for their country. Tim laughed in Grover's garage when he read that word *for* on the old guys' web site, the word that bothered the deserter so much. I'll turn you in *for* me. *For* money. Nothing ambiguous there. He knew that wasn't true. There were more *fors* than he could name.

EIGHT

Madeline spent one final hour in the Nebraska sunshine on Monday morning, October seventh. Then she emptied and deflated her pool and climbed into Randy's bus, riding shotgun. It was ten o'clock when they turned onto Highway 2, three blocks from the Pear Tree Inn, and the red bikini Madeline wore under her large Chicago Art Institute T-shirt was already dry. Henry sat in the short middle seat, his eyes opened to what Madeline guessed was a green and brown and gray swirl. The doctor in Nebraska City had told them all Henry's vision could improve, and if so, it would be gradual, and Madeline imagined that what Henry called a blur would shift, that shapes would separate themselves from the background. "Don't force it," the doctor had said to him, her voice so young and new it tinkled like the recording on ice-cream trucks that cruised Madeline's childhood street in summer.

She watched Henry now, imagined that what he saw from the middle seat was like being a witness at the formation of the Earth, watching the gas molecules bond and become liquid and thick mud and then some bonds growing strong enough to make solids, eventually lining up as recognizable trees and noses and license plates. At least he wasn't in total darkness. And every minute promised to be better than the one before.

Behind Henry, Wanda stretched out on the long seat, face up, and chanted nonsense. Did Henry hear her clearer because his sight was gone? Madeline knew senses compensated, one growing stronger as another weakened, and she knew in Henry's case, there was no benefit in that. Hey, not only can't you see, but sounds can now drive you crazy. She closed her

eyes and made and lost bets with herself about how long Wanda could
keep it up. By the time she counted to one thousand, Wanda'd stop. By
the time she counted backwards from one million, by the time she listed
for herself all B's specials. The toneless chants continued, filled with hi-yas
and ya-yas and lodged in her bones and joints, made her jittery and achy.
Wine, sweets, deep breathing, yoga, calisthenics—Madeline'd used them
all to calm herself, and each had failed her over the years, her inflatable
pool lately working best as tranquilizer, though best was relative, and
swimming had barely worked this morning. There was no cure, she knew,
for this agitation as long as the source of it spread, encroached, ooozed
over and through her, rode in the back seat.

Randy reached across the divide between their seats and patted
her bare leg, smiled at her. She wished she'd met him when she was
younger, but even as she made it, the wish seemed unfair to her other
husbands. Besides, falling in love required youth or a deliberate
blindness some put on to simulate youth, but at just sixty, merely sixty,
she was not too far gone to pretend. Love looked toward the future,
was based on a belief in the future, and she may have some future left,
maybe a large chunk of future. Who could tell? "Shut up, shut up, shut
up," she said, not loud enough for Wanda to hear, as if her hearing it
would have caused a change. "Stupid badger."

Henry heard, though, and he chuckled. "Stalking," he said.

She turned toward him. "Anything yet?"

He could be her grandson. If Trysh'd had a child, he could be as
old as Henry. On the other hand, the bad one, the obsequious waiter
with that deep mean streak who caused the blindness, could be her
grandson, too. And if Trysh's version of it was even close to being right,
he, the mean one, was the kind she'd end up with.

She remembered dancing a small jig, singing a made-up song,
"Trysh Dames is a-coming," and making Ollie laugh when the gift
arrived from Trysh sixteen years ago, a wedding gift. The name on
the return address, no matter it was a P.O. box, was enough from the
daughter quiet since 1982. "The self-centeredness has to stop," Trysh
had said on the voiceover she'd made to go with the video of her tubal
ligation. The genetic line Trysh came from, she explained, was full of
misery from the old squaw's mother—whoever or more likely whatever
that was—all the way through Wanda to Madeline. The other side, the

Dameses, merely appeared better, Trysh said, Louise Dames spreading as much misery about with her guilt-dripping disapproval as Wanda had with her violent attacks. "It stops here," Trysh said on the tape. "If you ever wish for grandchildren, that wish, like the majority of my own, will go unfulfilled. You probably think you weren't such a bad mother"—Madeline had thought that, had believed the meanness and insanity was being diluted with each generation—"but I may never get over you. I'll try. And you try, too, to get over me."

Madeline hadn't watched the whole video, destroying it with a hammer before tossing it in her trash. She got the gist of the message, and wasn't eager to hear more, to see her daughter's fallopian tubes cauterized. She did wonder, though, who'd done the filming. So there were no grandkids, something Madeline never had wished for or cared about, but now with Henry she felt oddly motherly. Grandmotherly. His sullenness was gone, or at least overshadowed by his distress. The attack had changed either him or her feelings for him. Maybe motherly feelings came with age just as the body could no longer do the job, the mind and the body not working in concert but perversely out of sync, as so much of nature seemed to be.

"Nothing but a blending of colors," Henry said in response. "I'll let you know."

Close behind Randy's bus, even after they turned onto Interstate 80 just beyond Lincoln, was B in his Cavalier. He'd said he'd stay close to monitor the VW bus for more failings, though Randy'd told him the Cavalier or any other car on the road was as likely to break down as the bus was now. B had Misery in his back seat, and Lisette in front, and though Madeline still disliked the groundless vision Lisette clearly had of herself—savior, heroine, fighting the world and, by the way, comforting pathetic old and misunderstood Wanda—she felt sorry for her now. Lisette or whoever she really was seemed stuck with a person she no longer loved. Madeline could tell she was itching to leave, had one foot turned in the opposite direction. That desire for flight made Madeline want to hug the girl who went by Lisette, tell her to go. Save yourself, she'd say. Flight is often the only way.

That was her modus operandi, after all. Run. Always run away. She would have run away from Iraq, too, as Henry had. But she may have planned it better.

In B's back seat Misery was talking about trephination, a way toward enlightenment, or at least the end of craziness. Though it was a prehistoric practice of using a chert blade to make one more hole in the skull, it was on the rise in modern times, she said. Some people did it to themselves now, using a tool much like an ice pick. Misery said they seldom got it right. "Well, they end up dead or vegged out. And you could say that's probably better than the way they were. If you're a veggie but don't know it, and naturally you don't, then maybe all you do is cause unhappiness and worry and disgust, mostly disgust, to those with the nerve to pretend to care, to love you. And they're likely the reason you wanted to put another hole in your head in the first place, so I guess it does sort of work."

Lisette turned in her seat, twisted her head around the side of the headrest to get a good look at Misery. "What is wrong with you?" she asked.

Misery smiled at her.

"The ultimate question," B said. "What is wrong with you? Who are you? Who do you think you are? I'd like to answer that one myself."

Lisette knew he was being kind. He had nothing wrong with him, or nothing overwhelming and unconquerable as Misery had. How could he be so calm and gentle in the face of such blather? Probably not listening, halfway listening at the most, and that was exactly what she should do, too, halfway listen. Why would she even ask Misery a question? An insane and hate-filled monster-like woman sat behind her, and when that monster-like woman wasn't talking about some variety of human pain, she was humming "Mack the Knife."

So not only had she been forced to turn from Anna, a person she'd come close to knowing, to become some blond girl called Lisette, a girl from someplace in Texas who was a third or some number cousin of Randy's, but she was stuck to Kenny by his blindness now, and heading west with people she hadn't known or imagined three weeks earlier. Adding to that list that one of the people she'd not heard of was a monstrous sort of crazy woman who sat behind her, almost made her laugh at the absurdity of it. She remembered last July 4th, the forced patriotism in her small Terra Haute neighborhood where old ladies flew flags from their car windows and young women had yellow magnetic ribbons on their bumpers, and the desire she had while listening to the high school band blast *America, the Beautiful* as if it were a march. The desire was to be somewhere else, to be doing something surprising. Listening to her grandparents' tales of doing without when young, of wanting to make the world a better place, of their mostly imagined and nonexistent hippie days, she'd wanted to shout. "Save it for the rest home. Tell it to yourselves." Three months later, she was doing something surprising, living some sort of adventure. Many of her aunts and cousins and those old gabbers would say the same thing to her if they knew of her life now and her wish then. They'd say, "Be careful what you wish for," as if it were the theory of relativity. She'd heard that so often, she was surprised it hadn't been put on a T-shirt, crocheted into a wall hanging. It was part of her family wisdom, one of the slogans they lived by.

Henry believed she'd take off, was poised for flight. She read that knowledge in his face, the resignation and martyrdom he'd worn since he could no longer see. But she wasn't going. She couldn't. She knew Henry, remembered the boy/man he used to be as Kenny. She couldn't abandon him to this caravan of weirdoes, him blind as a bat, and mean people still out to get him.

"Have you ever been in love?" she asked B.

"What's dear old mom calling herself now?" Misery leaned up into the space between the front bucket seats.

"Stalking Badger," B said.

"I was talking," Lisette said to Misery. "I asked B a question."

"It's just that I forgot. It's not an appealing name at all."

"This from the woman called Misery."

"Often," B said to Lisette. "Too many times to count. Or else, never."

Lisette laughed and waited for his explanation.

"Good observation. But this is something new," Misery said. "Another deviousness of some kind."

"I'm not being devious," B said. "One of those is true—often or never. Depends on what love is."

"I've been in love once," Lisette said. "But it turned out not to be the forever kind."

"I didn't mean you were devious. I mean the old she-devil is devious," Misery said. "Giving herself a Native American name is a new one. She used to say 'squaw' or 'injun,' and then spit in the dirt or on the floor immediately."

"My point exactly," B said to Lisette. "Probably not love if it's not the forever kind. 'Love is not love which alters where it alteration finds.'"

"Or bends with the remover to remove," Misery said. "Now think about what that means. Is the remover death?"

"She doesn't have an up side, does she?" Lisette asked B, jerking her head toward Misery. "But love doesn't have to be forever, no matter what the Bible or whatever that was you quoted says."

"People bore holes in their skulls to develop a third eye. Enlightenment. It's been attempted since the beginning of time. You try to do it where the skull grows together as you age, do it before you reach full adulthood and the bone is too hard."

"Shakespeare," B said. "But it's still likely wishful thinking. We want love to last forever because we don't want those few who love us to stop. We're comforted believing they're stuck no matter what."

"Madeline and I renamed ourselves," Misery said. "I think Lisette and Henry did too, though they'll deny it. Guess Satan's concubine got jealous, wanted to get in on the fun."

"Look," Lisette turned around again, knowing she should be perfecting her ignoring instead. "Mothers aren't perfect. How can they be? They're human." She gave herself a pain, sharp and hot in the area of her heart as she spoke. Her own mother latched onto trends, liked being in the know. "All the kids now go out to dinner before their proms," she'd say. Or "It's the new thing for the paintings in a home to be leaned against a wall, not hung on a nail." Lisette used to look away to keep from sneering when her mother took on that way, and once said, "Girls in high school give blow jobs now. It's the latest thing," and watched her mother's face cloud over. She was sorry for that then and sorrier now.

"I guess you're giving me a scolding," Misery said. "Using general statements like that. You think I should talk nice, pretty, sweet, lovey about dear old mom. Course, you won't come out and say it to me directly."

"OK, I will. Grow up. Be kinder. You cut your old mother some slack. It's hard work being a mother. I guess you'd make mistakes, too."

"Mistake is too nice a word for what I'd make. I'd make horrors. I'd be horrid at it. I should be locked up if I so much as say I want a child."

"Hasn't your time come and gone?" Lisette said. "I mean, your body can't reproduce anymore, right?"

"A rude question, but I'll answer. Just on the brink," Misery said. "I heat up like lighter fluid on a grill, but I still bleed. Stranger things have happened. I mean it would be possible if I were sexually active."

"Talk about strange," Lisette said, low enough for only B to hear.

"I'd be a miserable excuse for a father myself," B said. "Good thing I didn't reproduce."

"Yet," Lisette added. "Didn't reproduce yet. Men can be fathers much older."

"What's your real name?" Misery asked.

"Lisette. Just because you had to give yourself a noun and not a name doesn't mean any of the rest of us changed what our parents gave us."

"Names are nouns," Misery said. "Were you absent a lot in school?"

******

Randy led them to a gas station at the Grand Island exit, and while B and Randy filled up, Madeline and Lisette selected deli sandwiches and chips and assorted sodas from the attached food mart, and decided they'd stop at the state recreation area about ten more miles down the highway. But Wanda, whose chanting had finally turned to snoring just before the stop, woke up when the rattling and bouncing stopped and climbed from the bus. When she heard the plan, she forbade it. "That one is called War Axe recreation area," she said, jabbing one crooked finger at the map spread on the hood of the Cavalier and the place Madeline had pointed to. "It was named as a reminder of the war against my people. We cannot honor the slaughter."

"You don't know what it was named for or about," Madeline said. Her legs still shook from the vibration of the bus, and her muscles had frozen from being in one place for three hours. She wanted to get to a park and walk.

"Stalking Badger has spoken." Wanda folded her arms across her chest.

The others shrugged, Lisette and B saying it didn't matter if they went a little farther, and Wanda told them the great spirit of the plains would reward them for their goodness. She then took the map and studied it carefully. She said no to the next recreation area, Cheyenne, named she claimed after those who were slaughtered, the whole place like a tombstone. The next place was Fort Kearney, the source of the orders to kill, and so was absolutely off limits, and they finally had to go all the way to Sandy Channel Recreation area, nearly fifty miles from the Grand Island gas stop.

Wanda wondered if she'd known any of what she'd said. She'd surprised herself. And if she had known, how? What Wanda did know was her talk had caused a change in plans, minor but worth it. Any annoyance was better than none. Maybe she suffered from a version of Misery's curse, maybe small bits of useless trivia stuck to the goo in her head, too. If so, some of her reasons for pushing on could be based on truth.

"If we're going fifty more miles, Stalking Beaver should ride with B. Just to give us a break from the chanting," Madeline said. "Especially since she's probably mistaken about the places of slaughter and all that stuff."

"Badger," Wanda said. "And I don't like that car. I've watched it turn into a bear."

Once they were parked at the Sandy Channel recreation area, Wanda threw her head back and whooped a few times, and the whoops led into another chant that sounded to Madeline as if it were taken from a *Lone Ranger* episode. Wanda left the bus still chanting, the whoops and hi-yas getting louder until Misery climbed from the back of the Cavalier, turned to Wanda, and grabbed her by the shoulders, pinching the nylon of the running suit between her fingers. "We will not eat with that racket." She felt her funniness coming back, floating above the darkness inside like oil on water, and added, "You will chant no more forever."

"May your spleen become the appetizer for a black bear's dinner," Wanda said, and they all laughed, even Misery who then shook her head at Lisette. "Hey Whosit," she asked. "Is that curse just one of those mistakes mothers make?"

"It's a joke," Lisette said. She handed out paper plates as she spoke. "Even I can tell it's a joke."

Wanda walked around Misery so she stood beside the picnic table and Lisette. "Neither of my girls was born with a sense of humor. It's the Kneedelseeder in them. Phil's old mother wouldn't laugh if the pope himself tickled her."

After lunch, while Randy led Henry to the restroom as the others went to see the lakes, Madeline sat on the grass with her back against an elm, eyes closed. The sun was hotter than it should have been in October, and it burned her head through her hair. She smiled, imagining the molecules that made this thing called Madeline expanding and moving. The sun baked her joints, turned her tendons to liquid, made a flannel cloth of her tongue. Marvelous. She was a stranger in the world, or else the others were. The world became strange when you spent your life smiling at what was not understood. If she could sit against this tree until she died in a smoldering pool, her life would have a good ending, a better ending than it deserved, better than its beginning.

Henry was talking. "We were told we did good, were doing good, could do good. But it was that 'could' that bothered all of us. They said we *could* control others, and we *could* become models to be admired. We *could* communicate, boss, lead, establish a perimeter, load our weapons under fire, carry our food, control our bowels, that we *could* and would shoot when told to, when needed, that we *could* follow orders and *could* control ourselves. Most of that was not true, or if true, it was the word *could* that made it true. *Could* is not did. We could, but we often didn't. We were helpless. We couldn't control ourselves, others, not even our own bowels or our anger and fear. We couldn't make ourselves understood, and it was clear we couldn't command respect or obedience. We couldn't keep clean enough to be free from infections or toothaches." Henry's laugh was a mean-sounding chuckle, and Randy joined in. "The Army had not truly taken our incompetence into account. I mean, many of the recruits were there because they'd not been able to pay their rents, keep jobs, manage bank accounts, stay out of trouble. They or their families thought they'd learn to do most of that and come back as men or women, capable and disciplined. And maybe some got better, but mostly we were a bunch of fuck-ups appearing to outsiders as tough-guy heroes, a sort of comic-book persona, and we knew it."

Madeline opened her eyes and looked up at the two. "Isn't that true of youth in general? You spend a good half of your life hoping no one finds out how much of a poser you are."

"But we were supposed to control a group who may have loved or hated us—we couldn't tell. We were fuck-ups with guns, afraid for our lives.

"I once slapped and then kicked a child, a girl no older than ten, because she wouldn't leave my jeep. Pretended she didn't understand, but I knew she could speak English. I'd spoken to her before. Her perverseness made me suspect she was trying to distract us, make us pantomime and wheedle with her, jolly her into getting off our jeep, keep us distracted so we'd be good targets. I could almost see a gun trained on me, hear the roadside bomb that was being planted around the corner and would go off soon, sounding my death as we wasted time with her. My bowels clenched at what I knew. I yanked her up, slapped her, and when she dropped to the ground, I kicked her in the side. Twice. She screamed with the pain. "I'm not joking around, " I said. "I'm a soldier. You have to obey me."

"Oh," Madeline said, "Poor thing." She meant the child but was willing to include Henry in that, too. Yes, she would have run as fast as he was running. Faster. Maybe it was why she was along on this trip. She was the escape artist, passing the torch. See how to run, she'd say.

"Don't forgive me. They told us we could control our emotions." He sighed. "I wish I could be quiet. None of it is worth saying. There's no good response."

While Madeline listened to Henry, Wanda sat at the picnic table, her head in her arms, pretending to sleep. What she learned was that Henry had been a soldier, a somewhat whiney one at that. Oh, they made us do bad things in the war! Poor little me and my delicate self! I hit a little girl! Wasn't that the point of war? He'd not even admitted killing yet, which he must have done, a soldier and all. And wasn't this one a war you had to sign up for to be in it? She may not know much about world events, but she knew that. So why bitch and moan about it when you did it to yourself in the first place? It was like running a marathon and then saying, Oh it was so hard, it made my legs hurt. Henry was a wimp all right, but that wasn't the secret.

B, Lisette, and Misery followed a short woodchip trail that led from the picnic table to one of the many lakes in the recreation area, originally pits resulting from the work on Interstate 80 decades earlier. The water glistened blue in the afternoon sun, the wind from the west creating whitecaps along the shore. B said he'd heard the lakes were more than thirty feet deep and clear almost all the way to the bottom.

A scuba diving class was getting under way at the lake they stopped beside, four students hidden in gear and tanks. The instructor's voice carried across the lake, warning the class against stirring up the sand at the very bottom. When B said he'd always wanted to dive, Lisette shuddered, saying she was too claustrophobic to go underwater. "You have to listen to your own breathing," she said.

"Better than listening to your own thoughts," Misery said.

"Hearing your breath makes you feel how easily you could stop being. You realize there will be a last breath."

"But your thoughts never stop, cannot be stopped. An endless loop with no relief," Misery said. "You have no choice but to listen to them."

"Kneedelseeder, " B said. "When your mother was talking..."

"You mean Stalking Badger?" Misery asked.

"Yeah, sure. She mentioned Phil Kneedelseeder. Was he your father?"

"Not was, but is. At least as far as I know. Still is."

"The one who does the newsletter?"

"Yeah, I'm the youngest daughter of that font of wisdom and all-around jackass. But you know of that newsletter? I assumed anyone who actually paid for that thing was an inmate in a secure building."

B said he'd read a copy one of his customers had left lying around the café, and the one he'd read contained a report on small and mid-sized newspapers being bought up and owned by three giant corporations. B thought it was good to point something like that out, so perhaps out of boredom, he found the online version of the *Kneedelseeder Report,* and for the last four months, he'd found something in each that made him angry, and something that made him chuckle.

Misery sneered at that and when he looked into her eyes, he saw a mystery. A mire. He knew he wouldn't understand the tangles in her brain, but that they so clearly existed gave her a life worth the effort. He was curious about her real name, too, and had called up and discarded many already. He played the game with himself. He wouldn't ask her or Madeline. He'd discover it, would feel it. People could become their names. She wasn't a Marsha or a Jean or a Yolanda or any name beginning with C. Of that he was sure.

When the seven of them were finally ready to get into their seats, Madeline stood by the side of the bus, blocking the door, and said, "Please exchange Stalking Badger for Misery for a few hours. Give us

Misery, B. Or at least take Stalking Badger, too." She did it for Henry, she told herself.

Wanda spit in the dirt, and Misery said the bus was too bumpy for her.

Henry said maybe he'd ride in the Cavalier for a while, but Lisette said Misery took up too much room in the back so the Cavalier wouldn't hold four. B said he believed every one of them should be able to choose their seats and vehicles on their own without direction.

Madeline knew she was beaten when B spoke up, and even Randy didn't help, not then and not later once the bus got going down Interstate 80. He didn't smile at her as usual, didn't pat her leg, and she missed his attention.

Randy was trying to remember if he'd ever been involved in anything that'd begun so simply and turned out so wrong. Not just involved in, but in charge of. Nothing came to mind. He'd wanted to help the kid get to some relative safety. He and the engineering professor and B, as well as some others, had decided that the best way was to drive Henry to Canada, but had Henry set off hitchhiking, taken his chances with the bounty hunters and the patriots, he could be in Canada by now, his vision intact. And Randy wasn't often part of such screw-ups. Was it age? Was he letting too much slide? Well, he had to take the blame for the bus breaking down in the first place, for he had suspected the clutch was close to giving out and he should have put one in before they left. So that lack of planning ahead was his fault. The bus being vandalized, the angry waiter, those were what he put them in the way of with his lack of car maintenance. And what made this trip seem even more of a farce was the group he led. Even bringing Madeline along was maybe not the best idea, her moods darkening with every whoop from the back, no matter how fixed her smile.

"What's your next project?" Madeline asked, and he turned to her, surprised by her reaching out to him for a change, something she hadn't done since Stalking Badger showed up. He smiled then and she returned it, the world a bit less sad.

"The cost-effectiveness of high-speed trains. It's an interesting study by the center for transportation at the university, in fact, for the railroads need constant repairs, too, and while the costs for one person to travel by rail could be cheaper than the cost for one person to travel by auto, when you got many people, sort of like us, the cost of auto travel goes down." He suddenly wanted to get home and start working on the report, do something he knew he could handle, not make a mess of. When he finished the report it would be sent to the U.S. Department of Energy. It was a lower priority than the war and Homeland Security spending, and in fact, Randy didn't hold much hope of it making a difference, but it was fascinating anyway. "But that's direct costs. If you include indirect costs like carbon emissions and oil wars, the numbers change. Anyway, I'm just the writer."

"But it favors city people, no matter the costs," Madeline said.

"Oh-oh, oh-oh, oh-oh, oh-oh," came from the back seat.

"On the other hand, if we were on Amtrak, we could put train cars between ourselves and insanity," Madeline said.

"Insanity may be too prevalent for that," Randy said.

"OK." Madeline smiled. "I get it. I'm not special for having an insane family. But on a train I could at least get away from the insanity I know. I could maybe live with someone else's."

"Your mother has the contagious kind of insanity," Henry said.

"Yes," Madeline said. "That's great." She laughed. "You got it. You have to stay far away."

"Oh-oh, oh-oh, oh-oh, oh-oh." Wanda knew rhythm was important. The sounds or words or whatever they were meant zilch. It was the volume and the rhythm. It had to be monotonous, had to sound like drums. Earlier, before lunch, she'd used the hi-ya and the ya-ya sounds, but had switched to the ohs to make the others pay attention, thinking they would be looking for a pattern. She chanted so they wouldn't forget or ignore her, so they'd honor her heritage and past. She'd never done so and was sorry. The spirit she prayed to was strong, and by extension, so was she. Had she only known it sooner. If the old squaw had bothered to pass along some of the lore, the customs, the beliefs, Wanda could have led a powerful life. Juda with the black eyes and hairy chest would have loved her and wouldn't have broken up with her. She would've gotten out of Oklahoma sooner and with someone more interesting than Phil. If she'd had children at all, they would've loved her, revered her as the great mother, and given her gifts. They'd be honorable and sought after as strong oaks. By now, she could even be nationally, internationally, famous for her powers, a direct line to the help so many of the mere mortals needed. And she would know all the secrets.

If she chanted enough, one of them would tell her the main secret. She asked the gods to tell her, but no response so far. Who was Henry, and why were they taking that wimp north? If she knew, she could help. They continued to ignore her powers, to dismiss her prayers as coincidence or luck, but she was stronger than they knew. And more observant. Not one of them had noticed the waiter, the kid who'd sprayed spider killer in Henry's eyes, hiding behind the candy bar display in the center aisle of the food mart in Grand Island. He'd no doubt followed them to that picnic area by the lakes, though she hadn't seen him there. Her eyes were old, but her powers still better than all theirs put together. She now knew something they could use, and she would gladly share that knowledge just as soon as they acknowledged her as one chosen by the great spirit or spirits, as one blessed with whatever it was her people were blessed with, and as one with the will to use it. Someone could at least ask her advice. Until then, she was on the waiter's side. She stopped chanting and sat up, yelled to be heard over the rattle of the bus. "Are we in Oklahoma yet? I want to die in the land of my people."

NINE

"It's convoluted. That's what it is, and it's exactly what these liberals specialize in." Gerald spoke like a man hard of hearing with only one volume control, high. He'd driven into the parking lot of the Ogallala, Nebraska, Sioux Shack in a new Chevy sedan that did its best to introduce him to the world. Bumper stickers fighting magnetic ribbons for space on the bumpers and fenders and windows said She's a Child, Not a Choice; Pro-Life; God Bless America; United We Stand; Freedom Isn't Free; Support Our Troops; and POW/MIA. His passenger, a somewhat younger guy, closer to fifty than to sixty, introduced himself as Chuck something or other and wasn't much of a talker—even winced once or twice when Gerald's voice rang out across the diner. "Breaking a law and a solemn promise, then writing about it like it's the country's fault." Gerald poked the tabletop with a finger. "We don't want to hurt these boys for no reason, and I know how frightened you can be in a war zone. I was in Inch'on. But the letters he sent to the papers were taunts. Made it seem nothing means nothing."

Tim bit into his Sioux pocket, a western Nebraska version of an empanada he'd ordered only because Gerald nearly insisted—"Course you'll have one. The house specialty. Hand stuffed, full of energy"—and greasy juice dribbled down his chin. He wiped it with his hand, then wiped his hand on his jean leg. "Do I get my money now?"

"Money? Is that what you think you deserve?" Gerald poked the finger at Tim's face. "Gratitude's more like it. Thanks for doing your duty. Your country thanks you."

"But," Tim said, leaning across the table, ready to grab the poker finger and re-direct it. "I've done what you said you wanted on the web page."

"You'll get your money," Chuck said. "Gerald's just being Gerald."

"Good," Tim said. "Cause I'm almost out. Didn't bring much with me."

Chuck nodded. He was a big guy, broad shouldered and thick-necked like a former Cornhusker linebacker who'd not yet turned to all fat. He wore starched, creased jeans, a stiff, long-sleeved shirt with snaps instead of buttons, so white it seemed to jump around when Tim looked directly at it. Chuck's hat was a new-looking straw one with a high crown and a wide brim, and he kept it on as he ate. Though his clothes were clean and starched, his nails short and immaculate, his boots new looking, he smelled like a cow. Tim and his buddies used to make fun of the kids who came to school from the outlying areas smelling like cows, but one look at and whiff of Chuck and Tim knew you had to be tough to work with cows, not merely slow-witted and dirty as was the common knowledge back in his high school. Tim almost wanted the bovine smell for himself. And he could tell Chuck was embarrassed to be connected to Gerald, not just because of the quacking, but because of the white socks Gerald wore under his baggy, high-water khakis, the lime-green polo shirt with the American flag pin stuck on the placket. Tim's father would have hated men like Gerald, too, would not be sitting across a table from one for two thousand or a million dollars. "Silly men are more dangerous than the evil ones," Tim's father had said often. "The evil ones can be fought against, but silliness undermines the society." It was what he had against Disney and fast food and television laugh tracks.

When Tim had to talk to Grover to find out how much his father and he owed on the wounded VW bus, Grover, unlike Tim's father, was willing to help. "Check out the photo gallery if you want," he said. "I do it once or twice a week. Some of these who seem to be traveling through are running and hiding. Could be someone come into the restaurant you recognize. Look for the new ones and the old ones not caught. If you get no matches, I'll let you help me look for some guy I've lost track of, take a cut."

So with a half-hour before he'd be considered tardy, Tim sat at Grover's computer, clicking on pages of faces and descriptions, not sure he wanted to earn his extra money by being Grover's assistant, and not expecting to find anyone he knew among the photos. Killing time mostly but, he had to admit, interested nonetheless. The number of runners was what fascinated him. He'd no idea so many people were hiding from the law or the bondsmen. He looked at page after page of them until his finger got tired from the clicking, and he was nearly dizzy from one face blending into another, the noses growing or shrinking, fitting neatly between beady eyes or seeming lost between wide-spaced almond shapes. After more than an hour, he came across one he recognized, Jaco's old man. Jaco was a new dishwasher at the Cattleman's Reserve, and his father was wanted for skipping bail after he'd been arrested for dealing marijuana. Tim had only seen the guy once, but the face, with its long white scar from the bridge of the nose to the chin, was easy to remember. Tim tried to erase the scarred face from the gallery, hoping to give Jaco a break, not that Jaco'd ever said more than hello to him, but the link kept coming back. What was he doing anyway, looking at these poor pathetic losers, trying to make some money off their sorrow? He knew his father was right, had known it when he saw Jaco's father staring out at him, looking simultaneously lost and defiant. He was about to quit when suddenly he saw the unpatriotic jerk he'd sprayed. The hair was blond now, but it was him all right. He was wanted for being a deserter, and he had cocksure, arrogant, and patronizing written all over his face even before he left his fellow soldiers in danger.

"One of that VW bus group is on the list," Tim said to Grover, trying to sound nonchalant about it. He'd be a hero if he got the deserter. When he got the deserter.

"What do you know?" Grover said, leaning in to look at the photo. "Justice can happen. Worth two thousand, too." Grover read the web page out loud. "Two thousand dollar reward for anyone who aids in his capture by the U.S. Army."

"I could aid in his capture right now."

"The group offering the money's called Citizens Against Terror, CAT. It's a new one. Haven't heard of them before. You owe your dad twelve hundred for my bill, and he's taking that from your earnings, so seems like you have no spending money. Seems like you could use some of this."

"What do I do?" Tim asked. "Contact these guys?"

"Your prey's leaving town this morning, maybe already gone. So I hear from the Pear Tree. Whole group's pulling out. That means you've got to follow. If you tail 'em, you can call the Citizens Against Terror— oh, excuse me, the CATs—from the road, set up a place they can get to for the interception. Hopefully, you won't be too far out in the hills before you get your money."

"Should I just call the Army?"

"Yeah, do that if you don't want any money at all. See, if the Army gets him without the CATs being there, they'll welch, say they doubt you did much, must have been the Army found him on its own."

"The ad says 'aid.' I will have aided."

"It's a vague term," Grover said. "Usually a way to weasel out. Remember, putting a price on someone's head's not legal, not for a little unofficial group like this. It's not as if the notice is a contract."

So Tim left a voice message on the Cattleman's Reserve phone, said he was sick, guessing he wouldn't be back by evening. Then he parked down the hill from the Pear Tree, saw the VW and a white Cavalier leave. Before following them, he e-mailed an essay to his English teacher. English was his favorite class because the teacher let them argue their ideas, persuade others. And because he was one of the good students, his teacher let him get away with making jokes as he had in this paper against teaching intelligent design, arguing that there was nothing intelligent about intelligent design when everyone could tell evolution was true. Just look at Jason Wheeler, one of Tim's friends also in the class, and you'd believe his grandparents must be full-blooded chimpanzees. Tim was sorry he wouldn't be there to read his paper out loud, and he knew his teacher would pretend to be offended, though she liked a good joke better than most, and she wouldn't be able to fault him much, for his writing, as always, was good, every sentence diagrammable.

Tim guessed those liberals in front of him would be surprised he did so well in English class, surprised he could write at all. They probably fell for the stereotype that those who supported the war were not intellectual, or only did well in business classes, or spent too much time singing and praying to Jesus to think. He knew the categories, though he'd never figured out how they came to be, who'd come up with them.

In the Sioux Shack, he wasn't even four hundred miles from home, and if one of the CATS would just give him the two thousand and call the Army, he'd turn around and go back, drive all night and make it to school in the morning, work that evening, missing only one day of each. If he had to get a hotel, then miss one more day of work, the two thousand profit would be a bit smaller. What were they waiting for? He'd pointed out the VW bus, even confirmed that the whole group had rooms on the second floor of the Hiway Inn. Yet Chuck and Gerald hadn't wanted to stake out the motel, but had told him to go to the Sioux Shack across the street. Sure, they could see the VW from their booth, but what was the point? Tim hoped these citizens were picking up the tab, because a Sioux pocket was not something he'd ever eat on purpose, much less pay for.

"We called the Army," Gerald said. "Hell of a time getting through. Had to check us out. They can't afford wild goose chases. 'I have one of your deserters,' I said. I called Colonel Haynes, too. Retired. He's the one started the Citizens, lives in Florida now. Left a message. Someone'll call back soon."

Tim'd been watching the breast pocket of Gerald's lime green knit, noting how the phone made it droop, and he wondered now if it were set on ring or vibrate. Which would be better—a ringing or a vibrating breast? "So we can't do anything until someone calls you? You can't give me the money and let me get on with my life?"

"Being on the side of right and truth isn't a part-time job," Gerald said.

"Seems part-time to me," Chuck said to Gerald. "First work we've had to do.

Tim smiled. Even a CAT could be a bit funny.

When Tim left Nebraska City that morning, he'd taken the pages Grover had printed out. He knew the guy he was tracking was named Kenny, that he'd deserted, that the Army wanted him, and that the CATS would pay two thousand. He had a phone number to call, and he did call as soon as the VW turned west on 80. He got a voice mail and so left his number. Someone called back just before the Grand Island stop, and Tim gave his name and location. There was power in merely reporting he was on a trail. The gravelly voice on the other end of the line claimed to be coming from Georgia, but it assured Tim the CATS were all across the nation, had members in almost all the

Western states, and someone from Nebraska would contact him within the hour. When the whole group of them stopped in Ogallala for the night, even though it wasn't even four o'clock by then, and he'd still not been called, he called back, left another message. "What kind of lax organization is this? You guys want the deserter or not?" He'd driven nearly two hundred miles with no call.

It was another half hour before Gerald called, clearly defensive about the lax organization remark. "Nebraska's a big state," he said. "Course we want the guy."

"Easy to put some hogwash up on a web page," Tim said. "Easy to say you want him, but you can't prove it by me."

"Look here, boy, luck's on our side now. You're in Ogallala, and we got two members in Ogallala, another in Sidney. Only fifteen of us in the whole damn state, and nine of them are in Omaha, so you landed in the second best place for help."

"Well, want to know where I'm at? I'm in the parking lot of the Hiway Inn, just off Eighty. I'm in a purple eighty-four Jimmy. Guess you better get over here." After he hung up Tim knew he should have added, *And you better bring the money.*

Now he sat in the Sioux Shack and listened to Gerald explain that he had to wait for authorization from the retired Colonel, wanted to be sure of two things before he went to the bank and got cash money. One was that he'd be reimbursed, for the money would come out of his own account, and two was that it really was their man. For that, they'd have to get closer.

"We were closer in the parking lot," Tim said. "Why're we here?"

Gerald opened his eyes wider in surprise at the question. "We were hungry. I didn't get any dinner today, what with calling around and contacting the Citizens."

As Tim listened to Gerald quack and watched the way Chuck's lip curled up at one edge as Gerald's voice rose, his sense of toughness faded. He was a victim of his youth and inexperience, lacking any authority. It was like with his girlfriend, Marly, and her mean mother who threatened to bust her head open or rip her arm out of the socket and use it to beat her with. Well, they'd both been barely eleven at the time, just finishing the fifth grade when they started hanging around together, when she let him kiss her behind the maintenance shed at the baseball diamond.

She was his first and still his deepest love. Though his parents were not full of violent threats, lots of other parents promised ass beatings and head bustings, but Marly's mother's screeches were loud and constant, so much so they became a school joke.

Marly's insane witch mother, the kids said, and Tim knew how much it embarrassed her. He dreamed one night of killing Marly's mother, shooting her with a silver bullet to be sure she was dead. Another time he imagined driving a stake through her heart. By the end of summer, he knew what he had to do, so one afternoon, he left Marly in the municipal pool, snuck out through the boys' locker room, and ran the seven blocks to her house. He knew the witch was home because she was one of those rare mothers in the neighborhood who didn't work. When she answered the door, he stood up straight and took a deep breath. She wore white jeans and a pink-and-white checkered man's shirt, tied at the waist. He brushed past her into the mauve and white formal living room and told her to take a seat. The air conditioner was set so low he thought he could see his breath.

She did sit, smiling crookedly up at him as he paced the room, rubbed his hands together. Marly had her thick dark hair, but Marly didn't have the crooked, smart-aleck smile or that know-it-all glint in her eyes.

He stopped pacing and stood before the neighborhood witch, directing his gaze just above her head. "You're a school joke, and it hurts Marly. I know mothers never want to hurt their children, so I thought you'd want to know this. It would behoove you to change your ways." He was proud of "behoove." "The yellings and threats are way too much. Marly doesn't deserve it." He gave the speech exactly as he'd memorized it, practiced it while speaking into the bathroom mirror. He finished with his favorite lines. "I think you should treat Marly with more respect. She is a person, after all."

The witch mother clapped her hands together once, loud, and stood. The look in her eyes frightened him, and he tried not to back up toward the door.

"My business is not yours," she said. "Haven't your parents taught you the difference? Your business is God knows what—homework and playing ball and masturbating, I'd guess. Mine is my own life and my family's."

"Well," he said, hearing his voice shake. "Maybe. But still …."

"Maybe this is a courtship thing, your way of getting Marly's attention. But you've done it now."

Without intending to, he had taken small steps toward the door as she spoke, and when there he turned from her to see Marly walking across the yard, dragging her swim tote along the grass and heading toward the side door. He waved, and she blushed but kept moving. "She's not allowed to use the front door," Marly's mother said. "The living room is none of her business. And now," she said, pausing to give him a crooked smile once again, "now she's not allowed to see you. See what happens when you get helpful?"

When he cleared her front door, he took off, ran all the way to the next corner. He knew it was because he was young. That *my business* and *your business* had nothing to do with it. Had his mother or father paid her a visit instead of him, the witch would've been different, even if his parents had said just exactly what he'd said. Authority came with age and was what he needed. He knew the answers and had only to grow up enough so others would listen. He felt the same way now, talking to Gerald and Chuck. Were he fifty, even thirty, they'd be faster coughing up the money.

"If you're so hot on being all righteous and patriotic," he said, "you'd be willing to spend your own money whether or not the old colonel will cover it."

"What's to say this isn't a scam?" Gerald asked. "What do we know about you? And even if you're on the level, how can we be sure the guy is the one we want?"

"Beats me," Tim said. "Thought if your group went to the trouble of putting up a web page offering money, you'd have figured that out."

The two men shrugged. What they finally came up with, the two Citizens, was what Tim had suggested hours earlier and what Gerald called closer surveillance. The two of them positioned themselves in the lobby of the Hiway Inn, Chuck sitting on the sofa facing the check-in desk with the door to his right, and Gerald in an armchair with a view down to the laundry, the ice machines, and the elevator. The deserter would have to pass by eventually. Tim was sent to hang around the back entrance near the vending machines, risky because they'd recognize him, but if he saw any of them, he could duck into the men's room there, and it was more likely any or all of them would go through the lobby. Their two cars were parked just across from the lobby doors. If Tim did see the deserter coming down for a Snickers bar or something, he was to call Gerald, make his breast pocket ring. The whole point was to get a better, closer, look. Once they were sure, Gerald told Tim, they'd call the Army again, confirm the sighting. They'd also call the police, but the Citizens themselves would take control until someone official showed up. The three of them stood outside beside Tim's truck, the air that should have been cooling for evening still carrying heat.

"Then I'll get my money," Tim said.

Gerald shrugged. "Have to go to the ATM once it's all over and withdraw it."

"If I have to spend the night in Ogallala," Tim said, "you'll have to pay for it. I can't spend all my reward money in the getting."

Gerald looked hard at him, jabbing a finger toward him, nearly poking his chest. "You don't sound like a patriot to me," he said.

"Don't point that boney thing at me." Tim poked Gerald's shoulder.

"I'll get the room, all of our rooms if the time comes for that," Chuck said.

So as the two CATs sat in the lobby, pretending not to know each other and to both be very slow readers, Tim leaned against the wall near the back entrance, wishing he at least had a chair. He already knew he deserved more than two thousand.

******

Wanda's heartbeat was normal. As healthy as any hearts that have been beating sixty, seventy times a minute for seventy-nine plus years can be, she thought, healthier than most. She'd only said it was irregular, said she had shooting pains going up her arm and that the beat was so rapid she nearly felt whiplash from it so the group would stop. Riding in that bouncing bus was hard on her bones and joints and, if she had any left at all, her muscles, too. Weren't vehicles that were road-worthy supposed to have shock absorbers or some kind of springs to keep them on the road and to keep the passengers from being beaten near to death? That bus must have slipped through the inspections somehow.

She'd tried first acting crazy, "confused," as others said about the

elderly, believing it was a gentler word than crazy. "I see my ancestors
out there." She'd pointed to the sides of the highways. "All of them, lined
up, welcoming me back. We must be in Oklahoma. Are we near Felt?"

When no one answered, she was pleased. They were trying to ignore
her because they didn't know how to respond, weren't sure if she was
having a spell or not, and if she was, none of them wanted to be the
one to say it, to call attention to it. It was like when the clutch went
out in the beginning of the trip. Randy'd said just ignore it for now,
hoping not to stop, the normal first response to trouble. She knew they
wanted to get to their destination, wherever that was, with no more
interruptions or detours, and if she'd screwed up the journey as much
as they had so far, she'd be hell bent on the finish line, too. "Not all
my ancestors," she said. "Just the warriors. The brave." The young kid
started to say something, turned toward her, but changed his mind. He
was the one they had to take somewhere.

She knew no one could ignore her moans, though, especially if
they came from pains in her arm, from her heart beating wildly
without rhythm.

When they checked in, the nosy girl at the desk wanted all their
names, as if Randy saying six rooms for the group and paying with
his credit card were not enough. Why was it the Hiway Inn's business
what their names were? Nonetheless, Randy lied, said the young
people were Henry and Lisette and Wanda knew the boy wasn't Henry,
had her doubts about the blond girl's name, too. B said, "Name's B
Blaylock," and Angie gave that silly name she'd taken to using, Misery
Kneedelseeder. "It's my legal name," she said to Wanda when she gave
it. Madeline was Madeline Dames, and that still made Wanda angry.
The betrayal all those years ago, the jumping ship that told anyone
who cared to think about it that Madeline's home life was something
to escape from, so she said she was Stalking Badger. That was the one
the desk clerk wouldn't accept, Wanda the only one not allowed to
create her own name, so Madeline said Wanda was just an old woman
having a "mild attack" who was a bit confused. And maybe the attack
remark was true. For the last half-hour of so in that bucking bus, she'd
smelled buffalo, and not as if there were a buffalo farm somewhere
in the distance with its smell wafting in on the highway breezes, but
buffalo as if a wild one were sitting beside her, hiding under her seat. It

was not the smell of Felt or of Oklahoma, for long before the old squaw appeared on the plains, the buffalo were gone, and so the smell could only be provided by her far distant ancestors, a hunting party, meant as a greeting she guessed. Stranger was that she had never smelled a buffalo, yet she knew it for buffalo just the same. Part of her feared she may be what Madeline said she was, "a bit confused," but another part rejoiced in the way her ancestors reached out to her.

Once inside Room 218 of the Hiway Inn, with its view of the parking lot and the Dumpsters of the McDonald's next door, she prayed. She still had Alexandra's cancer to pray for, as well as the problems of a few clients of longer standing, and she continued to pray to find out the secret involving the boy. The bedspread at the Hiway Inn worked as well as the one from the Pear Tree Inn, and she wrapped up in it and pleaded and bargained with the supreme beings who listened to her. She added an extra request for her heart, not wanting to jinx herself by pretending it was giving out. When Madeline knocked on her door, and suggested calling in a doctor to give Wanda an examination, Wanda told her to go away, that all she needed was rest. "I was resting just fine, recovering, until you knocked. Now go away," she said. As she spoke she looked from the window at that waiter's purple pickup. Not one of the others knew what he drove, for no one else had seen him in the Grand Island food mart and so looked back to watch what he got into. She understood he was not too clever, that purple truck hard to hide, and that pleased her.

******

It was the kind of motel that cut corners, the rooms a few feet shorter than they should be, the vanity a few inches closer to the toilet, the tub a touch narrower than standard, so it had only one elevator, a slow one that seemed to be stuck on the second floor with the cleaning staff's cart, so Misery and B took the stairs to their rooms. Misery complained as they walked up that her hair kept falling in her eyes; the shoestring she used to make a ponytail with had come undone. Her hands were full, so she had to shake her head or try to blow the hair away from the sides of her face by sticking out her lower lip. It reminded her of Ginny, so she told B a story as they trudged upstairs. Their back yard neighbor was a beautician, and Ginny had gone to her once for a cut but hadn't liked it. Even someone as insensitive as Ginny found it difficult to tell the neighbor the cut was bad, that she would go elsewhere next time. Still, she was determined to do so, but before she got a chance, the neighbor was hit by a speeding car that ran a red light, killed immediately. "Ginny thought it a blessing," Misery said. "She said she would've had to hurt the neighbor, but luckily she died instead. Ginny said we all have to die sometime, and it's good when our deaths help someone, if by our deaths we avoid embarrassing situations."

They were standing outside Room 224, Misery's room, and B held one of her black plastic trash bags while she slid the card into the door. "Hey," he said. "Let's see what this burg has to offer, food wise. Just the two of us." Before she could answer, he added, "I mean this as a date. I'll pay. You comb your hair. I'll wear my cleaner jeans."

"Why not?" Misery said, surprised by her fast answer. B was a nice guy, though as Ginny used to say, they were a dime a dozen. Misery used to agree with Ginny about most things, believing herself lucky to have found someone smart and pretty, someone who didn't fit in with the so-called gay community either because she wasn't a joiner, cared nothing for how others managed as long as she did fine. Misery liked that honesty in her at first, just as she liked Ginny's copper-colored hair and gingery smell, liked it and Ginny until Ginny insisted on the pills that made Misery easier to be around and allowed her to hold down a job but changed her essence so completely she may as well have been someone else.

Misery knew she'd been putting it on thick so far on this journey, and was pissing off Lisette nicely, but B clearly liked her anyway. Well, at least he wouldn't be another Ginny. Not that she cared much for him, a former seminarian of all things. But this was merely a date, and dates didn't have to lead to anything, not even other dates, at least that was what she'd heard, not having had much experience in dating herself, with men or with women. She scowled at him and said nothing was wrong with her hair, and why should she comb it, but her "why not" echoed in her head like a shout. She told herself that if his offer pleased her, that pleasure was a temporary condition. Later, after she combed her hair and the two of them headed off in B's car, driving north toward downtown Ogallala, searching for something not a chain but with enough cars around it to appear good, she was nearly happy and almost missed B's news. "I read at the end of the *Kneedelseeder Report* that there's a big family reunion coming up soon. Phil probably sends the report to all his relatives, so decided to advertise the reunion. He's not in charge of it, not part of the planning, but he said he's going. You and your sister can go. It's a big deal. Your grandfather was one of twelve, you know."

Misery smiled. She'd never heard anything about her grandfather Kneedelseeder.

"They expect twenty-eight different families to show up."

******

Madeline took her mother's "go away" for a reprieve and returned to her and Randy's room. She'd not insisted on a doctor, because she'd not for a minute believed her mother was stroking out. She'd gone to check merely to appease Randy, who, though he was coming to see Wanda for the selfish old crone she was, still had some human feeling for the pitiful and continued to be almost fooled by the bad acting. Madeline put herself in his position, that of putting up with her mother day after day, putting up with Madeline and her increasing distress, too, when all he wanted was to help Henry and have fun with her, travel about the country and get back to work. He handled it all well, though, still hugged her, kept going forward, no matter the delays. She would have to make it up to him once they got back to Bourbon and to Highway N.

The peace that would bring! The two kids in Canada and perhaps safe, her mother back in her hole and back in Madeline's past, perhaps even Misery out of Madeline's spare room and on the way to somewhere. Somewhere happy, Madeline added, for her coldness had risen to the top, revealing itself in the way she had used Misery to avoid dining with Wanda, in her wish that is was a heart attack and not a stroke Wanda pretended to have. And the old fear from childhood was still there, even though Madeline laughed it away, ignored it away. The fear that some of it was deserved, that the old badger had seen this selfishness in her first daughter all along, had understood she was unlovable.

As she was entering her room, her cell rang, startling her, making her say "Trysh" out loud. But again it was Alexandra, this time with news, incredible though it was, of a remission miracle. Her doctors could find no sign of the cancer in the pancreas nor of it in any other organs. This was unheard of. "Zilch," Alexandra said. "Zippo. Naught." The treatments that were not expected to work but designed solely to make her more comfortable had even not started yet. The diagnosis was three weeks old, and no, there had been no mistake. The doctors at her Chicago hospital and those at the Mayo Clinic had come to the same conclusions. No one would say for sure she was out of the woods, but she'd had all the tests they'd come up with so far, and the results were good, the news great. She'd live. "Even the doctors are using the words *God* and *miracle*. Your mother may really be a miracle worker," she said. "I know you hate to hear that."

"If it means you'll live, I love to hear it, love it all."

"My life has two parts now," Alexandra said. "And the second part will be lived by a believer!"

TEN

Madeline asked Henry why, and he started talking. He said he couldn't remember exactly how long he'd been Henry, but knew it wasn't long, the weeks still countable on his hand. And the gray blurriness had been what his mother used to call a cross to bear for just over a week. Lisette helping him with the drops twice a day. He said he often tried to focus on Lisette's face. Madeline listened, knew what it felt to be new, to recreate oneself. When he was still Kenny, he explained, the decision to take off in a direction not toward Fort Jackson was both sudden and long coming. The proximate cause was a report on a television news show. Some old guy, shaking with the strain of Parkinson's that allows its victims to get old, had worked in a German Nazi hospital-like place during World War II, experimenting on prisoners. He'd been tracked down, exposed, called a war criminal, discovered after all these years, even though he'd changed his name and had been working in a charity hospital, doctoring for free in some cases for the past sixty years, making amends. He'd looked directly into the camera, rheumy eyes and cancer-splotched nose, and said he wasn't the one in charge all those years ago. He'd only been following orders. Henry was on leave, facing going back to South Carolina in a matter of days, from there back to Iraq soon. He was stretched out on the couch in his parents' family room that summer evening, watching television to numb his mind and avoid the mess that was his life. He'd fired into a crowd a few weeks before his first tour was over. He heard the cries. Imagined them at least. Henry's brother-in-law was sunk in the beanbag across the room, watching the same TV show, and just as Henry was trying to fall for it, the brother-in-law snorted.

126

"Not a defense, buddy," he said to the face on the screen. "Humans are responsible for their own actions."

Henry explained it that way to Madeline when she asked why he'd become UA.

After he left, he said, he'd written letters, six different ones, all with the same message. Lives matter. People are more important than governments. The innocent suffer. All that heartfelt stuff, he said. He believed then he could be a voice of reason, but his letters were called diatribes. A newspaper in Colorado made him into a cartoon, a soldier hiding behind others, shaking with fear, and typing. He should accept it, he knew, the fact no one wanted to hear from him, let uselessness spin around inside as his sergeant had told them all to do with their fear. Keep it in.

Madeline nodded, knew Louise did, too.

Madeline watched him eat his stuffed mushrooms, placing his left hand alongside the dish so that his thumb touched its rim. In good light, she knew, he could better guess the placement of dishes and cups and glasses, but in candlelight, he needed the extra testing to be sure he was digging into his mushrooms and not the basket of bread. She wondered if the doctor could be wrong and his sight wouldn't get sharper. Madeline knew Lisette feared the same. *Why* was no longer a question with an answer that mattered except as a conversation starter, yet Madeline had asked it, causing Lisette to wave her hand, an automatic dismissive gesture. Henry didn't see it, though and answered as if he truly could explain.

Madeline smiled at Lisette. "Sorry." She'd insisted on this celebratory dinner, her dying friend not dying after all, the Native prayers having worked.

"It's OK," Lisette said. "We're celebrating what you said, a miracle. My mom believes in miracles and angels and divine intervention. Says she saw an angel once."

Madeline knew that was true, seemed the sort of mother someone like Lisette would have.

******

Gerald and Chuck had both seen the young man being led, nearly dragged, through the Hiway Inn lobby. A pale, skinny blond girl pulled on his hand, said, "There's a table just to your right," said, "just one step down at the door." Chuck stood, ready to reach out and grab the young man's arm, but caught sight of Gerald's confused look. Gerald shrugged. Chuck nodded and kept his hands at this side.

Gerald nodded back, then called Tim.

"It has to be him," Chuck whispered to Gerald. "We know his hair's been dyed."

Gerald held the photo, a copy of the military ID, in his right hand, his phone in his left against his ear. It was the same photo posted on the Citizens Against Terror web site. "Lots of parts are not the same. This bozo down at the end of the hall may be mistaken. Just wanting some quick money."

When Tim answered, Gerald said, "Get up here. Now."

Chuck watched the VW bus pull out of the lot as Gerald spoke.

"One who may be our man's gone," Chuck said when Tim rushed into the lobby. "Course he'll be back, didn't check out. But he was driven away."

"Was he in disguise?" Tim asked.

"Probably not. Just the dyed hair is all," Chuck said. "But he didn't really match the photo."

"It was him," Tim said. "You had to see him before he was blinded."

"Blinded?" Gerald asked. "What?"

"Was his mouth hanging open? Was his head tilted up and to the side? Was he being pushed around like a feeb?"

"Seems you could've said all that about his being blind earlier today."

"Not blind, really. What I've heard is he'll see again, maybe get all his vision back. Not that I care."

Gerald grabbed Tim's arm. He looked like a man with a heavy gas bubble navigating the curves of his small intestine.

"Are you OK?" Tim asked. "Having an attack?"

"I'm disturbed. Very. Did the blinding happen over there?"

"If it did," Chuck said, "that changes everything."

"I did it," Tim said. "Just a little poison in the face."

"We don't want to hurt these boys," Chuck said.

"Not even deserters?" Tim said, noting Gerald's color was more normal, his grimace gone.

"What kept you so quiet? Shame?"

"Didn't want to be a braggart," Tim said. "Nothing to be ashamed of in hurting a traitor. And we can find him, I bet. Ogallala's not so large an old orange VW can't be found in some parking lot."

"Or we could just wait here," Chuck said. "Comfortable. No sense chasing about when we know they're coming back. And don't worry," he said before Tim could protest. "I'll get your room, breakfast tomorrow, too."

******

The Happy Lucky House had an all-you-can-eat dinner buffet, that fact announced by letters pasted across the window, a *U* for *you*. Misery chose it, deciding not to pretend with B, and that meant not pretending to eat like a lady or like a thin woman or man. Over her first plate, egg rolls and pot stickers and crab Rangoons piled precariously high, she told him she was a big eater. She was fat and out of shape because she ate lots and mostly fried or sweet foods. It was just what she wanted, and she hoped no one would try to improve her. Madeline'd been tempted, she knew, back when Misery moved into the Bourbon house, but had refrained, taking as always the path of least resistance.

B nodded, reminded her he ran a diner, lots of biscuits and gravy and fried potatoes, cinnamon rolls and lemon meringue pies. How could he criticize anyone's consumption?

His plate matched hers. "May I ask you something I've been mulling over?"

"Is it about me, my name, or my attitude?"

"No. Not even close."

"Good. Go ahead."

"Why do humans want to be lied to?"

She shifted in her seat, the red plastic covers of the booth sticking to her thighs.

"I mean, the word 'gourmet' on this menu has me wondering. Saying so doesn't make it so. We buy lots of stuff that doesn't work, spot cleaners and used cars. We elect people who've ignored us until the elections, have made messes of our worlds."

"I once bought a box of tissues named Soft and Silky. They were like rubbing my nose with burlap and sand. Guess I believed the name. "

"My mother wore white gloves once when we went out to brunch as a family."

"Huh?"

"The point is why? It's the same thing as wanting to believe a lie. Did she think they would turn her into the Duchess of Windsor? She was a Bourbon, Missouri, housewife. Why don't we live in reality? Why do we fall for these lies over and over? Promises and images?"

Misery unstuck herself from the booth and went to the buffet line for plate number two, one that was only the pork and beef dishes. She'd get the chicken and seafood entrees on number three. And she giggled as she walked the buffet because this was friendship, this sort of talk. No weather talk, no courting talk, no trying to sound wise or profound, but instead giving sound to the detritus that took up space in a brain. May as well let it out to a friend. Misery, even back when she was Angie, seldom giggled, was not the giggling type. Yet here she was, loading up on salt and fat and giggling about wishful thinking. She returned to the table, took a sip of her second glass of Chablis, her thighs once again sticking to the booth, and giggled more. "Ginny had this powder she shook all over her cat, Beelzebub. It was called 'Gee My Cat Smells Like a Meadow,' or something as silly. Gee, Beelzebub smelled like canned tuna and pee."

"Guess it's an odd subject," B said. "Sorry. I don't go on many dates."

"It's just that no one talks to me this way. I get advice, questions about how I'm feeling, pabulum about taking it slow and one day at a time. No one says what's rolling about his brain like that." Her heart beat in her ears.

"You must think this is some date!"

"Better than most," she said, and that was funny, too, for she couldn't remember any others. "I once dumped that Gee My Cat Smells stuff all over Ginny. Turned her white. Don't remember why any more, but I thought it was funny." Her laughter echoed harsh in her head and she knew she should be careful. She forced herself to calm down by counting the sugar packets on the table. Fourteen.

"I guess most have been with women?"

"What?"

"Dates. Most of your dates have been with women, right?"

"No. There is no most. There aren't any really. But since you think

I'm a lesbian—Madeline's telling I guess—why take me out at all?"

"I like you. And yes, I heard from Madeline you broke up with your life partner."

"Jeez. Ginny was not my 'life partner.' Talk about lies and our ability to swallow them. We spent nearly five years together, and my life's been a lot longer than that. I don't think either of us meant to share our lives when we hooked up, and surely not by the end. Get over that PC talk." Her words were like shouting in her head, but she wasn't angry or insistent. She hoped they didn't grate like that on the outside.

"What then? You're not a lesbian?"

Misery drained her wine and signaled for glass number three. It was a question she didn't have an answer to, no matter how often she'd asked it herself, usually without the negative he used to ask it. It was boring enough to let her calm down, take twelve deep breaths before continuing. Calm and quiet. Imagine her diaphragm like jelly. She could do the same job the drugs did if she concentrated. "If a lesbian is someone who can be happy with a woman's love, OK, I am one. But do I prefer women to men? I've not had enough men to know which I prefer. And since we're being honest, when I say "enough," I mean none. I've never made love to a man. If lesbian means I prefer one gender over the other, just in general, sex or no sex, I'm not one. For me, it depends on who the women and the men are." B smiled at her across the table, so she kept talking. "I once took a personality inventory test to determine if I was still crazy, or what kind of crazy I still was. One question was would I rather go to a small intimate dinner party or a large bash. I left it blank, and the therapist said it reflected poorly on my personality, was almost enough to tip my scores into the anti-social category. But how could I answer? It does depend on the people. I know some people I would rather starve than dine with, and there are others who are only acceptable at large bashes where their yahooism fits in."

He nodded, kept smiling, so she excused herself to get plate number three, chicken and seafood.

"I don't' know why I told you I was given a crazy test," she said when she returned.

"I had to take some of those when I left the seminary. My mom sent me to this counseling group." He ordered a vodka gimlet, and she decided when it was time, she'd go back for lemon cake, a few almond cookies and at least one dish of soft serve ice cream with sprinkles. "Don't know if I scored in the crazy range or not."

Not, she knew. His range was *not crazy*. He could joke about it, but he wasn't even close.

******

Alexandra was going to live; the cancer was gone, or maybe had never existed. The imminent threat was no longer one. The idea made Madeline giddy. A miracle had happened. Or a mistaken diagnosis. Or almost a miracle. Alexandra was surely not the first and only one to have her rampaging cells calm down. Odd things happened, and science had to make room for all eventualities. A death sentence one week, a cure the next. The dinner with Randy and Henry and Lisette was her idea. In her joy, she wanted to know the young people as people, not as a deserter and his girl, not as two on the run. As the dinner wound down, their napkins balled up on the table beside their mostly clean plates, the three of them who'd ridden in the bus laughed at Stalking Badger's chants. Alexander's cancer, gone now, had brought them Stalking Badger. A lingering side effect, Madeline said. Henry imitated the chants for Lisette who laughed a bit before saying, "Poor thing."

Lisette then told them about her grandfather who'd grown odder as he aged, too. "He has a ferret, one that wins awards at shows for the best groomed, the best natured, whatever," she said. "The ferret's name is Admiral Nimitz, and Grandpa takes him everywhere. Admiral Nimitz rides in the kid part of the grocery store basket, its little feet sticking through the leg holes. Admiral Nimitz gets to sit in the sidecar of Grandpa's Honda Goldwing, and knows how to press the call button at the Taco Bell drive-through. People who meet him have to call him admiral, too. Grandpa says the title means something, that Nimitz worked hard to get it, put his life in danger many times, and so deserves the respect of being called admiral. When Grandpa gets wound up, we're not sure if he's talking about his ferret or the real Nimitz, and not sure he knows the difference either."

Madeline laughed with the others, and while she was trying to select her entree, the subject changed. Randy was telling about his first year in Canada when he worked for a bakery and had brown sugar ooozing from his pores for months after he quit. He said hummingbirds tried to suck nectar from his ear hairs. Henry then told about winning a rowing contest at Camp Lakeside when he was ten, and that he kept the certificate that said he won under his mattress for years, taking it out every now and then to look at and remember how proud he'd been, how hard he'd rowed. The certificate was just red magic marker on cardboard but it was still Henry's greatest triumph.

Their stories blended as one. Before dessert, Randy told of his mother's last words about hating her flatware, and they all laughed even as they agreed it was a sad story. That the stories changed yet seemed the same fed Madeline's giddiness. She worried briefly she laughed when solemnity was called for.

When they were finishing their coffees and all four playing with their desserts, Lisette asked to borrow the bus.

Lisette did not say she didn't want to talk to Henry in a motel room, but all the rooms in whichever motels in whichever towns they stopped in represented the present, this trip, her anger and now sorrow at being with him, his sighs, his frowns, his damaged self. They were trapped in the motel rooms. Though they held each other in the nights in the rooms, even made love again every now and then as if trying to recreate their past, the rooms were not up to the talk she planned. She wanted an expanse. She knew if she could drive about a bit, she'd find a park, a riverside bench, a vista somewhere they could enjoy. Not that he could enjoy a vista, but she could, and she could tell him about it. She could and would tell him so much more. Randy and Madeline and Henry himself were all agreeable when, over the spumoni and coffees, she proposed taking Henry for a ride. "The bus's a bit hard to drive," Randy said. "Even with the new clutch, it has a long throw on the shift, and the gears, especially second, aren't easy to find."

Though Lisette had never driven a standard shift, she decided to trust herself. She was a full-grown adult woman with no handicaps and a fake passport, and if others, many virtually dim-witted, could do it, she could, too. So with a brief lesson from Randy, going forward and backing up three times, then making one complete circle of the restaurant parking lot, she took charge and dropped

Randy and Madeline at the motel, then headed north, away from the highway they came in on. They rode in silence, with Henry, she guessed, believing she was planning her break-up speech, and her not knowing what she was planning, not specifically. Within a few miles, Lisette saw the signs for Lake McConaughy and took being on the Ogallala Beach Road as a good omen. Who would have expected a beach in the middle of Nebraska? She didn't want to break up with him, not exactly. Her being with him, their romance and future, seemed secondary to his safety and recovery, to him finding peace after the tumult he'd set in motion. And even more than that, she wanted clarity, honesty. Neither of their feelings had to be spared, so long as they said what they meant. For most of her life, she'd wanted to fit in, and she knew that was normal. She'd also wanted not to fit in. She was annoyed by the lame jokes and stale ideas of her family, her so-called friends. She guessed that was normal, too, though how could she know for sure? No one said. No one confessed. She still wanted it both ways, the cake and the eating, coming to the path that diverged in a wood and taking both ways. Like now. Go with him and run away. Both appealed to her. She could flip a coin.

The beach road ended at the beach, and the wooden sign at the entrance said the park closed a half hour after sunset, but the gate was open, so she kept driving, not realizing at first she was on the sand and no longer on a road. She thought there was a path she was meant to stay on, but she lost it and ended up in a grove of cottonwood trees, the lake glistening twenty feet in front of her. She stopped the bus and the shudder told her she'd gone from third to off. She laughed at forgetting to downshift, but he kept quiet. "We're on a beach," she told him. "There's a moon that's lighting it up, and it could be an illusion, but the beach looks like white sand, the water too wide to see across. We're in a grove of trees, and I have driven across the actual sand. Course, it's dark, so I may be wrong except about the trees."

He nodded. "Smells like Cagles's Mill Lake. Like mud."

"But it's sand. And we are parked right on it." She laughed again. "Can't drive on the beach at Cagle's Mill. Now, don't worry. I'm not going to ask you any questions. I've asked them all. The answers aren't important anyway."

"Sorry."

"No. That's not the point either. One of my aunts knew a boy who drove his car off the road into a ditch on the way home from the prom. He ended up a quadriplegic. He'd been drinking, of course. Drove right into the ditch. But my friend Pam got drunk at the party we all had after our graduation, and she drove her car into a telephone pole. The car was dented, the pole knocked down, but she was unharmed. Some of us pay for our mistakes, and some of us don't." Well, that wasn't what she wanted to say, not really, but she could hear and see herself closing in on the point. The lake was a sheet of steel behind his head when she decided to try again.

"I don't guess any of us pay for all of them," he said. "We make so many."

"Right. Some girls get pregnant their first time, no protection. Others cross their fingers, toes, say prayers, whatever, and luck holds and they don't pay for their sins."

"You think you're paying for my mistakes," he said, finding her hand and squeezing it. "I really am sorry. Didn't think of you when I acted."

"No. I made my own decisions. Still am making them. But you keep paying, more and more. This blindness is the worst part."

"Not even close."

******

Before Lisette dropped them off at the motel, Madeline had made her stop at Spotlight Liquors for a bottle of champagne she would open in their room, drink to miracles. Louise said, Oh, yes, celebrate rarities, and Randy who had not met Alexandra, agreed. His laugh was stronger at dinner, his mood lighter. But though she'd said champagne, she wanted candy. And not some fancy and expensive candy in gold foil and velvet-lined boxes, but just the stale milk chocolate made with corn syrup, the mass-produced candy bars that lingered in vending machines for weeks or months. Snickers, Almond Joy, Kit Kat, Three Musketeers. Surely those went with champagne. She asked Randy what he wanted, and he'd laughed as she headed toward the vending machines, said, "Surprise me." The cheap candy craving was an old one, so old Chris used to tease her about it, so old she thought maybe on good days Wanda had laughed at it, too.

Something with nuts, she thought as she hopped down the motel back stairs, feeling like nine or ten or twenty-five or whatever age people still hopped. How old were you when you stopped hopping? Clearly older than sixty, she knew, for she hadn't stopped yet. She hopped over the last step and opened the door to the hallway, coming face to face with Tim.

"Hi," she said, knowing she knew him from somewhere. Then she knew where. "You're that mean kid," she said. "You're far from home."

"Not as far as you," he said. "I am a Nebraskan."

As she turned and hurried up the stairs without her candy bars, he called after her. "And I'm not mean. Just after justice."

"Justice," Randy said when she told him. "It's what all mean people claim to be after."

Randy sat on the bed with his head in his hands. "One more thing going wrong. What is this? How can I keep screwing this rescue up? It should be a simple trip. What's that guy doing here? What the hell is going wrong? Whatever it is, it won't be good for Henry. The kid probably thinks he can turn him in."

Madeline sat beside him, not sad enough yet, still up and somewhat giddy from Alexandra's news. But she rubbed his back, said it was not his doing, the whole thing not his responsibility. "I'll open the champagne, while you call Lisette," she said. "Tell her to take him to another motel tonight. We can walk to it in the morning, meet her there, and take off tomorrow, leave this mean kid sitting here waiting." She was a planner, yes, but she surprised herself with how good this one was.

Randy sighed and sat up straighter, his face wrinkled from where his hands had been, the bags under his eyes sagging to match the skin around his ears. He'd use her idea with just a few changes. The first change was that he couldn't call either Lisette or Henry as both had stopped using their phones when they'd gone into hiding. Henry'd mailed his to his mother who'd no doubt turned it over to the military police by now, and Lisette, who couldn't do that and keep the pretense of traveling by herself around the country, had thrown hers in the bottom of her suitcase, then eventually stuffed it under some sheets in a drawer in Madeline's spare room, giving Randy the battery first. Getting rid of the phones was for their own safety, the people who'd passed Henry on to Randy had said. The phones will get you in trouble, they'd said, the calls not only traceable, but even with the untraceable ones, the temptation to use them is great, and all talk gives you away.

So instead, Randy would call B, ask him and Misery to drive about and search for the bus, but first he called the front desk and asked about city parks or national parks, nice stretches with lakes or views. When he heard about Lake McConaughy, he guessed Lisette had found it. The road past the motel became Ogallala Beach Road, he'd noticed, though he'd not believed there was an actual beach nearby. He told B to drive around, but to head out the beach road, try the lake first.

"Lake McConaughy," Misery said when B explained it to her. "Named for an old grain merchant who proposed supplemental irrigation using the Platte River. It was back in the thirties, I think." B stared at her, so she worried she'd been talking too fast, too loud. "I read a lot," she said, hearing a tremor in her voice. "Usually most of what I come up with is useless. Guess this is, too."

******

Madeline knew people could think many things at once, the brain big enough to hold the world. You could plan a dinner party menu and drive a busy interstate and recall scenes from a favorite movie and wonder where an old childhood pal ended up and worry about the war in Iraq and more all at the same time. But what most people couldn't get around, were even embarrassed about, Madeline thought, was how easy it was to *feel* many things at the same time. She was worried about Henry and sorry for Randy, yet still joyful about Alexandra, and all that combined to make it hard for her to sit still, to remain in the room, champagne or no champagne. She had to get out, and not to run into Tim or to help anyone but herself. She said so to Randy. "Let's walk around town; let's go out and count trucks on the highway; let's find a grassy yard and walk across it barefoot."

"Can't," he said. "B will call."

"But you'll have your phone with you."

"But I have to think. Have to concentrate." He hugged her. "But you go out and howl at the moon, act like a giddy girl if you have to."

She took the elevator to the lobby, planning to walk across the parking lot and head toward the residential section, just for the walking. She hoped Tim was still at the back stairs, but if he'd moved to the front and if she ran into him, that was fine, too. She'd tell him what a mousey little creep he was, following a poor man whom he'd already hurt badly, skulking about in dark hallways for whatever reason, surely not a good one, and thus speeding down the path to ruin and destruction. He should be home doing his homework or talking to the flirty girls who hung around the Nebraska City pizza joints. Being here, he'd either hurt someone who didn't deserve it or hurt himself and ruin his chances for college by ending up in the hospital or jail. Or he could get by and remain safe and uncaught but already on the path to the next nasty thing, having killed his soul no matter if anyone else knew it or not. She wanted to tell him she didn't like him but if he shaped himself up he may in fact turn into someone she and others would like. But he was not in the lobby, and she was both relieved and disappointed not to give her speech.

It was like being in grade school, walking home with the lecture given by Miss Gruenlough still fresh in her mind: "Do not get in a car with a stranger, no matter how he entices you. Even if he says he knows your parents." Well, let anyone try, she would think as she walked home, daring the passing cars to stop and offer her a ride. She'd snarl, tell them off, scream, scratch, bite, hit, whatever it took to prove she was not a girl anyone should offer a ride to, was not an easy victim. No one ever offered her a ride, though, not once. Not even Mr. Parks who lived across the street and whom she knew. He once told her he'd passed her, but knew the walk would do her good, said he believed kids had it too soft, getting rides everywhere. Just as well, she'd thought as he was giving his speech. Someone should bite him, but she wasn't sure she wanted to taste that bitter hide.

As she started to walk out the lobby door, her glee wearing off already, tempered by Randy's frustration and her abandoning of him, she saw two men who'd been sitting there when she passed through both times already. She laughed at her joke to herself—didn't this town have a library for the homeless and dejected to sit around in, pretending to read? Both men looked at her from behind whatever they pretended to read, and that cheered her up even more. How could a sixty-year-old live with such vanity, be encouraged by two homeless old guys looking at her? It was Louise's ghost asking, and she told Louise *how* was a ridiculous question. And, well, she'd always been good looking, the way her body overflowed from her bikini now when she swam notwithstanding. She could eat all the candy bars she wanted to, for she had the kind of metabolism that could handle it, and she believed in her own good shape, or general good shape, whatever the scales or her age told her. And Louise should know it, too, for Madeline's looks, not drop-dead gorgeous but sweet and cute, had helped her escape Wanda, had made Louise take an interest, had first attracted Martin and Ollie. And now these two men watched her.

She strode out into the parking lot on this warm Nebraska evening, October not bringing the relief from the heat yet as it normally did, and crossed the street that ran at a right angle to the interstate, walking past the Red Roof, the Comfort Inn, the chain Mexican restaurant and the fast food burger place and the pancake and waffle anytime place. It wasn't pleasant, too many parking lots and gas stations to pass before getting to the tree-lined town streets they'd driven by on the way home from dinner. She recalled those streets, the residences that, like all others, fed her curiosity about the lives lived behind the curtains, lived in the rooms with the lamps burning and the nice-looking chairs before the fireplaces. How many were the kind of lives she'd always wanted, the Dames' kind? And how many were versions of the horror living with Wanda could bring? Did children at the tables feel their stomachs knot up even before their first bites? She tried to guess always when driving by the homes of strangers, knowing the outside gave no clues. She continued to walk toward the residential section and away from the motel, though she could still see the Hiway Inn a few blocks behind her, its vacancy sign lighting up first letter by letter, then the whole word blinking three times. It was a cheap but new place so at least the rooms didn't smell like those in the older chains, so full of smoke and sweat and anxiety no amount of pine-scented cleaner could cover it. And then she knew. Her joke to herself about the homeless men was not based on reality at all, and her rationalizations about her still good looks were the vanity Louise disparaged. Those men were up to no good and connected somehow to Tim. She didn't know how, but knew she had to go back and tell Randy about them still being there, about the way they studied her.

She went in the back way of the motel, more willing to see that little snot Tim with his toddler hair than the two men who were spying on them, but all she saw was the vending machine. Candy was still a craving, though how it could be with all else going on was a mystery.

Nevertheless, she stopped by the vending machines and got two bags of Peanut M&Ms, one for her and Randy and one to drop by Wanda's room.

She had a vague memory, the kind that at sixty she wondered if it had happened or if she'd wished for it, imagined it, dreamed it instead. Either way, it was real. She and Wanda had played "war," a card game for two in which the highest card put down won the hand, and the one with the most cards at the end won the game. It was a game a four- or five-year-old could play, and she was that age. The prize for winning a game was one M&M, and the two of them laughed, mother and daughter enjoying themselves one rainy afternoon, picking out their favorite colors, red for Madeline and yellow for Wanda. The memory or whatever it was reminded her she should tell her mother about Alexandra's cure. The prayers for Alexandra could stop. Of course, Wanda would take credit for the cure, but maybe the credit was deserved. Who knew for sure who or what controlled humankind, if anything did, and if it did, why it cared. Let there be a god that listened to her mother, no matter how upside-down that made the whole idea of god, and Madeline would use it. She'd ask her to pray for Trysh to call, to pray for a reunion. Then she'd ask for Henry's eyesight and his safety, for the end of war in order to save other boys like Henry. Maybe she'd ask her mother to pray for Misery, wounded beyond any but miraculous help, and finally she'd ask for prayers for herself, who wanted more than anything for Wanda to move once again to the background of her life, to be part of a past she never thought of, to be someone she sent a card to once in a while but never spoke to. Please pray for your own disappearance, she could say, and though that made her laugh a bit on her walk up the back stairs, she knew it was something the woman who'd laughed while playing "war" wouldn't appreciate, though the one called Stalking Badger may understand.

******

Lisette and Henry were sitting in the bus talking when Misery knocked on the driver's side window, making both jump. "Get down," Henry shouted, while Lisette said, "Go away."

"Don't come back to the motel," Misery said, when Lisette, still shaking, rolled down the window. B stood behind her and repeated the instruction.

"The guy who attacked Henry is in the motel, waiting for you," B said. "I guess he wants to turn you in. Maybe he wants to hurt you more. Whatever, you have to avoid him. Go to another motel, not too close to ours so he can't see the bus from the Hiway Inn parking lot." B gave Henry two hundred-dollar bills. "This should cover it. Give me your room keys so I can get your stuff and have it for morning. Call Randy in the morning, and we'll arrange a place to meet up with you. Maybe really far down the highway, not near Ogallala at all."

After B and Misery left, Lisette said she wanted to walk down the beach, thought that instead of another motel room, they could just stay up all night, listening to the water lap the sand, to the frogs call out in what sounded like desperation. They'd both said all they could say by then. Lisette'd said she loved him, but would probably not stay across in Canada with him. She wasn't sure why, but some of it was homesickness. She said she may regret not staying with him, but going back to Indiana was all she could do now. It wasn't rational as much as instinctive. Henry told her he lived with a disgust in himself and in the world he was part of. It was a brutal, petty, conventional, and false world, and he was a solid part of it. When he looked inside himself, he saw nothing better than what he saw outside. He said he would not be sadder or lonelier with or without her, and hearing him say so hurt more than she'd expected it to.

As they walked to the water, he asked her to tell him about Nebraska, having missed all but the tip of it before being blinded in Nebraska City.

"If you like space, it's beautiful," she said. "Full of newly harvested fields. It looks rich for that. But the towns seem the opposite of rich. At least these few along Interstate 80 do. Lots of strip malls, chain restaurants. I was thinking how inhuman it would've seemed to be brought here, back in pioneer days, I mean. Say with your husband or parents. Far from all you know, lost in the vastness, able to see for miles but not caring because it all looked the same. But at times, as we rode along, it seemed just the reverse. The vastness of Nebraska, the small hills and the chimney rocks sticking up so suddenly are breathtaking. Must have seemed so to the pioneers, too. It's the strip malls that seem inhuman."

"You're getting carried away. Disingenuous. We have strip malls in Terre Haute, the place you're running back to. Don't make it sound like the problem is less than universal."

When they went back toward the bus, the sky was lightening at the horizon, and the shore birds as well as the warblers in the cottonwoods were screeching. She held his hand and squeezed more than was necessary to guide him back. If her being there or not being there were all the same to him, maybe she'd stay with him in Canada.

There was only one grove of trees near the beach road entrance, and they'd been the only vehicle in it when they left, but as they approached the place where the bus should be, she was confused and then frightened and then angry. There were nothing but tire tracks under the cottonwoods now. The bus was gone.

ELEVEN

"I want to know your family," Misery said to B on the drive back from Lake McConaughy. "Or at least hear about them. For all my fifty years, I've told myself I missed a mother, but that's wrong. It's family I missed."

B's forehead had been reflecting the streetlights as they neared town, and when he shook it now, a circle of light flashed across his window. "It's never as interesting as it seems. Besides, your mother annoys you, so you already have that part."

"Not annoy," Misery said. "Don't belittle it."

"Sorry," he said and she chose to accept his apology, appreciating the blush that went with it.

"I yearn for family," she said, her voice high pitched. "I desire family." She'd never been the playful type. She knew it. But being with B now she felt that fleeting funniness that came with being off the pills, a humor surfacing rarely, but not entirely covered over yet. And though she was not calm—her fingers tingled with electric sparks, and she could see waves and red swirls in the air she expelled—she bordered on content. Content was rare and good. She had climbed a peak and wanted to enjoy the clear air, knowing the descent would be rapid. "It's an emotional need." She mock cried. "E mo shun al. After all, Madeline's had three husbands and I didn't know any of them. Well, I did know Chris, but I was six when they married, ten when he died. I saw Martin only in those oh-so-cute photo Christmas cards they sent out. I did meet old Ollie, who fancied himself a patron of the arts. He was at some large family gatherings, Dad's eightieth birthday, for example. Those were formal and false but few, thank God. I don't know his daughter. I don't even know Madeline's daughter except as a little girl. Am I pulling on your heartstrings?"

"Big time."

When they got back to the Hiway Inn, B carried his laptop to her room, opened the link to the *Kneedelseeder Report* and clicked on "Reunion." "See? You have a large family."

Misery wouldn't look at the screen. "I lost that family years ago. Never heard of any of them. For all real use, Dad left before I was born. When I was a kid, I saw a movie on TV about pod people, and after that, I wondered if Dad had been taken by aliens, just his shell left behind."

"Ha," B said as he looked at the screen. "He's talking about incompetence in this Bush regime."

Misery laughed. "You take old Dad's rants seriously? What good do they do?"

"What else can he do?"

"He's saying what you already know. Do you think anyone reading his newsletter is surprised?" Misery was slumped in the one upholstered chair in the room, so she couldn't see the computer screen even if she'd wanted to.

"I'll ask it again," B said as he clicked the mouse button a number of times, "What else can he do? Or me? Or you? Can we do more than say our piece?"

"Tell me about your parents."

"And because his so-called rants are linked to the family reunion, he's at least working the Kneedelseeder clan. Not many families read the same blogs, get the same facts to work from."

"Do you have any brothers?"

"One," he said. He closed the laptop and turned toward her. " John. He's an accountant. We get along as well as people with only the past in common do. He's got lots of kids, even a grandchild or two by now. He feels a bit sorry for me, and I feel a bit sorry for him."

"See? That's what I mean. You can be surrounded by a group, all ages, all beliefs, any time you want. You could invite the whole group to your house and they'd come, too, even if they didn't want to, because you're family."

He stood and stretched. "Ha! Some fun that would be."

"Grandpa Kneedelseeder was one of twelve."

He leaned over and mussed her hair, swung her ponytail. "You did know!"

"No. You told me. I remember everything anyone tells me."

"Think of all the cousins your father has." B sat on the edge of the bed, his knees touching hers. "And you. Second cousins, third, fourth. A cast of thousands."

"All assholes, no doubt. But you win. When we get back home, I'll go to the damned reunion. I'll go only if you go with me so you can meet dear old dad. And by home I mean Madeline's of course, in sweet Bourbon. I have no other one."

"I've been trying to tell you. It's not 'back home.' The reunion's in our direction. A small town in Washington State. One of your Dad's cousins is in charge. It seems lots of Kneedelseeders live in the northwest."

"See how little I know about my so-called family? I had no idea, just guessed they all hung around the St. Louis area. Silly to think that, I guess."

"Phil's father was the only one who ended up in the Midwest. Some of the clan are in California and a fairly large group's in Maine."

"You've been keeping up like it matters. Why?"

B shrugged. "Boredom. More interesting than most other blogs. And then I have an affinity to Phil."

"No you don't. When I was a kid, he was silent. Now he's just one of many old cranks. Anyway, Madeline won't go to a reunion. She stopped being a Kneedelseeder almost as soon as she got her first period. And we've got Stalking Badger with us."

"We've also got two cars. I'll go with you, and the rest can take the bus somewhere. I really want to shake Phil's hand."

"Good luck," she said and closed her eyes, trying to remember her father paying enough attention to shake anyone's hands. Had pod people ever shaken hands?

******

Madeline and Martin and Alexandra were throwing a party for someone, and whoever it was would walk through the door any minute. The door was a large double one, heavy, white-painted wood with gold handles and hinges. It was set in a powder blue wall and festooned with pink and white crepe paper and pink balloons. All the guests had streamers, ready to throw, and Louise Dames stood in the background, smiling at how nice it all looked. Alexandra said, "I can't wait," and hopped from one foot to the next. "Randy," Martin said. "Don't forget his name. It's Randy." Then they were outside and Louise was shaking her head at the VW bus, the seats duct taped together. Alexandra and Martin tangoed together, but the party mood was gone. An older Trysh said, "Mom, you should have known better. How could you?" Even angry, her voice was musical, and she did start singing. It began as Gregorian chant and turned into a dirge. "How could you?"

When the bus joined in the dirge, Madeline knew it as a dream, so when Randy's phone rang, waking them both, she was ready to awaken. Five o'clock meant trouble, though, and she wasn't surprised to hear Randy cursing.

Henry and Lisette had walked three miles from the beach to a twenty-four-hour gas station to call Randy. "How do you tell a nice guy like Randy you lost his car?" Lisette asked as they walked. "All he's doing, this whole thing, is trying to help."

"We didn't lose it. Someone stole it. A random, mean, senseless act, sure, but not one we're responsible for."

"I feel guilty."

"Stop."

"I can't help it."

"Try. Guilt over this is silly."

"You do the calling," she said. "I can't."

Madeline was proud that not one of them wasted time in anger or cried out woe-is-me. Louise was proud, too. Plans worked. Getting on with it, ignoring that emotional stuff, cursing and weeping later if there were time. And there was always time. Those were the foundations of sanity, Louise said. In this case, a plan was made quickly. Misery and Madeline went to Henry and Lisette's room to pack up Henry's stuff, leaving Lisette's alone. In one of the back-and-forth phone calls to the gas station, Lisette was given a choice—go to Canada with Henry or go to Washington with the women. She decided Ogallala was as good a place as any to say good-bye, and so would travel with the women. B picked Henry and Lisette up, but dropped Lisette again on a residential street five blocks from the motel and picked up Randy a block farther over. They hoped to sneak away without being followed by the two men in the lobby or by the kid in the back hallway. Stuffing the bags in the trunk was the trickiest part, but they did it fast, hoping no one was watching. B and Randy were taking Henry to Cut Bank, Montana, to the safe house, and then to Alberta, British Columbia, only twenty miles farther, where he would apply for refugee status. The women would stay around the Hiway Inn for at least one more day as decoys, and then rent a car and head for the Kneedelseeder family reunion. B and Randy would meet up with them there. You always were good at plans, Louise told Madeline.

Randy kissed Madeline good-bye in their room, and she closed the door behind him, not even watching him walk down the hallway. He was supposed to be going out for a morning stroll, nothing more. As part of the act, she wasn't supposed to draw the curtains and watch him walk across the parking lot. She knew they'd meet in three days in Ritzville, Washington, would be together for a time back in Bourbon, yet she wished she'd told him she loved him sometime other than when they were making love. She didn't ask herself if it she should call it love or like or infatuation. Maybe it was need, maybe attraction. She knew it was the same no matter the word, and knew, too, life was better with him.

He'd told her Lisette had been crying.

******

The deserter was slipping away. Tim could feel it. By the time he left his room, he knew they'd all gone. He'd said the night before that he and Chuck and Gerald should set up a schedule so someone was always watching. Not that any of them could sit up all night in the lobby without the desk clerks growing more suspicious, but the two CATs had views of the parking lot from their windows, and while Tim didn't, he claimed he wouldn't mind standing out by the side of the building for an hour or two when it was his turn. Course, because of the windows and all, it would be easier for the CATs to divide the watch. They'd nodded, said they'd take care of it, humoring him, he guessed now. Each of them must have been snoring and farting as the bus and car left the parking lot. The odd thing was by the time he made it to the lobby, the pretty girl who was with them was eating pancakes in the breakfast section, and the old woman who'd called him a mean kid was talking to the desk clerk about the beach road as if she were a tourist, almost proving his intuition wrong. The car and the bus were gone, though.

Tim knew a trick when he saw one, but Gerald and Chuck refused to chase farther when he explained it to them. Sure, they acted outraged, Gerald stating his disgust that the kid had deserted and in doing so left some other young man in harm's way, and describing his anger at living in a country where duty meant nothing to some. It was a boring speech, but Tim listened to the whole thing without smirking. "The thing is," Chuck said, "we have lives. I'm a wheat farmer. It's time to get the hard red in."

"I can't neglect my business any longer, either," Gerald said. "I have clients who need me. And you should get back to school."

Tim knew he should have taken them for quitters from the first. Neither of them even had a gun. "I'm in this for justice." Tim said. "And the money you owe me."

"Justice," Chuck said, "is a funny thing. You don't know if something is just or isn't until much later."

"Sounds like my dad," Tim said. "Who would've taken you for a relativist?"

"Take some comfort that you did the right thing," Gerald said. "You tried. Maybe it was us that blew it."

"Damn right," Tim said.

"Never thought I'd make a good lawman," Chuck said. "I just can't stay mad long enough. Besides, this motel trip's not exactly the highlight of my life."

"I wish we could continue trailing the kid, I really do," Gerald said. "Unlike Chuck, I can stay mad long enough."

"Hey, man," Tim said. "Let's do it without Chuck. I figured you for a true patriot anyway. Just from your bumper stickers."

"Ha! Again, I'd love to, kid, but I've got a business to run. I am a true patriot," he said, jabbing Tim's chest with his finger. "But it's my brother-in-law's car."

"Where's my money?" Tim grabbed hold of the finger, squeezed it. "I've earned it."

"Did you get the deserter?" Gerald asked. He yanked his hand back, wiped his finger on his leg. "I don't think so," he quacked. "No results, no money."

After they drove off in Gerald's brother-in-law's car, Tim called his home, knowing both his parents were already out for the day, and left a voice message. "Hey, Dad, I headed out with some friends yesterday. I know you're worried, but don't be. I'm fine. It was an impulse, a wild hair, see the West, go down Eighty as far as we can stand it, stuff like that. We're OK. I know I'll catch hell when I get back, but don't call the cops or anything. I'm fine." His father would know it as bullshit, but at least Tim's face wouldn't be on the six o'clock news: "Missing High School Student."

The next call was to Grover at the garage, and after Tim told his story of the CAT's incompetence, of getting nothing other than a night in Ogallala and a sad excuse for a sandwich, Grover called Tim a naïve, wet-behind-the-ears dupe. "What were you listening to those old buzzards for? Stop whining. Take action. Call the police on this deserter, make the cops give you a letter saying you called them, then get in touch with that head brother in the organization and make him pay up."

"But you said they wouldn't give me the money that way."

"Didn't do so well this way, either, did you? The thing is, nitwit, you have to change tactics if one isn't working. You tried what seemed the best way, but got stuck with dweebs, so try something else. A letter from the police should be honored by those citizens or whatever they are. You've come too far to quit now."

"OK," Tim said. "Think I should follow them, try to find the bus and the car, or call from here?"

"You call from there what's gonna happen? That makes as much sense as me calling and saying they came through a few days ago. Go get 'em, you idiot. Track 'em. Be a hunter. Are you afraid?"

"Of those old guys and the blinky? Hardly."

"I think you are," Grover said. "Wuss. Coward. Stupid, to boot."

******

Misery said she'd expected Madeline to be upset at being part of the Kneedelseeders once again, using the reunion as a connecting place, but she wasn't. Kneedelseeder wasn't the problem. Madeline remembered Grandma Kneedelseeder as a civilized and proper woman, probably much like Louise Dames, upsetting only Wanda, whom she disapproved of, and thus showing herself as wisely judgmental. It was being stuck with her mother now and still and what seemed forever that saddened Madeline, but she'd been a Dames long enough to try to make the best of a bad situation. Keep going forward. It was why she would wring some good from the bad and buy a car instead of rent one. After all, she would need one soon. Her Escort was hardly up to the Ozark hills, had struggled painfully on Route 185 from the beginning.

She set off on foot at close to noon, walking toward the business section of Ogallala, knowing there had to be a car lot in town with something she could use. Roughly a mile from the motel she came upon Zeus Motors, specializing, according to the signs, in new and pre-owned luxury cars. She walked about the front of the lot, looking in car windows, running her hands along fenders, even kicking an Audi tire, but no one came from the yellow cinderblock office. Though she was tempted to walk away, find another car dealer and thereby prove to Zeus he could lose a sale by being whatever he was—lazy or misogynistic or anti-pedestrian—she was warm, especially after her mile walk, so she went into the cinderblock building for air-conditioning. She hoped, too, for a cold water fountain or a free soda or lemonade as some of the dealers on Interstate 44 near Bourbon gave out.

Inside, she saw a sandy-haired man, just barely old enough to be called a man, in a salmon-colored sport coat and brown plaid slacks. He was slumped in his chair, his feet up on the only desk in the room. He was snoring gently, and the bangs covering his forehead blew softly in the breeze from the air conditioning vent. She coughed, and he opened his eyes, not seeming startled. "The walker," he said. "Saw you come up the road. Want to use the restroom?"

"I need a car."

"Ha!" He stood and brushed his bangs back. "Guess so. Walking about on a day like this."

"I want to buy one of yours."

He stood up straighter. "Really?"

"If I see anything I can stand, that is."

"Great. Sorry. We got some old ladies who come in here often, walk down from those senior apartments." He pointed behind him. "All they want is something to do. One thought we had free soda or coffee."

She nodded, and turned toward the door, took a few steps before he apologized. "I don't mean you're like them, not at all. They're crazy for one thing, and old, too. Not one is under sixty."

"I'm sixty," she said, and turned back toward him. "You do sell cars, right?"

"Yep. All you see are for sale. New ones, older ones, all one hundred percent guaranteed. Our family's been in the business for three generations, and we're as honest and trustworthy as you'll find. We wouldn't stay in business otherwise. My father goes over each pre-owned car personally, making more repairs than necessary, just as if it were his own. But then it may as well be. We're like a family here. We depend on repeat business, so your friends and family are as important as ours. My grandfather owns this one here in Ogallala and the Ford/Toyota dealership in North Platte, and no one knows more about quality cars. And really, no one beats our prices. That's the truth."

She raised her hand to interrupt him. "Can I see what you have in a fairly large sedan? A good highway car?"

He showed her a new Lexus, two new Volvos, one with and one without a sunroof, a few gently used Cadillacs, some Lincoln Town Cars, two new and one used, a Jaguar sedan she said was too small, and three Mercedes sedans. Though the prices for most were considerably more than she wanted to pay, "Ridiculously high," she told him, she looked at each one, listening to his claims of low prices while what she saw written on the stickers made his claims a lie. Unless, she thought, the word *low* had taken on an alternate meaning. He leaned in close at one point, his breath smelling like pecans, and glanced about the place furtively before speaking. "We upset the other dealers in the state by selling so low. Some are really out to get us because of it, but Grandpa just doesn't think it's fair to make honest hard-working people pay so much. He sells so low we barely make any money, lose, in fact, on some deals, but make it up in the satisfaction we get from seeing people happy with their cars." He said this as she leaned up against a 2005 Mercedes 300, a steal at $32,900.

"Gramps is all heart," she said.

"What do Americans love more than their cars?" he asked. "What gives more pleasure, says more about you?"

"Tough questions," she said, straightening up enough to spot a shiny red roof on a car back by the fence. She pointed. "Let's look at that one."

The salesman, Zeus' grandson, followed her as she wound through two rows of cars to the section for the really old ones. She'd been led by the red, her favorite color, and because it was in an area that was likely for the less expensive cars. The red one proved to be close enough to what she wanted. It was another Mercedes 300, but twenty years old. It had a sunroof that worked on a crank, and beige leather seats that had turned brown and black from the oil of previous bodies. It had cruise control, wipers that worked, tires with most of their tread, a working AC, and best of all, it was a diesel. Randy'd just been telling her how clean diesel fuel was compared to gasoline.

On the negative side, black lettering on a white background was part of a sign that covered both doors, each side. *ISABELLE BELLE IS NUMBER ONE IN SALES* was painted across the top, and underneath that, right in the center, in full color, one eye on each door, was Isabelle herself, a jowly but young woman, her face surrounded by dark curls. On the bottom of the front door was the phrase, in quotes, "Let her ring your bells," and on the bottom of the back doors was a phone number and the Rock Firm Realty logo, a jagged rock.

"I'll be honest with you," Zeus the third said as she walked around the car, comparing both photos of Isabelle, "It's a hard car to sell."

"Her eyes don't follow you," Madeline said.

"I don't know who she is. We got this at auction. Dad hasn't gotten around to painting it yet."

The whitewash on the window said $4,000, but after Madeline drove it around the block and heard the brakes squeal, she offered $2,000, and ended up agreeing to $2,200, her final offer. Not a great bargain for a car with 206,000 miles. Zeus the Third pretended he couldn't give her a title until her check cleared, but she called her bank from his office and erased all doubt of that. When he did give her the title, she saw it was stamped "Salvage," something he called "a mere formality." She took her check back and wrote another for $1,500 that made him scowl even as he pocketed it.

She hadn't meant to be cheap, she told herself as she drove out of the lot. Ollie would have scolded her for such dealing. "When you do that, you give money much more importance than it should have," he'd said to her more than once. She'd given him the same answer each time: "Only rich folk can afford that attitude."

All the new cars on Zeus' lot had been much too high, and this car she merely hoped would make it back to Bourbon had come with a salvage title, so it truly wasn't worth more than she gave for it. And since it cost her so little, she could now afford to play around with it, experiment. After they got back home, she'd get Randy to advise her on converting it to bio-diesel, and then would use the old cooking oil from B's place so it would smell like a large french fry sliding along Highway N. She looked through the rearview mirror into the back seat and wished the car were larger. For a luxury sedan, it wasn't as roomy as she'd expected. Stalking Badger would take up most of the back seat, had been known to suck all the air out of much larger places, and after a few miles the car would seem like a sub-compact. Madeline stopped herself. No use suffering ahead of time, Louise said as she often had. In three days Madeline would be back with Randy in Ritzville, and in a week she'd be back in Bourbon, the air maybe still warm enough for an hour or so in her pool, even if she only dangled her feet in it. A week was 168 hours, or 10,080 minutes, and she had used up at least one of those minutes with the multiplication. By that time, in 10,079 minutes, she'd have a new pool to replace her nice blue one taken with the bus. In 10,079 minutes plus two hours, 11,519 minutes, her mother would be back in her little house and Madeline could communicate with her the usual way, a Christmas card mailed just after Christmas. She pulled off the road in front of a home with a decorated front yard— gnomes and windmills and plaster deer filled the spaces in between the burning bushes and cedar trees. She closed her eyes, and forced herself to take deep breaths. Eventually she smiled. In a week she would change her life into one she could handle.

Before going back to the motel, she drove to a Kmart, then a Walmart, then a hardware store, and finally to a toy store, already looking for a replacement pool. She didn't insist on the kind she liked, three inflated blue circles, but was willing to settle for any kind that would fit in Isabelle's trunk. No one in Nebraska, though, was selling pools in October.

It was while driving aimlessly around Ogallala then, meandering in the outskirts, counting off minutes, that she saw a pool on the side of the road, wadded up into a small pink mound beside a brown plastic trash barrel. It was just like hers only in pink. She'd guessed that when she passed, but wasn't sure until she lifted it out of the grassy ditch, straightened it out, and spread it on the road. It was full of kitty litter she had to dump to see the two tears in the bottom. She folded it up and put it in Isabelle's trunk. A little duct tape and it would be as good as new. If the motel had a hose, she'd soon be swimming.

As she could've guessed, none of the others appreciated Isabelle. "We shouldn't be so easy to spot," was Lisette's comment, one that was totally wrong. They could be easy to spot. It was B who shouldn't be. And Stalking Badger chanted a bit, more of the hi-ya-ya with some foot-stomping thrown in, right there in the motel's parking lot. "It's cursed, " she said. "That white eyes on the side doesn't want us driving her around."

Misery merely laughed when she saw Isabelle, said nothing then, but later she borrowed a black marker from the desk clerk and drew large pupils on Isabelle, making them fit the inside corners of the eyes on the driver's side, so Isabelle was cross-eyed, and making them look from the outsides of the eyes on the other side, so Isabelle was wall-eyed.

Madeline was examining the eye job Misery had given Isabelle, when she saw the purple pick-up driven by the mean kid leave the parking lot fast. She hoped he'd come back, but just in case, she called Randy and told him to be on the look out. Randy said he missed her. He and B were nearing Casper, Wyoming, making good time. Suddenly he laughed. He said the mean kid was probably looking for the bus because it'd be much easier to find than B's car, and so he could be led in the opposite direction. Randy hoped the thief was speeding through Colorado or Kansas, but as he said it, Madeline heard other laughter coming from his end. B and Henry both repeated that word, speeding. "In the bus?" B said. "You do remember the bus, don't you?"

******

Grover must've enjoyed calling Tim stupid. Made him feel like a big man, just as his Dad had said. The same as busting down some poor nitwit's door. When Tim got back home, he'd snub Grover, concentrate on making himself into the kind of man Grover and his deranged sort wouldn't know. But what he felt now, what propelled him west and slightly north, was pure anger. Not only at the deserter, but also at Grover. He'd prove something to that cocksucker, collect the reward money, and do it by being smart, listening to no more advice from old men who pretended to know things, guided instead by his own intelligence.

Calm down, calm down, he said as he drove. Take it easy, be smart, get a grip. How long have they been gone? What was that old woman doing with the real estate car? Figure it out. He hit himself on the forehead as he drove. Think, Tim, think. They'd spilt up, of course. That was an easy one. What else? Where are they, the deserter and the two old guys? Headed to Canada, he knew. That was an easier one, but which way they were going to Canada was harder. How he could surprise them, if he could find them, was harder still. Their sneaking out, splitting up, meant they'd guessed what he was up to. Easy for them to figure that once he'd let himself be seen. So they were running away from him, maybe expecting him to follow. Too bad his purple truck was so easy to find. As easy as that orange bus.

But like his truck, the bus was too easy. It was a gamble, but Tim decided to take it. He wouldn't look for the bus, but would concentrate instead on the nondescript Cavalier the others rode in. It was one of dozens, the Missouri license plate perhaps the only distinguishing feature. But maybe they'd figured him out first, knew he'd be watching for the car and had ditched it somewhere, were heading straight for the border in the bus? How could he track that Cavalier anyway? The bus is one some people at gas stations would remember. And if he found the bus, the Cavalier would surely be nearby. But no, he couldn't second-guess himself so soon. If they had any brains at all, they'd ditched the bus someplace and were taking the Cavalier into Canada. But where in Canada? They'd be headed north or northeast or northwest. Washington, Montana, North Dakota, Minnesota. Those were the states bordering Canada. Assuming they'd not changed direction or destination, they wouldn't have traveled the width of Nebraska if they intended Minnesota from Missouri, so he could eliminate that one as a possibility. That left three. He felt proud he could come up with a fairly accurate map of the U.S. in his head, just while driving.

When he left Ogallala, he'd turned up Highway 26, too angry to make the decision, just instinctively moving north when Interstate 80 dipped south. By the time 26 changed to 92 without him noticing and he saw the main Chimney Rock Nebraska bragged about, that boney yellowish finger pointing to the sky, he believed he was going the right way, at least so far. He wished he had one of those fancy direction systems in the truck, so he'd know what happened to 26 and if it would reappear as he hoped. He saw a sign announcing the town of Scottsbluff in a matter of miles, and though his knowledge of his own state's geography was nearly nonexistent, he did know Scottsbluff was almost Wyoming, and so was where he'd have to buy an atlas, see what his and their choices were. How many roads went into Canada, anyway? Then he remembered Idaho. That was another state bordering Canada, wasn't it? He was almost sure.

******

The world was alive, a fact the white eyes never understood. The Earth breathed. The trees themselves turned their leaves away from loud noises and ugliness, listened to the chatter of humans as well as squirrels and cicadas and carpenter ants. Rocks mulled things over, and their man-made counterpoints, bricks and wooden boards and sheets of steel, exerted their wills. Clods of dirt worked in concert with concrete sidewalks and kept the records, took notes. The mirror in her room of the Hiway Inn was nearly suicidal from having seen so much humiliation and hypocrisy, also from having been so ill used. It was smiled into, winked at, puckered at, made faces at, but never for the mirror. Always for the one doing it. Fake, phony, and vain. The shower was angry. It sent hissing noises out with its spray, tried to burn her. The carpet was dying a slow death. No one but Wanda knew these things, for the white man was too wrapped up in himself to notice.

But Madeline was an eighth or more of whatever tribe the old squaw had been, so she had enough native blood in her to be more aware. She should've known you cannot drive safely in a car so obviously marked by someone else. There were two things to consider: The car was angry at being made so ugly, and would lash out, or the woman's spirit was still in it, perhaps fighting with the car, and they'd be caught in the middle.

Let the others act as if only what they could see and understand was real. Wanda would not get in that car.

She turned to her mirror to comfort it. "Don't be sad," she said. "Someone pretty may look in you with love after I'm gone. At least you're warm and dry, not a crack on you."

How simple and clear her own life used to be, back before she believed in her powers, before she made contact with the great spirits, back when she was miserable yet able to make them all quake, back when all she wanted was her daughters' adoration, even though they'd never know so certainly how much she deserved it. All she got then was their unspoken hatred, and she got the same now. Back then was better, though, for the gods letting her in and making her aware of how the world teemed with life, showing her how the atoms were forever talking trash about humans as they spun endlessly, made her days more strenuous. She never could take in enough air anymore, and each breath choked her.

TWELVE

By Wednesday morning, Randy and B and Henry were in the Crow Indian Reservation just south of Hardin, Montana, where they'd spent the night. The purple pickup hadn't been seen, and B said that meant the kid had gone home, back to Nebraska City, his adventure over. "By tomorrow, he'll be bragging about getting the best of us or some other fictional characters."

"Or," Randy said, "he hasn't quit. We had a four-hour head start."

They were driving south on a two-lane road, unnamed and unnumbered, thinking it would take them to Yellowtail Dam, a structure of engineering magnificence Randy had been told about by his engineering professor connection. "Yellowtail's the highest dam in the Missouri River basin, and it creates the seventy-one mile Big Horn Lake. Produces energy that's sent to the electric grid," Randy said. "Still does, even in the third year of the drought, though not as much as it could with some rain. The small plants in Missouri only produce enough energy to power their own visitor centers."

The other two grunted in response.

Henry said he would've been in favor of driving all the way to Yellowstone Park, knowing this may be his only and last chance to see it, but his eyes couldn't make out much other than half shapes and bright colors. "Glad you're willing to pass on Yellowstone," B said. "Cause we already did. That was yesterday's decision."

"This may be as good as my eyes get."

"Don't strain 'em," Randy said.

"We're backtracking south," B said. "If it were up to me, we wouldn't be.

'No backtracking' is the motto of someone who intends to get somewhere."

"This around here's where Custer got it." Randy rode in the back seat and he pointed to his left as he spoke.

"Got what was coming to him," B said. "Not just the Native Americans, even his own men hated him, right? Seems I've read that."

Randy nodded. "Can't think of anyone deserving scalping. Course, dead's dead."

"Did his own men deserve it, then?" Henry squinted out the car window, trying to tell the mountains from the hills and trees. "Probably someone's been killed on every inch of earth after all the years we've been human on it. As much as we kill."

******

Tim called the Citizens Against Terror's voice mail and said he was still on the deserter's trail, said he'd get back when he had the deserter in his sights, and then would have to insist on his money. He said the Nebraska CATs had been inept and chintzy and he suspected their patriotism. He called their big cat paw logo *cute* to make them angry. The message was long, but that meant it would stand out; someone would have to listen to it all, would remember Tim when he called and gave a shorter one—"I have the criminal. Send me the bounty." After looking at the atlas in Scottsbluff, he decided he could wait to make a decision until he crossed all of Wyoming and got into Montana. Billings would require a smart choice or a lucky flip of the coin. But for now, he was willing to bet the deserter and his handlers would stay on the interstate. For one thing, they thought they'd outsmarted him, and for another, they were strangers like him, not used to the back roads and hoping to make good time. They probably wouldn't stop for the night, but switch drivers and keep going. He'd do the same, keep driving, that was. His school's driver's ed teacher ended each semester by telling the class not to be afraid, even though they were driving what were lethal weapons, could even be called weapons of mass destruction, he'd say and laugh. He said because they were young, they were by nature the best drivers—reflexes sharp and fast, eyes clear, muscles at their peaks. They were equipped to ride all night if need be, could call on their own strength and youth to serve them. In fact, he suggested they sign on for long distance trucking, make big bucks and quit once they hit thirty and needed more sleep. Tim's parents had laughed at that, though some other parents who were lobbying for college for their offspring were angry at such statements. Now was the time to test the teacher's belief. Tim would drive all night with no relief driver, stare into the setting sun and then the black night, trusting he could see what he needed to and would react well when called upon.

Just before dusk he passed an antelope on the side of the highway, leaning against the high wire fence designed to keep it from being flattened by the rare passing semi. The antelope looked directly at Tim as he passed, and stood still long enough for him to back up and shoot it with his phone. He sent the picture to his father with a message: U evr see 1? He sent it also to Jason Wheeler and a few other friends and wished he could send it to his brother because he doubted there were antelopes in Iraq. Though his brother could call home every now and then, neither Tim nor his parents could call or send electronic messages back. He sent the antelope to his English teacher, too, coming clean with her about being sick. Please don't flunk me, he added. He was tempted to send it to his boss at the Cattleman's Reserve, but knew by the time he got back there, at least two more days, his job would be history anyway.

He stopped at the Sunrise Cafe in Sheridan, Wyoming, almost on the Montana border, for steak and eggs, his goal being protein and lots of coffee. He'd heard of guys being able to buy speed at truck stops or from truckers anywhere, but he understood that because he didn't know how, he'd likely ask the wrong guy and be either arrested or ripped off. And truckers seemed as scarce as antelope and all other people up here.

He cleaned his plate with one of his two slices of wheat toast, made it shine the way his mother's Pomeranian did their dinner plates, and finished his fourth cup of coffee, asking himself why he kept going in the dark. That Cavalier with Missouri plates would be easy to drive by, and he may have driven by it already since it'd been dark since before Buffalo. And in the few minutes it'd take to put the lights of Sheridan behind him, he'd be heading north in total darkness again. Just him and the low-hanging stars. But dark or not, he had to press on. At Billings, he'd rest, get a room for a few hours and hit the road at dawn. It was unlikely he'd passed them—they had a large enough head start—but he must be closing the gap. The waitress who poured his fifth cup of coffee and gave him his bill was about his age, pretty with dark hair in a lopsided ponytail, large blue eyes, and a wide mouth. She smiled at him, so he talked her into smiling for the camera phone, and then when she turned her back, he took another shot, her jeans stretched tight and smooth across her ass. He sent those to Jason, saying glad you're not here.

He noticed five new voice messages, three from his father, one from Jason, and one from the Citizens. He kept his phone off most of the time so he wouldn't have to explain himself to his father, but he'd listen to all the messages, read the few texts, knew he'd have time to do so as he drove through the darkness. Before hitting Interstate 90, he cruised Sheridan, pulled into every motel parking lot. No Cavalier with Missouri plates, but lots of Canadians acting like migratory birds, heading south in fall. Sheridan was one of those quaint towns his mother would like. After posing for him, the waitress told him it was a railroad town, plotted quickly on the back of wrapping paper by a former civil war soldier who named it for his hero, General Sheridan. What was she, a member of the tourist board, he asked, but she hadn't smiled. No, she was merely giving him some information, but if he preferred being ignorant, that was OK with her. As he drove around, he decided the whole town was mostly a museum to the past, the bars and restaurants with cute names like Straight Home and One For The Road were deserted by nine o'clock. Yeah, it was just his mother's speed.

The two hours of blackness between Sheridan and Billings were interrupted twice by well-lit Quonset huts with signs outside claiming they were casinos. Their parking lots were full. His ears popped a few times outside of Billings, and he smelled it before he saw the lights. Oil and gas storage tanks lit with high-powered spots and surrounded by fences toped with barbed wire seemed to be the Billings welcoming committee on Interstate 90. He checked into the first motel he saw, a small red stone one claiming to be American owned, just across from the BP compound. It was not quite ten o'clock, but when he rang the bell on the desk, an older woman in pink foam curlers and a quilted robe came to take his information and give him the key. She spoke around a short cigarette clenched in her teeth, and squinted as her own smoke filled her eyes. She said checkout was noon, and he nodded, knowing he'd be long gone by then, had no intention of staying in Billings.

When he got to his room, he spread the atlas out on the mauve-and-rose bedspread. The coupons on the back pages included one for a free "Discover Montana!" brochure, with information on beautiful cities like Billings. He laughed. Not beautiful from the side he'd come from. Flipping back to the Montana page, he discovered he'd been wrong. If the Cavalier was to stay on interstates, as he still believed, Billings was not where the road split, but rather Butte, one of the other towns beginning with B Montana was full of. Until Butte and Interstate 15, it was 90 all the way.

The next morning, Wednesday, at least two hours before B agreed to backtrack and take Randy to Yellowtail Dam, Tim left Billings ahead of those he was chasing.

******

Her mother could get in the car or not, stay at the motel, wander off, take a bus home. None of it was Madeline's responsibility. Nevertheless, Lisette, Misery, and probably anyone else, acquaintance or stranger, even old Stalking Badger herself, would expect Madeline to care, to worry, and to coax. After all, she was a daughter. Misery was, too, but few seeing her in her fuzzy sweaters and full black skirts would expect much of her. This caretaking Madeline was supposed to accept was based on payback, the cycle of life. The mother provides food and shelter, and then it's the daughter's turn. And Madeline had to admit she and Misery had never gone hungry. Though they hated and feared their home, it at least was one.

Five over-the-counter sleeping pills ground up and sprinkled in Wanda's sausage gravy from the nearby Hardee's did it. Three hours after breakfast, Misery and Madeline checked Wanda out of her room and half-carried, half-dragged her to the car and, without bumping her head on the door and roof more than thrice, arranged her in the back seat.

They left the city limits of Ogallala, Nebraska, at nearly 12:30, headed northwest, and crossed the border into Wyoming at close to three. Misery rode in the front seat and was the only one who talked at first, though she didn't talk to anyone, merely commented on what she saw from her window. A herd of cows, a shack, what were probably mesquite trees. "Wyoming's sad-looking," she said shortly after the border town of Torrington.

No one responded, but she continued. "Looks like Afghanistan does on the news, all brown and bare, hills and scrub."

They looked to the right, the three who were awake, and saw a freight train way off in the distance, underlining the horizon. "Must be five hundred cars," Misery said. "It's at least five miles away. No wonder the pioneers went crazy."

"I don't think I want another guy," Lisette said, her head leaning against the window, absorbing the regular bump bump bump of a wheel out of round.

"It's the forty-fourth state," Misery said. "The first to let women vote."

"Yeah, it's nice all right," Lisette said. "The problem is you fall in love before you know all the bad stuff, and once in love, you can't get out of it."

"No." Misery leaned around the headrest to see Lisette, directly behind her. "It's not nice. It's like Afghanistan without the history or as many people but with better roads. Equality's deeply rooted here, though, and that counts a bit."

Madeline felt Lisettte looking her way, knew if she returned the glance in the mirror, she would feel obliged to offer comfort in the form of meaningless words, platitudes Louise would have provided. Madeline drove on, though, saying nothing. Her eyes on the road. A comforting remark like *Sorry you're sad*, a gentle smile, even a wink in the rearview mirror seemed too much for her. She was posing, had long been posing, and wished for a way to stop. Lisette was wasting her time hoping for a connection. Madeline could tell her that. Lisette'd clearly wanted to connect with B and had transferred that desire to Madeline. Can't you be self-sufficient? Madeline wished she had the guts to ask. Do you need constant love? Are you that much of a wimp? How can you be lonely surrounded by us odd people all the time? We even eat together. Now and then Wanda's regular breathing changed to a strangled snoring, and Madeline would talk to Lisette. "Poke her. Make her stop."

"I guess they could train troops here," Misery said.

"I would've killed myself if I'd come out here to live, been dragged along by some guy looking for his fortune or something at least green."

Lisette's words came out jerky, her head still on the window. "Over every hill is just another hill."

"Yeah," Misery said. "If somebody was coming, though, you'd see his dust rising at least a day before he showed up."

"My God, " Lisette sat up straight and wailed. "Who would've thought he'd turn so sullen and sad? He didn't have that in him back when we were a couple."

"Maybe we all have everything in us, waiting for the right circumstance to bring it out," Madeline said, a Louise-worthy slogan of sorts, inspirational poster material. Well, Lisette could take it as comfort. "Poke the old woman. She's snoring again."

Lisette poked Wanda, then leaned up between the two front seats. "Another thing. Call me Anna."

Madeline nodded. "Anna." The sun would be in the windshield soon, and when it got lower than the visor, she'd stop, spend the night somewhere in Wyoming. She could see no other cars, though she'd counted thirty since Scottsbluff. Nineteen trucks. Three trains. Some cows but no ranch houses. A few shacks, a cluster of trailer homes. She'd seen many sheep who seemed as lonely as the cows, and she'd spotted three antelope. She hoped to see a buffalo before the day ended.

"You won't replace him," Misery picked at a spot of foodstuff, maybe dried gravy, on her skirt. "People aren't replaceable."

"My mother used to tell me to be careful with her good china," Anna said. "because it wasn't replaceable." She laughed. "How is a boyfriend like a Wedgwood bowl?" She leaned back and they rode in silence again, Wanda requiring a poke every five or so miles.

"Indian paintbrush," Misery said. "It's the state flower of Wyoming."

"What's Indiana's?" Anna asked. "That's my home. Not Texas."

"The peony. I don't decide to memorize things like state flowers or birds, just so you know. But if I hear it or read it somewhere, I remember."

"Peony's nice."

"I hate tamed flowers," Misery said.

"Why would anyone say I'm going to volunteer to go kill people I don't know?" Anna poked Wanda as she asked Madeline.

"Not sure where I ever heard or read about Wyoming. I can never remember the source. It's driving me crazy. I hate it."

"I just find it hard to imagine is all," Anna said.

Misery turned to face her. "Cause you're thinking about it the wrong way, nitwit. The killing is a surprise for lots of them. They sign up for the uniform and to be part of something. It's like when girls decide to be nuns, they don't think about all that praying and having to bow and scrape to the older nuns. They think of the little veils and that they're working as part of a group for God."

"Not many girls want to be nuns anymore," Anna said. "Guess they wised up."

"They don't wear veils anymore, either," Misery said. She'd bought five long black skirts for ten dollars at a cut-rate clothing store when she left Ginny, deciding to be in mourning for whatever had been her life that was now over, all the good parts gone or passed by anyway. They weren't even skirts nuns would wear. Looking down at her lap now, Misery saw her skirt as if for the first time, a thing that made her uglier than normal.

Silence reigned once again in the car, and even Wanda's snores seemed to have stopped. Highway 25 curved west a bit, then north, then west again for nearly forty miles, all the way to Casper. Isabelle headed into the light. Madeline considered stopping once they got to Casper, though they should be able to do more than four and a half hours. Isabelle's windows weren't tinted, so the sun bounced off the hood and made her eyes throb. Madeline recognized the song Misery hummed in the silence, the childhood song and rhyme about her name. It made her smile. What made her smile more, though, was the ever-present knowledge of Alexandra's cure. "Miracles rarely happen," Louise used to say. "You make the best of what you're given." But Madeline had encountered a near miracle, and merely knowing about it was uplifting. Like seeing a solar eclipse, a meteor shower, the Northern lights—none of which she had seen.

While soaking in her pool that morning, waiting as they all were for Wanda's pills to work, she'd had to close her eyes to imagine herself back on her Bourbon hill, swimming on Highway N. The pink pool had been placed in a small grassy area between the motel's parking lot and a Taco Bell parking lot, in sight of the motel's Dumpster and a gas station across from the Taco Bell. No one honked and waved as he passed. She missed Bourbon. But for the first time in many years, certainly since before the cancer cells began multiplying in Ollie's head, she saw the balance Louise Dames claimed existed. Bad and good together. Things got better as often as they got worse. Surprises were sometimes delights. "You can't control it," Louise said. "But you can control how you think about it. You can remember it's never all one or the other."

"Catalina, Madelina, oopastala, wallabala, hoka, poka, moka was her name." Misery sang just under her breath, her humming having grown words.

Anna sighed loudly in the back seat. "Odd this car," she said. "What kind of woman likes her face so?"

Misery stopped singing.

"Or maybe it's not *like* but *accept*. Maybe it's a good thing. I mean I saw you this morning in your bikini, and well, you know." Anna's laugh was nervous. "I don't mean it that way, not as an insult. But you aren't like a bikini model or anything

Misery snorted.

"My grandmother won't even wear a swimming suit that doesn't have one of those little skirts on it. She even stopped wearing shorts in favor of cropped pants."

"Yet I flaunt it, right?" Madeline broke her silence once more. "Where do I get the nerve, you wonder."

"Not nerve," Anna said, "but how do you learn not to care what you look like?"

"Ha!" Misery said. "Wonderful."

Madeline passed the Douglas exit and knew she'd pass the Casper one, too, at least make it to Buffalo before stopping. Though no one was speaking just then, the inside of Isabelle was noisy. Misery hummed, Wanda snored, Anna whimpered, and something rattled in the dashboard.

"I made a mistake," Anna said, but no one answered her. Five minutes later, coming up on the exit for Ayes Natural Bridge State Park, she wanted to stop. "Come on. We need to stretch. And we're hungry."

"We don't have a picnic with us," Madeline said. "No food at all

"Then let's pick him up," Anna said, pointing to the hitchhiker they passed, a short, chubby man with a red crew cut, a red T-shirt over tattered jeans.

"We could be the last car he sees today," Misery said. "His last chance."

"Poor guy," Madeline said, feeling the familiar guilt hitchhikers created. She'd never stopped for one and usually turned her face away from them to avoid the look of disappointment they'd likely give. Many were the stories of thievery, rape, and murder brought about by giving a stranger a ride. Hitchhikers must know the stories, too, so by not stopping she was saying to the hitcher, I don't trust you. I'm betting you're evil. I not only won't give you a ride, but will also question your character. "Shame our world is so scary."

"What're the odds he's a killer, though?" Misery asked, looking back. "One in a thousand maybe. Not many people are killers. I mean, has anyone ever tired to kill you?"

"Not that I know of, " Madeline said. "Other than Mom."

"And there are four of us," Anna said. "If he's dangerous, it's four against one. Your mother's no help, but the three of us aren't wimps."

"He'll never get a ride," Madeline said. "And it's hot out there."

"Or if he does, it may be with someone who wants to harm him," Anna said, as Madeline took the emergency vehicle turn-off to the eastbound lanes.

"One of the one-tenth of one percent," Misery said.

Madeline headed back toward the hitcher. She was a good and probably a stupid person. As she passed him, she looked carefully at the awkward way he walked, bigger steps than his short legs were meant for. His clothing was excessively baggy, too, looking as if it'd been handed down by a larger man. He looked like a child, a big child, a childish man. When she passed him, she saw he wasn't even close to childhood. The stubble on his chubby face was silver, and silver bristles were mixed in with the red ones sprouting from his head. Two miles later, Madeline found another turn-off and headed west again. He looked even sadder from behind.

"We're going up north for a hundred or so miles," Misery said out her window when Madeline stopped. "A few more hours. If you want to squeeze, we'll take you."

"Thanks," he said. "My name's Gene."

"Get in, Gene," Anna opened her door and scooted next to Wanda.

"I'm Gene," he said and extended his hand.

"Anna," she said, leaning back toward the door to shake his hand.

"Now, get in if you want a ride."

He did.

"We're probably going as far as Buffalo," Madeline said. "But we can stop anywhere along the way to let you out."

"OK," he said.

"Where are you going?"

"Buffalo," he said.

"Really, Buffalo?" Anna asked.

"Yeah, Buffalo." He smelled like cow manure, pungent and sweet and nose tickling, a smell Madeline connected to one old guy she'd once sat beside at B's counter.

"My name's Madeline," she said. "Madeline Dames. This is Misery, my sister. My mother's asleep next to Anna."

"Hello," he said.

They had questions, but it wasn't up to them to interrogate him. He was supposed to offer the information, and most hitchhikers would, Madeline thought, wondering how she knew what any, much less most, hitchhikers would do. This was her first. Still, she knew if there were a hitchhikers guide to behavior, road etiquette, it should say as much. *Tell the driver where you're going and why you're hitching, at the very least, tell the reason for your trip.* To ask seemed nosey.

"Going to see someone?" Misery asked.

"My sister," Gene said.

"And where does she live?" Anna asked.

"She died," Gene said. "I have to be there by tomorrow night."

"Be where?" Anna asked.

"I told you," he said, and reached for his wallet, raising up a bit to do so. He took out a card and handed it to Anna.

"Wallace-Steinlagge Funeral Home, Buffalo, Wyoming." Anna read it out loud.

"You'll be there a day early," Madeline said. "Lucky we passed by."

"Early's good," he said. His voice was soft, younger than his face.

"Who's jabbing me?" Wanda sat up. "Where're you taking me? Why's this girl so close to me?" She pushed an elbow into Anna's side. "I can jab back, see?"

"Relax, Mom," Madeline said, words as useless as any ever uttered.

"I get it. Kidnapped. Torture's next. My people understand that by now."

"You've been asleep," Gene said.

"That squirrel means death."

"Oh, Wanda, there aren't squirrels around here. Look," Anna said, gesturing out the window. "Antelope maybe. Some prairie dogs."

"The red squirrel is right beside you." Wanda leaned down, her head nearly on her lap, and glared across Anna's knees at Gene. "He means death."

"My sister died," he said.

"See? I'm always right," Wanda said. "Though my darling daughters think I'm crazy. We're in that haunted car, aren't we? Don't blame me when we all die."

"She called me a squirrel," Gene said.

"She didn't mean anything by it," Madeline said.

"Ha!" Wanda snorted, then reached across Anna's lap and tapped Gene on the knee. "I mean it."

"My Grandma used to call me squirrel," Gene said.

"See?" Wanda laughed, then said "At least the weather's changed. Won't be so miserable in this running suit."

"It's hot, Mom." Madeline looked into the glare, the cloudless sky. "Still hot."

"My bones know better. It's almost cold now."

Gene opened his window and a blast of cool air filled the back seat.

"Close it," Anna said, and he did. "It's because we're moving so fast, " she said.

"I'm famished," Wanda said. "Can we eat soon?"

"At Buffalo," Madeline said. "Not much more than an hour."

"I'll be in a coma by then," Wanda said.

"We'll have to risk it," Misery said.

"My sister died by falling off a horse."

"Where do you live?" Anna asked, turning toward him so her back was like a shield against Wanda's glares.

"Lost Springs."

"And do you have a last name?"

"Yes," he said. "And a nickname."

"Well, spit it out, squirrel," Wanda said, looking over Anna's shoulder.

He laughed. "Preedy's the last name. My nickname is Tomato."

"I'm Stalking Badger. My maiden white man's name was Preedy.

We're likely related."

"Tomato?" Anna laughed. "I guess it's the red hair."

"Just call me Gene, OK?"

"At least we're out of all that wheat," Wanda said. "Just dirt here. I can't stand wheat. When the wheat went down all the men jumped out of windows and it stopped raining and that meant me and the old squaw had to go hungry."

"The U.S. Supreme Court declared the tomato a vegetable in the eighteen-nineties," Misery said. "Though everyone knows it's a fruit."

"Maybe we're cousins," Wanda said to Gene.

He rested his head on the window, felt the same bump bump bump Anna had earlier. "I hate Tomato. Don't know why I said it. I'm tired. Can I take a nap?"

"Sure," Anna said.

"Feel free," Misery said.

"Preedy's a common name," he said, his eyes already closed. "I know I'm not related to you."

"And just so you know," Wanda said. "If I ever tried to kill any of you, you'd be dead."

THIRTEEN

The visitors' center was closed without explanation, but Randy was content to stand on the side of the road and look down the high arch of the Yellowtail, imagine the gorge without the dam, and the engineers who'd envisioned the concrete joining the boulders far below. Seeing amazing feats made him reevaluate his own place in the world. Funny, but when he was young, his grandparents, neighbors, teachers, other old people, had talked about the downside of age, mainly the way a body grows ugly and gives in to the tug of gravity, that the bones and joints hurt, that such little breath could be held in reserve, that memories tangle together. But not one had told him the real sorrow: the regret for another life, the desire for other paths than the one taken. He'd fallen into writing the way it was possible to back in the early seventies with a degree in liberal arts, and it'd been a useful skill, too, one he'd been paid for in Armstrong and back in the States wherever he ended up. He liked sentences, could spend sleepless nights moving their parts around. But working for the engineers at the University of Missouri had shown him his life could have been more. He wished he'd been a dam builder, a designer. He wished he'd experimented with wind turbines, understood hydrology and meteorology and the way energy was transferred through materials and from object to object. He understood the physical world as an amateur, even after sixty years of living by its rules, testing them at times without being aware of it. The areas of his ignorance were expanding daily, and his curiosity had arrived way too late.

Henry leaned on the guardrail, his eyes closed, his face to the sun, and Randy wished Henry could see the high smooth concrete face of Yellowtail. Even if B complained about it, the dam was an amazing endeavor. The perfect design, the accomplishment, the power. Man and nature combined way out in nowhere, Montana. Randy laughed at himself, getting carried away with words like those that were stuck in his brain from other things he'd written, inane brochures like those gathering dust in the locked visitor's center.

"Water reclamation," B said once they were back in the car, retracing their journey. "Fancy name, but not as nice as it sounds. They stop water meant to flow down to one place or places and direct it to others. They call it irrigation, but it's at the expense of a drought elsewhere, and a flood, of course, at the basin. Redirection maybe, but not reclamation."

"What's wrong with sending water where you need it?" Henry asked it to keep the old guys talking, to fill the void.

"Your needs aren't the river's. Redirection can ruin rivers. And your needs are usually at the expense of the needs of others. All in all it's a dangerous practice."

Randy had heard those arguments before, had taken both sides at times, but he joined in again. He'd been surprised by that side of B, the one who liked a good debate. The two argued the integrity of rivers and the water rights and the value of food production. Not reclaiming the rivers may result in starvation, Randy said. And man's reckless or thoughtless interference could lead to starvation, B said. Soon they were back at Hardin and ready to take Interstate 90 all the way to Butte.

Though it was Henry's question that started the discussion, he'd been quiet for all of it, for Randy's calling B a fundamentalist for not wanting to change the course of the rivers, as if there were a higher power that had set them and not an accident that could be corrected. B called Randy a tool of the capitalists for being willing to consider people and farms over the needs of the creatures living along the riverbanks who had adapted to its size and force. But Henry spoke up from the back seat once they were on 90, heading west.

"I don't think we're in a hurry. I'm not being chased, am I? Those Citizens against me probably have found someone else to be against by now."

"I'll check some sites when we stop for lunch," B said. "It's hard to second-guess these groups."

"But other than that kid I upset in Nebraska City, no one's been following or has seemed out to get me. No MPs, no police."

"Hard to know," Randy said. "Turns out there were a few guys wanted to keep me out of Canada back when. I didn't know it until later when one of them showed up in Armstrong, told me. It'd been a lark sort of—'Let's harass the peacenik' stuff. But I didn't know about it at all. They drank better than they pursued is what saved me. Drank with more seriousness."

"Strange to say this after what I've seen and done," Henry said, "but this leaving seems the worst step. Now that you're close to dropping me off."

"I thought you'd say that," B said. "Others have."

"If you expect to be lonely," Randy said. "That's good. Then it won't be as bad as you imagine. You'll be prepared."

"We can slow down a bit," B said. "If I discover no one's looking. We'll have lunch at Bozeman, and if there's nothing on the websites, we'll take another side trip. Surely the junior engineer here has other dams he wants to see."

"Ha! And why does the junior spy think he'll find out if we're being chased by checking the web as if it's the only source?"

"Not only," B said. "But they don't put this stuff in the newspapers, the bounties and such. There are print versions, and they can be calling each other, sending e-mails, too, but most of that will get posted pretty soon. That is, if they want to get him, want to expand the circle of those looking. Keeping it a secret isn't desirable. So the web's not a sure thing, but a good indication."

"Had an uncle once who went to prison," Randy said. "Talk of slowing down brings him to mind. His name was Bernard, but because he was the baby of his family, the youngest of six boys, and maybe because his mother, my grandma, wanted a girl, they all called him Bunny. A name he gave himself when he started to say his own name. He carried it through school and even as an adult. At least to the family he was Bunny. My sister and I called him Uncle Bunny. Mom hated him, I think, or maybe she was afraid of him. He was convicted of a brutal murder when he wasn't even thirty. Supposedly a robbery gone bad. The woman came home and he had to kill her with the only weapon he could find fast, her steam iron. Had to hit her many times until she died." Randy cleared his throat. "Word in our family, of course, was Uncle Bunny was innocent. He lived in one of the apartments across from the woman's house, and he had borrowed her iron, her vacuum, too, once or twice. That explained his fingerprints on it. He thought they were friends, and he claimed to be devastated by her horrible death. Her sons said he'd accosted her one night as she got our of her car, said he needed money, and she should give him what was in her purse if she knew what was good for her. 'Lurking' was the word they used. Said he was lurking in the shadows."

"A bully," Henry said. "The sons should have put him in his place then and there."

"Maybe. Dad said he was clowning around. 'That Bunny,' he said. 'Too much a clown for his own good.'"

"What's Bunny have to do with going slow?" B asked.

"That's the odd part," Randy said. "When he was sent to prison, we got his stuff. The five older brothers moved his apartment into our basement. The belief was he'd get out on appeal, or maybe get probation early once the court found out what a nice guy he was. And when he did get out, he'd want his stuff. So we had all of it crammed into our basement, and Mom had to dodge his dresser and this old yellow-painted desk just to get to the washer. She didn't take it well. 'Stubbed my toe on that murderer's dresser,' she'd say. 'Damn it. He'll end up killing me, too.' Once she said, 'No wonder he turned out so bad, crap like that around him all the time.' She tried shoving it around, and I helped her with it, but that old desk just wouldn't fit anywhere. She tried chopping it with an ax once, but didn't get very far. That was one of my parents' biggest fights, and it ended with Dad crying, saying she didn't know what it was like. Bunny was his baby brother, always such a cute and lovable kid. And Mom saying there, there, she was sorry.

"But I wanted to know for sure if Uncle Bunny did it. So I started going through the stuff in his desk and dresser, finding odd notes in the drawers. Nothing about stealing or killing, but things to do. He had to-do lists everywhere, even on the inside covers of some detective paperbacks. Grocery lists, too. And they said 1) bread, 2) cigarettes, 3) slow down. Or 1) buy newspaper, 2) call electric company, 3) clean refrigerator, 4) Go slow. Stuff like that. Some said only one thing—slow down. I didn't know what they meant."

"He still in prison?" B asked.

"Died there. Fifteen or so years ago. My sister'd long since given his stuff to Goodwill. I never asked if she saw the notes."

"Like Bunny, I would appreciate slowing down. I'll be a refugee soon." Henry knew the guy named Kenny lived inside the one called Henry, the one he'd turned himself into, the hopeless, lonely, quiet one. He pictured it like that, a man within a man. He'd live inside the Henry façade as long as he had to. At least he was no longer the simpleton who'd written those letters as if one person's understanding could help others, the naïve idiot who'd leaned up against a screen door to persuade a dumb kid. As if any of it would affect the world.

"You'll be a refugee if you're lucky, " Randy said. "It's not a sure thing. You have to apply. The mood of the person in charge of the paperwork that day will make the difference."

"So I'll get to be Kenny again. You guys may as well call me Kenny, now."

"I'd stick with the name on the birth certificate you have," B said.

"Yeah," Randy said, then laughed. "Take it from Adam Blaylock, otherwise known as B, the guy who prefers an initial to his given name."

"Call your lady friend," B said. "Save your wit for her."

******

Gene hadn't minded naming Lost Springs as his hometown, but decided to nap before they asked more. If he'd taken the bus as his brother-in-law expected, he wouldn't have to answer questions, wouldn't have to close his eyes to avoid telling these women he lived in the Village of Hope because if he did they'd think as everyone did that he was an idiot, though he was not. He was not mentally or even emotionally challenged. If anyone in the car decorated with the woman's face was fit for the Village of Hope it was the old one in the blue running suit. There were two like her in the Village with him, and others even worse off than she. He was there because he'd fallen from a horse, been thrown, and his brain had swelled up against his skull. Now that the swelling was gone, he was fine nearly sixty-five percent of the time. That percent had been given by one of his doctors. But the other times, he was confused. He'd lose whole days and weeks, end up in places he'd never even wanted to visit, usually dizzy and nauseated. He'd told the women in the car his sister was thrown by a horse, but that was him. His sister had died a more normal way—stomach cancer. He didn't know why he told them it was a horse that did it, but he thought horses deserved more blame in general than they were given— should be reviled more than they were.

Though pretending at first, he did doze off, his head bouncing on the car window, and woke up in Buffalo. They were stopped in front of the mortuary, and the cute blond one was shaking him. He looked at the mortuary, Wallace-Steinlagge, rubbed his eyes, then looked at himself. "She'll be in there tomorrow. I look like a vagabond. Can't go in there now."

"We're going to the Buffalo Courts we passed on the second street from the interstate," Madeline said. "Guess you could get a room there, too. Or wherever." He was not their responsibility, and when she'd called Randy and said they'd picked up a hitcher, he'd warned her to be careful, but said it clearly was too late for such a warning. He's harmless, she'd said. He smells like manure and looks like a big child. The only assaulting he'll do is on our senses of smell and sight. "Wish I was there with you," Randy said. "In case you're wrong."

"I'm not trying to tag along," Gene said, "but that sounds like a cheap place."

Inexpensive, Madeline heard Louise say, is not the same as cheap. Dameses never seek out cheap.

"You can eat with us, too," Madeline said. "If you want to." She shrugged, not wanting to sound too friendly. "I mean we all have to eat."

When Madeline opened Isabelle's door in front of the Buffalo Courts, the wind went straight through her skin to her bones and she felt the fluids surrounding her joints turn to ice. "Close it, close it," Wanda shouted, and Madeline did, then took a breath and opened the door once more, got out. Wanda'd been right about the change, sudden and drastic. That was likely a way of life in Wyoming. One minute the wind blowing down into the valley was from a furnace, the next from an ice flow.

The desk clerk in the Buffalo Courts, a round ball of a woman with purple spikey hair, pointed with pride to the lobby window. "Those streaks," she said, "are not man made. The wind blows the dirt and rock so hard it etches lines into the glass. Nature's the artist." She nodded her head at their amazement. She owned the motor court, she said, and answered to no one, so once she made sure Madeline's credit card was good, she said they could check in with whatever names they wanted, Stalking Badger as good as any. "Why do I need your identification? I see you standing before me." She chuckled and shook her head as she sorted out the keys.

Gene did join them for dinner at the Stevens Family Restaurant across the street, and when Madeline saw him in the same red T-shirt and tattered jeans, she remembered he hadn't had luggage, not even a plastic bag. She was tempted to offer him the flannel shirt she'd taken from Randy's duffel, the one she now wore over her T-shirt, but she knew she couldn't part with it. Sure she had sweaters to keep her warm, but the shirt smelled like Randy, tasted like Randy, was like being inside his hug.

Gene ordered a ten-ounce strip steak with a potato and green beans, a house salad, and a bowl of clam chowder to start. He decided he'd have a medium-sized dessert later, nothing too outrageous. Since his accident his appetite was voracious enough that soon after he was admitted, the Village administrator restricted his access to the dining room and kitchen areas. He was not allowed in the kitchen ever, and the dining room only the three normal times a day. He had to sneak the basket of dinner rolls, pats of butter, extra cookies, into his room. He'd found an all-night food shop and walked there once or sometimes twice a night for candy and chips, cans of chili and sliced bologna and angel food cakes. None of his old clothes fit, so he wore what he could find rummaging through the bin of donated clothing. Lucky for him, many people who donated were large. He wasn't concerned with his looks or his weight, but the eating itself embarrassed him. He'd been raised to call gluttony a sin, yet even when he overate so much his stomach rumbled for help and his breathing grew shallow, even when he felt his thighs rub together as he walked, even then, he was hungry. He told a few of the many doctors who examined him in the beginning as well as the one he was left with that he ate to fill a hole, the standard line about why people were fat, but in this case, the hole was large, was himself. He'd lost himself and the hole was where he used to be. All had nodded, one had said, "Perhaps," one had laughed and said that was way too easy an explanation. But not one had come up with a better reason. Embarrassed as he was by his eating, he wanted company for dinner and was determined to keep his eating within bounds. His sister, his only family and maybe his last remaining friend, was dead. He could call his brother-in-law who lived somewhere in Buffalo, but he didn't remember if they got along, had a vague idea that the word asshole had been used at their last meeting, for the brother-in-law or for himself wasn't clear. Besides, he couldn't show up at the bereaved household in cast off clothing smelling of cow shit.

Wanda cackled as Gene grabbed the basket of rolls, ate two of them two-handed, then two more before passing the basket on.

"Hitchhiking must make you hungry," Misery said, but she wasn't concerned with the hitcher's appetite or manners or whatever it was her mother laughed at. As she sat at the table, she was counting her breaths, in for a count of six, out for the same. It was an attempt to keep the anger from crawling through her veins, its tiny feet scratching her from the inside out.

"If I'd tried to kill you, you'd be dead," Wanda'd said. When Misery heard that brag, she was no longer riding about Wyoming in a car with a woman's face on the sides, but was back in Florissant, Missouri, twelve years old. She knew her age, for it had been her twelfth birthday, the one Madeline and Trysh were supposed to bring an ice cream cake for, but instead Madeline called an hour before the party saying they couldn't come. No reason, no apology, no lie that they really wanted to be there to celebrate Angie's birthday. So it was the three of them, and her mother was angry at Madeline throughout, but directed the force of it at Misery. Her face had been gray for some time—Misery remembered that. And Misery and her father had been mostly silent, trying not to upset Wanda further. They ate sloppy joes, and almost immediately after, Misery was running down her street while her mother followed in the old blue Studebaker, trying to run her over. More than once, Misery felt the bumper on her butt. "Goddamn you," Wanda shouted from the car window. The memory proved the boast. It was an example of Wanda trying not to kill Misery, trying not to and succeeding in not killing. Misery looked around the table in the Stevens Family Restaurant and kept breathing. When the Chablis came, she polished it off in one large gulp, but when the plate of chicken fried steak and cream gravy was placed before her, her hand shook so she couldn't move her fork. What had her father been doing when Misery was being chased by her mother? What had the neighbors thought? What made her mother stop? Misery remembered the laugh, Wanda's nervous, mirthless laughter rolling down the street behind her, and then Wanda's gum snapping later that night as she sat on the orange-and-green couch.

"Guess I showed you," Wanda said then. Snap snap. "Both of you. I'm the one who matters around here. No one else."

Gene ate two desserts that night at the Stevens Family Restaurant, three counting the chocolate shake, and Wanda cackled. "The red squirrel's going to eat us all up. It's a sign."

******

Tim tried to appear normal, a high school guy eating a burger at Denny's, a guy with enough money to cover the check. He'd left home with his tip money from the three nights before, one hundred and forty-eight dollars in his wallet, but that was two days ago and he'd filled up the truck three times and paid for his room in Billings, his dinner in Sheridan, his lunch in Scottsbluff, and so had eleven dollars and some change left. He'd ordered the triple-decker turkey club with a side of fries and a bowl of chili, a large Coke because this was all he'd had since the night before in Sheridan, and his stomach had been complaining all day. He ordered coffee, too, for the caffeine, and was tempted to go for the apple pie, already much over his eleven-dollar limit so he may as well get as much fuel in his gut as he could. But he didn't want to call attention to himself. At the Cattleman's Reserve, they'd often point out the big eaters, laugh at them. One man was known to them all as WA for wide ass. He routinely ordered two desserts. The cutest waitress, Kim, took diet pills to control what she called a gland problem, and more than once she broke a few up and dissolved them in his coffee she served with the desserts. So in Denny's, Tim passed on the pie, then watched the cashier's desk, trying to time his run.

He was going north on 15 out of Butte. North or northwest had been his choices and he'd made his decision by flipping a coin, knowing he had nothing else to go on. He called the CATs three times, asked if it had members in Montana, but no one had returned his calls. He'd called his home, too, knowing no one was there during the day, and he told his parents he was seeing real mountains. The Rockies made Nebraska look flatter, even counting the western edge of the state with some high plains and cliffs. I'm surrounded by peaks that are tens of thousands of feet up, he told them, and quickly corrected himself. *We* are surrounded. He remembered his story of traveling with buddies.

The quarter'd come up tails. Heads he would have stayed on 90, tails he was going north on 15. He'd been afraid of the result and had wanted to do two out of three, but talked himself out of it. He knew he'd be afraid of any result, each eliminating a good direction and cutting his chances for success in half. Now he had to figure the best way to sneak out. There was no window in the restroom, and he knew he wasn't fast enough to be in his truck with the engine running before anyone could stop him. And then, too, his purple truck was too easy for the Butte police or the Montana state police to spot. He sighed deeply, tried to think.

His waitress, April she'd said when he first sat down, had teeth so bucked out you wanted to hit her mouth hard with your fist, not in a mean way, but to push them back where they belonged. You seldom saw such bad teeth on a girl or on anyone except in old photos. His mother once said the fact of everyone having good teeth showed how far dentistry had come. Maybe so, he joked with himself now, but it hadn't made it as far as Montana. The rest of her was all right, pale skin and reddish-brown hair, lots of blue eye shadow. He winked at her as a last resort. One of the waitresses at Cattleman's Reserve had agreed to let some guy go without paying once, promised not to cry out for at least seven minutes. Of course she had to pay for the food herself, as April would when he bolted, but she'd been left a fifty-dollar gift certificate for winterizing her car. Tim had nothing to offer April, but decided to try to flirt anyway. He had to wink at her three times before she came over with a smile.

"That's some eye you got," she said. "What makes you think I care about your winks? We're all laughing about it."

"Ha!" He could've ordered the pie after all. "Clumsy of me," he said. "Just trying to get you to smile more."

"I do smile. We have to smile. Don't tell me I don't smile." She did not smile.

"I meant just at me. I like you," Tim said. In his own town with girls he'd grown up with, he wasn't smooth, but up here in the mountains, he'd flatter them to death. If that wasn't smooth, he didn't know what was. "You have nice eyes. In fact, you're too hot to be working here."

"I know that." She slid into his booth and faced him. "Once I get my teeth fixed, I'll try modeling. That or marry some rich cowboy. I'm saving up."

"I like your teeth," Tim said, surprised he meant it. "They grow on you."

"Ha. On me they grow." She laughed. "What's up really? You trying to get me to look away while you bolt?"

"No." He tried to look offended.

"Yes. Hell, yes. I've been through this before. But here's my question—what's in it for me?"

"I'll take you with me." He hadn't meant to make that offer, but there it was. He winked again, smiled, touched one of her hands as they lay on a laminated menu she'd forgotten to collect.

"Stupid kid." she moved her hand out from under his. "That's for you. What would I get out of hooking up with a raggedy-ass broke kid? Where're you headed anyway?"

"Canada."

"Oh, running away? Don't blame you. My brother says this place is going to hell faster than Stalin and Nixon put together."

He shrugged. "Not running," he said. "Chasing. I'm a bounty hunter."

"That so?" She stood. "I'll be back with your check. You go anywhere, I'll get the police on you faster than you can sneeze."

He watched her walk away. He'd have to try an escape, no matter what she said. If he ended up in prison, he'd have to flip a coin again. Heads he'd call his parents. Tails he'd tough it out, being careful not to let his being a bounty hunter slip because bounty hunters were likely unpopular in prison. Course, they'd probably take his coins away first thing. He downed the last of his coffee, stood, stretched, looked about as if searching for the restroom. No one was looking at him. He'd be at the door in twenty feet. His jacket was in his truck, left deliberately so he wouldn't have to put it on inside and signal his leaving. He took one step from his booth and stood in the aisle. Still no one looked up. A bald and very wrinkled man slurped a milkshake and read a newspaper in the far corner. His earlobes hung nearly to his collar. A young woman with four children under six or seven were in the booth behind him, all too occupied coloring the placemats and seeing who could whine the loudest to notice him. A young couple sat across the aisle, but stared out the window at the traffic. He took another step, moved closer to the cashier's station and therefore the door. The cashier's station was empty. The sign by the door said *Please Seat Yourself*. His way was clear. He took two more steps, not wanting to seem to be hurrying. If he could cover the last ten feet, sprint to his truck before the door closed behind him, he could disappear in the dark of the mountains. He took his keys from his pocket and faced the door, but felt a tap on his back.

"I have your check," April said, then added much louder, "I'm sorry you left your wallet in your truck, but the management insists I go out with you to get it." The young woman with the children looked at him, her pug face set in a scowl. "It's just our policy," April said, still loud. "Don't take it personally." She laughed. He noticed the cashier, a middle-aged man with a crew cut, was back at his station. "We won't be a minute," April said to the cashier, and pushed Tim out into the cold. "Let's go. We can leave before they catch on."

"You're going with me?" he was running toward the truck as he asked it.

"Slow down. If we're getting your wallet, you've no need to run."

He slowed, shivering as he reached his truck yards before she did. At least she had a jacket on.

"Get in and open the other door, doofus," she said.

He did.

"Yes, I'm going. Now you can rush. Go, go, go. Jesus," she said when he put on his blinker to turn out of the parking lot. "Some bounty hunter. What is it, a video game?"

"It's my first hunt," he said. "Why do you want to come with me?"

She directed him to take a street behind the Denny's and make a right and then a quick left, a shortcut to 90, she said, even though he'd planned to take 15. Once they were on 90 and headed west, she explained. She'd failed a random drug test that morning. She and the guy she lived with enjoyed pot, one of the few ways they were compatible, in fact. The tester Denny's hired took hair samples, not just urine, so she knew there was no hope. Denny's had a no-tolerance policy. Then there was the boyfriend himself, a sleazeball who was sleeping with the woman next door. "My life is all very Jerry

Springer," she said. She'd been in Butte for all of her twenty-six years, and though it was an impulse, now seemed a good time to go. "I would've gone right after the drug test, better than hanging around and being led from the place in humiliation, but I didn't have wheels. I use Roy's car, and today he needed it, so he dropped me off. Then you came along like fate. You may be a psycho, so you should know I have a gun in my purse."

"You're twenty-six?"

"The teeth make me look younger. Take me to Deer Lodge. Then you're on your own."

He nodded. "I wanted 15. I flipped for it."

"You can cut across later." She turned to watch the road behind them. "Not much of a run just up to Deer Creek," she said. "I know that. Imagine, running away a mere forty miles. I should go somewhere like Tahiti, and maybe I will. But for now, I've got a cousin in Deer Lodge. Don't like her, but hey, family's family and all that. She's a nun, so she can't refuse to help."

"Weird," he said. "This is all so weird."

"Who're you tracking for this first hunt of yours anyway? Some poor slob who skipped bail?"

"A deserter from the U.S. Army. Guy left instead of going back to Iraq."

"My God," she said. "You are an idiot."

******

Gene finished the breakfast special called scattered, smothered, and covered—fried potatoes and sausage smothered in scrambled eggs and covered with a thick cheese sauce—as well as the side order of three buttermilk pancakes before Madeline finished her second cup of coffee. They were the only ones in the Breakfast House so far, and he was the only one eating. After close to two weeks of road food, Madeline pictured herself giving birth to a twenty-pound gas bubble. Her clothes were snug, and two mornings ago in the Ogallala parking lot, her bikini was almost uncomfortably tight. So she was sticking with coffee only that morning, watching Gene eat enough for both of them and then some.

When he finished, he looked up. "Sorry," he said and blushed. "Can you buy me a suit?"

"Buy you a suit." She said it back to him slowly as if it would make more sense in her mouth, or he would see he'd said the wrong thing.

"For the funeral," he said. "I have the money, but I need help choosing."

"We're not hanging around here," she said. "We're on the way to Washington State for a family reunion."

"My only family is dead."

She sighed. She'd already done him a large favor.

"I can't go like this, can I? I'd rather not go than look like this."

"We passed something called a department store on the way in yesterday. It should have suits. Tell the salesman to help you. I'll drive you down when the rest are eating breakfast."

He shook his head. "I don't want to see her all pretty in her best dress, and me like a fat clown."

Madeline looked out into the parking lot, her eye assaulted by the sun glinting off a mini-van's front window.

"She'll be laid out on satin. I've got dirt encrusted in my cuffs."

How responsible was she for the hitchhiker anyway? Madeline knew the answer was not at all. The question was a joke in itself. Yet she felt she should help. Nothing about Gene made her want to help, nothing specific, but Louise had turned her into a nice woman, a surface condition, certainly, but Madeline wasn't eager to confront what was beneath the surface. She shrugged, sighed, and then agreed. "Hope we can get something fast." She drove them back to the motor court, roused Anna and Misery, being careful to tiptoe past her mother's room, and the four of them, Misery still wiping sleep from her eyes, went to Turley's department and fine clothing store. Anna said it was exciting, and Misery said she'd been thinking of buying clothes for herself anyway before the reunion. They picked out a dark blue suit for Gene in no time, and made him take two white shirts in case he spilled something on one of them. Anna picked out an electric blue tie and a pair of dark blue socks, and they told the clerk Gene would wear the new ensemble home. Anna said he would carry the extra shirt, but the store could burn the red tee and the jeans. She laughed.

"How dare you." Gene crossed his arms across his chest. "I need my work clothes. What gives you the right to get so involved in my business anyway?"

"Sorry," Anna said.

Madeline stood by the front door, ready to open it and make the bell ring so they'd all go, but Misery moved to the women's section and asked a saleswoman for help. The saleswoman's eyes sparkled behind her cat-eye glasses when Misery said she wanted an entire new wardrobe, a new look. The saleswoman was about Madeline's age, and her platinum blond hair worn in two high-riding pigtails along with her low-cut white angora sweater made her look like an aging starlet, the ingénue from a fifties television drama. And perhaps she believed Misery wanted to put on that look, too, for she brought out a few low-cut blouses and clinging sweaters, some with beading around the necks and cuffs. She paired the sweaters with velvet pants, georgette skirts, and animal print stretch slacks. Misery took the whole lot into the dressing room, and emerged close to tears, the stretch pants topped by a yellow sweater with teardrop pearls around the scoop neckline. "I'm a large decorated butterbean."

The saleswoman was undaunted. "We'll try another look," she said, and gathered khaki skirts and slacks, cotton blouses with tiny flowers on them, corduroy blazers, and Misery took those into the dressing room as the other three, including Gene in his suit, milled about, fingering price tags. The saleswoman added other looks, muumuu-like things, jumpers, crisp white blouses, handed them into the dressing room while the others wandered the store, checked the time. When Misery emerged, she wore her same black skirt and the blue fuzzy sweater she'd come in with. "I'm ready to go," she said. You could fancy up ugly, but you still had ugly. She should've understood that by now, had had fifty years to get used to it.

They returned to the Buffalo Courts to check out and load up at 12:10. Checkout time, the owner told them, was eleven o'clock. She reminded them the time was posted on the doors, as well as on a sign in the lobby. Not to mention she'd told them it was eleven when they checked in the night before. Sure, they could leave now, and it mattered little to her one way or the other, but she would have to charge them for two nights.

Misery wondered why in her dreams, her imagination, she was not as ugly as she was in mirrors, especially mirrors in department stores. In fact, she was continually startled by the monster in the mirror.

Did B care that she was ugly? Would he like her better if she were good looking? No, it wasn't for him, this need, but for herself. As she thought it, the word made her grimace. Need. It was far from a need.

Anna stood at the motel front desk, huddled in her sky blue fleece jacket, remembering the matching one Henry had. They'd bought the jackets together as a joke, some sort of irony and humor found in matching clothes for lovers. She closed her eyes and smiled.

Because the other two were quiet, likely not listening, it was up to Madeline to respond. "Maybe there's something to see or do in Buffalo," Madeline finally said, thinking she should smile as she said it, show the woman behind the desk she hadn't won. Louise would be smiling. "Mean and ugly though it is." They could still get to Ritzville in a day.

The owner of the Buffalo Court barked out a laugh. "Yeah. We're first on no one's list. But look at him." She pointed to Gene who leaned against the rack of tourist brochures. "Nice shoes, handsome."

They'd forgotten to buy him shoes, and Gene wore his brown dusty work boots under the new blue suit. There was nothing for it now but to lie. "Those shoes look fine," Madeline said.

"Hardly noticeable," Anna said. "Or else, I mean, we would have."

"Why couldn't he think of some things himself?" Anna whispered to Madeline. "It's not our place to dress him completely is it?"

The extra $392.00 on Madeline's credit card, four rooms for one more night each, was Gene's fault for asking her help with shopping, Misery's for suddenly wanting a sane look. Though they weren't rushing to Ritzville and the reunion none of them cared about, they could've wasted time in better places.

Gene glared back when they looked at him. "I don't want any of you to go to the mortuary with me. She's my sister and I want to see her by myself."

"Good," Anna said. "I hate wakes."

His face burned redder, and he pointed his finger as he spoke. "You all act like you can climb right in on my own sorrow and pain, act like it's your pain, like you want to get in on my tragedy. Get some of your own. You're too clinging," Gene said. "I can't take it. Get sad about your own lives."

They stood out in the wind in the Buffalo Court parking lot and watched him walk west, his new suit coat pulled up above his neck, his shoulders hunched and stiff for warmth. They looked at one another and shrugged. Another one slightly off center, Madeline thought. Or more than slightly. How well he fit in with the rest of them. Were there normal people in the country anymore, the ones television commercials were made for? Maybe. Probably lots of them, she decided. But not on their way to Canada with a deserter and side-tracked to a reunion of a family none felt part of, not hitchhiking on Highway 25 on the way to a funeral, and not any who considered themselves a direct line to deities. And that direct line should have been up by now, so Madeline walked down three doors and knocked at her mother's room.

Wanda made her knock seven times before answering. "An absurd time to be checking on me. I won't go away, you know, just because you ignore me." She was wrapped in the brown chenille spread with a mustard yellow stain on the edge, just under her cheek.

"We're staying here one more night," Madeline said.

"Good. Now get away. I'm in the middle of my prayers, trying to work another miracle or two before noon." She sighed. "Those of us who can, have to. It's wearing me down to nothing at all."

FOURTEEN

Madeline cried. Madeline was crying. It happened lately at three or so in the morning. Tears gushed from her with enough force she collected them in a bucket until they breached the rim and ran across the floor. It was a dream she wanted to awaken from, so she did, finding her pillow damp each time, her cheeks wet. What was she crying about now? Most sadness was behind her. She'd made sure of it. She remembered Trysh after Martin's funeral, accusing her of not caring. "You didn't save him," she said, and some years later, their last fight before she cut Madeline out of her life forever, she'd had the same complaint with a new refrain. "You didn't even cry. If you cared, you would've cried."

"I did," Madeline said then.

"Liar. Not one tear. I did not see one tear," Trysh shouted, her face a glowing coal of heat.

"You weren't looking at me all the time."

"Oh, I've heard all the rationalizations. Some people don't cry when sad. Some are Dames tough and hold it in. Some sorrow is too profound for tears." Trysh waved her arms, pushed air about and finally pointed one accusing finger at Madeline. "But all that's lies. I know if you were ever sad, you'd cry."

"OK." Madeline gave up then, threw her hands into the air, too, even as they trembled. Martin had been dead for four years. They'd both said it all before. "I guess you're right. I have never been sad. I've lost two husbands. I was born to Wanda and Phil. I have a daughter who persecutes me. But no. You got me. I have never been sad." She wanted Martin to be alive, to live, to have kept living, but Trysh was right. She hadn't cried. "I'm just not a crier."

Now she wept in her sleep, but no one cared. No one sat in judgment or gave her credit for her tears. She hoped it wasn't herself she cried for. Not only herself. Her story was a sob one, true enough, at least the way she told it to herself lately. And it bored even her.

Since the split three days ago, she'd talked to Randy at least a dozen times, calling him to say good morning, to report an antelope sighting, to describe her pink pool. She knew the three of them had stopped at Yellowtail Dam, and she knew Henry was already feeling lonesome. No one had seen the purple truck. She wanted to tell him about her three nights of tears, but did not. He's too new, Louise said. Put yourself in his place. What if he told you he'd been crying buckets full?

For their second evening in Buffalo, Wyoming, Madeline, Misery, and Anna dined at Broken Arrow, a Mexican-Indian restaurant close to the Buffalo Court. They chose the table in front of a window, ate in a silence broken only by rolling thunder, and watched rivulets of water glisten when lit by the occasional headlights. They finished eating by seven-thirty, but sat and watched the storm for lack of anything else to do. Anna said she hoped for something on cable later to help her sleep. Misery hummed a tune Madeline couldn't identify—a commercial for some kind of fast food, she decided—and she tried but failed to hum a different tune inside her head to drown Misery's out. She jumped at each crack of thunder. Survival was not much of a goal. She came close three times to saying that out loud. Suddenly, she saw Gene, his suit coat hanging on his head, the sleeves tied under his chin. He was in the window, illuminated by a passing truck. Then he was inside dripping beside their table, diluting their coffees.

His wet pants squeaked as he slid into the chair next to Madeline. He shook his head, sending puddles across the tabletop. He sneezed. "Glad I saw the car," he said. "I've been walking for hours."

"What happened?" Anna asked.

"Wrong week. Not just the wrong day, but the wrong week. I was off by a week. I lost a week." He frowned at them. "Well, it happens, but where do they go, those lost weeks? That's my biggest problem."

The funeral director, a small man with a smooth skull and skin the color of tar, had been nonplussed. He introduced himself, but Gene hadn't listened to his name. "Your sister was our special guest Wednesday last. She looked peaceful. The turnout was quite respectable."

"I tried to be here," Gene said.

"Things happen," the funeral director said. "Who knows that better than I?" His voice was soft and thick like velvet, pitched just above a whisper. He gave Gene directions to the cemetery, wrote them down and placed the paper in Gene's breast pocket, patted it. His moist eyes held Gene in place. "She's not truly gone, your sister. People never are really gone if they touched us, if we loved them."

"But she's not here," Gene said, tearing his gaze away to look around.

The funeral director rubbed Gene's shoulder, made him turn back to those moist eyes. "She never was here, you know. Even last week, you wouldn't have found her here."

"She was thrown by a horse," Gene said.

"Yes. The horse is some nasty animal."

In Broken Arrow, Madeline reached over and touched his arm. "So you missed your sister's wake? How sad."

"My sister doesn't care," Gene said, then asked for a menu. "What's good here?"

"Beans," Madeline said, feeling tears massing behind her lids. "All of it's just beans and something."

Gene ordered a plate of bean burritos and a side order of pinto cornpone. "I'll go back home after I eat," he said. "Hit the road, get a lift."

Madeline swallowed her tears. How would a man who lost weeks fare hitchhiking on a night like this? "What'd your brother-in-law say?"

"Scram. Beat it. Really," he said to the three who looked at him with open mouths. "That's a direct quote. We never got along. Even before."

"Before your sister died?" Madeline asked.

"None of your business," he said. He had not in fact talked to his brother-in-law, and sometimes he wondered if his sister had been married. He couldn't remember a husband clearly, though a guy with a dark beard loomed in the back of his mind, snarled at him. "I don't mean to be rude," he said because they looked at him harder, frowning in concentration. "I'm grateful for the ride and all, but some things are private."

"You're some kind of idiot, aren't you?" Misery asked. "You escaped from an institution, right?"

He shrugged.

"Likely we all are, some kinds." Madeline said, and while he waited for his food, she called Randy. "Guess who missed his sister's funeral?" she said when he answered. By the time she hung up, Gene's food had arrived, so she called her mother's room, got no answer as she'd expected and hoped. But knowing her mother was listening to the phone, likely staring at it as it rang, made Madeline want to cry more.

Wanda was tempted to answer the phone for no other reason than to find out what name she'd be called. When the ringing stopped, she left the bed carefully and walked into the bathroom to gaze at herself in the mirror above the sink. The face was familiar, and so was the blue running suit she wore, though it was clear she was too old to be running. Who are you? she asked. She walked back into the bedroom, her feet a bit numb, sounder asleep than her mind, and saw the purse on the bedside table. In it she found her name and address on a bill for electricity dated September 5. She wondered if she were the kind of woman to let bills get overdue or if it was still before September 5. Well, a newspaper or even the television would clear that up, but she wasn't ready to know yet. The bill told her she was Wanda Kneedelseeder and she lived in Florissant, Missouri. The phone book in the dresser drawer, underneath a fuzzy blue sweater, said Johnson County, Wyoming. The bed sagged. The mirror above the sink was cracked, the pressed board dresser had only one drawer as the narrow top one was fake. In short, the motel she was in was a dump. Whoever Wanda was, she wasn't rich. Damn. Old and poor.

Maybe she just had bad taste, as the fuzzy sweater would attest to. Perhaps she was eccentric. She looked into the parking lot, but none of the cars or trucks seemed familiar. Then again, she probably didn't drive, old as she looked. There hadn't been a license in her wallet. She sat in the only chair in the room, a brown upholstered wing chair that smelled of cumin and rubbing alcohol and faced the door. She wasn't afraid, so she guessed that meant she'd been confused before and was used to it. When she checked, her skeleton had been visible under the sagging crepe paper skin on her face, and her hands were mottled and veiny. She could be a hundred or more. Her lack of fear told her she'd probably snap out of it. The last thing she remembered was a dream of a woman who claimed to be her mother, a woman who smiled but in a mean way and not from happiness. The good news was that dream was finished. "And look at me," she said out loud to prove she was awake. "Any mother I had would be dust by now."

******

Attila was the ugliest woman Tim had ever seen, and when he said as much to April, forgetting they were cousins and may have some sort of blood loyalty, she told him he was young yet and would surely run across uglier. Attila was tall and boney, her hands and wrists chapped and raw. Her nose was bumpy as if it'd been broken in at least two places, and her eyes were small dark specks that seemed to stare at the bumpy nose. Her large and flat ears lay against her head like a pair of yellow earmuffs, made more pronounced by her pewter-colored crewcut. April said her cousin's name was Deborah, but she introduced herself as Attila and snickered. "Attila the nun. Get it?" Tim did, managed not to groan. "My peeps named me. I accept the comparison. I can be ruthless." Her peeps were the teenagers she worked with, mostly Blackfeet, many raised on the reservation just north. She operated a teen center for the Catholic Church, though she didn't ask the teens their religion and had no religious decorations about. The teen center was where they came for video games, craft projects, movie nights, poetry writing classes taught by Attila herself, and story night. It was a pre-fab metal building just north of the Deer Lodge city limits. Inside was one large room with a concrete floor covered by orange indoor/outdoor carpet, a few tattered couches and recliners, five long cafeteria tables with folding chairs, a kitchen and bathroom at one end, and next to the bathroom, a maroon curtain that separated Attila's cot and bureau from the rest of the room.

She'd been in the kitchen spraying for silverfish when he and April arrived, walked right in. The door was locked only after midnight, and it was just past ten when Tim pulled up. Five boys, maybe a year or two younger than Tim, sat at a cafeteria table sharing a laptop.

"What brand are you?" Tim asked after she said she was Attila.

"Catholic, you jerk," April said.

"I mean the different costumes and all. I know something about that from history class and the settlements in California. There are kinds who used to wear big starched hats, all pointy, and some wore only white. Most wore black."

"Ha! A scholar of ancient history," Attila said. "I'm a Franciscan. "That tell you anything?"

Tim shrugged.

"Exactly how I feel about it." She clapped her hands and the boys sauntered over, looking annoyed, sneering at Tim and April. "These're my peeps," she said. "They don't want to meet you, but they should. I want them to learn the social skills, which means when jerkwads come to your door, you have to be polite, at least at first. Smile and introduce yourself until you know for sure they're trouble."

"I'm not trouble," April held out her hand to whichever boy would take it. "My name is April. How can I be trouble? I'm family."

"Har de har har," Attila said. "Get it boys? Laugh at the lady's joke."

"I'm Tim." He held out his hand, too, but they looked away.

"They're Harvey, Maurice, Lincoln, Biggie, and Hedge." Attila pointed to each as she named them. "Now, what's your story? Listen up boys."

"I'm runnin' away," April said. "And Tim's chasing some guy. We met a few hours ago when he tried to skip out on the check. I failed a drug test."

"I'm a bounty hunter." Tim had never walked out on a check before.

"A lawman!" Attila snickered again, and turned to the boys. "He's probably after one of you."

"I'm after a deserter from the U.S. Army. An enemy of the state."

"He's like a narc," April said. "But he's leaving soon. He only dropped me off."

But Attila and her peeps were looking at him now with respect. He saw it in their eyes. Biggie dragged a chair over for him.

"I hate deserters," Attila said. "My father was a war hero. Purple Heart."

"My father died in Afghanistan," Hedge said. "His last words were 'Avenge me.'" Hedge was larger than the rest with coarser features, a protruding lower lip, thick and dark hair on his arms and hands.

The other four were olive toned and skinny, and one of them, Harvey, punched Hedge in the arm. "No," he said. "Your dad's last words were 'Aaaaaaww!'" He clutched at his heart and fell to the floor.

Hedge laughed. "When I'm old enough, I'll go kill some Afghanis."

"This guy I'm after," Tim said. "Refused to fight. Because of him, others are getting killed."

The boys all nodded.

"Blackfeet," Hedge said. "Probably some of those dying are ours."

******

"Henry named his new dog Kenny after himself," Randy said. He told Madeline they'd found the beagle at Canyon Ferry Lake where they'd stopped after B figured out no one was hot on their trail. Maybe no one was chasing them at all. They'd decided to slow down just a bit, add a day to the trip, ease Henry's impending loneliness. Randy said the dog'd jumped at them out of a stand of scrub trees beside the lake, nearly jumped right into Henry's arms. No collar. And though they made a halfhearted attempt at finding the owners, walking around the parking lot and part of the lake, calling out, they'd known immediately the dog was what Henry needed. No other cars were there anyway. It was nine o'clock and below freezing, what with the wind being driven down from Canada between the Rockies and the Big Belt Mountains. The moonlight let them see whitecaps on the lake, the wind was so strong. And the beagle was skinny enough to have been out for a while on its own. "Course it gets car sick," Randy said. "Puking in B's back seat just now."

Madeline cried a bit, thinking of the dog being lost and frightened.

Randy said they'd go to Helena for the night, then on to Cut Bank by the following night, drop Henry off finally, continue to Ritzville. They knew they'd meet up again in three days. "Looking forward to that Kneedelseeder reunion," he said. "Though I imagine I already know the best Kneedelseeder."

"I'm Dames," she said. "I don't claim Kneedelseeder, won't even for the reunion."

"They're still in Buffalo," Randy said when he hung up.

"Damn dog," B said. "This isn't an expensive luxury car, but what the hell. Dog vomit all over it."

"I'll clean it up when we get somewhere," Henry said. "He's just nervous."

"This way, you'll take a pal into Canada with you, to stay that is," Randy said. "We'll go in with you, but then come back."

"Did you ever try to come back after you got up there?" Henry asked. "I mean, if no one's looking for me anyway, why can't I go back and forth?"

"You can. It's not much of a risk once you're in. If the passport works once, it'll work every time. In theory at least. As long as no one's trying to get you. I didn't because I knew someone who knew someone who tried it and was arrested, got fifteen years in a military prison. I didn't have documents. Most of us didn't have false documents. And then I heard of another one who was shot trying to sneak back in. Don't know if any of those were true stories, but they were enough to keep me in my place, and pretty soon it really was my place." Randy turned around and petted Kenny, rubbed its head as it vomited once again on B's floorboards. "In your case, even being a deserter, you could get amnesty. People're fed up with this administration and this stupid war, and some people already think you're right to escape. You could even become a hero in some minds."

"That's Randy's take," B said. "Pie in the sky. Not something to count on."

"Are you guys pacifists?"

B shook his head. "Never knew fighting to help much, but no, I'm not against it. Just this war, and the ones like it."

"I decided very early," Randy said, "as a child really, that fighting was OK if personal, but not just because someone else wanted you to. I used to watch *Gunsmoke* and *Wild Bill Hickok* and those other shows where the sheriffs were always getting up posses to go catch the bad guy, and the bad guy had his flunkies, too, his own group. Well, the unnamed posse members who seldom knew why they were going after Bart got killed. One or two had their horses shot out from under them; others were just gunned down. Bart's guys got shot, too, from their perches on top of boulders or on the livery stable roof, and the main guys, ones with the actual grudge, they survived until nearly the end. Well, Bart eventually got it, the sheriff killing him or taking him in, but if it had started like that, all those other posse members and flunkies wouldn't have died. I may have been the only kid who noticed the nameless dead. I even remember them from the comic book version of the Trojan war. All those dying Greeks. So like B, I'm not a pacifist, and if there's reason for me to fight, I will."

"I've made a decision," Henry said. "I need to talk to Anna."

"Gag," B said.

"Sorry I'm a bother, " Henry said.

"Yes, you are, but I meant gag," B said. The stench rose from the back all at once. "That dog's a great addition to our trip."

"The kid can't see," Randy said. "He needs a dog."

"That still the situation?" B asked. "Still blurry?"

"Blurry's putting a positive spin on it," Henry said. "I'm losing hope."

"Be a blessing if you couldn't smell."

******

Randy called Madeline at eleven and told her they'd changed their plans a bit, just off by a day. They'd checked into a Quality Court in east Helena and would be waiting for the women, would stay there two nights because Henry wanted to see Anna. Randy pictured Madeline's shoulder bones, fragile and defined, as he talked, remembered her real and true smile—not the fake one she used often—delicate and fleeting and crooked. He said Henry wanted to talk to Anna, so Madeline took the phone to Anna's room.

"I miss you," Henry said to her. "And I have a surprise for you. They're changing their plans, letting me see you again."

"Do you expect something from me, some promise?" Say yes, she thought. Expect. Ask me.

"I can't expect anything. I just miss you."

"Me, too," she said. "This is all so silly." She meant the trip, the running, the plotting and fake names, missing him.

******

"When we don't show up in Cut Bank tomorrow, they'll worry, but won't do anything. They'll hope for the best. I can get one of those pre-paid phones and a card with minutes and call someone who will call someone else. I'll say sorry I'll miss the party. I'll ask see if we can stop by later when we're in the neighborhood. It'll work. We'll still get Henry taken care of."

"Cloak and dagger. Spy stuff. You enjoy it, don't you? Admit it." Randy was stretched out across one of the double beds in the room all three of them decided to share, saving money when they could.

"So what?" B asked.

"So nothing. That dog'll cry all night," Randy said.

******

Attila came up with the plan in minutes, making Tim understand how wasted his day and a half with Gerald and Chuck had been. Attila hated deserters, and so did the five boys. "We don't want any of your bounty," Hedge said. "We're patriots."

The boys would get paid, though. Attila'd won four thousand in the dollar slots at the casino the week before, and the government grant the church got from the bureau of Indian Affairs took care of all her needs, so the money was sitting around, waiting, as she said, for a cause. This was it. She offered half of it to whoever helped Tim catch the deserter, and if all five helped, she'd split the half five ways, four hundred per. "What about me?" April asked. "I'll help, too."

"How can you expect money?" Attila asked. "You're family."

Attila decided that they didn't know if the deserter was already in Canada or not, but if he wasn't there yet, they'd catch him, simple as that. If he was, of course they wouldn't. But why worry about the *ifs*. Point was, they may as well try. When Tim said he'd decided the deserter was taking Highway 15, and the reason he gave was a flip of a coin, Attila snorted, said the quality of bounty hunters seemed to have gone down, and suggested a more scientific method. They would station themselves at either end of Route 12, at Garrison on Interstate 90 and at Helena where 12 ran into 15. No one going either direction could get by if they watched both places. There were eight of them, so two at each place in the daytime and two at each place at night. They were looking for a Cavalier, white, Missouri tags, three men in it. Tim said they could also look for an older Mercedes sedan with a woman's face smiling out on each side, temporary tags. No telling where that car was or where it was headed, but if it came by here, it could mean something. And an orange VW bus, too, Missouri tags, still the likely escape vehicle. They all had cell phones, and were instructed to keep in touch constantly, if for nothing else but to keep one another alert and awake. It was ten miles to Route 12 from Deer Lodge, and then another forty-five miles east to Helena. As they drove to their posts, they should be on the lookout for the cars mentioned, especially the Cavalier, in restaurant parking lots. Attila was calm and decisive, very much in control. "No slacking off. No stupidity. No taking unauthorized breaks," she said. If the deserter or any of his group were spotted, they would all be told, and Attila would devise the capture. No one should be a hero. No weapons were allowed. That last order made Hedge wink at Harvey.

By midnight, Harvey and Maurice had set off to Helena, and Attila and April took first shift at Garrison. Tim was told to get some sleep, and though Biggie's mother pulled up outside the teen center and honked for him, he told her he was staying all night for an early class in Blackfeet lore and culture.

"She believes that?" Tim asked.

"She's coming home from the casino. She deals blackjack," Biggie said. "She's used to big lies so much she don't notice small ones."

"He's got no car," Hedge said to explain Biggie's mother coming by. "You do?"

"Yeah. One I found in a ditch and put wheels on. Runs fine, just needed wheels."

"Are you old enough to drive?"

"Old enough to do anything," Hedge said. "But not legally."

Lincoln nodded. "Me, too. I drive my brother's Cadillac whenever I want to. It's a convertible. He won it in a raffle."

"Why do you guys hang around this nun?" Tim asked.

"She's powerful," Lincoln said. "She got my pop on the list for a new liver, high up on it, too."

"She eats jalapeños like apples," Biggie said. "Big bites. No flinching."

******

Madeline lay on her side and kicked her legs out in front of her, first one then the other, sliding them back across the cool sheets. It didn't help; they ached. She'd had lots of exercise in Bourbon from hill climbing, the walk to her mailbox from her house itself a steep climb. Now her legs missed that. As she moved her legs, she thought about Bourbon as her destiny, a place she was born to be in, a space she was meant for. Not a nice space especially, surrounded by poverty and metal buildings as it was, but one she fit in somehow. When her phone rang, she welcomed the chance to sit up, knew it would be Randy, another part of her destiny. He already understood her so well, knew she'd be tossing, running nearly, in her sleepless state.

But it was Alexandra. "I remember you never could sleep until early morning," she said instead of hello.

"We're still driving around the West," Madeline said. "We're in Buffalo, Wyoming, now."

"Tell me about it some other time. Want to know why I'm awake so late or early?"

"What's up? Still healthy?" Madeline tasted the tears behind her nose.

"Perfectly. I've been given a rebirth, another chance. I do believe now, you know. God and all that."

"Yes. You said so. I have some hope it may not all be bull, too."

"No. I believe. Not just hope. I'm going to be baptized."

"But if my old mother's prayers worked, then help didn't come from any religion, but from some great spirits and spells and whatever—badgers and such."

"It doesn't matter. Lots of people were praying for me, and I think they all worked. All requests end up on the same desk, as they say in my new church. It's Methodist. That's what I'm becoming because there are so many different kinds of Methodist I can be. And they don't want much, not like Catholics. I don't have to study lore or rules. I'm born again, have been, but I don't want that sort of thing either, all that proclaiming and believing only one thing. I think it's all things together."

"Swell." Madeline laughed. "Did you call to give me your mush-brained theology?"

"I want your mother to come to my baptism, want all those who prayed for me to come. Is she still with you? When will you be back from the frontier?"

"Hard to say. A week I think, maybe longer if things keep screwing up. But you're insane, too. That old mother of mine is not one to invite anywhere."

"Can you just ask her? I think I have to include all the gods who cured me."

Was stupidity an after-effect of a miracle? A decade ago, Alexandra nixed the bachelorette party her bridesmaids had planned for her, and instead of traipsing through Chicago's dark and smelly dives, drinking and telling unfunny jokes about men and marriage, they all, including Madeline and the groom's mother, piled in rented johnboats and trolled the Chicago River, picked up Styrofoam and tires. She'd gotten each of them to swear it was better than annoying the habitués of those dark and smelly bars. Yet now she wanted to appease the gods.

"Ask her to come," Alexandra said. "I will if you won't."

"We're checking out of here as soon as we can get moving tomorrow, so call at seven our time and I'll give her the phone. It'll be an excuse to get her up. She hides out in her room all the time now, pretending to be sick."

"You've turned heartless," Alexandra said. "The West isn't good for you."

"I've always been heartless, just hid it well."

In the room next to Madeline, Anna couldn't sleep, either. Henry had said he wanted to see her, and her need for him was as large as the distances they traveled through. She believed now she could take enforced confinement in Canada without sorrow or anger. His near blindness made him pathetic, yes, but he could still be lovable. She hoped she could cope with it as well as he did. She yearned to be a strong woman who could endure all, be the pillar others leaned on. That kid with the baby hairstyle who'd sprayed the spider killer deserved as much pain as Henry, though, and she pictured spraying his face until his own eyes were wet clouds. His screams would delight her.

In the room across the hall from Anna, Misery was awake as well. How could anyone be tired when the days were so full of nothing? Walking about, watching the rain, hearing not one interesting thing. The brain grew as more information was given it, as more nerve endings connected to form pathways, and it was not information alone, but the purpose of the information, what could be made of it as it related to knowledge already stored in a few folds that swelled the brain in a good way. But it was the opposite, too. The longer one lived in boredom and ignorance, the smoother the brain became. By the time this trip ended, she'd be a few IQ points lower than when she started. Not that she credited IQ as anything, but this ennui was like a death. Oh, the mountains are pretty, Oh it's raining, Oh, Randy and the others are in nowheresville in godforsaken Montana. What's out there? Mountains, sky, wheat, antelope. Big deal. Wanda was mean and crazy and thought she was holy; Madeline wept easily now and had it bad for Randy; Anna mourned Henry and felt sorry for herself; the hitchhiker was as touched as the rest of them.

Wanda slept fitfully, waking once to find it was only midnight, not morning, then again at 2:22, at 3:30, and finally at 5:03, all according to the digital clock beside the bed she slept in in Johnson County, Wyoming. Each time she awoke, she expected to remember who this Wanda Kneedelseeder was, why she was in Wyoming if she lived in Missouri. At five-thirty, she turned on the television, hoping to discover the date at least, but no one said. Shows that were all new versions of themselves were coming back in two weeks, on next Thursday or Sunday, but never was an exact date mentioned. She knew it was no longer summer, for one news person said it had been the driest summer in Wyoming in years. She wondered if she were in hell already. If this hole in the wall had cable, she could check the Weather Channel and read the bottom banner for the date and time, but that thought was a clue: She was an old woman named Wanda who'd once watched the Weather Channel. Eventually television put her to sleep, and she didn't awaken until Madeline knocked at seven o'clock. She opened the door with anticipation, even hope, knowing she would soon know more.

"It's Alexandra for you." Madeline didn't enter the room, just reached the cell phone in to Wanda. "Since you cured her, or maybe had a part in it."

Wanda took the phone, but pushed Madeline back out of the doorway and into the hall, slammed the door hard and locked the deadbolt. One look at Madeline and she remembered all. She was herself and her life came flooding back. She could almost hear her heart break, like a twig snapping under a boot.

"We're leaving in an hour, Mom" Madeline called through the door. "Get ready."

FIFTEEN

Isabelle's windows rattled, and a cold stream whistled in, hitting Misery just above her right ear. She tucked her head down, and told herself that B was not a boyfriend, but rather a human being she liked to talk to, that in itself as rare as unsmiling newscasters. He was a friend.

Wanda was hunched down into her running suit. A towel she'd taken from the Buffalo Court was under the suit and wrapped around her middle for insulation. The haunted car was cold. She pretended to sleep, for awake she'd have to say things to annoy the rest, and though they were easy to get, she'd grown tired of that, her energy at an all-time low. It took effort to force air from her mouth.

As soon as she'd seen Madeline earlier that morning, she remembered her two hateful daughters, this haunted car, a mystery ride to nowhere, the long and tedious marriage to Phil, her connection to the gods, her sorrow and anger and an entire life of persecution. Never had a woman been so misunderstood by mortals, had so hard a life. At least the red squirrel was gone. The fake blond sitting next to her in the backseat was staring, trying to see if she was really sleeping, perhaps trying to determine if she'd passed on. Not such a frightening idea that, passing on, especially if she could come back with more power, maybe as a demi-god herself. She didn't know the fake blond's name because she didn't want to know it. Besides, it'd been changed during the journey, making it two names Wanda didn't care to know.

"Are you cold?" the blond asked.

"Where are we?" Wanda pretended to wake up. She stretched and asked it again. "Where are we?" She kicked the seat back, causing Madeline to jump.

"Almost in Oklahoma," Madeline said.

"Good. Wake me when we get to my homeland." The lie and pretenses were wearing thin, the joke of it boring. And Madeline's "almost in Oklahoma" was the same as none of your business or shut up and leave me alone. Of course they weren't going to Oklahoma, never had been. Wanda knew it, and that she merely pretended to want to go to Oklahoma was clear to all in the car, yet they continued the game. "Too bad this haunted car doesn't have a heater."

"It has one," Madeline said. "Just takes time to work."

"I'm not even cold," the blond said.

"Goody for you," Wanda said. "Thanks for the update."

Wanda vowed to say no more, to save her strength for the flight home she'd been promised that would spare her the reunion. She'd not known the Kneedelseeders except Phil's immediate family, his parents likely too embarrassed by her to have told any auntie or cousins about the beauty Phil had snagged. They wouldn't have said *beauty*, but if they'd been the kind to speak what they considered the truth would've said *tramp* or *trash* or *Okie*. Instead they told others Wanda was from a "farming community," and "of limited means." The Kneedelseeders were a family of snobs for and to whom boredom and conventionality were a way of life. She knew the whole lot of them, though they'd not met. That they were all Indian haters went without saying.

"Joe Pye weed was once used to treat typhus," Misery said. "I mention that because it's cold in here and the shivering made me think of fevers that come with chills. Don't ask how I know that."

"I won't," Anna said. "I don't want to know. Not about Joe Pye weed. I have other things on my mind. He said he had a surprise for me."

"Could be the dog," Madeline said.

"Dog? He has a dog? That's it. What a sweet thing he is. He remembers I used to be a dog groomer. It was one summer before we met. I once cut a terrier's toe nails so short it got an infection, but other than that I was good."

"Joe Pye weed's all around. Could even be in Montana. It needs moisture but not too much. Those large weeds with domed flower heads, the ones pinkish white. That's it."

"The dog's name is Kenny. It's a beagle."

"That probably comes from early French," Misery said. "From *beeguele*, meaning noisy person."

"It pukes in the car," Madeline said. "What's early French for puke?"

"It's not bad to know things," Misery said. "Don't be so proud of your ignorance. How can you get through life knowing nothing?"

No one answered, and the four of them rode in silence far into Montana, past the sign for Yellowtail Dam where Randy and the guys had stopped. Madeline understood the plan to meet up in Helena so the kids could reunite, but she didn't know why they were still aiming for the Kneedelseeder reunion. No one wanted to attend it, no one in Isabelle, at least. And surely no one in B's car. Maybe once they all got to Helena, they'd realize that and finally go to by-god Canada, where they'd meant to go from the beginning.

"I hope he doesn't get lost," Anna said, breaking the silence as they passed the Miles City exit. No one answered. They knew she meant Gene, and they all pictured his departure, the way he hurried out of the Buffalo Court with a backward wave that said go away, leave me. "See you never," he'd said.

"Or lose another week," Madeline said, adding only to herself that some weeks were worth misplacing, endurance being less than a virtue.

"Poor thing," Anna said, and for a moment, Madeline thought the pity was meant for her.

But two hours later, there he was, Gene, wearing his suit coat over his red shirt, carrying a paper bag, and thumbing a ride. "It's him, it's him, it's him," Anna cried, but Madeline and Misery'd already seen him.

"He did get lost," Misery said as they slowed beside him. "Why aren't we surprised?"

He shook his head at them at first, trying not to look inside the familiar car. He didn't want a ride with them. All rides weren't equal, and he'd hoped to be finished with these strange women who watched him like substitute mothers. In fact, he'd seen them as they came down and around the bend where the oil tanker had dropped him, knowing there weren't two cars with a smiling woman on their sides in the entire state. He'd seen them, but had no place to hide. That morning, he'd considered himself blessed to get a fast ride with the driver of the tanker. He knew they were going north, too, but thought he'd had enough of a head start. He waved them off when they stopped beside him, but they wouldn't leave, and because his suit coat was no match for the Montana wind being driven through the mountain peaks and already smelling of snow, he gave in.

"We thought you were going home," Anna said. "Or else you could've come with us. Where are you going?"

"That's the question," he said. "The big one. For all of us."

"Geez," Misery sneered. "Give me a break."

"North," he said. "I'm going north."

"How perverse," Misery said. "I mean you're clearly going nowhere, and nowhere south makes more sense then nowhere north."

"Sense," he said, "has nothing to do with it."

"Clearly," Madeline and Misery said together.

He knew it was perverse to go north, but south was the direction of his so-called home, the village where he was tired of being the idiot. Maybe his brain never would heal completely and he'd spend his days confused, but at least people wouldn't be smiling at him kindly, watching how much he ate, closing the kitchen to him after hours. He needed money, sure, but he knew he had a bank account, proof of that was two checks in his wallet, and they could be enough for now. When he got wherever he'd end up, he'd call the bank and find out what exactly he had. He'd probably have to get a job, but another advantage of heading north and west was the competition thinned out, and he'd surely be able to find farm work in Big Sky Country.

He sighed as Anna pulled on him, nearly dragged him into the car. "Leave me alone," he whispered as he was enveloped by the warmth. What fun, trapped in a car with four crazy female people. He missed his sister. That'd been one of her jokes. She called herself a female person when the word female became interchangeable with woman. "It's so male people or other female people don't think I'm a sheep or a cat." Four female people, he repeated to himself, nearly crying at his loss. At least he hadn't gone to her grave, a visitation she would've been embarrassed by. And if he'd talked to her, said "Dear Sis, I know you're not there, but ...," she would've been angry enough not to haunt him, and he yearned for that haunting. He wanted her spirit about, playing tricks or even trying to frighten him. He didn't care what she did, as long as she showed up.

******

"I'm Anna again," she said before she told Henry the three days of separation seemed like years, but after she kissed and hugged him, breathed in his sour smell. "Don't guys bathe when they travel by themselves?" she asked later, still unable to talk without touching.

He said, "Please, please come with me; join me and the dog in Canada. Please."

She nodded, wanted to say yes, but he kept begging.

"Please," he said. "Maybe you'll be able to return at will. The borders cannot be that solid. All you could ever be accused of is aiding a fugitive, anyway, and that's not likely. Once I become a refugee, I won't be a fugitive anyway."

"I will," she said. "I—"

But he interrupted her. "I need you. There's no doubt. But I also want you. I missed you more than I expected, more than when I was over there. Pay-as-you-go phones are nearly untraceable, so you can call home anytime. Your parents can come visit us. Mine, too."

He was nearly breathless when she placed her fingers on his lips to make him stop. "We may as well love the now. Love now. For now. Don't say how long we'll be there. Don't even guess."

"But we do have hope. That's all I mean."

"Hope's a trap.

He tried to swallow it, but his laugh burst out. "So melodramatic. And cynical. It's a new side of you. Not right, either."

She laughed, too, loving his, like a drumbeat, not quite rhythmical but deep. They tumbled to the bed in the Best Western motel, and the dog barked and wagged its tail. "Cute dog," she said, making them laugh harder. "Come here, Kenny." She patted the bed and the dog jumped up beside her, rolled on its back. "I'm letting my blond grow out," she said. "I hate looking so sweet."

He removed her shirt, pushed her bra up, and bent over her. He sucked on her left nipple, bit it, sucked again. "You are sweet," he said. "Vanilla-y."

"You should sue that doctor in Nebraska City. Your eyes should be lots better by now."

"And you should pay attention."

The bedspread in Wanda's room of the Quality Court in Helena,

Montana, was a satiny acetate, bronze and gold. It smelled like wildflowers in a can. Wanda wrapped it around her not for prayer this time, but for warmth. Her running suit was in a washing machine downstairs, Madeline having taken it because she was doing dark clothes so she could show up at the reunion in clean jeans. The group would be in Ritzville tomorrow, but at least Wanda wasn't going to that festival of ennui. She heard them laughing next door, Madeline and Randy, acting like teenagers. She hoped she'd not have to hear their passion. At their ages, they should've learned to be quiet. Misery was no better than her sister, smiling like a government worker at closing time, bobbing her ugly head, giggling, even blushing when B said it was good to see her and that he wanted her to ride with him again because he was tired of arguing with Randy.

Why had she yearned for her daughters' attentions and time? Not because she liked them, though in their long absence she'd nearly convinced herself she did or could. Well, she'd not fool herself again. When she returned to Florissant, Missouri, she'd appreciate the way they ignored her, enjoy their neglect. Now with recently cured Whosit coming, she'd be back in a night and a day. And she'd sooner pass over to the happy hunting grounds rather than go to any baptism, no matter what she promised.

"Whom do you pray to?" the woman had asked her early that morning on Madeline's phone.

"Who are you? What business is it of yours?"

"It's Alexandra. I had cancer."

"Is this a trick? Why are you asking me?" Wanda shouted as she spoke to the woman on the phone whose words echoed as if shouted back and down a metal pipe. It was a hard landing, remembering who she was and who she was attached to all at once. Now this hard-to-understand voice filled her ear.

"I'm a believer. In you. You cured me."

"Oh. One of my miracles?"

"Yes. That's what I am."

The woman could grant wishes and give favors. She could pay twice the going rate for the prayers, more than that, if Wanda wanted. In fact, Wanda could name her price. Who was the god that helped? Was it one of the regular ones—Jesus, Mohammed, the Holy Spirit, Yahweh,

Baal, Demeter, Persephone? She reeled off gods Wanda hadn't heard of. How'd Wanda make contact? How'd she get listened to?

Those were Wanda's questions, too, but this connection of Madeline's wouldn't know it. "It has no name. This god is a powerful one. I've always been special. I was born into a line of great spirits. It's in my blood. I am a sacred vessel."

"Thank you," Alexandra said. "My main reason for calling is to say thank you. But I also want to do something for you.

"I specialize in illness," Wanda said. "My ancestors were healers. I've prayed for other things, a connection to my daughters, for example, but those requests backfire. Because I am Stalking Badger, the healer. I am doomed to loneliness. No one can love me."

"I want you at my baptism. What do you want more than anything?"

"I want to go home. I'm on some sort of stupid trip, a tour of broken-down and worthless and ugly towns in the Western states nobody wants to visit. We're in a haunted car with a face on it, and no one wants me along. Come and get me."

Alexandra said she would. "Where will you be tomorrow evening or afternoon? I'll fly out, fly back with you."

"Call the number in my room in a hour and I'll tell you. Madeline will know."

But when Wanda hung up, and then knocked on Madeline's door, stretching the phone across the threshold as Madeline had done, and asked where they were going, Madeline said, "Oklahoma, Mom. Remember?"

Wanda almost slapped her, would have if it wouldn't have been the same as blinking first, ending the game. "Good. That woman I prayed for wants to know. Your friend. Give her a call."

So Madeline was on the phone to Alexandra as soon as Wanda went back to her room, and as the two, Madeline and Alexandra, made plans for the disposal and transport of Wanda, Wanda wrote in deep red lipstick on her bathroom mirror in the Buffalo Court, "I whelped two liars."

The plan Alexandra and Madeline made was that Wanda would stay with the group through Helena, but the next day, Alexandra would fly into the Spokane airport, and Madeline would meet her flight, hand her mother over, and Alexandra would then take the next flight back to

St. Louis, rent a car and drive Wanda to her Florissant home. Madeline liked the plan so much she crossed the hall to Misery's room and told her. "One more night of Mom," she said.

"So Mom'll miss the reunion," Misery said. "Those Kneedelseeders don't know the disaster that almost hit."

Madeline nodded, leaning in the doorway while Misery gathered her black plastic bags together for checkout. "Why will any of us go to the reunion anyway?"

"B's one of Dad's fans," Misery said. The sisters looked at each other for a moment, then laughed as one. "Who would've imagined?" Madeline said.

******

Attila found the deserter on the CAT's webpage as Tim said she would. He was Kenny something, a normal enough kid from Indiana. Not one who should've caused trouble. Links to his name took her to reports of his being UA, then being classified as a deserter. She learned of MPs and the sheriff looking for him and a girl named Anna Adams. Eventually his name led her to the letters he'd sent out, and after reading them, Attila said she was outraged. It was a direct assault on the nation, on stability, on the entire way of life that after so many thousands of years of civilization had proved to work. Enough little snots like him, she said, and there'd be anarchy. Her own teachers, nuns who back then did wear black robes and starched wimples, would've smacked him about the ears, beaten his hands with rulers until they bled, pulled his hair until his eyeballs popped out.

It would be a great pleasure to catch him. She printed Kenny's letter and made her boys read it. Her boys claimed to be as outraged, especially Hedge, whose father had died a hero and so had left him with no one besides a mother who believed you could predict your fortune by the length of your index fingers.

Killing, the deserter had called it. It was not killing in war. *Murder*, he said. Everyone knew it was not that, had known it since the Athenians conquered the Spartans. The Bible was full of battles in which the good guys destroyed their foes and were called holy for it. Killers! If the kid were from outer space, he could be forgiven for the mistake contained in that word. But he was from here, had partaken in all the bounty that came with being part of a strong and therefore tough nation. How dare he turn so childlike and pseudo-innocent.

"We have to get him," she told April after Tim and Hedge left for their shift on 90 and 12.

"I think I'll move to a warm and friendly place where no one fights or cares to," April said. "Isn't there a warm island nation somewhere the natives smoke opium and smile all day?"

"Catch this Kenny and the reward I'm offering will be enough for you to search for that 'do nothing' place."

"Wow. I'll get some money? You said no before."

"That was a joke. I forgot your side of the family doesn't have a sense of humor."

"Yeah. It's your side that's so full of clowns."

"If I were you, I'd get those teeth fixed before looking for nirvana."

******

The night before, when the women joined the men in Helena, they'd booked three extra rooms—one for Misery, one for Wanda, and one for the hitchhiker. "Why for him?" Randy asked, surprised to see the hitchhiker was a chubby man with a baby face and a scowl. Rude, too. He'd pushed Anna's hand off his shoulder once in the lobby, and sneered when Misery asked if he were stopping in Helena, too, and if so, why. But he'd not objected when Madeline gave her credit card for all three rooms. "Let me know when you guys decide to go to dinner," he said before carrying his paper bag into the elevator. He'd not said a word to Randy or B, not shaken their hands or so much as nodded.

Anna and Henry soon followed Gene upstairs, Anna clutching Henry as if she couldn't stand without his help, and Misery and B sat on a sofa by the travel brochures and sipped cups of stale coffee left over from the morning. Randy and Madeline went to his room, and he told her the same thing he'd heard Anna, whom he still thought of as Lisette, tell Henry. The three days seemed long, maybe not years, but long. He knew he sounded like a kid, but he continued. He'd missed her. He thought they could be serious. His ears pounded from the blood rushing to his head from his embarrassment. He'd thought he was old enough to be cool. She laughed and said she missed him and Bourbon, too, but at least she had a new pool. He said she shouldn't have been allowed to buy a car, for it was worse than he'd imagined, said he'd look it over later, but didn't expect much.

"Mom thinks it's haunted. The heater's no good. It rattles and bucks and rumbles, but it keeps going."

"So far," he said. "We'll see how impressed the Kneedelseeders are when we show up in it."

She kissed him then, running her hand down the front of his jeans, nibbling his ear.

Later, she told him the plan to drop Wanda in Spokane and explained what little she knew about Gene—that he'd missed his sister's funeral and for some reason was still heading north. As she laid it all out, he watched her eyes glisten. It was her talking, weeping a bit even as she shrugged at the strange turns they'd taken that made him see the whole trip as a continual forward movement with a few obstacles that had merely slowed but not stopped them. "Yeah, there've been screw-ups, but none total or too harmful," she said, but it wasn't her words as much as her presence that made him believe it.

After the reunion, they'd drive Anna and Henry up to Canada, straight north, no stops, nothing to get in their way. They'd cross the border as visitors, come back with two fewer. Nothing to it. No one was following them. They based their plan on that. Henry had likely dropped off the radar. "Short attention spans," Randy said, "are good things sometimes."

"Five days from now, we'll be back in Bourbon," she said. "I've been crying for no reason."

"Yeah," he said. "We'll turn around and drive as fast as Isabelle will go."

"Isabelle!" Madeline said, and went out to the car, dug the pink wading pool from the trunk, and carried it in. She blew into it for nearly a half hour before Randy had to take over, but the pool took shape and eventually filled the space between the bed and the bathroom. Madeline used the ice bucket to fill it with warm water from the tub. "Soon we'll be swimming," she said, as she put on her red bikini. "Swimming on Highway Two-Eighty-Seven," she said as she sat down in the pool, splashed about. "Swimming in Montana." If only she could be the person Randy saw when he looked at her as he did, the same way Chris and Martin and Ollie once had, seeing someone other than she. Inauthentic was what Trysh had called her, a descriptive-enough word. She wasn't sure why she wanted to cry all the time, but she doubted it was for Gene or Anna's sorrow or the stupid war boys had to run from. It was for her poor little self, nothing but. How did you become authentic? Not by trying, Louise's ghost said, and Madeline laughed once at the ghost's change of heart and tone. This from the woman who'd taught her the value of trying, preached pretense as a step toward being.

Randy stretched across the bed and watched her, wondering out loud how she'd empty it when she finished her swim. She laughed either at his questions or at something funny inside her brain, so he closed his eyes and sighed. Most of her laughs were forced. He believed Henry would get safely into Canada, and he and Madeline, once back in Bourbon, would be bound together by this trip. He'd have to buy a larger pool.

SIXTEEN

"Take you for a spin? Interest you in a wheel?" The antelope that carried Wanda asked it. The antelope was half dog, and it shook, tried to shake Wanda off. "She's heavier than my essence," it said. Madeline laughed. Wanda was one of the heaviest of elements. Madeline woke up enough to know she was dreaming. Not odd to be dreaming of Wanda, not at all, but to be laughing about Wanda: that was new. And hadn't Alexandra been in the dream too? Well, it all made sense, even though Alexandra had been wearing a mint green taffeta ball gown and eating a bowl of beans. Alexandra was saving her from Wanda, and Wanda could be laughed at now that she was virtually gone. Madeline kept her eyes closed, wanted to go back to the dream, pleased she could connect the dream world to the real and so it all made some sense. This one was not sad, either, no sobbing in it at all. The wind in Montana was no gentler than it'd been in Wyoming, blowing down from the snow-covered peaks and hitting the motel hard. She heard the windows rattle, and felt safe. They would hold. The cold could not get in.

Misery heard the wind, too, in her room across and down the hall from Madeline and Randy's. It came from the north, but swirled about the Quality Court, hitting all sides as if angry to be blocked. Misery would stay in bed all day, all winter, all her life. She recognized that desire as a bad sign, the depression creeping over her once again. This was what the pills had killed off, this longing for oblivion. To be no one. To exist inside her own body, deep within. You could call it a life or a death, but why call it at all? Her brain was tired. What good was it to make connections if they became words with no actions, no effects or force? Had one thing she'd done or said, ever, made a difference to herself or to any others? Not likely. Last night as she and B sat and talked about his favorite subject—the corruption and incompetence of the government and the blind eye citizens turned toward it all—she'd understood he'd picked her as his listener because he sensed her pain before she'd ever spoken, and he needed a wounded listener. And maybe he was right in his rantings, but her sorrow had deeper roots and she'd once hoped to be more than a place for his anger. He said it was good to see her, but she doubted he had seen her, had remembered her looks. And her remembering her looks made her burrow deeper under the covers and into herself. Big, thick bodies were ideal for hiding in.

B heard the wind, too, and when his bladder woke him at the usual five o'clock, he stumbled the toilet, stubbing his toe on the nightstand. On his way back, he looked through the heavy red drapes out onto the parking lot and saw that the snow had already covered the tires of his Cavalier and was coming hard. He smiled as he crawled back under his covers. Good thing they'd all managed to meet up before the storm so they could be stranded together. The group. The strange group. The irritating old woman. How like a family they were. He remembered Misery's talk of family back in Ogallala, what she called her need for it, meaning his at the time, and he smiled. He understood the idea of family better than he'd done when he distanced himself from his own. It wasn't a group you had to be proud of or like, but one you had a place in, a role to fill. Finding how you fit was the ultimate intelligence test. Forget that square-peg-in-round-hole stuff. It'd been harder to fit himself into his biological family than into this one, for he had a purpose here. He didn't have to like any of them, but he did like a few.

Anna held on to Henry, hugged him tight all night, not sleeping but listening to him snore, the way he struggled to breathe, and then let loose with a long high whistle. The motel air was dry, and his whistle originated deep in his chest. Such an old man thing, she thought and smiled. He would be an old man and she would be an old woman beside him, maybe in the U.S., maybe Canada, maybe someplace she'd never heard of, one of those new countries that didn't exist yet. The world was open to them. Their lives were new. She was free to think of him again as Kenny, though she was careful to call him Henry. She wondered when, as they aged, he'd drop that boy name and take on Ken or maybe Kenneth, become a fully developed man. She opened her eyes a tiny bit and even through the red drapes, she knew it was snowing, and the truth was she'd known it even before she opened her eyes. She could smell snow. Always had been able to. It was a game she'd played with her mother when waking in winter mornings for school. "Don't look outside yet," she'd say. Then she'd take a deep breath and say snow or no snow. "What does snow smell like?" her mother asked. "White," she said. And it was white now, solid white on the other side of the red. She knew it. If it piled up deep enough, they could stay where they were, and she felt the delirious happiness of a child on a snow day as she turned more toward Henry and hugged him. A cozy snow, a safe and protective blizzard.

Henry whistled in his sleep, a freight train at a country road crossing like the one less than a mile from his boyhood home. In his sleep he looked at trees and saw individual leaves, could read "no trespassing" signs from across the fields. The dog who'd rested quietly on the foot of the bed stood up at an extra loud whistle, turned around twice, and sank down again with a sigh. Henry liked having the dog in bed, but he wished it wouldn't sleep on his feet.

The water in Madeline's pink pool lost its heat overnight, and Randy stepped in it on his way to the bathroom. "Damn, shit, fuck, shit," he said. "Why is it right by the bed?" He had to take one more step in it before he was clear, so both feet ended up wet and cold. He looked back at the unmoving form under the covers. She had to be awake. He laughed then, louder than normal so she'd turn over, sit up. Nothing. "Are you dead?" No answer. "I stepped in your goddamned pool."

She did move then, snuggled down deeper into the covers, mumbling something.

He waded back through the icy water to the foot of the bed, gathered the comforter and blankets with both hands, and yanked until she was covered by only the sheet.

"Jesus." She sat up. "What's going on? Why are you doing this?" She scrambled to grab the edge of the covers, nearly falling out of bed, and he laughed again. His first wife told him on their wedding day why they were marrying. "It's because we're better together than apart." He'd agreed then, but had not understood it until now.

******

The doors were locked, front, side, and back. The porch light off, socks stuffed in around the pipes hanging on the living room wall that served as the doorbell chimes. The child called Angie, named for angels or their qualities, pounded on the front door, threw snowballs at the windows. She was nine, but large for her age, so her knocks were powerful, not possible to ignore. Madeline'd left three years earlier, was already divorced but still living in the Dameses' basement. Angie knew how to get there, but her goal was to get in her own room, to make her father hear her. Besides, if she told outsiders about being locked out, her mother would keep her from her own bed even longer. And the Dameses were outsiders, even if Madeline lived there.

The girdle caused this.

The snowman Angie'd built in the front yard needed something. Three balls on top of one another and acorns for eyes and the smile was not good enough, not for having struggled with the snowman for nearly an hour, not for losing feeling in her fingers and for all the snow lodged inside her boots, stinging her ankles. She would change it to a woman. She stuck half circles on its front, on the middle ball, and stepped back to look. Just a bit lopsided, but better with breasts. A hat, the one her mother'd bought to wear last Easter to the brunch at the Holiday Inn but had given to Angie for dress-up because old Mrs. Ferguson had driven by on her way to church in the same hat, making her understand it had been on sale at Fishers because it was out of style and good only for ugly old hags—that hat was what the snowwoman needed.

Angie found the hat in a cardboard box in the basement, a box that held other discards Angie was allowed to play with. It was a wide-brimmed floppy sort of straw with two bunches of red wooden cherries attached to the bright yellow ribbon surrounding the crown. Angie adjusted the hat at an angle, then went to work on the snowwoman's boobs and, finding two more acorns under the snow, used them as nipples. She laughed at that. The snowwoman looked better with nipples and wearing a hat, more like a person, more like her mother, Angie thought as she stood in the front yard across the street to get the full view. The snowwoman was fat, though, fatter than her mother, and fat women needed girdles.

Her mother was grocery shopping, but her father was inside watching a cowboy movie on the new console television bought with her mother's employee discount from Fishers. He seldom looked around, checked on anything not related directly to him, but still Angie tiptoed as she made her way into her parents' bedroom and took a girdle out of her mother's underwear drawer. Of course, she couldn't put it around the snowwoman, but she could stick it on the front and knock off some snow around the waist so the girdle appeared to be working. She stole something else, too, her mother's favorite necklace, a thick choker, glittery with ruby-colored paste and glass.

Angie was happy with her creation. Mom wearing a necklace, hat and a girdle, smiling. She hoped Madeline'd drive by, for she'd surely laugh.

But her mother didn't laugh. Nor did she raise her voice. But her face turned from green to yellow and then to blue, the skin around her eyes always a shade deeper than the rest of her face. Without a word, she took a shovel from the shed next to the carport and in five hard hits, the snowwoman lay in a heap in the yard.

Since then, for four hours, Angie'd been trying to get inside. She'd taken the ladder from the shed and climbed up high enough to raise the window to her first- floor bedroom, the only one besides the bathroom without a storm window because her father hadn't yet gotten around to putting it on, but she discovered someone, and she knew who, had locked that window. She banged, she shouted, she threw acorns and snow. She carried the ladder around and tried the bathroom window with the same result. When she was up on the ladder in the back of the house at the bathroom window, she heard the side door open and saw her father for a fleeting few seconds as he ran to the car. By the time she got down and rushed to the side door, it was locked up solid once again. But the car was unlocked, so she curled up in the back seat and tried to sleep. Dad, she said, Daddy. Help me. She'd known he wouldn't, just as she knew heading toward his assorted relatives now was a mistake.

Misery shivered and crawled deeper under the covers at the Best Western. The others were up. She'd heard them in the hall, and a few had knocked on her door. Snow, she'd heard. Stuck for at least one more day. The highways were closed. When she got to Ritzville, would she remind her father of the night he let his nine-year-old sleep outside? Not likely. If she were inclined to bring the past up, she could've done so at his eightieth birthday party, his seventy-fifth, his seventieth. His second wife's family seemed programmed to separate their lives into half-decades and then to celebrate with charred cow and soporific dinner conversation about the weather and road conditions. Misery doubted the second family read his newsletters, knew about them.

******

Madeline wanted to swim in the snow, so she'd refilled the pool with warm water and was sitting in it when B came in to say Interstate 90 was closed, 12 and 15, too. Highway 287 was open, but impassable, so the reporters were saying. Trucks were stopped on 12, their drivers having to walk into Helena or stay in the cabs all day.

"It's still coming." Randy sat at the table by the window, watched. "Can barely see which are our cars anymore. Snow's almost past Isabelle's eyes."

"Being warm and sheltered in the midst of such natural violence is like escaping death," she said. She reached out of the pool for the waxed paper cup of hot chocolate the girl at the front desk had given out. They all had to conserve, the girl had said. Nothing more would come in today. Coffee or hot chocolate. Not both.

"We may be warm but likely we won't be well fed," Randy said. "This motel's got no dining room, just gives out those packaged iced rolls they serve as continental breakfast. The girl says we have to conserve those, too."

B sipped his coffee and chuckled. "The kids dyed their hair. A wasted effort."

Randy nodded. "Those old patriots."

"Hardest thing they do," B said, "is getting all worked up on those blogs and webpages. But like us, all of us, they've got bad knees or emphysema or shitty retirements looming. If they're lucky, they can look forward to golf vacations with other old patriots, all wearing lime green or pink pants."

"Well, they made us change direction," Madeline said.

"Not to say they're totally impotent. But take that kid who blinded him. He acted alone, not one of those CATs, and there's no way to guard against that."

"Poor thing." Tears massed suddenly behind Madeline's eyes. Was she sorry for the blind or the blinder? Or was this more of the same cry-me-a-river crap she'd been suffering through. Enough tears to drown in. In her dreams she choked and gagged on all that salt.

"Hey," Randy said, noticing what she thought she'd hidden, "don't cry about it. That doc said his sight might come back."

"Could be she knows," B said.

Madeline surprised herself by crying harder, and was soon wiping tears off her face with both hands. She wanted to cry for the pain of the others around her—Gene's confusion and dead sister, the horrors Henry had suffered, Misery's misery. She made herself think of it all as she stood and wrapped herself in the towel Randy held out. Get a grip, Louise said. What's with all this now? No need to cry. You've made your life by being strong. Someone knocked on their door.

It was Gene, and he wanted to know if anyone was going to brave the snow for breakfast.

"Probably not," Randy said, then motioned Gene into the room and closed the door behind him. "I'm Randy." He extended his hand, but though Gene glanced at it, he didn't take it.

"It'll be worse later," Gene said. "The snow's not stopping."

"Afraid of starving?" Randy laughed, slapped his own stomach. "Guess I can take a day off."

Madeline swallowed and spread her lips into a smile. "His name's Gene Preedy. Gene, this is Randy and B. Gene was on his way to his sister's funeral when we picked him up. Now he's heading north for fun and adventure. Gene, Randy and B are the leaders of this expedition we're on."

Gene shrugged.

"Going to a family reunion," B said. "Her family."

"Roads are closed," Gene said. He shifted from one foot to the other, almost dancing. "Have to walk a ways for food."

"I'm up for vending machine fare until the snow stops," Randy said. "Much prefer it to tramping through a blizzard. None of us even has boots."

Gene sighed but continued dancing. "I never chose to be here."

"You don't even have a coat," Madeline said.

"Anyone have change for the machines?" Gene held out a hand.

"Ask the girl at the desk," Randy said, holding the door opened for Gene.

"Let us know what's good," Madeline called after him.

"Strange guy," Randy said.

"Head injury," B said, and when they looked at him, he shrugged. "I'm guessing. His eyes are blank."

******

Attila the nun and April had the midnight shift, and as they sat in Attila's SUV, they saw the first flakes blowing about in the wind, clearly harmless as they landed on the windshield and melted. "It's only October," April said. "Flurries. Nothing more." Two hours later, she begged to go back to the community center. "I can't see the road. Can you even guess where the road ends and the ditch begins? The rocks on the side? The drop-offs?"

"You can't see now cause it's dark. No different than any other night. You can feel where the road is. But it would be crazy to go now. Much easier in the light."

"By morning it'll be worse."

"The road crews'll be plowing all night. By morning, it'll be as clear as it was yesterday. Smooth and dry."

About a half hour later, they felt the ground tremble, heard the rumble, saw flashes of bright light. The road plows had arrived. Two spotlights passed by, but the second set stopped, trained on the SUV. The driver sat facing them, his window rolled down, yelling for them to do the same. "Trouble?" he shouted. He sounded like a young man, a voice coming through the lights they squinted into.

"No," Attila shouted. "We're waiting for someone."

"Go home. No one's coming out tonight."

"Do we have to? Can't we wait a bit longer? For them I mean. Be a shame if they managed to get this far, and we were gone."

"Don't you people have cellphones?"

"They're old people," Attila said. "They don't. But they've probably stopped somewhere safe. We'll wait just another hour and go back."

"You're nearly stranded already. This keeps up, the road'll be closed. This is a four-wheel drive?"

"Naturally," Attila said.

"Where's home?" He had to shout that twice before they understood.

"Helena."

"Half an hour," he said. "Give them a half-hour. Call nine-one-one if you can't make it. But we don't want to be rescuing you."

"Go, go, go," April said when he rumbled away. "We can freeze to death out here."

"This is a good situation for someone running from the law. It could seem safe for the deserter tonight."

"God, you're a small brain. If he's out here tonight, he's already punished, and you're not necessary."

"A small brain, huh? Just like your lover boy who's cheating on you?"

"Not at all. He's good-looking."

"OK, then. Is my brain as small as yours was when you chose him? And this new one's too young for you."

"He's just a ride. *Was* just a ride. That is until you got off on this cops-and-robbers craze. Why do you want to catch some poor kid anyway?"

"He's not a poor kid." Attila banged her fist on the steering wheel. "He's a soldier. A bad soldier. Call him what he is, and you'll get over feeling sorry for him."

"You call him what he is."

"Pretend he's that guy you left behind. The good-looking lover boy jerk."

"Shut up."

"Or pretend something else, whatever you have to in order to be some help."

"Let's go." April's whine was close to crying. "I don't want to die before I can get to that warm place full of pleasant people."

"Yeah, right," Attila said. "You know where that place is? That place full of pleasant people? It's in your brain, your soft and squishy brain. Nowhere else."

When Attila did turn her SUV around and head east on 12 a half-hour later, it was not to shut April up, though that was a bonus. It was to keep the plowmen from coming back and telling her to leave. The sole authority she wanted to obey was herself. She would go home when she decided. Her inability to take orders, even suggestions, was why she'd become a nun in the first place. It was also why she'd nearly been tossed out as a postulant and as a novice. Was why she lived out in the community center rather than in a convent or house with other Franciscans. The sixty-something-mile drive back to the community center took three hours, and the SUV went off the road, noticeably so, a dozen or more times, the women in it feeling the tilt as they teetered on the edge of what they hoped were ditches, holding their breaths. They saw no other vehicles, no animals, and only one or two lights far off in the distance. Engulfed as she was in snow, April believed in death. In her death. She'd been in blizzards before, and had reacted to each the same way, claustrophobic, suffocating, drowning in white. The world disappeared and nothing took its place.

When Attila and April struggled in the door amidst blowing snow, Tim had an excuse to hang up. He'd spent the last quarter hour listening to, trying not to listen to, and lying to his parents. "Have to go. Be home soon," he said and clicked his phone off. It was Attila's fault that he'd had to talk to them at all. Because she'd ordered all of them to answer their phones, day or night, until they captured the deserter, Tim'd answered his. The caller ID was blocked, but he'd guessed that was one of Attila's tricks.

"Come home now," his father said.

"You are driving us crazy," his mother said, making crazy a three-syllable word. "I cannot sleep. I cannot eat. My eyes are ringed with worry."

"I'm fine," Tim said. "Go ahead. Sleep and eat."

Clearly they had not wanted his assessment. "No. You are not fine. You are stupid and irresponsible. What's all this about a bounty?"

"You talked to Grover?"

"Hell, yes. You didn't think we believed your story, did you?"

"Then what can I say? You know all about it. Why ask?"

"Smart answers won't make this easier. And if you think they're appropriate, that's more proof you're too stupid to be out on your own."

"I've had a headache since you left," his mother said. "My eyes are throbbing from it."

"I'm sorry, Mom."

"Come home immediately and you'll only get grounded. Fool around too much longer and you'll be in serious trouble."

"An ungrateful son," his mother said. "You've lost our trust."

"Your ass is in big trouble. We'll get the police involved if you aren't home by tomorrow night."

"Your brother called two nights ago from Iraq. He said to tell you to get home. He doesn't want to risk his life so you can put yourself in trouble." His mother's voice cracked

"Where is he? When will he call again?"

"Come home and we'll tell you," his mother said. "

"Give me two days, and I can make it."

"One and a half. Noon by the day after tomorrow, or the police will be looking for you."

"I'm in Utah," Tim said. "Just so you know."

When he hung up, even before asking April and Attila how the roads were, Hedge laughed. "Not going, are you?"

"No. Another thing I'm not doing is answering my phone again."

******

By the time Madeline called, Alexandra was already at O'Hare, her flight to Spokane delayed, but not cancelled. She said nothing was landing in Spokane at the time, but the ticket agents expected the runways would be clear by afternoon. "I'll get out when I can. You get there when you can. We'll just keep in touch and it'll work out. And by the way, I'm not getting baptized."

"The glow of the miracle gone already?"

"No. But I can't pick a denomination. The Methodists have lost their glow. The easy religions to get into are sort of boring, and the ones that I have to take instruction for are too dogmatic. I think I'm a religion generalist. I can't even decide if there is one god or many. Not that I worry about it much. I can't see that it matters."

"Back where you began, then? That conversion and loss of faith as whirlwind as your diagnosis and cure."

"Not at all. I *am* a believer. I believe. I'm just not sure what I believe."

When Madeline went to her mother's room to tell her the snow had caused a delay but not a change in their plans, her mother grabbed her wrist and pulled her into the room, tugged at her to make her move to the window. The drapes were wide open and the room was bathed in white. "Look," she said. She pointed out the window. "I want you and your sister to know what I've been a victim of. What I've had to put up with."

"What, Mom? Snow?"

"Yes, you moron. It's snow. But that's not it. Snow's an example."

"Of?"

Wanda threw Madeline's wrist down and turned away. "Of them, the Kneedelseeders. What do you think? Who else would plan a family reunion in a blizzard? None of those upstanding folk has a lick of sense. Yet you girls continue to blame me for your wrecked lives."

Not wrecked, not mine, not wrecked because of my escape. Madeline started to say it, but instead she reached for her mother's shoulder, gave the royal blue nylon a squeeze. There was little under the fabric but bone.

SEVENTEEN

Tim and Hedge saw the deserter at ten o'clock Sunday morning.

"Odd," Hedge was saying, "the interstate's so empty you could play a whole game of hockey on it before a car'd come by, yet there go four cars and a truck all grouped up."

Tim's eyes felt scratchy and dry from the video games, *Super Soldier I* and *II*, he'd played through the night with Hedge and Biggie, not concentrating much for trying to guess the exact moment his parents would call the police. They'd give him some time, and then it would occur to both, maybe simultaneously, that he was lying, that he wasn't in Utah or on his way home, and that the solution was to have him driven home by officers of the law. It was the ultimate unfairness, and as such it wouldn't leave him but kept circling about his brain, the same words and outrage each time it came by: He was chasing a criminal, yet he was being chased by the police. If he were in English class reading about it happening to some poor fool, he'd laugh at the irony. He was the good guy. He was doing what the military and the cops and the other bounty hunters hadn't done, and he wasn't in it for the money, either. Not entirely. This wasn't more of that mercenary crap his father and even he was disgusted by. Each separate point of his argument rounded the same corners of his mind in the same sequence, a pattern he indulged rather than listen to Hedge tell the entire plot of a thriller he'd seen recently. So he would've missed the Cavalier if Hedge hadn't pointed out the grouping. A UPS double trailer, a white Corolla, the white Cavalier, the car with the woman's face on it, and a yellow Jeep.

The Cavalier was in the outside lane, passing and almost hidden by the UPS trailer, and the face car was right behind. He counted seven or maybe even eight heads in both, and knew he had the whole group—the blond who'd insulted his brother without knowing him or knowing if he were dead or being shot at that very minute, the old woman and the really old one, the retarded one, the bald guy, the other one. "A sorry bunch," he said out loud, and took off after them. "Call Attila," he said to Hedge, who was already dialing. "Sorry but intact. We have them all."

Yes, his purple truck would be known to them now that they'd seen it in Ogallala, that is if they paid attention, and surely at least one had. But so what? They'd be frightened to see him in the rearview mirror, but fear would only help him, not them.

After Hedge told Attila where they were, reported their pursuit, he called the CATs and got voice mail. "We've got that guy, Kenny from Ohio," Hedge said. "Call back fast. We can get justice."

"Indiana, stupid," Tim said.

"I mean Indiana," Hedge said. "The one wrote the letter and dishonored us and made everyone mad. We're in Montana. Heading west on Ninety in a purple Jimmy. Call back. We're right behind him. "

"We don't need those old coots," he said when he hung up. "Attila's getting the cops." His brown eyes glowed electric. Tim looked at him and understood. His own blood was racing. No way was that bastard getting across the border. Being with Hedge was like having a younger brother.

Henry and the girl who was now called Anna took the back seat of B's Cavalier, and Misery rode up front, listening to them. After a snow day, what B'd considered a benign slowdown and a chance to rest and maybe even play, the atmosphere had changed. The kids whose desire to be reunited had caused this part of the detour looked fragile, their faces paler, their voices weak.

"Good boy," Anna said to Kenny as the dog sat on the seat between them. "You have to sit still while you ride."

"Want a treat?" Henry asked. "Good dogs deserve treats."

"He does," Anna said. "His tail's going so fast, I'm surprised it doesn't break off."

"You're happy because you don't understand what people are capable of," Henry said to Kenny the dog.

"He's happy to be getting a new home, to be almost a Canadian dog."

"You're a fool," Henry said to Kenny. "That's why you're happy."

"You know that some people are capable of good, don't you, boy? You know we rescued you and are feeding you treats," Anna said.

Misery, too, had slipped into a sadder place. From the beginning, B'd been fascinated by her name and her attitude, thumbing her nose at the world and propriety, caring little if Anna was put off by the talk of mother hatred or people boring holes in their skulls, dressing to appear odd. She was independent of the whole world. He admired that. But now, she'd crossed a line and tripped on the edge. Her supply of some needed brain chemical was low, and she'd become pitiful in the way crazy could be. Her days of deliberately not smiling and talking about unpleasantness were over. Her few sentences needed unraveling. He'd been annoyed and then worried that she'd not spent the snow day with him or anyone, but had stayed locked in her room, not responding to knocks or phone calls, and this morning when he asked what she'd done all day, knowing she'd been trapped by her own mood, she said, "Lumpy bed warm was but."

He laughed and was ashamed.

"Next stop, Spokane," he said when they pulled out of the parking lot, and she said, "Giddy go go," and scowled as it if were his fault she couldn't connect words and meaning. So he drove in near silence for thirty miles, the kids talking to the dog once in a while, then sighing big and full of wind.

Anna understood what life with Henry would be. "I wish I had the guts to kill myself," he'd said. They'd been walking around the edges of the parking lot the day before, stepping into snow up past their knees. "It's good exercise," she said. She tried to make the best of it, playing in the deep white. Her face was beginning to hurt from smiling so constantly. "Indiana snows aren't often like this."

"This war is not an anomaly," he said. "Seeing how it was over there and hearing what's said about it over here has shown me something. I'm embarrassed. No, not embarrassed. Disgusted. To have fallen for it, yeah, but more than that. Disgusted to be human. We're not smart.

We're not good. Our lives are cheap, even to ourselves. No matter our nation or tribe or religion."

"You went through something unspeakable. But you came out on the other side." She took a giant careful step onto the recently plowed asphalt, kicked her legs to knock off the snow that clung to her jeans. She kept smiling, her face hurting more.

"There is no other side. I did not come through."

"I'm not like you say. I'm human. I'm smart and I'm good. Don't say we're all no good."

"I wish I had the guts to kill myself," he said. "It's the only answer."

Even then she kept smiling as she reached for his hand to keep him steady as he moved to the plowed parking lot. "I can't see either," she said. "I'm snowblind, so we're nearly even."

"Ignore me if you want to. But I am serious. And by acting happy, you show your ignorance."

In the back seat of B's car, the beagle snuggling up to her, warming her thighs with his puppy heat, she decided she'd have to carry the whole burden of cheer, would have to be even more positive and hopeful until he got better. He could go ahead and accuse her of ignoring him, dismissing his pain, but it was really the opposite. She paid so much attention, that she nearly understood what it was like to be him, felt herself trapped in his mind and by his experiences. She had headaches from wishing so hard. Not all traumas were war traumas. Each life matters. Hadn't he said something like that in a few of his letters? But it was her job to be happy. Or leave. Be happy or get out. If anything made her sad, she'd swallow it, at least for now. She'd embrace what he called ignorance for a time, wallow in it. Plenty of time for her to be sad once he got better.

Misery knew the pills would help her talk sense, but sense had never helped anyway. Her brain cells were Mexican jumping beans, popping up and down but not in sequence. "There's lots we don't know about the gray matter," one doctor told her, an excuse why he couldn't explain her problem better. Gray matter, she'd thought then and again in B's car. It should be gray only if the brain were dead. Alive, the brain should be pink, right? Too bad she hadn't been able to ask it. And it wasn't the snow or seeing B again or the trip or any of it. It was merely time for the confusion to take over. She'd felt it coming way back. She'd gone to sleep a number of nights ago in Ogallala with the sense of something dark covering her like a net, but B was similar to a friend and thinking of him had delayed but not stopped the fog made of fear and anger and a yearning for something she couldn't name, something that remained shadowed.

******

When Randy carried their bags out to Isabelle that morning, he'd worn a black knit cap pulled down to just above his eyes, covering his brows and much of his head. Gray hair hung out on the sides and back, trying to wave or curl. "Yes, it's that cold," he said when Madeline rolled her eyes at his look. "Luckily for you, I packed two of these." He took a red one from his jacket pocket and stretched it over her head. "It's good cover, too," he said. "Being seen in this face car could ruin my image."

Wanda wouldn't sit next to the red squirrel in the haunted car. "My people were slaughtered by Injun haters. Just for being who they were. Yours, too." She poked Madeline in the middle of the too-thin jacket. "You're a descendent of great but persecuted people, too. How can you ignore the signs?"

"Get in the back seat," Madeline said, and pushed down on her mother's shoulder to make her sit. Her mother's spine was strong, though, her joints unmoving.

"That hurts," Wanda said, "but I won't sit in this thing, not even if you torture me more, not if you take me apart piece by piece and pile my bones back there. Even then, I'll jump out. No matter that he is related to me, I cannot sit by him."

"I'm not," Gene said.

"It's cold, Mom," Madeline said. "B's leaving. We have to go."

Wanda knocked Madeline's hands from her shoulders. "Well, I have to ride in front."

"You're a selfish old hog," Madeline said.

"And you're one of those self-haters. Calling your own kind names and going along with the persecutors."

Once they hit Highway 12, the white Cavalier in front of them, nearly lost in the whiteness all around, Randy laughed. "This is reverse of what Dad used to call German style. Now the women in front and the men are in the back."

"I'm old and I need comfort," Wanda said. "Amazing the stories I have to tell to get my daughter to care about my old sore body."

Madeline stepped on the gas, and Isabelle's speedometer needle moved to ninety.

"Don't kill us just because you feel guilty," Wanda said. "This front seat's not much more comfortable than the back anyway."

"The highway's likely got icy patches," Randy said, leaning up between the front seats. "Be careful."

"We could skid and slide over the rocks and land in a gully, upside down. Wonder if we'd live through it?" Gene said. "It'd be a good way to go. Pain for a moment, then peace."

"The squirrel's suicidal," Wanda said.

"I think my sister committed suicide," Gene said, though he didn't really think that. If he'd had cancer of the stomach, he would've, but she had a husband and children and a reason to keep living. Or so she said.

"Thought it was a horse," Madeline said.

"All three of Madeline's husbands killed themselves," Wanda said. "She didn't even try to stop them."

"Keep your sights on Spokane, Mom," Madeline said. "Mine are."

"Why's that red squirrel telling stories?"

"I'll get out and get another ride if I'm a bother," Gene said.

"I guess we'll take you as far as Spokane," Randy said. "After that, we're going on our own."

"I appreciate that," Gene said.

Madeline noticed that thanks of sorts, Gene's first. Not that she'd been counting, she told herself. Ha. Of course, she'd been counting. Days, hours, minutes, but not about Gene. She'd been delayed, but in one more week, which she knew to be 10,080 minutes, she'd be back in Bourbon, Isabelle stationed on the steep gravel drive, smiling at those who passed above on Highway N.

******

Attila wanted to take Biggie with her, but Biggie said he'd wait for Harvey and Maurice, and April declined to be part of the chase, period.

"Don't see how you can hunt down some poor kid," she said. "Christian as you swear to be and all."

"Thank God we found him," Attila said. "Really. I've been praying for this. God wants order. God wants the bad guys punished. He leaves it to us, but we have to do it, even if it's no fun."

"But for you it is fun," April said.

"So sue me."

Attila left Deer Lodge alone, a mere twenty miles behind Tim. Thank you, God, she prayed as she drove. Thank you for delivering the deserter to us. To me. Yes, it was good to do God's work. Old women like her understood all else was vanity, but being part of a larger purpose was the reason for living, and whose purpose was larger than God's? You didn't have to understand it all, just accept and act.

She'd seen it over and over in the first convent she lived in. Those old crones who believed they were brides of Christ died in peace and with bravery. They knew they'd see the glory of god the bridegroom soon and would be surrounded or consumed by other good souls who'd given up one life for the next one, the big infinite one. And the others, those who thought too much, who came to see the stories as merely expedient or purposeful, the God as tricky and inconsistent and whimsical, or the afterlife no more than a story told to children with as much truth as the one about Santa—those who thought like that died with scowls and sneers, angry at being duped. Attila understood even when she was young, was Deborah the postulant, that too much thinking was not healthy. What was gained by dying with questions and fear? Keep all the rules and dogmas, the so-called articles of faith in a small corner, dust 'em off for comfort now and then. Otherwise, leave them be. Besides, the old categories worked as well as any new ones. You stuck with your team. If your country was at war, you took its side. If your religion was under attack, you defended it. If the Franciscans were criticized by the Dominicans or the Society of the Most Precious Blood, you attacked back for the Franciscans. If Montana were attacked by Idaho, you fought for Montana. All of it was simple. You were a member of a number of groups, and families counted. Why else would she have fed April, and why would April have come to her? You accepted your group and that was the first step toward happiness. Then you fought for it, and with God on your side, you kept order, kept kids too stupid to know their own group from giving chaos an entry into the world and taking civilization down. It's what life had taught her. And yes, she was an oddball in some of the groups she claimed membership in, but that didn't mean she hadn't gained from each membership. If the U.S. didn't police the world, didn't control the major wars, would she have a SUV and grant money and a good pair of glasses? God was order. God was the way and the truth. She was happy the powers that be allowed it was a God-given right to have a gun, hers a Smith & Wesson .32, small and neat and loaded in the glove compartment as she drove. If she lived in one of those no-account countries without big weapons and power, she'd have had a harder time getting such a good gun.

******

As they passed Elliston, approaching Interstate 90, Gene said the best, fanciest, most expensive meal in the world wasn't worth a bucket of mashed potatoes covered in cream gravy. He said he'd once had veal Cordon Bleu and baby asparagus tips and a Parmesan risotto and it'd been good enough that he'd had seconds of everything. But still, he'd take a bucket of mashed potatoes over that and all the other foods he'd ever had, including pancakes.

"What size bucket?" Wanda asked, and Gene said bigger was better.

"I don't even care if I can lift it," he said. "Or if I have to put the gravy in another bucket."

Madeline looked in the rearview mirror to see if he were smiling, to catch Randy's smile at Gene's talk, and instead saw Tim's purple truck. "We're caught! That mean kid's behind us."

Randy called B and said the same. "We're caught. We're caught."

In the discussion that followed, one between B and Randy with comments and ideas from Madeline, going to the airport and buying two tickets to anywhere in Canada, wherever the first flight was heading, was the first plan mentioned. B said anyone following could only go so far, and the kids would be safe once through the security screening, but that idea was quickly discarded. Security was never fast; there were always lots of cops at airports. "Sorry for the dumb idea," he said. "Just thinking out loud." Splitting up was discussed, as was dumping Henry somewhere, a gas station or even a wooded area, then getting the mean kid to follow one of the two cars while someone else, maybe the owner of the safe house in Cut Bank, came down and picked up Henry. But Anna said she and Henry had to get dumped together and then what about the dog, and it was very risky, the kid in the purple truck staying close to them the whole time. Splitting up was still a good idea, they decided, at least make the kid choose which car to follow and there was just a chance he'd choose Isabelle.

"They," Madeline said. "There're two in the truck. He's found help."

"Well, he didn't see us leave Helena, or we would've seen him. He doesn't know for sure which car Henry's in, and he can see two heads in the back seat of this one." Randy read B the map, the numbers of roads and distances, and B said he'd get off 90 at 141 and go toward Helmville, then up toward route 200 and eventually pick up 93, take that straight into British Columbia. Isabelle would continue on 90, but if the kid followed B, Madeline'd get off at the next exit and head back toward Route 200 and meet up at the juncture of 200 and 93, maybe trapping the kid between the two cars and if not frightening him, at least being close to help out if needed.

Henry, feeling the weight of being the object and cause of the sudden speed up, the veering off onto the back road that though it had been plowed was white and slick and bumpy, slumped in B's back seat. For two days, since he and Anna reunited, he'd wanted to lash out, curse, at everything. How was it possible for him to have a girl who cared for him, a chance for a new life? No matter how helpful B and the other guy were, even if they could help him somehow, life had to end. He knew calling this group for help to get to Canada had been a mistake, one of many he'd made over the past few years, but not even close to the biggest. He'd seen life end for some already, and it wasn't profound. Some didn't even look different than they had a second earlier. But even for those who died with pain still on their faces, or the ones ripped to pieces, the Earth didn't shake and nothing changed. "Let the mean boy have me. Stop this nonsense." That'd been his contribution to the discussions going on between the two cars. There was no logic except punishment, and he deserved punishment. "Turn me in. Let that boy get me."

Anna said of course they wouldn't let him be captured, and that "boy" was nothing but mean, meanness incarnate. In fact, she said, if she could shoot, if she'd ever learned how to use a weapon, she'd gladly kill that kid, but instead hoped a semi would overturn on him, push him to the side of the road and over into the gulley below. The road was rough and it made sense someone would die on it. Innocent people were killed all the time, so why not let one who was guilty die, especially if others could benefit? The guy in the passenger seat, whoever he was, would have to be sacrificed.

"For the greater good?"

She turned away when he asked it and looked into Kenny's big and blank eyes. "I got carried away, didn't I, pup? We'd never hurt anyone would we? Would we? Not even meanies. No, we would not."

When the Cavalier turned off, Tim followed it. No one would be stupid enough to hide the deserter in a car with a face on it. He was exuberant. He'd been hunting the deserter for six days, but this was different, a chase, a race to the finish. Without old geezers like Gerald and Chuck he'd get his man, be a hero to Hedge and the other boys, to his classmates even to his parents and that pinhead Grover, and to his brother in Iraq. When one of the CATs called back, he wasn't surprised it was just some other old guy with no passion for the chase. Snowed in was this guy's excuse. His name was Andy Curly Bear and he lived up near Swan Lake on Route 93, which was closed. No one was going anywhere on it in a car or truck for a few hours at least, maybe not for a day.

Tim hung up without saying good-bye. These CATs should have called themselves WATs. Wimps against terror. What sort of name was Curly Bear anyway?

A storyteller name, Hedge told him. "The Curly Bears keep our people's stories, know how everything started."

"Why say 'our people'? If everything began for some, it began for all. I don't get that stuff. What's your point?"

"Sorry," Hedge said. "Don't get mad at the truth."

"Not mad," Tim said, but he let it drop. He couldn't get sidetracked now. The bald guy driving the Cavalier must have a map with him, and Tim needed one, too. How many roads went anywhere? "Did you call the cops?"

"Attila said she would," Hedge said, then corrected himself. "She will if she has to."

"She has to. Call them now."

"I can't go against her. But wait and see. What she says will work out."

"Get the atlas, OK. It's behind the seat. Reach back and get it."

Hedge had to kneel on the seat to reach behind it, and he jabbed both his elbow and his knee into Tim's back before he had the atlas in hand. "What should I look up?"

"My god, you're ignorant. Where are we?"

"Don't call me ignorant," Hedge said, his voice deepening, full of menace. "What do you want to know?"

"I'm not afraid of you, just cause you make your voice go all deep. I want to know what this Road One-Forty-One goes to, and what would be the way to Canada from here. Can you handle that, dummy?"

Hedge opened the atlas to Montana and traced a line with his finger. "I won't tell you unless you apologize."

"Did you call the cops?"

"I said I won't."

"Call them and I'll apologize."

So Hedge called and reported he was in a purple Jimmy in pursuit of a white Cavalier with a criminal in it. He was heading north on 141, and he expected the Cavalier to turn onto 200.

"Chases by civilians are not allowed on Montana roads," the dispatcher said. "Stop chasing immediately."

Hedge hung up and told Tim what he'd been told. "See? Attila's always right."

"The world is full of idiots," Tim said, hearing his father's voice in that line.

"You have to apologize."

"Yeah," Tim said. "I'm sorry the world is so screwed up. We're lawbreakers now. Good for us. I'm sorry it's come to that."

"I accept," Hedge said.

EIGHTEEN

As it always did, snow enlarged the landscape, smoothed out the view, and even on the narrow roads broken only by twin tire tracks, Montana grew. But Madeline hadn't the time to notice, to appreciate the change. She was the driver, putting Isabelle through her paces on the roads slicker than owl shit. That a phrase of Ollie's that he often used to describe the downtown Chicago sidewalks. It came to her while driving fast, while doubling back, even when she twice passed B going the other way, all in some sort of madcap race. It came to her because she'd been thinking about Ollie for a day or so, remembering that a year ago he cried in pain, cried for a week before he died. And she'd done the nothing she could do, squeezed his hand, stroked his forehead, argued for more and stronger painkillers, told him soothing stories about falling in love with him when they met, all the while understanding she'd been loneliest with him than at any other time in her life. And then and now as she drove Montana roads, she knew that was not self-pity, not Wanda's kind, at least. She and Ollie went to dinners, shows, parties. They laughed often, his jokes corny groaners he'd send her by text. *What happens to little girls* who *eat bullets?* But she saw the two of them as painted papier-mâché dolls, or as that cute set of salt-and-pepper shakers he had, an old couple who clacked against each other in the whatnot drawer.

Once, as part of the effort to escape the mean boy in the purple truck, they pulled into a parking lot and switched passengers, the boy and girl and dog swapped for Gene. Madeline had turned to Randy then, wanting to tell him about Ollie and the loving emptiness they'd lived with, but of course it was not the time or place. Speed and concentration were needed, not talk.

After the switch, they drove for miles through diminishing snowfall, so by the time they crossed the border into Washington, the snow was gone, the roads and fields clear. They headed to the Spokane Airport to hand Wanda over to Alexandra, but Alexandra's flight had been cancelled. They were in the parking lot when Alexandra sent a text telling them what they'd just discovered. She suggested they go on to the reunion and as soon as she got in, she'd rent a car, find her way to Ritzville, see them with all those other needle-butts. Randy wanted to drive straight to Canada, get the kids to safety once and for all, but Madeline had argued for getting rooms in Ritzville first, by then no longer thinking about Ollie who'd been replaced by Trysh. The reunion had been going on for most of a day, and Trysh's presence was tugging her toward it. And yes, Trysh was more important than Henry/Kenny, and she said as much to Randy. She, Madeline Dames, was better than that self-centered woman Trysh left. The mother Trysh was hiding from did not exist, was not driving on eastern Washington roads in a car with a face on it. Madeline based her argument for a break in the action, for stopping in Ritzville, on the furious driving of the past few hours. The mad back-and-forth drive had been worthy of a road-chase comedy, she said, but a comedy flop. No one was laughing, certainly not Randy, who hadn't smiled since Helena, the worry lines across his forehead like strands of barbed wire. She told him he needed a break more than any of them. He wasn't convinced about checking in at the reunion first, though, not until B called and reported that the border by Gardner Cave State Park was blocked by state troopers. And B had even odder news: When he'd been stopped at the state park that hugged the border, the purple truck had been stopped, too. But instead of the mean boy, it was being driven by an old woman who said she was a nun from Montana. She'd told the police the truck belonged to a bounty hunter, and they'd switched in Missoula, and he was driving hers. She'd been held for further questioning because the truck wasn't registered to her and she had a loaded Smith & Wesson in it. But she had told on Henry, said the deserter trying to sneak into Canada was in a Mercedes with a woman's face on it.

"She sneered at me," B said. "Said, 'We switched, too. And my partner saw the face car at the airport.' Haven't had a nun sneer at me since I sang *Tantum Ergo* off-key at my first communion."

After Randy said Ritzville probably made sense, Madeline suggested dropping Henry and Anna at one motel and staying at another. The car may be identified, but Henry still wouldn't be found. And he'd be in the Cavalier tomorrow, a car the troopers, the mean boy, and what could be an entire order of nuns had already dismissed.

Randy checked into the Best Western, chosen because it had outside entrances to the rooms, and then gave his room key to Henry and Anna. Dogs weren't allowed, so to avoid trouble, Madeline and Randy kept the dog for the night. The other motel in town, a Comfort Inn, was full, so Madeline and Henry and Wanda and the dog ended up at the Top Hat, a low gray building with eight units, a refrigerator in each room, and powdered sugar doughnuts for breakfast. They took the only two vacant rooms, the second one for B and his passengers who'd be arriving later that night, and they parked Isabelle so it could be clearly seen from the street. Madeline even looked forward to the police knocking on the door. They'd be able to make the old nun seem as demented as B had guessed she was. She knew, of course, the biggest threat was the other car, and she hoped if the mean boy showed up, he'd also see Isabelle from the street.

Once they were squeezed into the Top Hat room, one double bed for three adults and a dog, Madeline tried to locate Trysh by calling the other hotels in town—the Comfort Inn and the two other motor courts like the Top Hat—asking each time for Trysh Dames' room. Trysh was not registered anywhere. Then Madeline called the phone number B gave her for the reunion planners, and was told no one by that name had registered. "Trysh Rankin," she said, thinking Trysh may be using Martin's last name. Or maybe she'd married. "Or anyone at all with just Trysh?"

Wanda sat in one of the two small wooden chairs, her back to the window, and cackled with each attempt. "Pathetic," she said. "Your little excuse to get away from me has turned her back on you. How does it feel? She won't be here. Wouldn't have anything to do with Kneedelseeders. Runs in the family. You won't, either. You're like me. I hate them all."

Randy said maybe Trysh went by Patricia or Pat by now, maybe she'd changed her name entirely, or maybe she was staying in a nearby town. "Who would want to run from you, cut you out of a life?" he asked. Trysh could be arriving tomorrow, he said, or the next day. It was a three-day reunion, after all.

Madeline smiled, said he was probably right.

B called and said he would have come to their room, but didn't want to leave Misery, who was in a bad way. He thought it serendipitous that the kids were in the same hotel as the reunion. "Luck," he said and made Madeline laugh. What straws they all grasped at.

She tried to sleep that night huddled beside Randy on the floor, the dog snoring near her head. The extra blankets they'd asked for added no cushioning. She wanted to drop off, for she believed she'd dream about Trysh, and a dream could be a close second to having Trysh in the flesh, an imagined touch better than no touch. When they'd lived together, just the two of them before she met Martin, they'd had names for each other that made them laugh. Trysh was Peach Pit, and Madeline was Doofus McGee. When they met again, Madeline would say nothing but "I'm sorry." For what? For everything.

Wanda had the bed, her bones even older than Madeline's, and Madeline had known if her mother got down on the floor, she'd not likely get back up. Old Stalking Badger had survived the poverty and harshness of her childhood, and though her bones were old, her muscles worn out, she retained a toughness, an indomitability. Yes, her mind was becoming mush, and her vision and hearing as poor as her judgment at times, yet so many of her ailments were phony—the bad heart likely an excuse to get her way, the bad stomach a reason to complain about poor cooking, the stiffness an excuse to get the best chair or in this case the bed. The old woman would probably outlive Madeline, complaining of being poorly up to the end, even having a spell at Madeline's funeral if too much attention were paid to the corpse. Thinking of it made Madeline smile. Well, maybe there was a triumph in survival, Madeline thought, and her mother deserved credit for beating the odds. Many children raised in the Oklahoma dust had starved, or as adults were weakened from early lack of nourishment. And the beatings from the old squaw would have permanently maimed many children, have set them up for the rest of their lives as handicapped. But not Wanda. And even if it were pure luck, Wanda deserved some recognition for her strength, for surviving. Madeline almost admired her for it.

Wanda lay under the comforter, snuggled deep into it. The Top Hat was a cold place, and she'd rather be in the motel with the kids. B and Misery had taken the room next door, and they still had the Red Squirrel with them, saying it was too late and cold to put him out. Besides, typical of them, the Kneedelseeders had taken up most of the other rooms in town. Still, she was the only one who understood the danger he posed, his power. She prayed for her heartbeats to become regular. Red squirrels meant death. She knew sleeping beside one, separated by a thin wall, was tempting the gods who, for a lark, may take her breath. And traveling with one was a taunt. Any minute now a god could decide he'd had enough of Wanda and her powers.

In the morning, Madeline spoke to the reunion organizers once again. One hundred and thirty-one attendees had checked in so far. Not a Trysh or a Pat or Patricia among them. A brunch buffet was scheduled from ten to noon at ten dollars apiece. After that, the clan would gather and play some sort of game designed to let them find their relatives. A woman who identified herself as Ike's granddaughter told her all that, and Madeline asked how Ike was, said it would be good to see him. The woman checked her sign-in sheet one more time and said yes, Phil Kneedelseeder was there, and staying in the Best Western.

Madeline sent B a text. "He's here."

Misery responded to the text meant for B. "Co la ba rater."

The six of them, seven counting the dog, squeezed into B's Cavalier for a three-block drive to the Best Western, Gene with them because B'd offered to pay for Gene's brunch. Gene told Madeline he'd agreed, but he was leaving after that, as soon as he could.

"We're not twisting your arm," Randy said.

"No. It's fine. I'll go. I've been hungry for three days. But once I finish eating, I won't get sucked in by you people again. The men are as odd as the women." He said sure the chase had been exciting, but he didn't approve of helping a deserter. One of the residents of his village had lost part of an arm and all of his mind in the first Desert Storm. "I won't get sucked in even if my choices are you or nothing."

Madeline, smushed up against the door, a seat belt buckle digging into her hip for the six-minute ride, thought again of Ollie. He'd once said close to the same thing, said his choice had been Madeline or nothing. He'd said it to Alexandra, the daughter Madeline had not met yet, the one who must have said something over the phone like getting on with your life does not have to mean marrying a woman you barely know. Ollie had winked at her, then, the dimple in his chin deepening as he spoke. And what would Ollie think of her now, almost a year since his death? She had no idea.

******

Attila had found Tim and Hedge during the night, and all three watched now as the two old guys, the really old woman, the other two old women, a fat red-headed retarded-looking guy, and a beagle got into a tiny white car and pulled out of the Top Hat parking lot. The deserter was not with them, nor was the rude blond. "Damn," Hedge said. "They got away after all."

"No," Tim said, and wished he believed it. "They're here somewhere. These people use lots of tricks." Tim and Hedge and Attila followed the group to the parking lot of the Best Western and into the lobby.

******

When they stepped into the ballroom, Kneedelseeders everywhere, Madeline imagined the warmth of family, connection. She saw a sea of orange, the color T-shirts sold at the check-in, KNEEDELSEEDERS RULE in black blocky letters across the front and back. She bought three shirts, one for herself, one for Misery, and one for Trysh. Randy bought three, but though he and B put theirs on immediately, Gene refused, said orange made him look fat. She asked Misery to find some seats at one of the round tables for them, but Misery shook her head and stared up at the chandelier, at least five feet in diameter with hundreds of tiny crystals shaped like tears hanging from it. Madeline saw her lips move, but no sound came out. Rather than worrying so about the kids or Trysh, she should concentrate on her own sister, find a good doctor, therapist, drug combination. Wanda struggled past her and took a seat at a table with three women as old as she, all dressed in knit slacks and twinsets in earth tones, orange Ts across their laps. One wore a string of pearls. "I'm Stalking Badger," Wanda said to them. "I'm Native American. Your family tried to wipe mine out." The three nodded and smiled, and Wanda smiled back. "These here are like that old Louise Dames," she shouted. "All this time, Madeline, you thought you was running from the Kneedelseeders by clinging to Louise Dames." She turned to the three women, continued to shout. "You failed. I survived after all. Some stains cannot be cleansed." She stuck her tongue out at them, Phil's sisters, she guessed. "Dried-up sticks," she said. "Sour as all get-out."

Hours, minutes, days, measurements of Wanda time—Madeline had lost count. Escape would come, release would come. Odd to yearn for release and belonging at once.

******

Anna lay on the bed beside Henry, hugged him from behind. "Don't leave me," he said. "Please. Keep touching me no matter what." They were under the purple-and-green flowered comforter, fully clothed. He even had his shoes on. "I know I'm an ass, but please stay."

"We'll get some land, a nice place," she said. All around in this part of the world was land, wheat fields and high plains, soy and lentils and corn. When she closed her eyes she pictured it all upside down, the brown harvested fields on top, the faded blue on the bottom. "We'll get more dogs, raise something like horses, cows, sheep. Whatever we can. It'll be a good and fulfilling life."

He shivered. "Hug me tighter."

She did. "We'll survive just fine. We don't even know what we can do yet."

"Tighter," he said, and her arms ached.

******

Madeline walked through the room, imagining the lives lived separate from her own all these years. All her kin. Some must have had peace and normalcy. She smiled at those who looked at her and some smiled back. She soon located her father standing alone near one of the buffet tables loaded with fruit. He looked bored and broken. In the too

242

small orange T-shirt, he was as insubstantial as always, his eyes dull and his face immobile. She waved and smiled. "Dad? Dad, is that you?"

He looked up and gave her a half-smile, the one that said seeing her reduced his boredom minutely. Misery and B followed Madeline, and B bounded up, took Phil's hand and shook it. "*The Kneedelseeder Report*," he said. "Good rag."

Phil shrugged. "I do what I can."

"Is Trysh here?" Madeline asked, hoping to sound casual.

"Haven't heard from her for years, decades. How's she doing?"

"Here's your other daughter," B said, and pulled Misery up beside him.

"Angie," Phil said, and B laughed. Never would he have guessed *Angie*. "Thought you were in a hospital someplace. Had a breakdown. Mental."

"Co co co, " Misery said.

"You look good, Dad," Madeline said. "Good crowd." She grimaced at her attempt to turn her father's gaze, now touched with pity, from Misery. She held the T-shirt out toward Misery.

Phil nodded again. "Lots of Kneedelseeders."

"Co lab a rate," Misery said.

"I never knew there were lots of us," Madeline said, still trying to sound pleasant, not accusing. "You seldom said anything about your kin." She and Misery were the leftovers, the Kneedelseeders no one wanted.

"You. Did. Not. Help." Misery spoke slowly, stopping for a shallow breath between each word. Her face glowed and a vein above her eyebrow throbbed.

"Well, we all just do our best, I guess." Phil's eyes were aimed above their heads, searching for a more interesting group.

"Can you introduce us to some of the other Kneedelseeders?" Madeline channeled Louise: Shield Misery; make dad act as if he cares.

Phil reached out and took her hand. "Oh my dear, What's the point? Just a bunch of people you'll never see again. Besides, they all have name tags on."

"Co co co co co," Misery said.

"Angie," Phil said. "Why don't take a break? This nice man will get some breakfast for you."

"Name's B. And her name is Misery." B said it as a challenge.

Phil raised both eyebrows at that, looked as interested as Madeline had ever seen. "That right? I like it. Your mother give it to you? Mine would be *Useless* or maybe *Disgusting* coming from your mother." His laugh was almost silent, air pushed passed his teeth.

"Colab, colab, colab," Misery said.

"Mom's here," Madeline said.

"Where?" When he asked, she saw it in his eyes, in the tilt of his chin. He still loved Wanda. She'd laid claim to him all those years ago in Tulsa, had carved her initials deep into his heart, and there was no room for others, not his children's, not his next wife's, not the friends' he'd never had.

"Where?" he asked again.

Madeline shrugged. "She's got a name tag. Goes by Stalking Badger." She looked across the ballroom, the ostentatious chandelier glowing above more than two dozen large round tables covered with white cloths, a gray/brown carpet with a faint pattern of squares within squares, beige walls. She'd picked up a postcard at the Top Hat: an aerial view of Ritzville surrounded by high plains full of wheat. She'd seen some of that wheat in waves at the end of the street where the town suddenly gave way to fields of it, most already harvested but some still golden and stretching to the horizon. What a waste. Being in the lovely town and stuck in a ballroom that could be in Chicago or Houston or even Bourbon.

The wheat would make Wanda sad. And Trysh would not show up. As Louise so often said, a hope without support was merely a want.

******

While lines of her orange-clad kin snaked about the buffet tables, Madeline and Randy took Kenny the dog from the Cavalier to Henry and Anna's room. "Soon we'll come and get you," Randy told them.

"I'll help him," Anna said. She stood just inside the door, holding Henry by the arm, and as Madeline watched she saw the youth fall away, saw an Anna twenty-five, thirty years older, saw what her mother must look like. The bones underneath her flesh more pronounced, her eyes duller. Yes, she'd been crying, but that wasn't it, not all of it. She looked like a person who no longer fell for her own lies, who moved carefully and in a straight line from one problem to the next. "He still stumbles about in the wrong sort of shadows, but we're up for a whatever it takes," Anna said. Then,

244

keeping hold of Henry, she squeezed Madeline's fingers. "Thanks. For all of it."

Madeline nodded. She wondered if Anna saying *still* meant Henry's sight was returning, at least a bit, but didn't want to ask. If they had good news, they'd surely have said. She and Randy left them cooing over the dog, and on entering the lobby of the Best Western the second time, they both spotted the mean boy. He was sitting at a desk in an alcove off the dining room, visible through the mirror behind the check-in desk. Randy called B, told him to come out to the lobby, said they had to move now.

When Tim stuck his head out of the alcove, Madeline knew they'd been spotted, and when she saw him send a text, she knew things were about to happen. She ran into the ballroom then, trying to find Misery.

Attila, dressed in the ubiquitous orange T-shirt, walked up to the microphone in front of the buffet tables, smiling at many of the Kneedelseeders as she moved. "A deserter from Operation Iraqi Freedom is in this room," she said. "Hiding out among you good Kneedelseeders. He is likely not one of you, or if he is, he's a black sheep. I'm working with two other bounty hunters, and we're going to take him in now. You can help us best by pointing him out if you know him, or by staying out of the way if you don't."

By the time the speech was finished, Madeline located Misery, her head down on a table, her eyes open. "Could she be the nun?" Madeline asked Misery, who remained quiet.

Madeline sat beside her then, rubbed Misery's back, making small and complete circles as she had once done for baby Trysh. "It'll be all right," she said, as she so often had to Trysh and to herself.

Misery filled her cheeks with air, and blew out.

Madeline heard B and Phil just over her left shoulder.

"This is your chance to do more than preach to the choir," B said. "The deserter's in a room upstairs. He and his girl and dog can be at your car in less than a minute. Can you get them to Canada?"

She turned and saw her father turn pale, saw him swallow hard. "Tell them it's a green Chevy station wagon," he said. "Missouri plates. In the middle of the line facing the road."

"Dad's going to do something," she whispered in Misery's ear. "Something brave."

"Go up by Midway," a young woman passing by said. "They barely look at your papers up there."

Phil nodded. After that, Madeline felt time speed up.

B sat down in a corner to call Henry's room, and Phil walked toward the lobby.

"Where do you think you're going, Grandpa?" Hedge said, blocking the door.

"That's right. No one's leaving until we get the deserter," Attila said. Some of the talk died down, the buzz quieted.

"What the hell?" someone said.

"Can she do that?" someone else asked.

"I have a gun. My associates do, too."

"Not me," Tim said from his position near the entrance to the lobby.

"I have a gun, too." This from a young blond man almost leaning against the wall cattycorner from the entrance into the lobby. He held his pistol up in the air for all to see. "Don't expect havin' a gun's much of a claim in here," he said.

"Look, kids," Phil said to Hedge and Tim, "I have to pee. Do I look like the kind who'd hide a fugitive, who'd be able to outrun you two? I just need to pee." He was acting even frailer than he was, Madeline knew. And at the same time, he was standing up to someone. Too bad Misery was too far gone to watch this amazing show.

Someone in the crowd laughed. An old woman, her hair a gray curly cap, stood up from a table near the door, said "Let 'im go pee. And don't expect a guy like him to hurry, either." That was followed by more laughter.

Tim and Hedge continued to block Phil's way, but Misery shook off Madeline's hand, stood, and walked toward Phil.

"Dad, it's Angie," Madeline called. "Help her."

"She's one of them," Tim said. "Stop, stop," he moved in from the doorway and grabbed Misery by her blue sweater, but she jerked loose.

Attila fired into the drywall above the entrance to the lobby, but Misery kept going. Madeline knew how that went. Misery was waiting for the next shot, wondering as she often must have, as Madeline often had, what it'd feel like when it came, the searing pain in her back.

"Stop ruining things," Madeline moved toward the microphone and pushed Attila aside. "Let my sister go. She's disturbed." She saw a sea of

Kneedelseeders gazing at her, wished she could feel part of them. "I'm Madeline, the daughter of Phil and Wanda. Phil's the one has to pee." A few Kneedelseeders tittered at that. "My poor sister is suffering some sort of breakdown. She shouldn't be shot at. This woman here, whom I do not know, is not one of us. She's chasing a nice kid who couldn't go back to Iraq. Whether you think that's OK or not, you can see how deranged she is, how little she cares about life. Don't let her ruin this, your family reunion I came all the way from Bourbon, Missouri, for. Those of you with guns, can't you take hers away?"

"We don't want to hurt anyone but the deserter," Tim said.

"I care about life," Attila said. She'd climbed onto a chair, stood above the crowd and slightly behind Madeline. "I shot above the so-called disturbed one's head. I can aim, for God's sake."

The young blond man responded by standing on his chair, his pistol still pointing up at the chandelier. "I can aim, too," he said. Another Kneedelseeder, a woman with two white braids down to her wide hips, also stood on her chair. She pointed her pistol at Attila. "Drop it, sister," she said.

"I will when you both drop yours." Attila said, and added. "We just want the deserter. We're after justice for all Americans."

"My family," Madeline said. "You are my family." She knew it wasn't so as she said it. She was an outsider. She knew they all knew it, too. "Can't you help?"

"My brother's in Iraq right now," Tim said. "He's doing his duty."

"Ha," one of the men near the buffet said. "Where's that old radical Uncle Phil when you need him?"

"I'm here," Phil said. "But I can't do anything."

Two young men, nearly twins with pinkish complexions and fringed jackets, now stood on chairs, too, about ten feet from Attila, between her and the entrance to the banquet room. "We're packing heat, too," one of them yelled.

"Stop it, kiddos," the woman with the gray braids shouted.

When Misery came back in, the old .22 in her hand, Hedge shouted. "Now *she's* got a gun."

"Bang bang," Misery said. She looked at Madeline, shrugged her shoulders, and said "Bang bang" once again.

"Put them down, all of you put your guns down." This came from B who also took a chair. "Please. What kind of family reunion is this?"

"Attila," Tim called from the door. "Drop it. We can't shoot anyone."

"I won't shoot anyone. Not anyone who doesn't deserve it." She shot at the chandelier, making shards of the tears fly about.

"Shrapnel," someone said, as some others ducked and someone screamed.

The pink-skinned twins shot at the same time, also aiming at the chandelier, spraying more pieces of it across the crowd. Madeline got down on all fours, covered her head.

So far, Gene had sat through the scene with guns and people on chairs. He ate his sausage links, eggs Benedict, fried potatoes. He wanted to return to the buffet for Belgian waffles. When Misery came by, he touched her shoulder, pointed to a table on his left. "Your mom," he said. He meant give her the gun; he meant she's one of you crazies so she can help you; he meant to end it all so he could get to the buffet table. He wanted to stop pieces of the chandelier from falling in his food. His hand was already bleeding. He had tried to get away from these people, but was still stuck.

Misery found her mother and pointed the gun at her chest, inches from the royal blue. "Bang, bang."

Attila, still on her chair, laughed. "Yeah, she's disturbed all right." She took aim at a sconce across the room above the buffet table. As she shot, her chair was jostled and she lost her footing.

"Nothing's more evil than an ungrateful child." Wanda said, Misery's gun inches from her. "My eyes are going, but I want to tell you all, even those of you cowering under tables." Me, Madeline thought. After all these years, I'm one of the cowering ones. She looked to her right and saw Gene slump forward, but she crawled toward her mother. "This is normal," Wanda said. "Being singled out on the streets. Kids who got to go to school pointing and calling me smelly. Like Phil's old mother who disapproved so of me that even as a Catholic she prayed for a divorce."

"Bang, bang," Misery said, the gun now pressing into Wanda's stomach. "I'm the one it's OK to throw sticks at."

Some idiot fired into the chandelier again, so crystal tears rained down harder on the Kneedelseeders.

Wanda cried out.

"Bang, bang," Misery said, then dropped the .22 and watched her mother crumble.

Madeline had dodged feet and table legs as she crawled across the brown carpet to her mother, was nearly there when she saw what seemed a crystal arrow head hit Wanda's neck and turned her into a clump of royal blue pooling on the floor. She found Wanda's head, lifted it, making pillows of her thighs. "It'll be OK, Mom." A survivor. A tough survivor. As she stroked the cool and dry forehead, she thought it could be the first time she'd ever touched her mother in comfort. Oh my, Louise's ghost said, looking sad. Madeline's jeans warmed from the blood flowing from Wanda's neck. Wanda dying amongst the Kneedelseeders. But so what? There was no value in where or when, no real triumph in surviving. Toughness was less than nothing. Madeline knew it then. It was not toughness but fate that made any of us keep going, one foot in front of the other, day after day, even if each step was leaden, each day more useless and humiliating than the one before. No real direction was possible but forward. Steps of sorrow. My God. Madeline laughed, a loud guffaw. She was becoming Wanda, nearly channeling her. Each day bringing another want or need that would not be answered or acknowledged. Like it or not. Yes, she discovered, it was an easy attitude to put on. Had her mother's soul found a new home already, squeezed inside Madeline, taking over so soon? She pressed a palm hard into Wanda's neck to catch and hold in the flow. She knew it wasn't right, laughing as her mother's blood ran through her fingers, but this was funny: doom, despair, and anger coating Madeline along with the blood. Louise's ghost was not on hand to say tsk tsk as expected, so Madeline's laughter gushed out as fast as Wanda's blood. "Help's coming, Mom." She turned to Randy who knelt beside her. "She had thick and shiny hair. Back when I knew her, I mean. She was proud of that." Poor thing. Poor poor poor poor poor thing. She heard someone say Gene was dead. "Hear that, Mom. The red squirrel." Even that was funny, and her laughter was not hysterical, not the kind Trysh or someone else sitting in judgment would forgive. Odd that Louise wasn't on hand to tell her to shape up, get a grip. Act right. Good that Randy was holding her shoulders. Without that pressure, she was light enough to float, hover about the ruined chandelier, go even higher, still laughing.

Wanda's neck was full of needles, her arms hurt, bricks were stacked high on her chest, and she swallowed sharp pieces of what felt like glass. She couldn't see or breathe and she wanted to vomit, yet this one, this oldest daughter, the one who believed she could control her life, the one who had chosen Louise over her, was babbling. More of the same stuff. It would all be OK. Even laughing as if pretending were enough. Showed how much she'd ever known. *Shut up, shut up.* It never had been OK. There was no help, never had been help. Wanda knew she was dying. Painfully dying. *Juda.* The word and his face were a surprise. She'd sometimes wondered what her last thought would be, and here it was. *Juda.* He hadn't loved her. She'd not been fooled. But he'd wanted her, and she'd loved that wanting, how strong it was. She saw once again the delight in his black eyes. She, Wanda Preedy of Felt, Oklahoma, had been worth wanting. Baby cakes, he'd called her. Sweet baby cakes.

NINETEEN

After the police reports and the decision to have Wanda sent to Bourbon for burial, Alexandra being told she needn't fly into Spokane after all, a quiet descended on the room in the Top Hat. Attila would be charged with something, manslaughter was Randy's guess. Her bullet had gone in through Gene's left eye. Gene had been missing from a home, a search had been under way, and now his brother-in-law was waiting in some tiny town in Wyoming to receive the body. Misery slept in the adjoining room, B. keeping watch, telling Madeline and Randy he knew she'd eventually be up for the ride back. Madeline had turned Ollie's .22 over to the Washington state troopers. It always had been unloaded.

The evening of what they all called the shootout, a contingent of Kneedelseeders knocked on the door. Five of them, all women near her age. Each one took a turn entering the small room and wrapping Madeline in a hug. Their names were Gladys, Helen, Carey, Sheila, and Genevieve. Some said they knew the emptiness of a world without mothers, some said Phil was someone named Regina's cousin, but others said it was Phil's father, Joe, who was connected to Regina. One, Sheila perhaps, was sure Joe was Regina's stepbrother, not cousin. They said too bad Ike was poorly and hadn't made it to the reunion, for he could clear all up. Regina was Ike's daughter. Three of the hugs lasted long enough that Madeline could imagine being under her down comforter back home, burrowing in for a nap. Two of the women smelled of cinnamon and something fried, and Helen was obviously a smoker. Madeline hugged each one back. Genevieve said it was silly to say too bad Ike wasn't here, for the display in the ballroom would've killed him, and then Carey apologized for Helen's insensitivity. They were sisters, she explained, so she knew firsthand how often Helen said the wrong thing. Madeline tried hard to tell them apart, but knew what mattered wasn't their separateness but their togetherness. They were Kneedelseeders or Kneedelseeder-connected, and that was enough. They all wore orange Ts.

They said most of them were leaving the next morning, cutting the reunion short, but as long as they were still around, Madeline and Randy should come to the Best Western, the hotel restaurant and bar, not the infamous banquet room. Had Madeline heard about the family tree drawn out on a poster one of Gladys' grandchildren had created? It was meant for the wall where the buffet tables had been, was to have been put up after brunch. Lots of missing boxes and lines on it. They stroked Madeline's arms, squeezed her shoulders, hugged Randy around the waist. Come, they said. Really, we're family. "What's family for?" Sheila asked, and Carey laughed. "Don't get me started," she said.

Tim and the younger boy he'd been with, one Madeline learned was called Hedge, sat on a couch in the lobby across from the registration desk. Both had their heads down as they typed into their phones. Tim looked up when Randy and Madeline arrived. "I've been surrounded by lots of incompetent people on this quest," he said. "That or crazy."

"Attila wasn't crazy," Hedge said without looking up.

"I guess the deserter's gone to safety by now," Tim said to Randy. Randy shrugged.

"You were lucky," Tim said. "That's all. You guys screwed up a lot, too. That you won is not down to anything but luck."

Randy nodded. "Don't really see it as winning," he said. "But you're right."

Tim stood and walked toward Randy, his orange T-shirt hanging nearly to his knees. "You may remember I'm Tim. We had to introduce ourselves in the restaurant. But I don't know your name." He held out his hand.

"Randy, Randy Roma."

"You know," Tim said, as he shook Randy's hand. "I had nothing to do with those two dying."

"Come," Sheila said, and Madeline let herself be pulled into the bar. "Red or white?" Carey asked. Once they made room for her at a long wooden table, more Kneedelseeders introduced themselves. Glen and Archie and Bert. Francis and Clara, Stella and the already mentioned Regina. Madeline knew keeping track was futile. And maybe they knew that, too. She leaned against the wooden chair back, letting her eyes unfocus a bit so she could adjust to the darkness. She knew Louise would be pleased Madeline had found family members who hugged. And she missed Louise, had felt her leave as Wanda died. Sure, she knew Louise had never been there, and she also knew Louise's advice, admonitions, words of comfort, were in her, could always be called up, and would be. But she'd been able to hear the soft voice, to close her eyes to see that gentle half-smile that signified an unflappable calm. That Louise, the one who'd lived just under Madeline's skull, skimming the surface of her frontal lobe, was gone.

One of the Kneedelseeders refilled Madeline's glass and leaned closer. "An Indian Princess was what we heard. Joe's son, Phil, had brought home a Cherokee from Oklahoma."

"Yes," another said. "We heard she was a beauty, wild and lovely."

"I had an Indian Princess doll," another one said. This one Madeline recognized from the shootout, the woman with two white braids and a pistol. "I named her Wanda after Cousin Phil's bride."

They wanted Wanda stories, wanted to know Wanda too late, wanted to know if life for the daughter of the Cherokee princess had been special. She looked at Randy who sat at the bar with a few orange-draped men. He smiled at her. She imagined saying *Yes, Wanda was Cherokee, her mother full blooded. Wanda's father, a white man, had used and abandoned a lovely Cherokee maiden, White Star, and White Star raised Wanda all by herself. She was brave and honest and loving.* Or maybe the grandmother Wanda had spit about when mentioning her would be called Little Fawn. Nothing ugly like Stalking Badger the First or Big Stalking Badger. The tragedy of Little Fawn's tale that would include an early death, would be all the sadder for Little Fawn's and then Wanda's goodness, a goodness carried to St. Louis and passed on to Madeline.

Even as Madeline created the stories she'd never tell, the ones already boring her with goodness, she remembered the feel of Wanda's birdlike bones beneath the royal blue, the angry green and gray that came with rage, grew and changed in Wanda's face, highlighting her cheekbones and deepening her eyes. "She didn't fit anywhere," she said. Her audience was silent then, each Kneedelseeder looking at her. "Some thought she communed with powerful spirits."

Madeline knew she would tell Randy she wanted to stay in Ritzville for a few more days, would say she wanted to watch over Misery, eat powdered sugar donuts, walk in the evenings to the edge of the town, to that street bordered by houses on one side and wheat on the other. She knew she would watch the wheat as she told him about using Chris and ruining his life instead of her own, about Martin's suicide, and the loneliness that had been her life with Ollie.

EPILOGUE

Phil stopped less than a mile from the border. As he drove, he'd been telling them about Wanda. "You met her, no doubt. She's really something. Isn't she something? Tough and sort of mean. Always was. Sometimes I thought she hated me. But she had reason to hate it all," he said. "Beaten as she was every day of her life." He held his right hand up above the steering wheel. "She once broke my thumb." He wiggled his fingers. "Still doesn't move right. Yeah, she really is something."

Anna tried not to listen. She knew Kenny wasn't. Kenny the man. Nice that she could call him Kenny again, had been able to since they got in the old guy's car, so there were now two Kennys in the car. Why should she or Kenny the man care about ancient problems, the old man's or the old woman's either, their long gone and over troubles? She and Kenny the man were young and soon enough would make their own troubles.

"Look, I cannot go across," Phil said after he stopped the car. "You have passports and the bad guys looking for you seem to be back at the party. Or maybe not. Maybe others are at the border. I don't know. I can't promise you safety. Perhaps you can survive a challenge. But the truth is, I'm afraid. I can't be an accomplice." He faced to all three of them in the back seat. "Hike up the road alongside these woods. Look innocent. It could work."

"We're not frightened," Anna said. "We'll be fine. It's a new life for us."

Someone had to say it. She helped Kenny the man out of the station wagon, trying to keep the dog leash from tripping him up, but Kenny the dog jumped out first, whined as it strained against its leash, nose to the ground. "For us, it's a beginning. We'll do fine, better than you or we can imagine."

Phil got out, too, stood beside Anna, and reached for his billfold. He counted out two hundred dollars in tens and twenties, folded the pile in half neatly, and handed it to her. "It's nearly all I have."

She nodded. Men used money to cover their cowardice. Who said that? It sounded like her own father's wisdom. She stuffed the cash in her back pocket.

"You won't like it any better up there," he said. "I do hope you know that."

"We have people to contact. Randy gave us a list," she said as Kenny the man squeezed her hand so hard she heard her bones crack and pop. She closed her eyes and smelled snow. It had followed them, would be deep by morning.

"I mean, they killed the native population up there, too, shot any people in the way of progress. Same kind of people up there as down below."

"We don't want to hear that bad stuff, do we, Kenny?" She made her voice light, a teasing tone. "We're starting from scratch. " If he could see her, she'd smile as hard and as wide as she could.

He dropped her hand and spread his arms out wide. "Something's finished," he said. "Something's over."

And though he wasn't smiling, she made herself laugh at that, louder than normal, heard her laugh bounce off the trees and return to them. The gloomy old guy looked worried, so she laughed again, louder. She'd have to let the coming snow, the dog tail that hit her calf with each fierce wag, the two hundred dollars, Kenny's outstretched arms—let all those be signs of hope. "Yes," she said. "An end." And a beginning, she whispered. An end *and* a beginning. And why not? It was true that something would happen.

THE MISSOURI AUTHORS SERIES

2014: *The Empire Rolls* by Trudy Lewis

2015: *The Teeth of the Souls* by Steve Yates

2016: *Swimming on Hwy N* by Mary Troy

CPSIA information can be obtained
at www.ICGtesting.com
Printed in the USA
FFOW05n2237070317

9 780913 785898